TEEN
FIC
Giles

W9-BAW-447

PRAISE FOR LAMAR GILES

SPIN

New York Times Book Review Editors' Choice
YALSA Quick Pick for Reluctant Young Adult Readers

"The first test of a whodunit is how heart-stopping and strange a thing has actually been dun. In *Spin*, Lamar Giles nails the murder . . . What's even more impressive is the subtle stuff you almost don't notice because Giles wears his intellect so lightly: the masterly knowledge of hip-hop and R&B; the command of technology's uses and abuses; the discerning ear for the way high schoolers talk. . . . A two-time nominee for an Edgar award, Giles is a terrific plotter . . . *Spin* champions the resourcefulness of teenagers and pities the grown-ups—villainous or just clueless—who underestimate them." —*New York Times Book Review*

★ "Not to be missed." —*Kirkus Reviews*, starred review

★ "*Spin* delivers everything you could want in a book: lush, complex characters; a spine-chilling plot; a vividly drawn world; and, best of all, hip-hop." —*Booklist*, starred review

★ "This novel transcends its genre." —*School Library Journal*, starred review

★ "This fast-paced tale seizes attention from the first thrown punch to the final curtain call." —*Publishers Weekly*

"Lamar Giles has spun together a fast-paced, music-forward whodunit."
—*School Library Connection*

OVERTURNED

YALSA Top Ten Quick Pick for Reluctant Young Adult Readers
A Kirkus Best Book of the Year

"Giles, a founding member of We Need Diverse Books and two-time Edgar Award finalist, is in top form, weaving together the threads of his whodunit-and-why and resonantly depicting his characters' home and school lives. As a poker genius Nikki may be a singular sort of teenager, but she's grounded in desires and motivations that make her story as moving as it is thrilling." —*New York Times Book Review*

★ "An utterly compelling whodunit." —*Kirkus Reviews*, starred review

"Another Giles winner." —*BCCB*

"A fast-paced, endlessly intriguing mystery." —*Booklist*

"Giles excels at pulpy crime drama, including a romance with a wealthy casino heir, scattering a trail of clues and bluffs to keep readers guessing." —*Publishers Weekly*

"A fast-paced, compelling mystery." —*School Library Journal*

THE
GETAWAY

THE

GETAWAY

LAMAR
GILES

SCHOLASTIC PRESS / NEW YORK

Copyright © 2022 by Lamar Giles

All rights reserved. Published by Scholastic Press, an imprint of Scholastic Inc., *Publishers since 1920*. SCHOLASTIC, SCHOLASTIC PRESS, and associated logos are trademarks and/or registered trademarks of Scholastic Inc.

The publisher does not have any control over and does not assume any responsibility for author or third-party websites or their content.

No part of this publication may be reproduced, stored in a retrieval system, or transmitted in any form or by any means, electronic, mechanical, photocopying, recording, or otherwise, without written permission of the publisher. For information regarding permission, write to Scholastic Inc., Attention: Permissions Department, 557 Broadway, New York, NY 10012.

This book is a work of fiction. Names, characters, places, and incidents are either the product of the author's imagination or are used fictitiously, and any resemblance to actual persons, living or dead, business establishments, events, or locales is entirely coincidental.

Library of Congress Cataloging-in-Publication Data available
ISBN 978-1-338-75201-4

1 2022

Printed in the U.S.A.   23
First edition, September 2022
Book design by Maeve Norton

FOR THE VISTA WAY CREW, SPRING 2000

THE FUNNEST
PLACE AROUND

Official Karloff Family Archives
from *TV Guide*, June 4–10, 1972

**BE SURE TO TUNE IN
TO THE OPENING OF**

An Exuberant, Coast-to-Coast, 90-Minute TV Special

Highlighting the Dedication Ceremonies for

"The Funnest Place Around"

NBC-TV

June 4

8:00–9:30 P.M. EASTERN STANDARD TIME

CHAPTER 1

"No one has ever died in Karloff Country."

That's what Zeke told us his dad told him. Mr. Johnson told Zeke a lot of wild things about our home.

"That's ridiculous," I said, forcing my voice to stay even so this remained a debate instead of a fight. When it came to Zeke's conspiracy theories, I'd gone from amused to over them a while ago.

"I'm telling you, Franklin Karloff made a pact with the Virginia tourism board back in the day."

"A pact? With a tourism board? Why?"

"Jay." He looked as incredulous as a math prodigy explaining two plus two. "Money."

All of Zeke's sinister deductions about the world had foundations built on coin.

Continuing this nonsense, he said, "If someone has a heart attack or falls down some stairs wrong anywhere in Karloff Country, the paramedics gotta wait until the body's *outside* the wall to pronounce them dead."

"How can that possibly affect the resort's money?" I said.

"Do paramedics pronounce people dead?" Connie asked, tugging a hunk of meat off the saucy rib staining her fingers before popping it in her mouth like a pork nugget. She often challenged Zeke's mess, but softer, like maybe we should spend more time digging deeper into his paranoia. "I can see your point about why the resort wouldn't want bad press if there were *a lot of deaths* on-site. No one, though? *Ever?*"

Zeke inhaled for a rebuttal. There was always a rebuttal. But I

1

didn't want to keep giving this nonsense air. "Bro," I said, "this is like the secret prison for rowdy guests you told us about before. Or how all the birds are really surveillance drones. Or how the animatronic puppets in PatriotScape 'watch you back.'"

Connie spoke through half-chewed food. "Them puppets do be creepy."

Zeke's attention was 100 percent on me when he dropped his half-eaten burger on his overloaded paper plate. It landed on a french fry mound and almost toppled to the ground. My insides cinched tight as shoelaces and only relaxed when I knew his food wasn't going to be lost to the grass and ants. I still remembered what real hunger felt like.

He was really on one, though, so he didn't care. "Whatever, haters. No one's died here. It's never happened. Facts!"

"Raising your voice and yelling *facts* don't make it true," I said.

"You being a Karloff superfan don't make you right all the time either," he replied.

Air whistled through my nose, and I held on to the question that was becoming more aggressive and slippery each time we went down conspiracy road. Zeke might be my best friend, but the thing I wanted to ask, that would definitely shift us into fight mode, was simple: How could he be so ungrateful?

Zeke kept going, talking with his hands, breaking down more players and motives for the No Deaths scheme. My attention drifted to movement on the stage erected fifty yards or so from our pavilion. There was plenty going on between here and there, so saying the *movement* onstage drew my attention and not the *person* was, well, a lie. I forced my focus elsewhere.

Closer to us, my dad was among the adults working a line of

sweltering grills, serving up hot dogs, burgers, ribs, and chicken with no food-ration concerns—something that still hadn't sunk in completely, even after three years of safely living inside the Karloff Country walls. When Dad talked about *his* dad barbecuing meat every summer weekend when he was a kid, it sounded as wild as Zeke's no-one-ever-died-here story. Too unbelievable to be true.

Closer to the stage, Mom hung with a bunch of ladies. Some—like her best friend, DeeDee—I knew; others were likely getting recruited for Mom's book club. Off to the side, younger kids played a lawless game of football in the big field that made up most of the Treat (short for *Retreat*, which was short for the *Jubilee Residents' Association Neighborhood Retreat*, which was long for what could've been called a park), while some of the older crews dispatched to semi-exclusive areas in the bordering forest. None strayed too far. Because that stage was there for a reason.

A DJ blasted playlist tracks that ranged from ancient times to . . . slightly *less* ancient times. Up-tempo R&B and the kind of hip-hop Dad rolled his eyes at before Mom got on him about "not appreciating happy rap." The music was all Black everything for today's event, clean edits only. Because while the Karloff Country Resort embraced all the world's diverse cultures, vulgar music was not on brand for Karloff Entertainment Company proper. Facts!

A roving video crew that'd been capturing B-roll of the festivities during the previous hour was now set up near the foot of the stage, ready for their real job. They documented our benefactor's generosity as they did at every big sponsored diversity/inclusion celebration here at the Treat. From Passover in early spring to the start of Pride Month a couple of weeks ago, to today's Juneteenth party.

The blond, tanned woman the cameras tracked was Blythe Karloff. She signaled the DJ, and Montell Jordan's "This Is How We Do It" cut off abruptly. Blythe slipped a wireless mic from its stand, thump-THUMPED it, then did a dramatic spin that made her flowery dress fan out like a parasol for a second. She had everyone's attention, except ours.

That was reserved for her partner onstage. Her daughter. Seychelle.

"Good afternoon," Blythe boomed into the mic, her voice smoky and crisp like on TV. She doubled her volume and shouted, "And happy Juneteenth!"

Joyous applause followed, then tapered off. Connie put down her rib. Zeke twisted on his bench for a better view. We all watched Chelle to see if she'd actually do the thing she claimed she would.

"She. Looks. Miserable," Connie said.

She did. Her face was expressionless, her hazel eyes on her mom's shoes.

I said, "I don't think she's going to do it."

Blythe grasped the mic with two hands, a solemn and caring kind of grip. "On this day, we celebrate the liberation of those subjected to the horrors of chattel slavery in the United States. When I was growing up, I attended the best prep schools in the country and never had a single lesson about the significance of June 19, 1865. When I went to Princeton, I didn't learn about it there either. I'm ashamed to say I was well into adulthood, and the mother of a Black child, before I became *aware*."

Blythe cast a meaningful look Chelle's way. What the meaning was, I didn't know, but it was full of something. Chelle did not look back.

Reciprocating the gaze wasn't even a speed bump for Blythe's delivery. "I say *aware* because me knowing about a thing is not the same as *understanding* it. Even a basic white girl like me knows that." She paused for laughter. Got it. Never looked directly at the camera capturing the charming self-deprecating moment.

"Let me tell you what's not basic," Blythe said, transitioning from the comedy portion of her speech. "The desire of the Karloff Entertainment Company to recognize how Black people have made this country better despite the pain and suffering caused by white Americans. And while I celebrate this wonderful occasion with my daughter and my whole heart, I also recognize it's not *my* place to be front and center today. So, I'm handing the mic over to Seychelle so she can speak directly to you. Her people. Come on, baby."

Chelle loathed this—and really any of the various public duties—that were required of her as a member of the Karloff family. None of us could ever comprehend the burdens of being a billionaire heiress, but we still felt for her being dragged in front of the world by her wealthy family. Was any amount of money worth being a living, breathing prop? This was the one area where I allowed myself some disdain for the Karloffs. They didn't appreciate what they had in her.

Chelle shuffled to the mic. "Thanks, Mom," then, to the crowd, "Thank you for having us, Jubilee."

Jubilee was us. Our neighborhood. Where everyone who lived in Karloff Country, except the Karloffs, of course, resided. The utterance of the name elicited more applause for the same reason Zeke never actually condemned Karloff Country for supposedly throwing dead bodies over the wall or whatever. He knew no matter what he believed the company did or didn't do for money, we were all lucky to be here.

Chelle said, "It really warms my heart to see so much of Jubilee come out to celebrate Juneteenth. Being Black, and being a Karloff, has always endowed me with a sense of responsibility, and extra drive to—"

Chelle stopped talking.

Connie, Zeke, and I leaned forward.

"Y'all didn't really come to hear me give a speech. As my mom said, she doesn't understand what this particular moment in time requires. But I do." She brought the mic closer to her lips, cupped her free hand over it, and began to beatbox.

Bom-bom-ba-ba-ba-tah! Bom-bom-ba-ba-ba-tah!

Oh. My. God.

She did it.

We hopped from our seats, cheering her on. "Ohhhhhh!"

Because Chelle was actually good at beatboxing—don't ask me why—and the song she was performing, another classic from a long, long time ago, sounded like it should sound, the crowd had no trouble giving up those cheers too.

Chelle ended her assault on the mic and told the DJ, "Hit it!"

Music resumed, the real track she'd been performing. She crouched at the end of the stage and said, *"When they say calm down . . ."*

She extended the mic to her audience, and the crowd responded, *"WE. TURN. UP!"*

Turn up we did.

The residents of Jubilee were shaking and grooving and celebrating a holiday that represented a spark of hope in a horrid national history. I caught Chelle's eye while she swayed onstage, killing it. Then my gaze slipped past her, to her mother.

I knew the Karloffs had impeccable public training, but I was still beyond impressed. Chelle's mom's smile remained fixed. Like she wasn't pissed at all.

CHAPTER 2

The Juneteenth celebration ended at dusk. We wasted no time piling into Chelle's car and escaping the wrath of Blythe while the sun sank behind us.

"My mom's never going to lose it in front of people," Chelle said, reassuring herself as much as informing us. She was our getaway driver, checking the rearview like cops were in pursuit. We were out of Jubilee in record time while somehow maintaining safe(ish) speeds. "When I get home, she'll be halfway into a merlot. The pain will have dulled."

"How mad do you think she is, though?" Connie only seemed half-interested while she scrolled through playlists on Chelle's phone.

"About as mad as a 'basic white girl' could be on Juneteenth."

"So . . . *very*," Zeke said.

Connie was taking too long. I grabbed Chelle's phone and hit play on something aggressive that nearly drowned us in bass.

"Yoooo!" Zeke wrenched the volume left, decreasing the boom by half. He was tallest, so we granted him shotgun and, thus, easiest access to the dashboard. Something Chelle loathed. She nudged his hand off the knob. "I like it loud."

"I like working ears."

I said, "He's right, Chelle. He's never going to finish his musical if you blow his hearing."

Connie and Chelle snickered. Zeke got *mad* mad. "Here y'all go."

My first day in Jubilee, almost three years ago now, I met Zeke in the Treat under the same pavilion where we'd been gorging ourselves this afternoon. He was rounder then, about six months from the growth spurt that would stretch him into long lines and sharp angles. Hunched over a laptop with earbuds screwed in, he'd been spouting questionable rap lyrics that I never planned on letting him forget. It wasn't his suspect rhymes that got me caught staring. It'd been a long time since I saw another kid with any weight on him.

I was fourteen years old, five foot seven, and roughly one hundred pounds then. That's how bad the food shortages were before we became part of the extended Karloff family. When he spotted me and asked what I was looking at, I asked him what he was listening to instead of the question I *really* wanted to ask: Did he have any food on him?

Now he hated me bringing up his magnum opus ode to Lin-Manuel Miranda, but what he did next was not a safe path for escaping ridicule. He pulled down the visor, examined himself in the mirror, and said, "I think Ramona Hanshaw's working her merch stand tonight. How I look?"

"Ashy," Connie said.

"Your dreads look dusty," said Chelle.

I leaned over his seat, sniffing. "Bro, when was your last shower?"

"Whatever," he said, "I'm the most handsome dude any of you know."

"Ewww," Connie said, "*Handsome?* You know I don't like that word. It creeps me out. Almost as bad as *moist*."

We all shuddered. I don't know if everyone had certain, mostly mundane, words that they didn't like, but our crew did. *Moist* was on everyone's Don't Say It list.

Zeke said, "Fine. I'm the most *sultry* dude y'all know."

9

Chelle gripped the wheel with both hands. "Add *sultry* to the list!"

Noted.

Chelle's phone was still in my hand, so I felt it spasm with rapid incoming texts.

> **Mom**
>
> What the flip was that, Seychelle? Have you lost your mind? What did we rehearse? WHY did we rehearse?

> **Mom**
>
> Will you ever get enough of embarrassing me?

> **Mom**
>
> You have RESPONSIBILITIES whether you like it or not!

More messages shook the phone, but I put it to sleep and slipped it into the cup holder for Chelle to check later. Karloff family business was none of mine.

Night came fast, but not where we were going. A neon haze from dozens of restaurants, shops, and bars created a misty dome over our destination, the resort's entertainment district, known as Downtown Karloff. Traffic thickened into the usual Saturday evening slog for space in the parking deck.

We were on Karloff Country's main stretch, nicknamed Banner Road for the numerous flags flying high on either side of the asphalt. There were flags of the nations around the world. Pride flags. Black

Lives Matter flags. Fight Hate flags. The same flags you'd see pinned on uniforms around property by workers who wanted to show you where they came from and who they were, supported and encouraged by the company. I knew them all now. From Colombia to Kazakhstan. Nigeria to Nauru.

I rolled down my window and stuck my head out. The flags flapped like beating wings over our four eastbound lanes bottlenecking to two. We were twenty minutes from reaching the deck even though I could hit the entrance sign with a rock if I wanted. "The busy season is here."

Chelle uttered the resort's famous slogan with heavy sarcasm. "Funnest place around."

I kept quiet. Despite the stalled traffic, heavy exhaust fumes, and general sameness of every weekend spent inside the walls . . . I kind of thought it was.

Being the "Funnest Place Around" maybe wasn't so hard considering the state of the world beyond the Karloff Country walls. What's wrong outside is what's been wrong my entire life, so I gauged the severity by comparison to my parents' childhood stories. Even when their nostalgia felt like fiction.

There was stuff I couldn't wrap my head around. Like pay phones and video rental stores. Other things they told me about, though, I wanted to feel with my entire being.

For example, sand.

Mom said when she was a kid, her family spent a week at a beach house in the Outer Banks of North Carolina every summer. I was little and laughed because it must've been a joke. We'd done a geography unit in school, and I knew the place she was talking about was completely underwater. When Mom started crying, I cried too. I knew my laughter hurt her feelings even though she said she just missed the old days.

Every part of the country felt the climate adjustments differently. Out west, the perpetual wildfires left untold miles of formerly lush forests as smoldering ember wastelands with half-breathable air. In Middle America, droughts and hurricanes took turns punishing the people, crops, and homes. For us in the East, the flooding that pushed tides miles inland created the New Coast.

Then there was the people toll. The increasing poverty. Protests and riots. Violence. Racism. Fewer and fewer places earning the government's coveted "safe city" designation, which determined so much about the resources those who lived within them were allotted. Or maybe things have always been that bad, but we just stopped working so hard to ignore it.

As painful as losing the Old Coast must've been for anyone who knew a different time, there was no comparison to how bad things got with the food.

Not everyone felt it. America was better off than most countries— that's what I was told. In some states where the leaders maintained different priorities and agendas, ample stores remained stocked for the few who could afford the price of meat, and for those who couldn't, other kindnesses allowed them to make a way. *My* state wasn't one of those.

Right after my thirteenth birthday, Mom and Dad told me about a new routine they were trying. Intermittent fasting. Supposedly there were a lot of health benefits. Supposedly.

Our lives weren't different from our neighbors'. We weren't better or worse people, not special or cursed. Life was what it was.

Now it was sometimes difficult recalling the constant misery of the old days. Much easier remembering Penny Pup and his pals' adventures in Karloff Cartoons comforting me like a friend's hug. Dad cursing out bill collectors was background noise while streaming a Penny Pup movie on a cracked old tablet. The nights my parents and I huddled under two musty comforters in a drafty apartment were also nights a stuffed Milo Mole nuzzled my nose until I dozed off. The Karloff characters lived in my heart and in a magic place offering a one-in-a-million chance to lucky families, something we never were.

Until.

Zeke's no-one-dies-inside-the-walls conspiracies were exaggerated trash, but life has been lost over Karloff Country's enviable promise of housing, food, safety, and security. People have died waiting to be part of what we have here. People have killed.

For a fortunate few, like us, they simply opened the gate and let you in.

"Dude," Connie said, "why are we standing in Ramona's line?"

Zeke said, "She's working."

I said, "It is weird we're standing in line. You're not, like, going to buy something, are you?"

He didn't respond.

"No. Zeke. That's *not* your opening. This is a T-shirt stand." It was an unspoken rule that people who lived in Karloff Country did not rock the merch. It'd be like New Yorkers rolling around in those I Love NY shirts.

Sheepish, he said, "I got a lot of Pup Points, okay."

Pup Points. On-property currency that could be used in lieu of dollars. Or dignity, in this case.

I threw my hands up. "I can't be a part of this."

Connie chose to participate as videographer, putting her phone in camera mode to memorialize Zeke's shaming.

Stepping from the line put me in the bustle of Downtown Karloff. Wide lanes between an eclectic mix of shops and eateries that had you brushing shoulders with folks from all over the globe on a busy night like this. Downtown Karloff was a more accurate snapshot of daily life outside our neighborhood. A heavy mix of guests enjoying the nightlife away from the more kid-friendly amusement parks, and on-duty resident-workers attending to every tourist want and need.

People came here from as close as the next town over to as far as China, but not from all walks of life. Everyone here who wasn't an employee had two things in common: some love for the world-famous Karloff experience and money. Lots of money.

The resort served roughly eight million guests per year, about 0.1 percent of the world's population, but since a lot of that was repeat business from wealthy guests visiting more than once a year, that math wasn't precise. Here's what was 100 percent true: Most people would never have the means to peek inside the Karloff Country walls.

Through a break in the crowd, I spotted Seychelle sitting on the lip of the Penny Pup fountain, the hood on her sleeveless hoodie casting half her face in shadow. The other half grimaced at her phone screen before serial-killer-stabbing it with her thumbs. I assumed her mom was still text-scolding her. Slithering between guests, I made my way to her and sat.

She turned her phone facedown on her thigh and forced a smile. "Real talk, what are Zeke's chances here?"

I wobbled my hand. "Iffy. Ramona's a senior and ridiculous hot."

"You think she's hot?"

"I mean. Sure. She's attractive."

"What do you think is hot about her?"

To answer the question: Ramona was objectively good-looking. Dark brown skin. Great smile. She made her Karloff Country–mandated khakis and polo shirt look so good I wouldn't have been shocked if Dad's department used her as a model in the resort marketing materials. I could've articulated that to Chelle; I didn't want to.

Used to be talking with Chelle about a girl wasn't much different than talking to Zeke or Connie. When she dated that cornball Dale Tannen for most of sophomore year, and I was with my old girl Steph, it was whatever. Steph and I broke up last summer, though. We weren't a good fit, and that was okay. Then Dale's family moved off the resort a few months back, and Chelle was tore up about it for a while. She sulked. Made too many sad-song playlists. A lot of girl talk with Connie while Zeke and I got it in on his PlayStation 6. Before long, she was back to her old self, but things didn't go back to the way they were. Not for me.

I don't know, it sounds stupid, but I saw her in sunlight one morning and it was like seeing her for the first time all over again. More often than I wanted, I wondered how she saw me.

Like I said. Stupid.

Pushing those thoughts away, I shrugged off her question.

Four girls, maybe ten or eleven years old, sprinted to the fountain, giggling. I couldn't tell if they were siblings, cousins, or vacation buds, but one flung a whole handful of change into the fountain, creating a heavy splash like she'd blasted the surface with a shotgun. She immediately caught flak from the others, all insisting they were supposed to pitch the coins one at a time and now the wishes were ruined. Before it got out of hand and they tossed the overzealous flinger into the water after the money, Seychelle said, "You know doing it that way means you all get to make bigger wishes."

"Is that true?" one of the angry kids said.

Before Chelle could respond, recognition hit the girl, then spread to the others. "Wait, are you—"

Chelle pressed a finger to her lips, shushing them like they were all in on a big secret. I'd seen her do this before.

She lowered her finger and said, "Don't scream. If you do, everyone will come over and we won't be able to take a selfie."

The selfie offer had them wide-eyed but obedient. Tears streamed down one girl's face.

"Come on," Chelle said, her demeanor super serious, though I knew she was having fun with her fame for once.

The girls crowded around but seemed confused about how to handle the picture subtly. This was where my job training kicked in. I shot pics of no less than ten families per day during my shifts.

"Give me one of the phones," I said, my hand extended.

The girl who flung the change handed me hers. After four quick shots, Chelle sent them on their way. Before they disappeared into the crowd, one said, "Your show was my favorite. I miss it a lot."

When she was gone, Chelle mumbled, "I don't."

"Hey, hey." I tapped her shoulder and motioned toward the T-shirt stand. "It's happening."

16

Zeke had reached Ramona. Connie turned her phone sideways like she was shooting Oscar bait.

Immediately things went bad. Zeke smiled. Ramona did not. She said something that made his smile evaporate. She pointed to a T-shirt. Solid red, with Gary Gator from the *Gator Gang* cartoon dressed in a James Bond tuxedo. Zeke's shoulders slumped so low the shirt he had on could've slid to his ankles. He nodded, Ramona bagged it up, and Zeke swiped his resident wristband across the scanner.

The *cha-ching* sound of Pup Points leaving his account chimed in my head.

He scuttled from the line with his shirt, and Connie cut her recording. His slack face said it all. Train wreck.

Zeke flopped onto the lip of the fountain next to Chelle. Connie plopped down on his other side. I said, "That looked rough, bro."

Zeke stared at the bag containing his new wardrobe purchase resting between his shoes. "The guest in line ahead of me was doing like guests do. Yelling at her about not having a specific shirt they wanted or something. You know how it go."

We did. Well, maybe not Chelle. The rest of us worked in Karloff Country's most popular park—Enchantria—where guest tantrums were a regular occurrence.

"When I got to her, she was annoyed. I could see it in her face. I wanted to abort the mission, but it was too late. I was like, 'Hey, Ramona,' and she hit me with a real dry 'Can I help you?' I said, 'I'm thinking about getting a shirt. Any recommendations?' She pointed to Gary Gator like, 'My boyfriend looks good in this one. I got him the last extra-large, though. Wait, what am I saying, you're like a medium, right?'"

I choked back a laugh; he hit me with a death stare.

"I told her a large would be fine. And I paid. End of story."

Chelle stared at the bag like someone staring at a mound of dog poop. "How many Pup Points did that cost you?"

"Two hundred."

I hissed, feeling the pain. It was hard racking up Pup Points, harder than getting actual money. Pup Points were a reward system for good service and guest compliments. Zeke had made a lot of people happy to lose so many in a trash-fire attempt to holler at Ramona.

We sat quietly in his grief and let Downtown be loud around us. You couldn't be sad in the joyous churn for long. Connie rubbed small circles in Zeke's back—the crew grandma soothing us after a skinned knee. "How about a milkshake? My treat."

Zeke beamed.

Before we got going, I said, "Zeke, that story you were telling us about no one ever dying on property . . ."

"What about it?"

"Does what happened with Ramona mean you're the first?"

Connie pressed her mouth into her shoulder, stifling her giggles. I met my disgruntled friend's gaze with a wide you-know-I-had-to-say-it grin.

Took a moment, but finally, he grinned back.

Staying salty in the funnest place around was counterproductive.

CHAPTER 3

Connie peered into her cup like a scientist looking through a microscope the whole ride home. She took short sips from her half-finished milkshake while the rest of us slurped the dregs of ours. She sipped, she looked. Sipped, looked. "They changed the recipe."

"Okay." Zeke popped the bubble lid off his strawberry shake, tilted the cup to his lips, and shoveled leftover whipped cream into his mouth with his straw.

"You can't tell?"

I'd gotten a caramel cashew shake. I peeked into my cup too, but I was hoping more of that ridiculous salty-sweet goodness had magically reappeared. "Mine tasted fine."

Chelle dropped her empty cup in her cup holder. "Could be your flavor."

Connie said, "I got chocolate like I always do. It's different."

"Bad different?" Chelle asked.

"Just . . . different. Maybe they're using a powdered mix instead of real ice cream."

Zeke groaned. "There's nothing wrong with that shake. You do this all the time."

"You have a caveman's mouth. I can't help if my palate is more sophisticated than yours."

Thing was, she really couldn't. Her dad was a chef. *The* chef here in Karloff Country. Mr. Chambers ran the best restaurant in the most expensive hotel, and Connie was on track to follow him into the family business. Not that she had much say in the matter. Her dad was recruited specifically to bring his signature style of cooking to Karloff Country. Part of the deal gave him naming rights to that fancy swank restaurant. He called it Constance.

It was written.

Connie wasn't a picky eater, exactly. She'd try anything. She *was* a harsh critic. I'd never heard her compliment any meal. The most she was capable of was supporting well-prepared food with her silence.

Chelle slowed to posted speed limits at the sight of the neighborhood entrance. The road ran past two huge brick marquees featuring brushed-nickel signage lit by landscaping spotlights planted among the tulips. Left marquee read: JUBILEE. The right: A KARLOFF RESIDENTIAL ADVENTURE.

We sailed the quiet streets, ready to call it a night.

"Tomorrow," I said, bringing up the unpleasantness we'd been avoiding all day. "Presentation practice."

"Do we have to?" Zeke twisted in his seat so I could see his pleading face. "We all pretty much know what we're doing."

"What we doing?" Connie challenged. "Your part specifically?"

"I got the middle . . . ish."

I said, "It's thirty percent of our grade. Mr. Lattimore deducts points if you say *um* too many times. So we're practicing."

Chelle turned onto our street. "I'll make sure our slides look good."

"Excellent," I said.

Zeke and I lived directly across the street from each other. Chelle passed our houses and four others before busting a U-turn and stopping in front of Connie's place. Connie climbed from the back seat and said, "Seven thirty tomorrow?"

Chelle said, "I might be a little late. We're having a State Dinner."

State Dinner was crewspeak for VIP meals at Karloff Manor, the big house you could see lit up on the distant mountain slope above Jubilee. Famous people. Political people. Rich people no one's ever heard of. They took vacations too. When those trips brought them to our world, they sometimes requested an audience with Franklin Karloff, Chelle's grandfather. Or maybe *he* summoned *them*. I never was clear on how that all worked.

Whatever way the State Dinners came together, Seychelle's attendance was mandatory.

"Girlllll," Connie said, "who's coming? Is it that delicious boy y'all cast to play Veil-Man in the new Garrison Cinematic Universe movie?"

Chelle shook her head. "Investors. I'm surprised you didn't know already."

Connie looked confused.

"Your dad and his A-Team are cooking."

"News to me. He's been grumpy lately so that explains a lot. No offense."

"Why would I be offended when I'm grumpy too? Those dinners are a whole pretentious mess."

Zeke said, "How late, though? I'm not trying to be waiting at the Treat all night."

"Eightish."

"We'll wait," I said.

Zeke shot me a look.

"We *will*," I said just to him.

While Zeke and I had our little moment, I was somewhat aware of a vibe between Connie and Chelle. Connie's eyes were wide, her stare pointed. Chelle looked twitchy.

Then Connie opened Zeke's door and snatched the bag holding his new T-shirt from his lap. "Let me get a good look at this undoubtedly appalling piece of apparel."

"Give it back! That shirt represents a significant part of my life savings." He hopped out while Connie skittered backward playing keep-away.

They darted, juked, and circled back to the car, where Connie kicked the door closed. "Go on, Chelle. Bye, Jay!"

Connie tossed Zeke's bag on her lawn like a game of fetch, and I watched him go full Fido as Chelle nudged the gas.

"That was . . ." I almost said *weird*, but knew it wasn't the right word for whatever this was. My hands were sweaty.

Chelle didn't say a word when she stopped in front of my house. Through her back window and the red wash of brake lights, Zeke was in no hurry to get home. Maybe at Connie's prompting. My heart beat hard. In my throat.

"I don't know what's wrong with Connie." Chelle's eyes were on her rearview mirror.

"Me neither. She's wild."

"Right."

It was too quiet. The car was electric, so not even engine noise.

I said, "You, um, sure you're gonna be good with your mom?"

She swatted an imaginary gnat from the air, looked unbothered. "I am not worried about Blythe."

"Good."

Good? Really, Jay? That's all you got?

She said, "You never did tell me what you thought was hot about Ramona?"

Wait. That was still on her mind? Had I been a jerk and not

realized it? "I shouldn't have said it that way. That's, like, objectification or something, isn't it?"

"I know you meant she was pretty. She is. Everyone knows that. I'm messing with you."

I wasn't imagining this. Something was happening here. Something Connie was in on. So, it wasn't only me who felt different lately. Was that a good thing?

"Hey, I'm getting out."

She gripped the wheel with both hands, stared straight ahead. Expressionless.

Crap. Did she take that the wrong way? "I mean, I want to talk face-to-face."

I exited the vehicle and crouched by her open window. She kept her eyes on the road, toward Jubilee's exit, and said, "You've got your shift tomorrow. I should go."

"Yes. I mean yes, I have a shift. But you don't have to go."

"I should, though. It's not cool to keep you up."

Girl stuff might be somewhat mysterious, but *Chelle stuff* I was well versed in. She was in embarrassment mode. When she got like this—felt like she'd said the wrong thing, or maybe inadvertently flexed some Karloff muscle too hard around people who relied on her family for their livelihood—her light complexion burned at her cheeks and forehead. The freckles on the bridge of her nose stood out. Even in the evening gloom, I saw.

My mind . . . blank. What to do? What to say?

"See you tomorrow." She began to drive.

"Chelle!" I blurted, unexpectedly desperate.

The car lurched when she stomped the brake. Waiting.

Crickets chirped night song around us, and moths fluttered in the streetlight haze. This felt like a moment, the kind where if you got it wrong, you didn't get it back. I felt it in my gut as keenly as my phantom hunger pains. I said, "Ramona's pretty, but she ain't you."

One dimpled cheek turned up in a half grin. "That was so corny, Jay."

"I know who you used to date. You *love* corny."

"He's got jokes!" Full grin.

This was a moment too. The quit-while-you're-ahead kind.

Backing away from the car, I said, "Text when you're home. Let me know you got there safe."

I'd never asked her to do that before. Just like she'd never engineered some weird one-on-one drop-off with Connie's help. It was a night for new.

From my porch, I watched her turn the corner. Then I swiped my resident wristband over the lock pad. A red diode blinked blue, and my front door unlatched. Inside, Sandrina greeted me from invisible speakers. "Welcome home, Jermaine. Wireless charging is on."

My wristband turned orange, and the haptic servos in the band double-tapped my wrist at the pulse, indicating a sync and charge had begun.

Mom was on the couch, holding her phone for a video call.

Animated and talking loud on the screen was her friend DeeDee, saying, "Girl, I heard they're about to open a new neighborhood to house new Helpers. S'pose to be nicer than Jubilee. I don't think that's right. Seniority should get you better amenities, don't you think?"

"Hold on a sec, Dee." Mom looked up. Her head tilted. "Hey, guy. What's up with you?"

"What you mean?"

"You look . . . energized."

I held up my glowing band. "I'm charging."

"Ha-ha."

That's all she was going to get. "G'night."

"Good night," Mom said.

In my room with the door closed, I said, "Sandrina, play Game Time."

The pyramid mounted to my desk chimed and glowed purple at the tip. "Playing Jay's playlist Game Time."

A heavy guitar riff kicked off the mix of rock and rap as I booted up my PS6 and fell into the beanbag chair in front of my gaming monitor. I got lost in a futuristic battlefield, firing infinite rounds into infinite space ghouls and lobbing sticky grenades because those were the goriest. Lost in digital blood spatter splashing my screen, I almost missed the incoming text.

Chelle
Made it.

Me
Good. Today was fun.

Me
All of it.

Chelle
It was. WYD?

Me
On the sticks.

25

Chelle

So. Boy. You're shooting
monsters aren't you?

Me

Nope. Game's called Kitten
Cloud. I'm a kitten hopping
between clouds.

Chelle

It went back and forth like that for a while. Banter! I could've kept going, but Chelle had her Karloff responsibilities, and I had mine. Long shift tomorrow.

We called it a night. I put the PS6 in rest mode, peeled off my clothes, and fell into bed.

The shrinking piece of my consciousness still in the waking world registered my Game Time music fading before the playlist cut off completely. Sandrina sensed I was no longer listening and shifted to energy-saver mode.

So helpful.

I slept well.

Excerpt from *Pillars of the Community: A History of American Industrialists* by P. J. Wayne, published in 2012 by Harbinger Press, Boston

JACK OF ALL TRADES

There may not be a family with a more eclectic business history than Breckerton Karloff and his offspring. Having earned his initial fortune through coal-mining ventures in West Virginia and managing to keep most of his wealth through the Great Depression—a boast many of his contemporaries couldn't make—his fellow magnates were surprised when Karloff pivoted into not one but two new industries: candy and film.

His turn to the world of confections was inspired by his admiration for Milton Hershey, aka the Chocolate King. Although Breckerton's interest in the budding film industry had a more salacious catalyst—a long-term tryst with a silent-film actress. Regardless of his motives, he made quality gains in both arenas, producing small batches of popular high-end candies for an upscale clientele and becoming a production partner on several hit movies, eventually forming his own studio, Karloff Pictures.

Breckerton was pleased with the success he'd found diversifying his assets and sought other lucrative prospects. At any given time between the 1930s and 1960s, you'd find the Karloff family dipping their toes into telecommunications, agriculture, government contracting, and other miscellany.

When Breckerton's eldest son, Franklin, took over company operations in the early '70s, he continued his father's practice of seeking inspiration from other successful men. And one drew young Franklin's eye more than any other . . .

The late Walt Disney.

CHAPTER 4

Whenever people thought about janitors, the grossest parts of the job came to mind. Picking up nasty trash. Scrubbing toilets. And, yes, those things could be disgusting. Not gonna lie. So, whenever I told people being a janitor in Enchantria Park was the best public-facing job in Karloff Country, they scoffed, super skeptical.

It was true, though.

Forget about the gross stuff—not the easiest thing to do, and I had some stories that'd give you nightmares—but toss the nastiest bits aside and listen.

First, we weren't called janitors. We were "Helpers." The idea was, we're giving Karloff Country guests a fantasy. An expensive fantasy. That money and trust meant everyone with a Karloff Country name tag was responsible for *helping* meet guest expectations. Within that, there were categories. Like, Zeke and his dad worked in engineering and maintenance, making sure rides and other critical systems remained functional. They were "Attraction Helpers." Connie worked the legendary Penny Pup's Weiners stand in the SafariScape section of Enchantria, while her dad was a big deal chef. They were "Culinary Helpers." See how that worked?

My janitorial role made me an "Immediacy Helper," as in I dealt with a lot of in-the-moment stuff. If a guest dropped an ice-cream wrapper in my line of sight, the ice cream staining that wrapper should still be cold by the time I deposited it in a nearby receptacle. If a guest looked lost, I offered assistance without being asked. If the heat got to someone and they fainted, I had a medical team rolling up in their golf cart before a crowd gathered.

Probably still didn't sound all that appealing, right? It's all relative, though.

Connie was pretty much bolted to the same spot all day, every day, doing the same repetitive work of taking orders, grabbing hot dogs and onion rings, and passing them through a window to a guest who'd probably yell at her for taking too long even when she was fast. She took it in stride because she saw it as paying dues . . . the path to food supremacy like her dad.

Zeke rarely dealt with the public, since the attractions his team fixed were usually closed to guests until operational again, but that meant he rarely saw sunshine. His grease-stained maintenance coveralls weren't conducive to the mystical fantasy guests paid for, so he traveled the tunnels beneath Enchantria and in the Helpers Only corridors behind every Enchantria attraction, like a phantom with a toolbox.

Me, though . . . every day a different adventure. Aside from the hourly cleaning schedules of whatever restrooms my boss, Harry, assigned me, I was free to roam the various sections of our park. Like, FuturaScape was supposed to be the future, but the look and feel was like some guy from the 1970s' idea of what the year 2000 would be except we still had no teleportation booths and everyday people weren't walking around in aluminum-foil space suits. Guests often complained about the outdated forecast, but a bunch also found the utopian charm appealing.

There was ArcanaScape, which was magic themed, wizards and faeries and whatever. PatriotScape, an ode to the founding of America. SafariScape with its mix of jungle and desert themes and so on.

Unlike the Helpers who worked restaurants, rides, and retail in those sections, with their area-specific space cop, eldritch witch, or American Revolution costumes, my plain gray, almost-invisible Immediacy Helper outfit was universal. Nothing about me broke the fantasy.

I strolled through ArcanaScape late that afternoon. Thickly sweet cotton candy made every breath like snorting straight sugar. A grease-spotted food wrapper blew by guests' feet like a tumbleweed. As I was jogging to catch it, an elderly guest holding the hand of a freckle-faced child wearing a seventy-five-dollar sorcerer's hat (that's real-world currency; in Pup Points, it would've been, like, four hundred) waved me over. It was an aggressive, hurried wave, like the universal gesture for impatience. Widening my smile, I approached the woman. "Hi there. My name is Jay. How might I help you?"

"Where's Elf Penny?"

Penny Pup, Karloff Entertainment's most popular character, rocking the elven look featured in the Karloff classic animated film *Enchantment Eve*, was likely a hundred feet beneath me, disassembled in the character shop, with his big bubble head hanging on a wall hook for tonight's steam cleaning since the Character Helper who wore that costume had already made their three appearances for the day.

Character costumes were made of heavy latex foam and fiberglass. Sometimes covered in fur. When it's 110 degrees outside, it's 130 in those suits. The performers could roam their allotted realms for, like, ten minutes at a time before they had to be escorted underground into lifesaving air-conditioning. They emerged from those suits looking like they'd been thrown into a pool, they sweat so much. Most spent an hour chugging Gatorade only to repeat the process for however long their shift dictated. The job that, arguably, brought children the most joy, best photos, and forever memories was pure torture for the people making it possible.

Most guests knew nothing of that—those who did probably didn't care all that much. Their concern was the memory; pleasing the crying child who wanted to shake a four-fingered cartoon hand.

This was about to be awesome.

"I'm sorry," I said. "Elf Penny isn't visiting Enchantria anymore today. He will be back tomorrow at ten a.m., one p.m., and four p.m."

The kid exploded in a predictable tantrum, throwing his hat on the ground, then curb-stomping it.

The woman, just as predictable, said, "I paid an obscene amount of money for my grandson to see Elf Penny. Is this really the best you can do?"

A veteran in my Helper role, I recognized the kind of Irate Guest I was dealing with by tone alone. This lady was a negotiator. Probably a Karloff Country regular who understood an unhappy child was currency on par with actual money—or Pup Points. She didn't berate me and didn't make an outright request. She wanted to hear my offer first.

Kneeling at eye level with the kid, I produced a pad from my back pocket. Grandma recognized it; any Karloff regular would. She salivated.

"Hey, friend," I told the kid while I tore a golden sheet free and scribbled a number. "I'm sorry Elf Penny won't be back today, but this Karloff Coupon will let you pick out any item, from any gift shop, up to one hundred dollars in value."

Those tears dried instantly. He snatched the coupon fast and retrieved his mangled hat.

I waited on what I knew was coming.

Grandma said, "We were planning to celebrate his big day of meeting Elf Penny with a nice meal before we flew home in the morning."

"I thought we weren't going home until Tuesday, Grandma!"

"Be quiet, Timmy," she scolded. To me, "As I said, we're leaving tomorrow and won't have the chance to see Elf Penny. The meal would've been a celebration."

The coupon I gave her was for $150. "Might I suggest Constance in the Grand Virginian hotel? Best food in the resort."

She had Timmy by the hand and was already diving into the late-day crowd. I mumbled, "You're welcome."

Back to enjoying my stroll. Guest interactions like that happened more than I liked, but all things considered, there was still magic in the air.

Enchantria closed to guests at 6:00 p.m. on Sundays, but my team and I started final cleanup at 5:15 so tasks were completed quickly, all equipment stowed, and we were descending into the tunnels beneath the park to shower and change by no later than 6:30.

My boss, Harry, took the stairs with me. He tapped through screens on the tablet he used to track everything from shift schedules to resupply these days. "Hey, Jermaine, got a guest comment about you."

"Oh yeah?"

"Nice little compliment. Said you're highly professional, attentive, and you have a nice smile."

For some reason, Grandma and Little Timmy came to mind. I was certain that stellar review *didn't* come from them. "Service and joy," I said. "It's the Karloff way."

"That it is."

Harry never recognized my sarcasm, and I don't know that I actually wanted him to. So maybe it wasn't sarcasm?

Whoever it came from, the compliment was a nice end to the day.

At the base of the stairs, Harry tugged me aside so other teammates could pass us. "Lemme see your band."

My resident wristband lit up orange, like everyone else's since the Enchantria tunnels were equipped with wireless charging. When I rotated it toward Harry's tablet, he tapped a command and my band flashed green, accompanied by a sound like jackpot tokens spilling from a slot machine.

Harry said, "One hundred Pup Points for you, kid."

I would not be spending them on any T-shirts.

Here, under Enchantria, it was amazing how not-magical and un-fun the place seemed. Dull green floor tiles, thick pipes, wire conduits, ventilation shafts painted eggshell white to match the walls, and, above it all, black foam insulation. The main tunnel was a loop that ran the perimeter of the park. Do a full lap, and you'd clock five miles for the day. Every dozen yards or so were doors leading into the center. Mini tunnels, like the spokes on a wheel, that took you to different departments and storage areas. There were three cafeterias. Four laundry services. A huge IT department that, supposedly, took up most of some central hub. And other necessary things—an infirmary, inner wall security, executive meeting rooms. Really, who knows what else? Zeke had all kinds of theories about secret labs, hidden gold, props from a faked moon landing, whatever.

In that moment, after a long day in the sun, all I was concerned with was the locker room and a shower—both a few yards ahead.

Harry had other things in mind.

He grabbed my shoulder. "Walk with me a sec."

"Am I getting more Pup Points? Please tell me I'm getting more Pup Points."

He caught the sarcasm that time. "This is serious, Jay. Big news."

Jay? He rarely called me by my nickname. We kept on down the tunnel. "What's up, Harry?"

"This is between you and me. I mean not a word."

"Got it."

He made the exaggerated gesture of checking our surroundings as if every square inch of the tunnels weren't in the sight lines of one or more security cameras—but I guessed he was more worried about eavesdropping. This must be *very* good. With the coast clear, he whispered, "Sheri Poe jumped the wall."

That straightened my spine. Somewhat horrified, I said, "Why?"

Resuming his normal volume, he said, "Who knows. Not my business, really."

Jumping the wall was the euphemism Karloff Helpers used when someone left the company. Whenever it happened, it felt like a big deal. Almost like they should be mourned. Unless, of course, their absence meant good things for those they left behind. Sheri Poe had been *Harry's* boss.

Ambition crackled off him. "I'm moving up the ranks, Jay. God's plan. I'm telling you. Been praying on this a long time."

"Congratulations." I was so used to Harry's divine attributions for everything I barely heard them. Everything in life was God's plan. God's good all the time. Folks outside the Karloff Country walls would likely disagree. When my family was out there, I would've disagreed.

I nearly asked why he was telling me all this when the answer was obvious.

He wanted me to move up the ranks too.

"You're my best Helper, hands down. Your work ethic's great. I count on you to be squared away. I want you to know that when I'm able to make the recommendation, I'm throwing your name in for an assistant manager slot."

Assistant manager. That meant planning, scheduling, dealing with the department's budget. I'd transition away from the worst parts of the job. No more wiping pee and crap off toilet seats because folks couldn't aim or simply chose not to. No more getting hustled when Elf Penny didn't operate on some entitled guest's schedule.

"How soon?" I asked.

"Couple of weeks. I'll be doing double duty for a while since Sheri left so suddenly. Be ready when the time comes. You get your legs under you over the summer, then we'll work around your school schedule in the fall."

I grinned at the possibilities if I did get this new job and crushed it. "That sounds like a plan."

Gaining a place in Karloff Country was a gift. The possibility to secure a higher position, more status—more security!—almost had me turning to religion like Harry. I couldn't quite get to "God's plan," but my family had been on a run these last few years.

Why not keep the winning streak going?

CONNIE

Freshly showered, in my street clothes, and so ready to catch the shuttle home, I was a little annoyed I had to shoo some basic chicks away. Shuttle Shelter #4 has been my crew's bench since forever, and the Gift Shop Barbies should've known better is all I'm saying. One was bold enough to suck her teeth as they scuttled away. Whatever. I flopped on the bench, waiting for Jay and Zeke.

The shuttle loop was a brightly lit lot that butted against loading docks with big bay doors where supplies got off-loaded. Boxy dumpsters for trash and recyclables were nearby, and with it being a warm night, those smelled lovely. Bus, hurry!

Jay emerged from the tunnels first, which was perfect. Me and him needed a word.

He sat, grunting in a way boys seemed to think passed for human communication, and was immediately in his phone.

"You texting Chelle?" I said.

He looked up, clearly annoyed. "I'm playing *Two Dots*. It's a puzzle game where you try to connect—"

"I don't care about your stupid puzzle game, Jay. Are you a grandpa? What's up with you and Chelle?"

Really, I mean, what was up with *him*? Because if anyone was going to be a problem in this matchmaking perfection I'd set in motion, it'd be Jay Butler.

He shrugged, proving my point, and really tried to get back to those dots.

I snatched his phone.

"Hey!"

"You get it back when you assure me our good friend is someone you're going to pursue instead of what you usually do."

"Usually do? It feels like you insulted me, but I'm not sure how, exactly."

Deep breaths, Con. Long days at the hot dog broiler got you on edge.

I said, "You drag your feet, Jay. Or you don't move them at all. My mom has this real country saying, 'So and so will stand still in a hurricane if the water's fine.' That's you."

"That doesn't make any sense."

"It does and it doesn't. Like a lot of country sayings. It's like you're scared to move because you're afraid you'll end up somewhere bad, even if you're already somewhere bad."

"Am I somewhere bad?"

Don't slap him, Con. He knows not what he does.

"Okay," I said, "maybe I've overcomplicated this. Chelle's into you. I sense you're somewhat into her. Whatever dumb calculus you're doing to not move the needle on this probably-good-thing, stop it. Constradamus has spoken."

He hit me with a strong eye roll. "Constradamus?"

"Modern-day prophet. It is I."

"Well, prophet, you're wrong. I'll have you know I kind of accepted a big promotion today. Does that sound like someone bathing in your mom's hurricane water or however that saying went?"

I slow blinked. "*Kind of* accepted is wishy-washy, Jay. My point stands."

At that moment, Zeke showed up with a group of engineers. Mostly large men with rough hands that had Zeke looking like a gazelle hanging with rhinos. He was frowny and sort of stomping. His typical after-work mood, but the grumpiness was magnified. His phone was out, thumb tapping, then both phones in my possession vibrated.

Jay grabbed his back, and I checked mine for the group text.

Zeke

We'll be home in like 20. What's your ETA?

Chelle

idk. Dinner's running long.

Zeke huffed, while Jay responded.

Jay

We'll be around.

Chelle

I know. 🤍

"Good job," I said. "You should send a heart emoji back."

"Why would he do that?" Zeke sounded genuinely confused. The World's Greatest Detective he was not. Then he changed subjects abruptly, shifting gears between his various annoyances. "Cosmos Sled went down today."

"Oh." I softened at the news. My hot dog hut was on the other side of the park, but that wasn't far enough to miss the implication of Enchantria's most popular ride malfunctioning on a busy weekend at the start of summer season.

For most guests in the park on Sunday, it meant their last day at the Karloff Country resort. A lot of Monday morning flights back to reality. If anything sullied that Last Day Experience for the most wretched vacationers, any employee in earshot heard about it.

Zeke said, "A gearbox in the sled's loading area blew. Of course, Sandrina dropped the ball on the resupply, so the parts that we needed and should've had are on back order. No fixing it today. Maybe not tomorrow either. When Skynet screws up, guess who gets candy thrown at them?"

He gained more of my sympathy. "A kid threw candy at you?"

"A parent."

Jay said, "Skynet was from *WarGames*, right?"

Even I knew that was wrong, and not because Jay always confused the old movies Zeke made us watch when it was his turn to pick how we spent a Saturday night.

"*The Terminator*," I said before Zeke did because maybe we could move on from it easily. Ha!

"WOPR was the AI in *WarGames*," Zeke said.

"Okay," Jay said, smug, "then comparing WOPR to Sandrina makes more sense than Skynet."

"How, bro?"

Here. We. Go. Ugh!

"Because Skynet did exactly what it meant to do—send a cyborg to the past to kill Susan Cooper."

"Sarah Connor."

"Yeah, her. WOPR was meant to do a thing one way, but did something different and worse. That's Sandrina."

"Except, I was going for an analogy for evil, not incompetence. *That's* Sandrina. And if she gets me killed out here, does it really matter?"

"Exaggeration," Jay countered, clearly ready to go the distance on this, and I'd had enough.

"Boys!" I shouted. "Keep this up and I'm using my karate."

I didn't know karate. They knew I didn't know karate. Still, they knew it was best to fear me, so they quieted down. Not that they didn't make valid points about the buggy nature of Karloff Country's proprietary artificial intelligence. Truth was, anything beyond cueing up a playlist or turning the lights off when I forgot to do it, and Sandrina was sus. We still didn't know if our missed hot dog shipments were about the system messing up or the meat shortages outside the walls. Fortunately, we were well stocked before, so we didn't feel it. Much. But another couple of weeks and I'd be dealing with irate guests too.

"Connie, how was your day?" one of them finally asked. I didn't even catch who because that new girl who worked the River Rescue ride sashayed by.

I turned on my selfie cam to poof my hair and get a longer view of that cutie inconspicuously. "Lotta hot dogs. Lotta fries. The usual."

The crowd around the benches got denser as more and more workers gathered for a trip home. The shuttle bus arrived with a single word flashing in the LED sign mounted to its side: JUBILEE. The doors squeaked open, and we filed on.

The "bus driver" wasn't a driver, or a person. It was hard-molded fiberglass mounted behind the steering well . . . like a statue of a driver, but with a tablet for a face. On the tablet was the hazy outline of a woman's hairdo and a soft jawline, like looking at a face through shower steam. As each of us passed it for a seat, it gave a soothing "Welcome" in the voice we all knew.

Über creepy if you hadn't lived here forever like us.

That was a lie. Sandrina the Driver was still creepy no matter how many times you rode along.

CHAPTER 5

In Jubilee, we walked dead center in the road, the kings and queen of our domain.

No need to worry about traffic because few cars ever drove this path. Neighborhood ordinances didn't allow for parking at the curb or in driveways. Most resident traffic stuck to narrow alleys behind the homes leading to two-car garages that didn't obstruct the manicured view of each house's facade. There were seven different designs and twenty-plus approved color palettes that made up the Jubilee homes, staggered and alternated so the sameness was barely felt.

Grass was lush and uniform, no taller than a quarter inch per yard, except for one home we passed, where the length and visible weeds had gotten that owner a bright yellow flyer affixed to their front door: a warning from the JRA—Jubilee Residents' Association.

We turned the corner and passed my house. The porch was crowded with women, Mom's book club. They were in animated conversation about the new N. K. Jemisin novel. Or possibly the wine bottle making the rounds to refill empty glasses. Mom leaned against the porch rail and called out, "Heyyyyy, kids."

"Hey, Mom," I said.

"Hi, Mrs. Butler," Connie and Zeke said in syrupy-sweet unison.

Mom waved at us.

I said, "We're going up to the Treat. Work on our presentation."

"Good luck. If I'm asleep when you come in, I left you a plate in the microwave."

Temps dropped rapidly at night here, and even though we'd

sweated through a scorcher of a shift today, Connie shuddered at a cool breeze that whistled between us. At her house, she said, "I'm running inside to grab a jacket. Meet you there."

She veered off toward her front door, swiping her band and ducking inside. As soon as her door clicked shut, I said, "You good?"

"I'm good." Zeke plunged both hands in his pockets and wouldn't meet my eyes. He did not seem good.

"You've been quiet the whole ride home. That usually means you have a lot to say. Spit, yo."

A few steps ahead, he turned so he was walking backward, putting us face-to-face. "It ain't really my business—"

"Never stopped you before."

"Cool. I'll keep it a buck with you. Chelle's the homey and everything, but it's a bad idea, bro."

We walked several steps while I processed it and tried not to show he pissed me off. "I know you ain't done."

He sucked his teeth, into it now. "Dale Tannen."

"Her ex ain't even on property anymore. If he was, they been through. Wouldn't mean anything to me."

"It really should."

"What are you talking about?"

Zeke yanked his hands from his pockets as if he were about to start making shadow puppets or something. When he talked with his hands like that, I knew something wild was going to come out of his mouth. "His whole family is gone, Jay. Over the wall. Done."

"So? People leave. They broke up *because* his family was leaving."

"I think you got it backward."

I spread my arms, clueless and waiting.

Zeke said, "I heard—"

"Oh, this should be good."

He stopped walking. Directly in front of me. Blocking my path. "I heard Dale was messing around with Hayley Brock and Chelle caught him. That's what broke them up. Then, all of sudden, Dale and his family aren't in Karloff Country anymore."

"Who is Hayley Brock? I don't know her at all."

"And you won't. Ever. Her whole family gone too."

"This is the first I've heard of it, so it didn't come from Chelle. How did *you* hear it?"

He started walking toward the Treat again.

"Zeke!"

Over his shoulder, he said, "Panopticon."

"You—you're serious?" I jogged to catch up.

Panopticon was—I don't know how to explain it. A message board? A person? A cult? Conspiracy theories and crap like that, so right up Zeke and his dad's alley. Panopticon's whole thing was trash-talking Karloff Country, Karloff Entertainment, the Karloffs themselves. If Zeke's dad told Zeke no one ever died in Karloff Country, I now knew who told Zeke's dad.

I said, "You don't be on there posting stuff about Chelle, do you?"

He scoffed. "Naw, man. That'd be foul. Plus, if anyone down with Panopticon knew I was that close to a Karloff, I'd probably get kicked off the board anyway."

That he seemed more concerned about continued access to that trash board than the possibility of betraying one of his best friends didn't sit right. "You don't really believe Chelle had whole families

44

removed from Karloff Country because her boyfriend cheated on her? You know how ridiculous that sounds? How cruel?"

He answered slowly. "No. I don't think *Chelle* would go that far. What about Blythe, or her grandpa, though?"

"Oh my God!" I wasn't going to think about it. Not if this was coming from those Panopticon lunatics.

We arrived at the Treat and found our pavilion empty. We sat in our usual seats, while Connie shuffled over in her poofy jacket. Before she was in earshot, Zeke said, "Be careful, Jay. Getting with Chelle might be a good thing, if it lasts. If it doesn't . . ."

He didn't complete the thought.

He didn't have to.

For a half hour, we did a loose run-through of our presentation, claiming responsibility for a specific subtopic and agreeing on the approximate order and handoff. Connie called intro because she got stage fright and wanted to get her part over with. I was second. Zeke third. Since Chelle was late, she was strapped with the responsibility of closing strong. Show up late, get the worst assignment. Even if there was something budding between us, I couldn't go soft on that particular group work rule.

The sky had darkened to turquoise when a pair of headlights floated straight at us, silent, like twin ghosts. Chelle swung her car sharply, its profile as slick and glossy as a soap bubble.

"Finally," said Connie. She wanted a real rehearsal with our actual presentation slides. The more prepared she felt, the less nervous she'd be. There was some logic to it, I guessed.

Chelle parked along the dead-end curb and exited the vehicle awkwardly, her agility restricted by her unexpected attire.

My chest seized.

Her hair was pulled back in a high, tight bun, and a for-real diamond necklace twinkled in the yellow light from a streetlamp over her head. Shuddering slightly from the evening chill, she snatched a leather jacket from the passenger seat and shrugged into it. The jacket's worn hide and the golden ball gown made her look like the heroine of some monsters-attack-the-prom movie.

With her backpack, she scuttled over, unconcerned that the expensive gown that had obviously been tailored for some sort of heeled shoe now dragged along the grass because she'd driven over in red sneakers.

"Hey, guys," she panted. "Sorry, Grandfather wouldn't let me go until dessert was finished and his guests were well into discussing whatever they needed to talk about."

Zeke spoke with a bad snooty British accent. "You mean once they retired to the parlor for brandy and cigars?"

She sneered, clearly not here for Zeke's snark.

Given our earlier conversation, I wasn't into it either. "Let's work."

Chelle removed her phone from her bag, popped the kickstand on the case, and said, "Sandrina, show social studies slide deck."

A wide blue beam fanned from the projector in Chelle's phone. Our presentation's title slide lit the broad wall of the Treat's public bathrooms, and whatever tension was lingering before slipped away. Beneath our project title ("The Vertical Farms of Karloff Country: Creating a World's Worth of Sustainable Food"), on a colorful custom background that was going to crush our classmates' plain came-with-the-program templates, was us. An old picture from like the first month we met, taken in the exact spot we occupied now.

We were on the table. Seychelle, still rocking braces and two big braids, lay on her side, with one hand propping up her head. I sat behind her, knees pulled to my chest. Zeke was next to me, head cocked, looking typically cynical about the whole affair. Connie was on my other side wringing her hands.

I was surprised how much the memory of those days affected me. How much Chelle in that gown, perfume like flowers and what I imagined the ocean from Mom's stories smelled like, affected me. She rooted through her bag for something. When she glanced up, she caught me looking. I didn't turn away. Neither did she.

Connie ended the friendly staring contest by waving her index cards between us. "Hello! Can we start, please?"

We went through our twelve-minute presentation three times. Everyone knew their part, we had smooth transitions, and Chelle was the appropriate closer, for sure. We *never* talked about how her and her family used to be on TV every week, but the confidence—or maybe indifference—that came with being "on" like she had to be when cameras trailed her 24/7 never went away. She'd completely discarded her index cards by the second run-through and never fumbled a single word. Unlike Connie, who finally got her act together by the third run but was going to be an anxious mess until the moment we finished tomorrow.

Zeke and I packed up our stuff while Chelle massaged Connie's shoulders like the cornerman at a boxing match. "We'll be right up there with you. You'll be fine."

"If only public speaking was like yelling at people in a kitchen. I'd be all over that."

Zeke said, "I once heard this joke about public speaking that said at a funeral most people would rather be in the coffin than give the eulogy."

Chelle, scolding, said, "Did someone tell you that was a funny joke? Because they lied."

Changing the subject before that went too far, I said, "Your dinner was good?"

"The food, yes. Everything else was extra dull. Saw your dad, though."

I thought she was talking to Connie, but Chelle's gaze leveled on me. I said, "*My* dad?"

"Yeah. Grandfather wanted people from the business departments present to talk shop with the money folks."

Had *I* even seen my dad since yesterday's cookout?

Zeke gathered his things. "Y'all keep talking about dinner, and only one of us has had it. I could eat one of *you* right now. We good here?"

Connie said, "My dad's been doing some test cooks on a few new recipes. We have leftovers. If you're that hungry, I'm sure he'd appreciate the feedback."

She said it with her sly grin while flicking glances Chelle's way. Guess me and her weren't invited.

Zeke perked up, until it sunk in for him too.

He eyed me. Took a noticeably heavy breath, then joined Connie. He'd said what he had to say and knew better than to push it further.

"See y'all in the morning," Connie said, the two of them exiting the Treat with quick steps.

"What kind of test recipes we talking about here?"

"Ever had gator tail?"

Zeke flinched but did not change course.

So. Me and Chelle. She sat on our table, her sneakers on the bench beside me. I climbed up next to her, backpack between us. She said, "This wasn't an awkward transition at all."

"Nope," I said, with a rush of heat to my face.

"Can we talk? I'm not too good at subtlety and I don't want to feel anxious about—" She made wavering hand gestures that I interpreted to mean *us*.

What she suggested for anxiety relief had the opposite effect on me. *Can we talk* . . . typically not the prelude to awesome things, and despite Zeke's ominous warning and Connie's overzealous manipulations, I wasn't without agency here. Chelle was crew, yes, but I've never seen her like a sister the way I saw Connie. I didn't have to be tricked into feeling what I feel and couldn't force myself away any longer.

It was shaping up into a cold night. The temp drop made her quick breaths puff. I exhaled slow and ignored the heavy thumping in my chest. "We talk about everything else. I don't want that to ever change."

"We are talking about a change, though."

"Seems that way."

"We're still being subtle-ish, huh?"

I laughed. "You look good in that dress."

"I know." She grinned. "Okay. Okay. How about this? We say the thing we've been avoiding. In our own way. No judgment from the other."

49

"Who goes first?"

"Call heads or tails."

"Heads."

She lifted her phone near her face. "Sandrina, flip a coin."

The AI said, "Tails."

Chelle said, "Crap."

Twisting to partially face her, I tucked my hand under my chin, attentive. "Go ahead and tell me how you admire my muscles."

"If I admired muscles, I'd be somewhere else."

"Ow."

"Gimme me my banter points." She waved both hands in the air like she was wiping away the last thirty seconds. "Okay, stop. We're doing this. I like you. Lately, more than how I've always liked you. I think you like me back, and I don't know what to do with that. Because that can get messy. Your turn."

Her *I like you* had my skin tingling. Truth: In what world would I, minuscule-to-the-universe Jermaine Butler, have a chance with Seychelle Karloff of the world-famous Karloff family? That she was even my friend felt ridiculous whenever I thought about it too hard. Those were the notions I'd operated on all this time. She was her, and I was me, and how would that make any sense? Except, I was here and so was she.

I liked her too. More than a friend. It felt okay to admit it today.

My turn. "It's been hard to be around you this year because I'm also worried about a mess."

"Okay. We agree there's something between us. We also agree we're worried about complicating everything."

"Accurate."

50

"We should kiss."

"How did you get from mess to there?" Not that I was complaining. The night wasn't cold anymore.

Her eyes widened. "I'm saying, like . . . like a test recipe. We kiss. See how it goes."

Zeke's voice invaded my thoughts: *Getting with Chelle might be a good thing, if it lasts. If it doesn't . . .*

That he was still in my head angered me like he'd interrupted this moment in person. I pushed him away, then pushed forward, maybe out of spite. "Okay. Let's—"

She swept her backpack aside and leaned into me. Her lips—God, they were soft—meeting mine. As quick as she'd acted, she snatched away. "Well?"

"I'd like to continue the recipe." I leaned into her, placing my hand on her shoulder, while one of her hands found its way to my cheek. We kissed again. Long. Sweet.

Phantom Zeke sounded off again: *It's a bad idea, bro.*

Maybe.

I wasn't exactly thinking pros and cons in that moment.

A breath and an eternity later, we parted. I said, "Recipe a success?"

"I would say yes."

That triggered our last batch of laughs for the night. The last for a long time.

She gathered her things and climbed from the table. I joined her, hip to hip, and she hooked my pinkie with hers. It was as good as the kisses. "I can drop you at your house."

I accepted the ride, of course. Now that we weren't warming each other, I fought to keep my teeth from chattering. On the short trip, she steered with one hand while the other remained intertwined with mine.

When I was halfway to my door, Chelle rolled down the window, called after me, "We're going to crush that presentation tomorrow."

"As long as Connie doesn't get freaked out and bail," I joked.

"We'll need to take her for milkshakes after."

"Definitely."

She pulled off, yelling from her window, "MILKSHAKES!"

All in all, it was a mild end for the last normal night we'd ever have.

Not every devastation comes with an omen.

KARLOFF COUNTRY RESORT *HOLLER!* PAGE

TERRENCE R., PHOENIX, AZ
5 OUT OF 5 STARS
FOUR MONTHS AGO

Nothing like that mountain air and top-tier service. I'd spend the rest of my life in Karloff Country . . . if I could afford it. LOL!

ANONYMOUS REVIEWER
2 OUT OF 5 STARS
ONE YEAR AGO

This is a tough review to write. My family absolutely loves Karloff Country—or at least we did. We've been blessed to go yearly since our children reached an appropriate age (one where they'll remember these trips, ha!), and though we don't opt for the most expensive lodging and restaurants on the property, we have still spent a great deal of money there. The experience has always been worth it. But, this last trip, I sensed a shift in the culture—what some of you other reviewers have brought up—that's really rubbed me the wrong way. Not only have the traditionally cheaper accommodations become as prohibitively expensive as the luxury options USED TO BE, but there's clearly been a shift in leadership for this new more "woke" agenda to be implemented throughout the property.

There's so much attention paid to waving those silly rainbow flags, inclusive hairstyles, and all sorts of other cultural sensitivity crap that it had me wondering if the Helpers were serving me, or if I was serving them? It felt like if I even THOUGHT something that wasn't in line, I'd get kicked out of the place. Don't get me wrong, I love everybody. But I don't pay a ridiculous sum of money every year to make THE HELPERS feel comfortable. Really, I miss the old days when MY FAMILY'S comfort was the most important thing. The days when the company didn't use all that famine conspiracy, global warming, left-wing-scam nonsense to triple the price of a hamburger and a bottle of water.

As much as I have loved the safety, security, and fun of being inside the Karloff Country walls, I'm seriously considering canceling next year's booking.

JANET T., MINNEAPOLIS, MN
4 OUT OF 5 STARS
SIXTEEN MONTHS AGO

We had a wonderful time exploring the resort. The kids loved Enchantria most, of course. Me and the hubs got some great hiking in. If you can swing it, because it IS pricey, you gotta do the seven-course chef's menu at Constance in the Grand Virginian. Simply divine! The only reason I'm not giving five stars is I felt the security teams were a little overzealous. When we were out on a long hike, we came across some new construction and the perimeter guards got really nasty about us being in an unauthorized area and how we could be expelled from the resort without a refund. I get Franklin Karloff's gotta protect his intellectual property but come on. Otherwise, had a great time.

CHAPTER 6

Jet noise woke me. Rare, but not extraordinary in Karloff Country. Among the many luxurious amenities on-site there was a private jetport and several hangars. The biggest was a permanent home for the Karloff family's two private planes, the rest were reserved for appropriately wealthy guests who scoffed at commercial flights. That morning it was a departing plane, judging from the engines growing faint. Probably the investors from last night's State Dinner going back to wherever their money was.

"Sandrina," I said reluctantly from beneath my comforter, "let's get it."

The pyramid on my desk double-chirped, confirming the start of my customized morning routine. The lamp and ceiling lights flicked on. The smart glass in my windows snapped from opaque to translucent, allowing in light while sustaining a privacy mode. Sandrina pyramids had decent subwoofers, so I felt that morning's random music selection in my soul. Before I could identify the artist, a familiar chime sounded.

Sandrina said, "Parental override volume control."

The song became less loud, and I imagined Mom shaking her head downstairs in the kitchen.

Groaning my way into the shower, I got my mind right, my clothes on, grabbed a waffle from the toaster—thanks, Mom—and stepped outside into a thick wall of mist.

Morning fog was common at this elevation. Across the street, Zeke exited his house too.

No Connie yet. Usually, she'd be sitting on one of our porches.

The thick gray wall of moisture between us had Zeke looking like a chalk smudge instead of a real boy. I braced myself for what would definitely be an interrogation/lecture over what happened with Chelle last night. I'd decided in the shower that I was going to be straight-up stern with him. Shut down all that dumb conspiracy talk and let me have my thing with Chelle.

Rehearsed lines flitted through my mind when I met him in the street. My stomach churned, though, because confrontation really wasn't my thing. I didn't want it to be a fight. I delayed the inevitable by fishing my phone from my pocket and hitting the group chat. Some backup would be nice. "I'mma text Connie."

Me
C, we out here

Connie
You guys go on without me.
I will have my father drive me
to school.

I squinted at my phone. Not that what she texted was *weird* weird. It *was* different than, like, every other day for the last three years.

Zeke read the same message on his phone. Shook his head.

"Why she sounding like a robot?"

Zeke didn't respond . . . or seem surprised. "Bro, let's go."

Because of the fog, I couldn't even see Connie's house, four lawns down. And I wanted to see her house. Like, an invisible hook in my gut tugged me that way. Zeke moved in the opposite direction, toward the bus stop, nearly vanishing in the fog, and this strange voice in my head said, *Don't lose him too.* Jogging to catch up, I snagged the handle at the top of his backpack.

"Dude!" He tried, unsuccessfully, to jerk away.

"What's going on?"

Finally, he surrendered. Stopped moving. "Fine. Mr. Chambers was being extra last night, and Connie's probably dealing with it, okay?"

Zeke quick-stepped toward the bus again, leaving me in a physical and mental fog. I jogged to catch up. "What do you mean *extra?*"

"Extra *tense.* I don't know." He huffed, clearly not wanting to get into it.

Checking my watch, I said, "We got ten minutes before the bus gets here. Dude."

Zeke angled toward the sidewalk, waving me along. A few class-mates shuffled past, hunching against a chilly breeze, but paid us no mind. He sat; I joined.

"When I got to her house, no one was there. Her mom had left a note about visiting some friends. It was just us destroying that gator, something she called prawns, but they were really like the biggest shrimp you ever seen in life. This cheesy garlic bread—"

"I ain't ask for the menu."

He kept talking like I didn't say a thing. "We were watching TV while eating on the couch. Overeating. Got so full I closed my eyes. Knocked. Out. Probably would've crashed there all night. Wouldn't have been the first time."

Another topic we didn't discuss much in the crew was how Zeke's dad didn't always come home at night, and Zeke didn't like to be in the house by himself. I said, "You fell asleep on the couch. What's the big deal?"

Zeke snapped. "If you stop interrupting, I'll tell you!"

My knee-jerk reaction was to tell him to take some of that bass out his voice. But this wasn't a regular grumpy Zeke explosion. He was shaking.

So no, I wasn't going to interrupt him anymore because I couldn't come close to guessing what the next twist in this story was.

Zeke said, "You know how it is in their house. You can only see the back of the couch from the front door. When he bust in, he's yelling their names. Connie's. Her mom. It scared me. Connie—"

Another classmate passed us with earbuds in, yet Zeke waited until they disappeared into the mist before he went on. "She gets up, and I stay flat because I'm shook. When she rounds the couch, he's yelling at her. 'Where's your mom get her right now we gotta—' Then Connie blurts, 'Zeke's here.' Like she's . . . she's . . ." He fumbled words and made jerky moves with his hands, looking for the right way to say it.

I knew what he was getting at, and the morning got considerably cooler. "She warned him," I said, "so he wouldn't say something someone outside the family shouldn't hear."

"Right! I sat up then, like, 'Hey, Mr. Chambers.' He's frozen, total disbelief that I'm there. We're staring at each other, and it feels like a month goes by until Connie says, 'Daddy?' Then he unsticks and is fake calm when he tells me I need to go home. He has things to discuss with his daughter. So, I rolled. Didn't even tell Connie bye."

A quick glance at my watch. We needed to get down to the bus stop. I stood and asked, "She didn't hit you at all last night?"

He stood too. "Nope. I tried her a couple of times, but she didn't respond."

"It's probably nothing for real. She'll tell us at school. It's fine."

It had to be. Right?

CHAPTER 7

Seychelle was parked in the student lot binging an audiobook in her car. Zeke and I climbed off the bus and approached. He crouched by the bumper of the closest car, angling away from me and taking a roundabout path to her passenger door. He beat me to her by a few seconds, startling her. Chelle scowled but warmed when she saw me. Her window whined down.

"You still listening to *Dreamweaver*?" I asked.

"No. Finished that last night. It. Was. *Incredible*." That emphasis on *incredible* and a held gaze suggested we maybe weren't talking about books at the moment.

Zeke's stare burned the side of my face. "You book nerds get real excited."

Facts!

Seychelle grabbed her phone and joined us outside. She craned her neck toward the drop-off loop. "Connie's not here yet?"

She was on the group text, so she knew Mr. Chambers was bringing Connie in.

"Y'all text last night?" I asked

Chelle, perplexed. "Were we supposed to?"

"I thought maybe—" I stopped short, letting it go. Chelle hitting Connie up after our make-out session at the Treat seemed inevitable in my head. Girl talk, you know. It clashed with the story Zeke told me, though. Whatever Mr. Chambers's deal was last night would've probably occupied Connie's attention. No need to obsess over Chelle telling her whether she had fun with me, if she thought I was a good kisser, that my breath was fresh the whole time. Move on, Jay.

The morning bustle was typical. Graduating seniors huddled by the display cases in the foyer, a Karloff Academy tradition. Those cases might've held accumulated academic and athletic trophies at a different school on the outside, but here they were filled with Karloff memorabilia, mostly from Chelle's family's movies, like a museum exhibit. Next year, we'd be the ones congregating around those framed film cells, classic costumes, and awards while most of the upperclassmen went on to prestigious colleges in safe cities and states.

The sweetest part of graduating from Karloff Academy was if you agreed to return and work for the resort for five years after you got your degree, you could go to college tuition-free. It was only for certain majors like engineering, information technology, and a few others, plus you had to keep a high GPA, but that scholarship made the impossible possible for a bunch of us. I'd already decided I'd major in business management—another qualifying major—and come back to my dad's department when I was done with school. I mean, why not?

The warning bell rang, and the crowds dispersed to our respective destinations.

Zeke, Chelle, Connie, and I had separate homerooms and wouldn't connect again until our third-period social studies class when we presented our final project.

I arrived first. Seychelle showed up next, flopping in her seat.

"Showtime," she said, game face on.

"Yep." My stomach swished from mild nerves, but I kept that to myself.

Zeke entered with a few of our classmates. He saw the empty

desk, then backpedaled into the hall, his head whipping both ways, clearly expecting a sprinting Connie to beat the bell.

It rang with Zeke at the class threshold, still waiting.

Mr. Lattimore said, "Ezekiel, care to take a seat?"

Slowly, reluctantly, he left the doorway, locking eyes with me and transmitting his concerns telepathically. I palmed my phone under my desk, at risk of having it confiscated, to check our group texts. Nothing new from Connie. As far as her last message was concerned, she was still on her way. Maybe her dad was bringing her by piggyback.

Seychelle radiated concern. She didn't know about Zeke's Mr. Chambers story, so her worries were more immediate.

Chelle
If Connie doesn't show, who's
doing the intro?

Mr. Lattimore spoke to the pyramid on his desk. "Sandrina, dim the lights."

The room darkened, and a cone of blue light shot from the ceiling projector onto a screen covering the whiteboard. The burgundy-and-gold Karloff Academy *K* displayed.

"Group One," Mr. Lattimore said, "you're up."

The first group made their way to the front, flanking the projection on either side, two by two. Their group leader—Aiden Harper, a white kid who lived three streets over from Zeke and me—placed his thumb drive on the illuminated pad beside Mr. Lattimore's keyboard, activating Sandrina's smart interface. The pad rimmed the drive in purple light, and that group, a quartet of student athlete buddies, presented "The New Champions: Karloff's Contributions to Sports Science and Human Performance."

Aiden read from handwritten note cards. "The Karloff Corporation, primarily known for entertainment ventures, does a lot more for the world than people realize. Profits are often invested into other business sectors, specifically those on the cutting edge of biotechnology that will one day aid the world's elite athletes, as well as everyday laborers, by maximizing hydration, endurance, and strength through consumable supplements that'll make Gatorade look like Kool-Aid . . ."

His voice became a background drone while I was facedown in our group chat.

Zeke
C, where you at?

Zeke
For real.

Group 1 finished, and Group 2 set up their presentation: "Breathing Easy: Clean Energy, Clean Air, the Karloff Way."

Still no word from Connie.

Seychelle got fidgety and fired off the next text.

Chelle
Hey, we're really worried about you.

Group 2 wrapped to polite applause, and Mr. Lattimore called Group 3. Us.

The wary looks bouncing between Seychelle, Zeke, and me would've been pure comedy in any other situation. Not with Connie missing in action and Mr. Lattimore mouthing our group count. "Where's your fourth?"

Nobody wanted to put Connie's business in the street or throw her under the bus. Crew Code of Silence remained intact.

"Constance was aware this presentation is thirty percent of your final grade?"

"I believe so," I said.

Classmates shifted, some amused and some sympathetic.

Ultimately, Mr. Lattimore said, "Well?"

We trudged to the front of the room, where I placed my drive on the Sandrina pad interface. Our presentation topic filled the screen: "The Vertical Farms of Karloff Country: Creating a World's Worth of Sustainable Food."

When class final presentations were explained, each group was assigned a topic at random with a common theme. How did it relate to Karloff Country, our home? Mr. Lattimore reasoned if we'd been paying attention throughout the year, any topic of his choosing could be addressed by any group. The thing is, at the time, we thought we'd lucked out. It was always going to be Connie up first even if she hadn't volunteered, because she'd resonate with the class, and more importantly, Mr. Lattimore. Everyone knew she was, essentially, food royalty here in KC.

We had a quick huddle that accomplished little because all we did was shrug and give each other pointed looks.

Mr. Lattimore said, "Group Three. Sometime today."

With a deep breath and wicked eye roll for Zeke and me,

Seychelle took the lead. She leapt into an improvised version of Connie's introductory speech on how a perfect storm of food scarcity, climate change, and economic policies had already thrust billions into peril all over the globe. Such circumstances would only get worse without responsible citizens and corporations stepping up. "With continued inaction, the world's food supply could collapse at any given time," she said, wrapping up her introductory remarks with no sign of nerves whatsoever. "Fortunately, here in Karloff Country, idle hands aren't our way. Our Vertical Farms, consisting of five cylindrical towers, each specializing in a different area of crop production, raising livestock, and other areas of food sustainability may be examples for the future of farming. The innovations in AI-driven automation combined with the greatest minds in agriculture already provide a portion of the food within the Karloff Country walls and could, one day, play a critical role in eradicating hunger worldwide . . ."

When final bell rang, there was no discussion or hesitation. We met at Seychelle's car and beat the buses out of the school lot. No music. No idle chatter. The one and only time anyone spoke was when we passed the Jubilee marquees and Zeke said, "She's going to hate Mr. Lattimore making her do a solo presentation."

That's the kind of hopeful we were choosing to be.

The power of positive thinking lasted all of the twenty seconds it took for Seychelle to navigate the Jubilee streets so Connie's lawn was visible in the distance. With that morning's fog long gone, seeing what—or who—was in Connie's yard made me queasy.

The sun was ahead of us, backlighting his unmistakable silhouette.

The pointy ears that protruded like horns. The snout in profile. The suspenders on his slim shoulders holding up those too-big pants. Awaiting us as we pulled to the curb before the Chambers residence, six feet and looming, was Penny Pup.

The car hadn't come to a full stop before Zeke leapt out.

He ran up on the dog—really a fiberglass standup mounted on a two-foot pike that had been driven into the lawn. We all knew this depiction of the animated dog, had seen him and the sign he held, in Jubilee many times. Usually on the lawns of newly constructed homes. The placard in the cartoon's puffy, four-fingered hands said: NEW NEIGHBORS COMING SOON.

Zeke sprinted past the dog onto Connie's porch. I was out of the car by then. Seychelle too. The overlapping chimes from Zeke smashing the bell could be heard mid-lawn.

And the sound was wrong.

If anyone was home, they would've opened the door by now, if for no other reason than to preserve their hearing. Zeke must've recognized the same thing because he abandoned the doorbell for the nearest window, cupped his hands around his eyes, and let his forehead touch the glass.

Zeke backed away from the window, startled, and I purposely avoided the glass, afraid to see what he saw, though my imagination was already sketching horrors in red.

Seychelle jabbed the doorbell like maybe it'd work better for her. That time, being that close, I knew why the chimes sounded off.

They echoed.

Seychelle peered through the window. To Zeke, she said, "You were here *last night*?"

I got to the inevitable, looked for myself, and tried not to wretch on the porch planks.

The Chambers house was completely empty. Like no one lived there.

Not yesterday.

Not ever.

CHAPTER 8

Alerting Karloff Country Security was my idea.

Zeke clenched his fists, stomped across the porch, and kicked a wall. On a loop. Anger was the emotion he'd always been most comfortable expressing. Seychelle . . . she shrank. Hugging herself so hard and tight, she could've wrapped her arms around her torso twice. Surprisingly, my Helper training kicked in. I took charge, treating this like I would any incident that occurred during one of my Enchantria shifts, because it was my best chance not to spiral.

When KC dispatch picked up, I said, "My name is Jermaine Butler, I'm calling from Three Fifteen Ashe Street in Jubilee. I've got a Code Fifty."

Whenever we called problems in from the park, we used codes so as not to panic guests who might overhear. You didn't want folks on the most memorable vacation their family would ever take to know someone had vomited (Code B) in a corner of the Fantasy Food Court. Or had a heart attack (Code E) on the ride you'd just gotten in line for, or you'd found something crazy like a bomb (Code 7) that might require the park be evacuated. So, my training took over and I called in a Code 50—lost person.

Usually this was reserved for a kid who'd gotten separated from a parent, so I understood the dispatcher's confusion. "You're on Ashe Street in *Jubilee*?"

"Yes. It's a Code Fifty, in Jubilee."

"Are we talking about a child?"

"A teenager and her parents. The Chambers family. The *whole* family."

The line went silent. She'd muted me.

When she returned, she said, "And your name is Jermaine Butler?"

"Yes. Could you"—I fought the gut feeling that I'd overplayed this somehow, that there would be consequences for this call—"could you please send someone?"

"Immediately."

My phone gave the double chirp of a disconnected call.

"What'd they say?" Zeke asked.

"They're sending somebody."

"Good," Seychelle said, still hugging herself. "Good."

We waited on Connie's porch steps. Seychelle at the top, me on the next riser, and Zeke pacing the walkway while the Penny Pup standup seemed to mock him.

"Tell Chelle about last night," I insisted. "Connie's dad."

Chelle's gaze bounced between us. Waiting.

Zeke didn't stop moving, but he delivered the recap. When he finished, he addressed Seychelle. "What happened at the dinner last night?"

Seychelle's knees bumped my back hard when she leaned forward. "We ate. I told you that."

Zeke wasn't pacing anymore. He was pointing. Sharp jabs with his index finger that would've put an eye out if you were close enough. "Mr. Chambers came from *your* house. Whatever had him freaking must've happened *at your house*. Everyone knows y'all do weird stuff up there."

"Excuse me? Weird?" Chelle was on her feet, her voice raised. "Weird how?"

I threw myself between them. "Hey! Hey! Stop it!"

She tried to skirt around me, but I sidestepped and raised my arm like a crossbar, cutting her off. She said, "Who's talking trash about me, Zeke? Your jealous behind?"

"Jealous? Of you?" Zeke closed the gap. "The literal *black* sheep of the Karloff Empire?"

Seychelle went completely still, the fight knocked from her by that low, stinging remark. No one knew how to hurt you like your friends.

I did not punch my best friend, but I wanted to. He'd gone too far. He knew it and tried backpedaling. "Sorry. Sorry. I shouldn't have said that. I was mad, and I shouldn't have."

My mom always says *sorry* is like pulling a nail from the board: The hole's still there no matter how much you want it not to be.

"Jermaine!"

That was my other parent. Dad, home early, strolling from our house. First time I'd seen him in two days. *Why* was he home early?

He was in his usual suit, loosening his tie as he drew near, the expression on his face was . . . something.

He gave the Penny Pup sign a cursory glance before joining us. I wanted to be glad to see him, to explain to him, fast, because time was of the essence, that Connie and her family had disappeared, and none of it made sense, except I was stuck on the way he looked at that sign.

Not surprised. At all.

"Seychelle," Dad said, tipping his chin in her direction. Then, "Ezekiel."

They returned his greeting with skepticism.

To me, he said, "Did you call the security dispatch, son?"

"I— How did you—"

"They called me. Or rather they called Janice. She pulled me from a meeting."

Janice was Dad's assistant. I called security about my missing friend, and they'd called my dad's office at the Karloff Executive Center. Now he was here. The logic of these related-when-they-shouldn't-be occurrences bounced around my skull.

"Is the security team coming?" I couldn't think of anything else to say.

"No, Jermaine. There's no reason. The Chambers family isn't missing. They left."

A golf cart rounded the corner, two familiar Jubilee Residents' Association officers, Fletcher and Burke, crammed in it shoulder to shoulder. They wore gray polo shirts and khakis. Both sported deep year-round tans from riding their cart up and down Jubilee streets as if they were real police.

Their weapons of choice were the clipboards where they noted neighborhood violations and the pads from which they issued citations about grass length and window treatment color. They pulled in close to Seychelle's bumper, Fletcher already scribbling something, while Burke hopped out, assessing our gathering.

Burke said, "Can't have you congregating on the lawn, Phil. Kills the grass."

Dad said, "Sorry. We're on our way."

"We know," Fletcher said.

Zeke, unable to control himself, mumbled, "Fake cops act like they don't live in Jubilee like the rest of us."

Fletcher, short and wide, left the cart, caressing the extendable baton housed in a sheath on his belt. "Something on your mind, young man?"

Dad's expression darkened, and he slid into the wide gap between Fletcher and Zeke.

"Let's go, *kids*. Seychelle, you may want to head on home as well."

Chelle said, "Mr. Butler, do you know why Connie's family would leave like this? She's not answering our texts. We're worried."

Dad nodded, sympathetic. "She might be embarrassed. It's not easy getting into Jubilee. It's even harder to leave. Usually when it happens, it's not under great circumstances. That's probably no fault of Connie's, mind you. But no one *wants* to be on the other side of the wall."

"All their stuff's gone. How could that happen so fast?" asked Zeke.

"You'd be surprised, Ezekiel. Everything here is next level. Even the movers."

"It's the Karloff way," said Fletcher, in the most unfriendly tone I'd ever heard the phrase used.

"Come on." Dad's hand fell on my shoulder, gentle but firmly guiding me to the street. Zeke trailed Seychelle to her car, mumbling another weak apology, but her attention shifted between Connie's house and the Penny Pup sign, her true concern.

Fletcher and Burke kept a watchful eye on us to ensure the safety of the vacant home's lawn.

I slipped Dad's grip to see Seychelle made it into her vehicle. "Text us when you're home."

She nodded, busted a wide U-turn in the street, passing us slow on her way out of Jubilee. Zeke paced Dad and me until we were at the midpoint between our houses.

"Later," Zeke said, which I interpreted as "expect a text inside of thirty seconds."

"Wait." Dad stopped us from parting ways yet. "Don't you two go

71

making a big deal of this, okay? You're good friends to Connie, I'm not mad you're trying to look out for her, but the truth is, Karloff Country is a temporary stop sometimes. If her dad found another opportunity and had to make a quick move for the family, that's life."

I said, "You *know* that's what happened? Mr. Chambers got some new job or something?"

"I'm guessing."

"Did he say anything to you last night?"

Dad's head tilted, as did his mood. "What about last night?"

"You were at that dinner thing at Karloff Manor. I thought maybe—"

He cut me off, not mean but not happy. "Look. I didn't get a chance to hang with Connie's dad last night because I was at work. Providing for our family. Calling security and bringing unwanted attention *at my office*, in front of my boss, it's not great optics. I'll ask around about your friend, but you gotta give me a little time. Okay? Can you do that for me?"

Zeke and I exchanged glances, and I worked hard to not let mine show doubt. I said, "Okay. We'll wait."

"Thank you. When I know more, you'll know more. Promise."

SEYCHELLE

At home, outside of Grandfather's study, I silently rehearsed one of several speeches I'd composed during my panicked drive from Jubilee. The most abrasive version—*You've treated me like crap my whole life and you owe me this*—got nixed immediately. As far as he was concerned, any treatment I viewed as harsh, because it was always my *perception*, never objective fact, was refuted by my lavish accommodations, significant trust fund, and last name. Whenever I expressed any displeasure over anything in his presence, he wasn't mean and never flashed anger. Those tirades were reserved for my mom, who'd "brought home a half-breed baby."

A half-breed baby who was the heir to a $24 billion fortune.

Maybe.

I mean, Mom and I *were* Franklin Karloff's only heirs. Not for his lack of trying, but for reasons both tragic (his only son's overdose before my birth) and completely unexpected (exposure to experimental chemicals in one of his industrial plants leaving him infertile). The *maybe* had to do with whether we'd actually inherit anything.

It's the classic rich man's threat he's held over Mom for as long as I've known what a will was. "I'm taking you out of the will!" Or, "I'm not going to add you to my will!" Which made me wonder, was there *really* a will? Because you seemed confused about its status, Frank.

For me, I wasn't worth the effort of a threat. He exuded a sort of helplessness over my existence and spoke in the gentler tones one might reserve for a conversation with a beloved pet. "None of this is *your* fault. The family's fortune ending up with a . . ." he once mused, stopping short of whatever ugly thing he thought of me. "Well, they won't say the Karloffs didn't change with the times, will they?"

Even though there were only three of us, he spoke our surname like we were some grand conquering dynasty and not the survivors of generational tragedies and profitable self-destruction. Which is why I also abandoned the pleading version of my pitch—*I try my best not to ask you for anything, but please, please help me find my friend.* The king of the Karloffs abhorred weakness. There was no way he'd assess those words from my mouth as anything but. A Karloff did not beg.

There were a couple of remixes in there, combos of forceful and meek, but I eventually settled on indirect: *There's a vacant home in Jubilee now, and I was thinking it'd be a nice incentive to attract some top-notch talent . . . Is there a file on the property?* He'd been insisting I "step up to family responsibilities" and pay more attention to "resort concerns," so he *might* inadvertently give me what I wanted because he'd count it as *his* victory.

I hated him.

I didn't regret the hate. Didn't try to interrogate it. Didn't care if he did or didn't leave me the fortune he couldn't take to whatever gruesome afterlife awaited him. My family had so much money, even accounts I had access to *right now* could buy an apartment building in New York City.

Yeah.

That's what I'd imagined often. When I was old enough to escape. Buy a building somewhere. If not New York, then Paris, or Johannesburg, or a dozen other places I scoped when I was most fed up. I'd gift an apartment each to my best friends so we could meet on the roof in the summer and share takeout containers of street food at sunset.

None of them knew I'd thought of this. But I wasn't going to keep it from Connie anymore. That's the deal I made with myself. When I got to the bottom of where she was, why her house was empty, when we could laugh about this unfortunately terrifying day, I'd tell her there was an apartment—a home—waiting for her, from me, always. I only had to game my horrid grandfather first.

As much as he detested half of my genetic makeup, he'd be pleased to know his conniving gene remained dominant.

I barged through the polished teak double doors, ready to make my play, but stopped short when I spotted Mom kneeling before my seated grandfather, adjusting the lapels of his suit coat. That was strange on its own, made stranger by him staring into space like he didn't even know she was doing it.

She stood quickly and looked past me like she expected more people.

No, not expected.

Feared.

"What?" she snapped.

"I was hoping to speak to Grandfather." I stumbled a bit, thrown off by the whole thing. "There's a vacant home in Jubilee, and I . . ."

An orange pill bottle sat on the desk next to a half-full water glass. Mom moved the pills to a drawer.

"Um . . . It'd be nice if some top-notch talent . . ."

"Chelley, I don't have time to think about those people in Jubilee right now and neither does Dad."

"But Grandfather wanted me to pay more attention to resort concerns."

Mom groaned. "There's a Board of Trustees call in three minutes, and we have to get ready. Get out of here right now, Seychelle!"

Banishing me wasn't a new thing in this house. I backed off, sealing the office, already cataloging other options for tracking down Connie. Despite what Grandfather thought, I'd paid *some* attention to resort concerns, and I knew a few people in the human resources department who wouldn't be opposed to making a little extra money. But at the moment, I was more focused on what just happened.

Grandfather, who usually greeted me with sneers and eye rolls, never acknowledged I was even in the room.

Take your resort experience to the next level with customized small-group experiences for your family or those closest to you.

Available packages include:

- Dedicated door-to-door concierge service
- Priority amenity privileges (no lines/no waiting)
- Guaranteed reservations for the finest dining experiences
- Private villas for the duration of your stay

*Draft copy for unreleased VIP Tours Ad Campaign webpage.
(**Developer Notes:** Page shelved in favor of a more selective word-of-mouth approach prioritizing top-tier repeat guests.)

CHAPTER 9

The phrase *summer break* felt like a scam that last day in June. Karloff Academy was done until I started my senior year in the fall, but a *break*? I was working harder than ever in Enchantria because, on top of it being our busiest season, my Helper team was notified of an unscheduled inspection by the Big Bosses.

It happened sometimes.

The difference between this short-notice inspection and all the ones I'd been through before: I was Inspection Prep Leader now. Because Harry hadn't quite been promoted as expected, he was doing all the stuff his predecessor used to but with his same old job title still in place. With the promotion I hadn't officially been offered dangling between us, I was doing part of his job and all of mine to stay in his good graces.

As Harry joked, grimly, when explaining how things were going to be for a while, "It's the Karloff way."

Mercifully it was a cooler afternoon. That didn't keep me from sweating my gray work shirt into a shade closer to black. I'd checked on the Helper teams in FuturaScape, PatriotScape, and ColoniaScape. The sterile tunnels beneath the park were my preferred path between the various Enchantria Dreamscapes. When I emerged from a hidden Helper entrance that was covered in plastic vines and faux-jungle foliage, the rancid stench of an overflowing trash bin punched me in the nose. The bin in question was bad when I'd spotted it—and avoided it—earlier, hoping one of my fellow Helpers would get to it.

Head down, trying for laser focus on the task, I approached the receptacle positioned near Penny Pup's Wieners, Connie's old gig. Of all the good work I'd been doing as Harry's second-in-command, I'd done my best work *not* thinking of Connie.

Window #5 used to be hers. Some blond kid I never met sat in her old perch now, the New Connie. I tried not to be angry at them.

It wasn't easy. Not after that last text we got from her.

Connie
Some tough family stuff is happening.
I need some time and space. Will be
in touch soon.

We got it three days after finding her old house empty. During those three days, Seychelle, Zeke, and I had blown up her phone a thousand times telling her how worried we were she'd been dragged off and murdered by some cult or something.

Zeke was a mess, showing up to the bus stop on day two with his hand bandaged from punching a tree in his backyard. Seychelle barely slept these days, evident by the dark half-moons beneath her eyes. The night of our kiss, in the moments before things got insane, we never spoke about again. There sure weren't any repeat kisses. Was I trash for thinking about that more than Connie lately? Sometimes I thought, yes, I'm trash. Other times I thought, life goes on. Connie didn't seem too worried about putting our minds at ease.

Chelle's especially.

The last text in our group chat was Chelle responding to that "tough family stuff."

Chelle
Don't do that.

That being . . . what? Disappearing? Being shady with her responses? Ghosting?

Done. Done. And done.

When I pressed my dad about his promise to look into it, he said, "I'm still waiting to hear more, but word is, Martin Chambers got a great new opportunity somewhere over the wall."

Seemed to be the trend these days.

Now that I couldn't avoid present duties, I concentrated on the Penny Pup trash instead of the garbage circumstances of my actual life, so the words spoken loudly and directly to me while I hunkered over discarded and spoiled food didn't register right away.

Someone said, "You're covering a lot of ground solo. I'm impressed."

The person sounded genuinely happy, and that's the only reason I glanced up—because the usual Karloff-endorsed "joy" of guests flaunting wealth and bossing me around hadn't done it for me lately. I'd been hungry for something positive. Something good. Somehow I managed not to flinch when I identified the source of this endorphin boost. "Mr. Barnabus."

The president of Karloff Country operations. Dad's boss. Almost everyone's boss, really.

Mostly I saw him on TV or YouTube uttering some faint praise for the latest Karloff superhero film. The few times I'd seen him in person was some employee thing Dad was forced to bring his family to.

Barnabus was tall and white, with smooth tanned skin that made it impossible to guess his age. Could've been anywhere from forty-five to sixty, though the sporadic gray slithering through his hair suggested the high end of the range. Then he'd been dripped out in a James Bond tuxedo, but the way he looked, and the way he was built, made it a toss-up between the tuxedo making *him* look like the famous spy, or his physique proving the attire worthy of a 007 mission.

Now he was in his trademark Karloff button-down shirt, no tie, with a Penny Pup logo over the heart. Stiff khakis and casual shoes. Didn't look all that different from JRA Officers Fletcher and Burke.

Dad said Barnabus was a good boss who cared for his employees, but Dad also said the man didn't have an off button, and when you were around him, you needed to be on too. I didn't know exactly what that meant for me right then, but I was wary.

He was *tall* tall; he had at least seven inches on me. He bent at the knees for a better look at my name tag. "Jermaine. Wait a sec—is your last name Butler? You're Phil's son, right?"

"Yes." I felt a twinge of excitement in my gut. This dude partied with actors, rappers, senators, and movie directors, yet he kind of knew who I was.

I said, "Can I help you with something, sir?"

"You're aware of the pending inspection?"

"Sure."

A few yards away, at the New Connie's wiener window, an irate voice got louder. "Are you serious? I can't even get one of Penny Pup's legendary wieners! From the *wiener* stand! This is supposed to be the best customer service in the world. Come on!"

If Barnabus cared about the disturbance, I couldn't tell. He flashed perfect white teeth. "Would you be kind enough to show me around?

I'm ashamed to admit it, but my memory of Enchantria's layout isn't as sharp as it used to be." His soft but heavy hand landed on my shoulder. "Let's keep that between you and me, though."

"No problem, sir."

Barnabus and I left ExploraScape together while the New Connie explained to the angry guest how we were temporarily unable to provide Penny Pup's wieners due to the nationwide meat shortages, but there were several delicious vegetarian options available.

Barnabus followed me through the scaled-down ivory columns of Early America in ColoniaScape to the dome-shaped, laser-and-hologram-enhanced dwelling of Tomorrow Town in FuturaScape with some random stops at supply closets, restrooms, and not-too-crowded attractions along the way. We were close to the Time Tube roller coaster, so the periodic banshee screams of guests hitting that first drop punctuated Barnabus's questions about our current supply stockpile.

He quizzed me about our latest shipments—arrived two days ago. Distribution throughout the park—everything balanced nicely. He tried throwing me a curveball with "How would we do if we had a string of max-capacity days back-to-back for two weeks straight?"

We'd taken the Employees Only door between Lunar Lands Ice Cream Parlor and the Solar Flare Gift Shop, so we were "out of frame"—the Karloff Country euphemism for the area off-limits to guests. Back here was such a vast difference from the obsessively detailed Dreamscapes guests frolicked in all day. They got curated excess. We got bare essentials. Black asphalt. Tan walls. High opaque fences. Zeke always said out of frame felt like those mazes scientists put test mice in. All walls and turns.

Barnabus and I sat at a picnic table shaded by a worn nylon umbrella while I tackled his trick question. "We'd be fine if we had two weeks of maximum-capacity days. We'd be fine if we had two months of maximum-capacity days. Last week's supply shipment was the first of the summer, and that shipment is always three months' worth of stock, so we're only doing small re-ups throughout the season."

Barnabus snapped his fingers like he wanted me to talk faster. "Why do we do that?"

That follow-up nearly froze me. "Uhhh, the first decade of the park's opening saw a couple of different oil shortages, which had a ripple effect on what goods were available when. Never wanting any guest to feel there was a shortage on anything while in Karloff Country, Franklin Karloff bought way more supplies than what was needed. That become the standard model for the parks."

It was one of those weird things that stuck when I went through my initial Helper training. Also, Dad, a business and logistics expert, ranted about it often because it was inefficient.

Actually, the word he used, spoken like a curse, was *hoarding*.

The New Connie explaining the meat shortage to that irate guest came to mind . . . Hoarding didn't work on everything. Not these days.

Barnabus nodded. "Good job, Jermaine. I got one more question that's a tad bit trickier. You ready?"

I knew the right answer was yes. Even if I wasn't.

"What if we only ran the park at one-twentieth the capacity? How long would our supplies last?"

My eyebrows bunched together so hard I nearly cramped in that little space above the bridge of my nose. "Run the park at one-twentieth the capacity? Why?"

His smile shrank at me answering a question with more questions. "Jermaine."

"Uh," I stammered. "I'd probably need a calculator to figure—"

"Guess." He was insistent. "Ballpark."

"Years."

That was the broadest answer, I think. For my department, we didn't deal in anything that went bad. So long as our supplies stayed cool, dry, and neatly stored, we could go for years.

"Excellent." He stood fast, not waiting for me. There was a plain door marked TUNNEL ACCESS that he walked toward. "Good job. As far as I'm concerned, keep doing what you're doing. It's the Karloff way." He checked his watch. "I'm meeting with park security in a few moments. Take care, Jermaine. I'm sure we'll cross paths again." He swiped his wristband over the lock, then disappeared below.

Beneath the umbrella's shade, I might've contemplated his odd questions more if not for realizing security's office was directly below FuturaScape. For someone who'd forgotten the layout of the park— and presumably its tunnels—he was in convenient proximity to his next meeting. Then I had to ask myself a question that I honestly couldn't answer.

Did I lead him here, or did he lead me?

The rest of my shift went by undisturbed. The new Garrison Cinematic Universe movie was playing in Downtown Karloff. It was iffy, but maybe I could get Zeke and Chelle on board for a viewing.

At the shuttle bus stop, I looked for Zeke, who was not in our usual spot. I was, like, 99 percent certain he had a shift today.

While my phone powered on, I ignored the sinking feeling of not seeing him. I made myself not think about the last time one of my friends wasn't where I'd thought she'd be.

All those thoughts derailed when I noticed my missed messages.

Chelle
We gotta meet at the Treat. Tonight.
Can you bring Zeke?

We'd abandoned our old group text without ever talking about it. Connie's last underwhelming message retired it for us. Not lost on me, Zeke and Seychelle hadn't talked much since that "black sheep" comment he'd made. I'd figured, like, back of my mind, if I convinced them both to hit the movies tonight, maybe we could, I don't know, get some of what we lost back. Hadn't expected *her* to request his presence in Jubilee. I mean, *why*?

It was 8:15 now. The shuttle was pulling up, and it would take ten minutes to get home.

Me
I'll hit him and will be at the Treat
in 20 minutes. If we got time, the
new Garrison movie's playing.
We can catch the 9:30.

Chelle
The movies? No. So unimportant
right now. I'm leaving my house
immediately. See you at the Treat.

85

I replied with a few question marks, expecting clarification. It didn't come. So I did what she asked and hit Zeke's phone. Didn't tell him about Chelle acting weird because, the way they'd been lately, he might stay home.

Me

Yo, meet me at the Treat in 20

Zeke

For what?

I couldn't think of a good explanation, so I didn't respond. He'd be as curious as I was. He'd come.

CHAPTER 10

Zeke beat me to the Treat. I spotted him from fifty yards out and slowed. He was stomping in front of our pavilion. His lips moved at the speed of conversation, talking to himself.

Embarrassment pricked my cheeks and forehead like I'd peeked in on something private. I called his name more to announce myself than get his attention. He stopped in his tracks like I'd startled him.

Recognizing me with a nod, he took his seat at our table.

"What's up?" he asked when I sat.

"Thought you had a shift today." I was still hesitant to mention this was Chelle's thing.

"Wasn't feeling it. Up late last night."

"Doing what?"

He blurted, "Did you know at least seventeen families have gone missing in Karloff Country in the middle of the night and their neighbors found their houses empty the next day? But nobody saw any trucks or heard any movers."

"Seventeen?" I was already skeptical because I could guess what he'd been doing all night. "This was on a Panopticon board, wasn't it?"

"Yeah. So?"

This was exhausting. "You gotta leave that dumb stuff alone, man."

"Why's it gotta be dumb, Jay? Because it's not that go-along-to-get-along mess you be on?"

He wasn't just mad, he was in my face. Squaring off. Maybe a split second from hard shoving me in the chest. I could feel it.

Because I wanted to do the same. "'Go along to get along'? You serious right now?"

"You don't even hear yourself because you a Karloff fanboy. It happened to Connie. You saw it with your own eyes. So what are you even disputing?"

"I—I'm not. I'm just saying, there's a lot of exaggeration on that board."

"Dumb stuff." He poked his finger in my sternum. "You said dumb stuff."

He went for a second poke, and I knocked his hand away. That's when headlights flashed toward us.

His attention went there, then back to me. His sneer was a whole silent movie about me not mentioning Chelle.

She parked and got to us quick, her gaze whipping between us, sensing the tension but having no time for it. She sat next to me but not close. I was not the priority here. "You need to see this."

She turned her phone so we all had a view. It was lit with messages, the blue speech bubbles for a lot of outgoing texts. *A LOT* a lot. No responses, though. She said, "I've been texting Connie."

"That's apparent," Zeke said.

Among the messages were phrases that made me shift uncomfortably. *Why are you acting like this? Don't do this. Please. What is wrong with you????* The desperation in the outreach read like heartbreak. The scary, unhinged kind. That Chelle wasn't self-conscious about it made me wonder—not for the first time—if I understood friendship differently than other people.

She scrolled down with big flicks, turning all those bubbles into an unbroken blue blur until a gray response finally interrupted.

Zeke leaned in. "She hit you back?"

Connie

Hey.

Chelle

Wait! You're answering now?
Connie! Where are you?
HOW are you?

Connie

I'm fine. I'm sorry I've been
out of touch. It's all been a lot.

Chelle

What's been a lot? Me, Jay, and
Zeke have been FREAKING OUT!
I went by your dad's restaurant.
They changed the name already.
The staff were like he didn't tell
them anything.

Chelle had gone by the Grand Virginian hotel and talked to the cooks at Constance—or whatever it was called now? They really changed the name?

Zeke took over scrolling, scrutinizing the conversation.

Connie

My dad is opening a new
restaurant.

89

Chelle

Where?

Connie

Cleveland.

Chelle

That's where you are now?

Connie

Yes.

Chelle

Why'd it take you this long to
respond? You had to know
we'd be worried!

Connie

I was embarrassed. It was
hard to leave Jubilee.

Chelle

That's it. That's all I get?

Connie

I told you I was embarrassed.
I should probably get going.

> **Chelle**
>
> Did something happen at
> the state dinner?

> **Connie**
>
> Steak dinner?

> **Chelle**
>
> Yes. The steak dinner. For that
> VIP party. Did your dad ever
> find the right meat?

> **Connie**
>
> Oh that. The steak was
> fine. I gotta go now. I'll
> be in touch soon.

That was the end of *their* conversation.

Ours was just beginning.

Chelle said, "Don't you see?"

I reread those last few exchanges again. Missing it.

"She didn't know we call the big-deal meals at my house *State Dinners.*"

Zeke stood, stomping again, getting it.

Chelle's face creased, frustrated with me. "Because that's not Connie."

CHAPTER 11

"It's not . . ." I couldn't finish the thought. *"What?"*

Zeke, buying in 100 percent, no doubt whatsoever, because this was the sort of thing he lived for, said, "If it's not Connie, then who?"

"If I knew that, I wouldn't be losing it right now," Chelle said. "Or maybe I'd be losing it more. I don't know."

I grabbed her phone, scrolling through the messages again. "Could she be confused? This is coming from *her* phone. How could it not be her?"

"Yeah, Jay." Zeke was stone-faced. His voice low, but the sarcasm loud. "Find the rational explanation for us dummies."

Seychelle's mouth opened, but she closed it and shook her head, choosing not to get into whatever was going on between me and him.

I kept scrolling and didn't take the bait. "Maybe her dad has her phone? She was radio silent for over a week, and he was acting weird before. The only time any of us go dark like that is when our phones get snatched. We never really stressed it because we catch up in school."

Chelle would see the sense in it. She'd have to.

"No," Chelle said, "that doesn't seem right."

"Exactly," said Zeke.

Their sudden camaraderie unsettled me more than what Chelle suggested with the texts. I placed the phone facedown on the table and took a few steps away from them to think. "Fine. What y'all got?"

Chelle said, "Why would her dad play along with me like that? Those messages are *supposed* to be from Connie. Like they were meant to . . ."

"Calm you down," said Zeke. He reclaimed his seat and waved me back over, his mood swinging to problem solver. The same way he got when he was excited about something he and his dad fixed, and we let him even though we really don't care about wiring or timing belts or whatever. He said, "Why Cleveland?"

I said, "Huh?"

"That's the city whoever sent that text named. That's real specific, but also who leaves *Karloff Country* for *Cleveland* to open a restaurant? They have some of the worst food shortages, don't they?"

I didn't know, but that didn't sound *wrong*.

"Connie's grandma lives there." Chelle retrieved folded papers from her back pocket and flattened them on the table. A map. "A nursing home on the east side of the city."

Zeke and I locked eyes. Guess he didn't know that about Connie either.

"Connie told you this?" I asked. "Before, I mean?"

Chelle shook her head.

Some bird cawed in the woods, making the hairs on my arms stand up.

Zeke said, "How'd you get this?"

Chelle exhaled heavy. "I got someone to look into Mr. Chambers's HR file."

Zeke stiffened, and I worked to keep my face neutral. She . . . could do that?

She spoke fast when she started up again. "Anyway, I called the nursing home and her grandmother is still there. They wouldn't let me talk to her directly because she was in VR therapy, and that probably wouldn't have been helpful anyway because the records indicate she's dealing with advanced dementia."

Zeke said, "Okay."

Chelle focused on me, upbeat now. "There are other relatives in Cleveland. Addresses but no other contact information. I think we should investigate this further. Don't you think so? Don't you want to know what's really going on with Connie?"

"Investigate?" I said. *"How?"*

"Just tell me you're in. Tell me you want to know as bad as I do?"

That maybe wasn't the truth, but I said it anyway. "Of course."

To Zeke, "You?"

"I'm in."

Chelle nodded, jerky. Her chin stabbing the air. "Can you get out of work on Friday morning?"

I said, "I'm already off."

Zeke smirked. "I feel a cold coming on."

Chelle gathered her bag, headed for her car fast. Over her shoulder, she said, "Give me an hour. I'll text you."

Her taillights flared when she took the turn for the Jubilee exit.

"Bro," Zeke said, "what was that?"

An hour later, we knew.

Chelle
Be ready EARLY Friday morning.

Chelle
We're flying to Cleveland.

CHAPTER 12

It was muggy at 6:00 a.m. Friday morning. The humidity pasted my shirt to me the moment I stepped on my porch, and the burnt tar smell of the asphalt heating up had my nose rabbit twitching. Yesterday was breezy and wet, ending my Enchantria shift with a storm bad enough to shut down some attractions during the last hour before closing. As usual, the mild inconveniences of nature did not go over well with the guests.

Many had objected to mandatory sheltering inside shops or breezeways during the worst of it. A few reminded me how much they paid to come here, that they paid my salary (I'm hourly, but whatever), and they would be contacting management about my "aggressive" behavior. Never mind that my insistence was an actual policy because the hail clinking to Earth had been responsible for everything from cuts to concussions during prior storms.

Anyhow, I was glad the ridiculous weather seesaw we lived with had dipped down to the pleasant side today. At the same time, if another hailstorm caused us to postpone Chelle's plan, I would've been okay with that too.

I hadn't left Karloff Country in years.

I never thought I'd be leaving like this.

Zeke stepped out and crossed his lawn but didn't make it to the street before Seychelle arrived. I'd halfway expected her to pull up in a Ferrari limo or something equally Rap Mogul because that was the only comparison I had for what we were trying to pull off.

She stopped directly between Zeke and me. Normally, he'd drift to shotgun seat automatically, but given the general messiness between us all right now, I relieved him of the choice, opened the passenger door, and flopped inside. Still, Zeke hesitated climbing into the back seat. Chelle rolled down her window.

"We're really doing this?" Zeke said.

She said, "We're going to find Connie. One way or another. Now get in."

Chelle drove us away from Jubilee, the parks, and the hotels toward the remote, northeastern sector of Karloff Country. Where the jetport was.

My family never flew much. The few times it happened, I hated it all.

The lines to check your bags. The ten-point security barricades that seemed to add an extra point every time someone threatened some innovative way to sabotage a flight and take lives. They scanned your retina and pricked your finger for a blood sample, then a full body scan. The cheek swab. The temperature check. And so on.

All that to say, I knew what we were about to do wasn't anything I'd experienced before. My stomach churned. I was already nervous about this unsanctioned flight, but also nervous I'd do something . . . *basic?* In front of Seychelle.

The trees lining the narrow road to the jetport abruptly vanished, replaced by flat green miles of land. In the distance, razor-wire fencing bordered the runways and butted up against an unimpressive brick building that could've been anything from an industrial warehouse to an auto parts store.

Seychelle stopped yards short of the gate, where a pyramid mounted on a concrete post stood next to a sign that read PRIVATE ENTRANCE ONLY and threatening spikes protruded from the ground. She leaned toward her open window and said, "Sandrina, this is Seychelle Karloff arriving for my morning flight."

The pyramid flashed red. "I am unable to process voice commands at this time. Please enter your jetport access code."

Seychelle shrugged off the minor inconvenience, then punched a code as long as a social security number into the keypad below the pyramid. The motorized gate retracted.

She nudged the car forward slowly. Her tires thump-thumped safely over those spikes.

The gate closed behind us, and she parked in one of the designated spaces next to the squat brick building.

Zeke said, "Is anyone going to think it's weird we don't have, like, bags?"

"No," she said. "I used my mom's credentials to book the flight as she normally does. They're used to us taking day trips. No luggage won't seem unusual."

"She keeps those credentials lying around?" I asked, curious about how this part of Seychelle's life worked.

"Don't tell the cybersecurity team, but the woman doesn't know how to create a strong password to save her life. She uses the same one for everything. This wasn't difficult. Come on."

At the door was another keypad, but no code from Seychelle this time. Instead, she thumbed a plain white button, then tipped her chin to a camera I felt silly for not noticing.

A buzzer sounded, and the lock clacked. Seychelle tugged the door handle, and a gust of cold air hit us like a full-body snowball.

As we crossed the threshold, most of my thoughts flitted away when I saw what awaited inside.

Plush leather couches on a white fur rug thrown over glossy wood floors. Six TVs were arranged in a grid, broadcasting sports highlights, while smooth jazz played low enough to allow for conversation. There were more flourishes—oil paintings, a coffee table that looked like a giant hunk of rough quartz—but my attention was snatched by the woman who said, "A pleasure to see you again, Ms. Karloff."

She was brown and beautiful—maybe one of the most beautiful women I'd ever seen, like someone who'd crack the top three in the Miss Universe pageant easy—with deep black hair that fell across her shoulder in a neat ponytail. She wore a tailored gray blazer and matching skirt that stopped below her knees. She worked a tablet and on her left lapel was the same Karloff Country name tag everyone wore, with a drawing of Penny Pup holding up her name the way a chef might hold his most delicious entrée along with an India flag.

Seychelle said, "Nice to see you, Farah."

"I'm so sorry to hear your mother was called away last minute, but I do hope you and your guests enjoy your time in"—she tapped the tablet and tried to remain upbeat when she saw what she saw—"Cleveland."

"I'm sure we will. My mom ordered a six-forty-five departure."

The digital clock hung over the TV grid read 6:37.

Farah's enthusiasm faltered slightly. "Yes. Of course. Captain Lucio is performing final safety checks, but there's going to be a slight delay due to an unusually busy—"

"How slight?" Seychelle asked.

Farah's manicured nails clacked her screen like tiny hammers. "Updated departure time is seven seventeen a.m."

Seychelle heavy sighed, then angled toward the nearest couch. "A caramel macchiato, please."

"Very well," Farah said. "And for your friends?"

Zeke stuffed his hands in his pockets. "I'm good."

I said, "Orange juice is fine."

"Of course." Farah hopped to our drink orders.

We sat and didn't talk. When Farah delivered our drinks, we sipped and watched highlights from Game 4 of the NBA Finals where Bronny James Jr. was *cooking* the Chicago Bulls. Ten minutes before our departure time, the TV grid went completely black.

"Farah?" Seychelle called.

The hostess arrived right away, remote in hand, first flipping to other channels—Home Shopping, the Cooking Channel, NBC—all black screens. She quickly powered down the TVs and powered them back up. Only the Karloff streaming services remained functional.

Farah sputtered an apology. "I'm sorry. I—I'm—maybe *the satellite* is having issues."

It was 7:12 then, and an Argentinian man in a dark gray suit with pilot wings and a small flag pin on his lapel entered through a door leading to the runway. Seychelle stood and greeted him. "Hi, Captain Lucio."

"Seychelle! More beautiful each time I see you. We're all prepped and ready."

Seychelle followed Captain Lucio through the door, and Zeke followed her. I grabbed Seychelle's empty cup and handed it to Farah with my half-drained orange juice. "Hey, thanks for everything."

She smiled tightly, still preoccupied with the malfunctioning TVs.

It was a longish walk to the staging area where the Karloff jet was . . . parked? Did you park jets?

A suitably long red carpet ran the path from the lounge. Captain Lucio helped Seychelle climb the plane's steps. He didn't offer Zeke or me any assistance, his eyes glossing over the moment Seychelle was out of sight.

Inside the plane, the opulence was . . . a lot. After the lounge, I couldn't say it was *surprising*. Cream-colored leather seating for maybe twelve people. Polished woodgrain throughout. There was even a flight attendant. Another beautiful brown woman, in a blazer and skirt like Farah's, but gray like Captain Lucio's suit. Her name tag said VALENTINA.

She offered me a pillow and blanket, but I declined, my attention shifting to the open cockpit door, where Captain Lucio's copilot adjusted his headset and did pilot stuff. Zeke chose a couch running along the left side of the plane while I picked a seat across from Seychelle. Captain Lucio boarded, and Valentina sealed the cabin.

"If you don't need anything preflight," Valentina said, "I'll be in the galley prepping for a breakfast of Chesapeake omelets, roasted new potatoes, and a summer corn hash."

"That sounds lovely," Seychelle confirmed over the sound of the engines revving.

Valentina disappeared through a door I didn't even know existed, it was so well hidden. Seychelle's neck craned as if to ensure the flight attendant was gone, then she said, "I know what you're thinking . . ."

Oh, I doubted that. What I thought was there are different worlds—different *universes*—all on the same planet.

Seychelle explained what no one had asked about. "I was aloof with Farah because I had to be. Without Mom here, it would've seemed suspicious if I was overly friendly. She might've sensed there was something off about this trip."

Zeke adjusted his seat belt. "Is *aloof* the rich people's version of *a jerk*?"

"Where, exactly, did you tell your dad you were going today?"

"Splash Zone."

"Right, you acted like you were going to a water park. I acted like a jerk. We don't want to tip anybody off, do we?"

I told Zeke, "She's gotten us this far. All that matters is Connie."

Seychelle gave me the most grateful look. My stomach fluttered. Zeke's expression was less generous.

She said, "I'll see to it Farah gets an incredible holiday bonus this year."

The plane began a slow taxi toward the runway.

Seychelle said, "What'd you tell your parents, Jay?"

"Enchantria."

"It'll be easy to tell you ain't working today," Zeke said, annoyed and concerned.

"Naw, not work." This part was a tiny bit embarrassing because hanging in your park on your days off was as taboo as buying Karloff merch. I never told anyone that I sometimes chilled in Enchantria when I wasn't on the clock. I got in for free. And I liked it there.

Zeke shook his head like I'd said I enjoyed scooping up parade horse poop with my bare hands.

Seychelle peered through her window, her forehead nearly touching the glass. "Why aren't we moving?"

This was another part I remembered from the few commercial

flights my parents had taken me on. A lot of waiting. Sometimes sitting on the runway an hour because twenty other planes had to take off first.

There were no planes ahead of us here, though.

Then we were in motion. Not the fast, push-you-back-in-your-seat acceleration before going airborne. More slow taxiing. Back to the hangar.

"Oh no," Seychelle said. "No. No. No."

Through my window I saw them too. Three black SUVs with opaque windows. Franklin Karloff—Seychelle's grandfather, Karloff Country founder—and his entourage.

"How did he know?" she mumbled.

It was a silly question when you thought about it. Everything here was his. If there's information anyone close to him felt he should hear, the better question was, how did he not know sooner?

The plane turned at an angle that put the Karloff caravan out of my line of sight. When we were parked in the hangar, Valentina and Captain Lucio emerged from their respective areas at nearly the same moment. The flight attendant's expression, confused. The captain's . . . less so.

"I apologize," Captain Lucio began, speaking directly to Seychelle. "We've been commanded back to the hangar and told the Karloff family planes are grounded for today."

Seychelle's light complexion took on hints of green.

I felt sick too. If freaking Franklin Karloff, who hardly anyone ever saw anymore, came all the way down from their estate to collect his wayward granddaughter, who he had very little affection for to begin with—what did that mean for Zeke and me? For our parents?

What if we got kicked out of Karloff Country?

Valentina unsealed the cabin, lowered the stairs, and the vibe among me and my friends was like, Can't we hide in here forever? Zeke, radiating defiance, flung off his seat belt and exited first. I went next, Seychelle behind me. I expected Mr. Karloff and his crew to greet us on the tarmac with handcuffs or at least yell at us. But they weren't even looking our way.

Their eyes were skyward. An engine grew louder on approach. A jet painted in bold red, white, and blue descended toward the landing strip, and its tires touched down with a screech of friction and gust of smoke. It zipped past, air howling against the raised wing flaps, its speed decreasing, and I caught the logo blazoned on the tail. NFL.

As in the National Football League.

We gazed after it until it taxied toward one of the empty hangars. Clearing the landing strip in time for another incoming plane.

While that second plane descended, I looked straight up, catching the contrails of jet exhaust from a third aircraft sailing way above us. That couldn't be another jet coming here. Could it?

Seychelle, resigned to her fate, approached her grandfather's entourage, who he addressed with slow, intense hand motions, and we had her back. Barnabus saw us first, breaking eye contact with Mr. Karloff, and thus drawing the old man's attention our way. When Franklin Karloff faced us, I forced myself not to cringe because he looked about a thousand years old, with wispy cotton-strand hair lightly covering his scalp and dark burgundy liver spots peppering his flesh like buckshot. His yellowed eyes widened at the sight of Seychelle. Total surprise. "What in God's name are *you* doing here?"

Barnabus's face remained flat. If he remembered we'd spent a couple of hours together in Enchantria two days ago, he didn't let on. He turned away from our conversation completely and watched the sky.

Seychelle responded to her grandfather, "I—I mean we . . ." She railed off, perhaps rethinking how much she should say. He hadn't come here for us.

Mr. Karloff said, "Get home to your mother. I can't deal with you right now. Go!" He snapped his fingers, dismissing us and regaining Barnabus's attention in a single gesture.

Seychelle motioned to her car, urgent. As in, let's get away while we can. We didn't speak again until we were past the jetport gate and on our way to Jubilee.

While Chelle drove, Zeke and I watched more private jets—the most I'd ever seen in a single day—enter Karloff Country airspace on their way to a safe landing. Yet, the unease I felt, you'd have thought them flaming wrecks crashing to earth, and the sky would fall next.

SEEKING THE PERFECT KARLOFF COUNTRY ADVENTURE?
NEED A GUIDE TO THE BEST TIME OF YOUR LIFE?
LOOK NO FURTHER!

A Certified Karloff Country Vacation

Planner can assist you with:

• Acquiring Park Tickets

• Selecting Accommodations to Suit Your Family's Particular Needs

• Booking Air Travel Through Your Preferred Air Carrier*

*For a personalized quote on private air travel options, <u>CLICK HERE</u>.

CHAPTER 13

Our phones were blowing up.

"My dad's telling me to come home," Zeke said, tapping a response.

I said, "My mom's telling me the same thing."

Actually, my mom's messages—plural—were a little more disturbing.

> **Mom**
> I don't know where you are,
> but you get back here right now.

> **Mom**
> I'm serious, Jermaine!

> **Mom**
> WHERE ARE YOU?

> **Me**
> On my way.

"Check mine," Chelle said. "Maybe my mom's said something."

We left the isolated jetport road and merged into the five lanes leading not only to Jubilee, but to Enchantria and all the other parks. On a Friday, this close to Independence Day, the road should have been bumper to bumper. Yet we were the only car.

On the other side of the road, the five lanes leading *out of* Karloff Country were packed.

I grabbed Chelle's phone from the cup holder. "No new messages."

"Oh. Okay. Good, I guess." She didn't sound like she believed this was good. It didn't feel good to me.

"Zeke," I said, "check online. See if something"—I swallowed hard, started over—"something's happened."

Chelle gripped the wheel tighter. Zeke responded with a shaky, "Yeah. Yeah. Okay."

What if there was a shooting like the kind we drilled for in school? Or something like the 6/14 terrorist attack on the nation's capital that happened during my family's first year in Jubilee? It was the last time Karloff Country shut down, the last time the roads in and out of our home looked anything like this.

Zeke said, "I'm not seeing anything."

Relieved, I said, "Awesome."

"No," he clarified, "I can't get to any sites. Phone's saying *network down*."

I checked mine again. I had a *network down* message, same as Zeke's. I couldn't even send another text to my mom.

Chelle turned off toward Jubilee. "What do you think is happening?"

"Don't know," I said. "After you drop us off, go home, see what's up on your end. Then let's meet at the Treat at, like, four this afternoon. Compare notes."

We passed the Jubilee marquees and pulled up in front of my house. Overhead, more jet noise, multiple engines overlapping, like they were ripping the sky.

Zeke ejected from the car, slamming the door behind him, and slow-jogged across his lawn. Fumbling my handle, I shouldered my door open, but before I left, Chelle slipped her hand into mine and squeezed.

"See you at four?" she said.

She wouldn't let go until I said, "Yes. Definitely. Four."

Inside my house, Mom was on our couch, the *Pup Tales* cartoon playing with the volume muted. Penny Pup and his ragtag team of animal friends were dressed in old-timey soldier uniforms, armed with paintball guns, and ducked behind tractor tires while Penny's nemesis Carter Cat and his gang fired paint pellets at them.

I said, "Mom, what's going on?"

She jabbed buttons on the remote hard. "Nothing's working right this morning."

There was irritation in her voice, directed at the TV, not me. Footsteps thumped upstairs—Dad—with no real urgency.

This vibe didn't match the panic in her texts. It didn't match all the people leaving Karloff Country, or the ramped-up air traffic. The back of my neck tingled. I said, "Why were you blowing up my phone a few minutes ago?"

Mom, perplexed, muted the TV. "What do you mean?"

"Your texts." I held my phone up as evidence, even though the screen was completely black now.

"I didn't send you any texts. I thought you were still asleep in your room until now. Where are you coming from anyway?"

My stomach sank, and I thought of what Chelle said the other night after showing us the suspect texts put a trip to Cleveland on our itinerary. *Because that's not Connie.*

Dad descended the stairs, his phone in hand. "Tish, I was on hold with Media Services about the TV, but the line went dead. Weird. Hey, Jay, are you okay?"

So many things were clacking together in my head. Somewhere

above, more jet noise as yet another plane passed. I wanted to be outside, wanted to confirm that I wasn't imagining all this strangeness. When I tried to exit, I couldn't. The door was locked.

"Sandrina, unlock door."

Instead of the pleasant confirmation chime, the pyramid on the coffee table flashed red and gave an angry buzz, like when someone guesses wrong on a quiz show.

I spoke louder. "Sandrina, unlock the front door."

Another red flash. Another buzz.

"Dad?"

Dad nudged me aside and jiggled the knob. There was no give. "Sandrina, this is Philip Butler, PIN 9301, unlock all doors in Butler home."

No change.

Mom abandoned Penny Pup's paintball game and crossed into the kitchen, going for the back door. "Sandrina, open the door right now."

In the living room, I spun in a slow circle, telling myself there was no way we were trapped in our own house. That's just dumb. Dad kept messing with the lock and went from giving Sandrina commands to yelling them. At the window nearest the door, I pulled the drapes aside and peered across the street to Zeke's house.

I spotted him through the window by his front door. His mouth stretched in a silent yell, both fists pounding the glass.

Then the smart panes in every window in my house snapped from transparent to opaque, hurling us into sudden and complete darkness.

SEYCHELLE

"Mom!" My voice echoed in the cavernous corridors of our home before I opted for the nearest intercom panel. Pressing the talk icon, I said, "Mom, where are you?"

The speaker squawked immediately. "Come to your grandfather's study." Her voice slurred, followed by the jarring sound of shattering glass.

I ran and found her at Grandfather's desk, her face in her hands and a bourbon decanter broken dangerously close to her bare feet. I gave the shards a wide berth, noting there was no bourbon on the floor. Mom faced me, and her breath suggested *she* was the new bourbon decanter.

"What's wrong with you?" I asked.

"Not just me, Chelley. Not just me."

"Does this have something to do with all the planes landing at the jetport?"

Her red eyes rolled hard, and her mouth turned up in a grin. "You're my little Getaway Adventure. You know that, don't you, Chelley?"

My insides twisted. Every time she told this story, she made it sound brave and warm and empowering. When our reality show was on, she told the Getaway Adventure story in the middle of the first season, right around the time our renewal was in jeopardy; it became the highest-rated episode and got us a second season. She'd been drunk then too.

"I was a young romantic. Got swept off my feet by a gorgeous basketball player the night he won his first championship. Ended up on some beautiful islands for a week"—she palmed her stomach, like she'd done for the cameras—"came home with you. I named you Seychelle because you're as beautiful as those beaches. I knew you would be before I ever saw you."

There was more to the story, of course. The part I'd only heard once, when I was seven and she was still partying way too hard. Grandfather had threatened to cut her and her "mongrel" off if she didn't start behaving in a way he approved of. That terrified her, and instead of blaming him, or herself, she went in on me.

"Your trifling father chose his fiancée over us. Called us a mistake. Said I tried to trap him. Like I didn't feel trapped. Like I didn't have options that wouldn't have blown up my life. But you're here, and now *my* father wants to kick me to the curb. Aren't we two of kind, Chelley?"

The next day, she claimed she didn't remember saying that. When she got out of rehab a month after, she said it never happened at all. Then she invented the clean, made-for-TV version. The one she told when she wanted sympathy. Or a reprieve. Maybe both.

She'd get neither from me.

I snapped my finger an inch from her nose. "Drink yourself stupid later. Now's not the time, Mom."

She still seemed groggy, so I did a full-force clap next to her ear. It echoed like a gunshot.

She jerked away and spoke through a sniffling whimper. "Jeez, Seychelle."

I thought of it as tough love, the only kind available in this house.

Whatever it was, Mom was scared. As scared as Grandfather was relieved when he saw I was almost as light as the white babies in the nursery after my birth. That part she'd told me when I was seven too.

Her face fell in her hands again, and I thought I'd have to become more drastic to make her make sense.

She spoke clearly, though. "Sit down. You need to know what we've done. What we really are."

She pressed the power button on the TV remote and the eighty-five-inch display mounted on the wall flared on to some war movie. Only, it wasn't a movie.

This was Grandfather's preferred news network, known for its exaggerations. The chyron across the bottom read: *Coordinated Attacks Worldwide.*

Something exploded in the deep background of the chaotic footage. A second explosion knocked the feed to static, followed by *PLEASE STAND BY.*

I pried the remote from my mother's hands and flipped to a different news network. More chaos, but in another country. Went to another news channel. Same. Gunfire and screams.

She said, "My little Getaway Adventure. There's no getting away now."

"Mom?"

"I didn't believe he'd ever really do it, Chelle. You have to understand that." Her gaze kept flicking to the carnage on the screen. Rampaging crowds, people carrying other blood-covered people to safety, presumably, though nothing in the frame looked safe. "He—they. Us. Tore it all down. We kicked the chair out from under the world."

"You're talking nonsense, Mom."

Her voice steadied. She explained, simply, a number of insane things. Decades of planning, machinations, safeguards put in place by Grandfather and people across the globe whom he deemed worthy for their money, success, and ruthlessness. Prophets of finance and politics who saw society's collapse coming, smiled, and asked, "How might we leverage this?"

She spoke for hours, it seemed. I kept changing the channel because the carnage on-screen countered my continuous need to dismiss her. Bloody food riots in the Middle East. Bombings and shootings in Asia. Civil wars in South America, and apparent coups in our various states' capitals. All at once, a chaotic storm so perfectly orchestrated, could it really be described as chaos?

Then newsfeed after newsfeed went black at sporadic intervals until, finally, there were no more. For all I knew, everything outside the study had ceased to exist. It would've been no less crazy than what Mom had revealed.

She was sobbing again. How could she not when she'd admitted our family's legacy wouldn't be chocolates, or theme parks, or cheesy sci-fi movies?

The Karloffs would be forever linked to the most significant event in human history. The apocalypse beyond our walls.

But what did that mean for us, here, in Karloff Country?

To Grandfather's sentiment about the circumstances I was born into, I hadn't asked for any of this. Yet here I was. The heir to doom.

By the time Mom finished laying it all bare, I was sobbing too.

**CLOSED FOR A
PRIVATE EVENT**

THREE YEARS EARLIER . . .

My parents told me to stay out of the way and let them handle everything.

While Mom directed the movers to stack our boxes in the appropriate rooms and Dad spoke quickly on conference calls that made him look like he was talking to himself because of how tiny those new Sandrina-enabled earbuds were, I was set free to explore our new, kind-of-famous neighborhood.

The houses were only visible in the gaps between eighteen-wheelers parked curbside at every property. The Karloff Coordinated Moving Day had the street looking like a whole truck stop. Some twitchy weird lady from the Jubilee Residents' Association assured Mom "this is the only time vehicles will be allowed to obscure the sight lines of our beautiful homes."

Every mover at every house wore matching blue coveralls with a Penny Pup patch embroidered across their backs. They were clean-shaven. Their rolled-up sleeves revealed swollen forearms with no tattoos. If I happened to make eye contact with one of them, even if they were straining against the weight of a heavy sofa or dresser, they paused and smiled. Service and joy. It was the Karloff way.

My earbuds were in, not the fancy Karloff ones Dad had—Christmas, though, he promised—and a bass-heavy soundtrack guided me deeper into the neighborhood. I'd been looking at the colorful planning map for weeks, imagining how wild it was to be *living in Karloff Country*! If I kept going the way I was going, I should end up at a park called the Retreat. According to the map, there would be big fields. A couple of playgrounds. Pavilions with grills and stuff.

When I turned onto a dead-end street and saw an odd, boxy white trailer at the end, I thought maybe I'd gotten it wrong. I kept going anyway and realized the truck was blocking my view. Closer now, I read the sign on the trailer door—KARLOFF COUNTRY WELCOME STATION: GET YOUR RESIDENT BANDS HERE.

My parents and I found our bands waiting on the kitchen counter in our home, with a note to "activate and sync immediately for worry-free access to your personalized Karloff Country experience." Mine dangled on my wrist, snug but light. How cool!

Rounding the trailer, I got a full view of the park I'd been looking for. It was smaller than the map made it seem. A few parents and kids were already out here testing the swings and slides.

The sun beamed. So I slipped under the shade of the pavilion, where a dark boy with plaits in his hair leaned over a notebook, tapping his pencil on the page, with an earbud cable snaking from one ear.

He looked my age. Maybe. I kind of wanted to say what's up but didn't know if it was cool to interrupt whatever he was doing.

He spotted me, though, and spoke too loud in the way people do when they're trying to hold a conversation and listen to music at the same time. "Yo, you know anything that rhymes with *pyramid scheme?*"

"Huh?"

"Pyramid scheme. It's this thing where one person scams people out of money, then gets them to scam other people and give them a cut. It goes level after level, spreading out wide like a—"

"Pyramid," I said, getting it. Though I didn't have a rhyme, and didn't know why he wanted one.

"Fear a kid?" he mumbled, answering his own question. He looked at me wide-eyed like he wanted a cookie.

"I mean, that does rhyme with *pyramid*. What about *scheme*, though?"

His brow furrowed with the challenge. He snapped his fingers. *"Pyramid scheme . . . Hear a kid scream."*

Dude rushed to scribble it down, and I wondered if he was okay. "What are you doing?"

"Writing a musical."

No response seemed appropriate, so I sat across the table from him. This was going to be interesting.

"My show is gonna be called *DeVos: An American Musical*. It's the story of Betsy DeVos, the first United States education secretary who didn't know anything about education. Told through hip-hop. It's inspired by Lin-Manuel Miranda's *Hamilton*. Have you seen it?"

"A long time ago, I think."

"It's bars. Except for the part where they left out slavery, but I mean, the rhymes were good. I'm Zeke, by the way."

"Jermaine. People call me Jay, though."

"So, Jay, how you feeling about being in the rat maze?" He waved his hand in the general direction of the houses.

"It's kind of cool, I guess."

He sat up straight, skeptical. "Please don't tell me you're one of those super hype Karloff Country fans who clips a puppy tail to the back of your pants and wants to collect all the limited-edition Penny Pup pins."

"Naw, nothing like that." Mental note: Never let him see any of Mom's photo albums where I had a puppy tail poking from beneath my shirt and was rocking a lanyard heavy with Penny Pins. I was five!

"Me and my dad moved in yesterday, and it was mad creepy last night. I looked out my window at a bunch of dark and empty houses. Too quiet. Horror-movie level."

He didn't mention his mom, and I knew better than to ask. My parents taught me everyone's family wasn't the same as ours and I shouldn't assume. I stuck to our story. "We got here today. A bunch of others too. So maybe it won't be so quiet now."

"According to the rules, it has to be. The association talks about how you gotta stay under so many decibels or our parents get a fine."

"How are you supposed to know what your decibels are?"

"I guess the point is don't be loud. Or we'll— Hey, hey!"

The way he jumped up and shouted, I thought we were being attacked. When I spun in my seat, I spotted a dark-skinned girl with short braids emerging from the resident band trailer. She wore a tank top, denim shorts, her own dangling resident band, and waved back.

She joined us under the pavilion and told Zeke, "It's *Connie*. Not 'hey!'"

"My bad. My bad. Connie, this Jay."

"Hey, Connie!"

She tilted her chin at me, then spoke to Zeke. "Told you."

I said, "Told him what?"

"That the Black kids always find each other."

"Oh."

She kept going. "Been that way every place I moved. Cali. London. Hong Kong. Now here."

"There are Black kids in Hong Kong?" I asked.

"Not a lot. I went to an international school, so it wasn't out of the ordinary there."

Zeke said, "Connie's dad's a famous cook."

"Chef," she corrected.

He cleaned it up. "Chef. She got a restaurant at the fanciest hotel on the resort."

Connie groaned. "Should've never told you. And it's not *my* restaurant."

"Your name's on it."

What they were talking about, I wasn't really following, and Connie seemed anxious enough to change the subject that she asked, "How's the musical coming?"

Zeke said, "Good now. Jay helped me with *pyramid scheme*."

He spit some lyrics that were not, indeed, good.

Connie shook her head, laughing. "Bruh, your raps are trash but also funny."

Zeke stopped rapping abruptly. "Whatever. Hey, Jay, what your parents do for Karloff?"

"My dad works in business affairs handling, like, money stuff for the whole property. My mom's an industrial designer working on the Serengeti Shadow expansions at Karloff Pictures. Her interests in Afrofuturism is, like, a big deal for the project."

"What's Afrofuturism?" Connie said, her eyes intense and curious.

Where we moved from, I was usually around more white kids than anything and I avoided talking about Mom's area of expertise, afraid of an inevitable eye roll, some racist "joke." Or worse, simply having her passions dismissed as something frivolous when most folks' main concern was their next meal.

"Um, my mom can explain it better than I can, but think of it like you mash up technology and futuristic stuff with ideas from Black history and culture."

Zeke said, "Like the Serengeti Shadow movies."

Connie sneered. "Isn't that what he just told us?"

Zeke snapped back. "I'm confirming."

When I finished, Connie relaxed on the topic of her dad, the chef. Once she started talking about him, I realized *I knew him*. He'd been on some of the Cooking Channel shows Mom watched when I was a kid, before they started getting canceled because of people's complaints about wasted food during the shortages.

Connie got shy again when she got to the TV cooking part of her dad's career, and I sort of figured whatever happened after that is why she moved all over the world before landing here. I suspected a lot of Jubilee kids could tell the kinds of stories like her dad's. Like my parents.

Zeke's dad was an engineer, but an in-the-trenches guy. Meaning he worked with, and managed, the numerous maintenance teams that kept Karloff Country functioning. We sat there an hour talking about our old schools, old friends, how our parents all acted like champions when they got a spot in Jubilee, an accomplishment akin to winning the PowerBucks Lottery. Then we theorized what we thought Karloff Academy would be like when Zeke made a chopping motion with his hand, shutting me and Connie up. "Look, look. That's her again."

A bike trail ran along the far side of the park, and the only cyclist on it must've been the "her." She was a sun-kissed shiny brown, like a new penny (the coin, not the Pup), a light sheen of sweat glistening. Her hair was in a tight ponytail that swung like a pendulum, and she was pumping the pedals hard. No helmet. No pads. She'd probably kill herself if she wrecked, but otherwise I didn't catch what was so interesting.

Connie explained. "That's Seychelle Karloff. You know who she is?"

"The last name's kind of self-explanatory." Also, I'd seen her before. From that reality show about her mom. Always thought she was pretty.

"What's her deal?" Zeke said.

Connie explained, "We saw her yesterday doing the same thing. She's riding that bike like something's chasing her."

I said, "She lives in Jubilee too?"

Zeke's are-you-stupid? look answered the question. In case I didn't get it: "Her people worth billions easy, bro. They have a *House on Haunted Hill*–type crib you can see if you look up the mountain."

Which made her suicide bike race even odder. Why run from that?

The trail would bring her within a few yards of our pavilion in about thirty seconds. I prepared to look at anything else so I wouldn't seem rude, but Connie said, "Screw this."

She hopped off the bench and ran to the edge of the bike trail.

Zeke and I followed, staying a few steps back.

Connie waved her down like someone signaling a helicopter, making big sweeping Xs with her arms. "Hey!"

Seychelle squeezed her hand brake and slowed to a stop right in front of us. "Hey?"

"I'm Connie. That's Zeke. He's Jay. We find our people, so let's be friends!"

And like that, we were crew. That's how easy it was. After some hard years, I deserved easy.

Life in Karloff Country was everything promised. Maybe more.

I never wanted to leave.

Why would anyone?

CHAPTER 14

"Hey!" Dad beat on the door with his fist. This had become part of his ritual. Every few hours assault the door. He hadn't won a round yet. "Hey! Let us out!"

Our windows were still opaque. There was no way to track the sun's rise or descent, and because we'd gotten used to asking Sandrina everything, including the time of day, we didn't even have watches to judge by. Our phones were bricked, so no clocks there either.

Mom said, "In Las Vegas casinos, they don't have clocks and you can't see outside. You lose track of time gambling. It's part of the game. I don't know what game this is."

Dad said, "Don't talk like that! It's a malfunction. That's all. Like getting stuck in an elevator."

Mom flopped on the couch, pulled her knees to her chest, and hugged them to herself. If she'd spoken to Dad since, I hadn't heard it.

A stuck elevator. That made perfect sense. This was bad, but nothing more than a glitchy AI doing what she does best. Glitch. What else could it be?

Occasional jet noise roared overhead, but no way that could be related to us.

No way.

Our resident bands were still somewhat functional. They glowed orange, signifying a wireless charge. Every hour you're charging, the haptics in the band double-tapped you. I started counting those doubles to time our lockdown. It worked okay until nine double taps in fatigue overtook me. When I woke, it could've been midnight or midday.

So it went. Time became fluid and immeasurable. Was there ever a case of someone being trapped in an elevator forever? I wondered.

Then light flooded my room so suddenly it felt like having my eyes gouged with a laser. I ratcheted up in my bed and vampire-flinched away from the sun. Realization overrode my comfort when I ran to the window and looked onto the alley behind our house. Across the way, an older neighbor squinted through her window at me. She waved gratefully like a shipwreck survivor clinging desperately to floating debris, greeting a rescue boat. I waved back.

Heavy, rushing footsteps thundered toward me. Dad crossed the room in two strides, grabbed my arm, and dragged me into the hall-way and down the stairs. "Come on, come on."

Mom was on the porch, with tears streaming down her cheeks. She bounced on her heels, urging us toward her like she didn't think we'd make it. Like the door would slam shut at the last second, cutting us in half.

We crossed the threshold without incident, and Dad put himself between us and the house. "Get on the lawn now."

Mom pulled me along, her nails so deep in my arm, blood wouldn't have surprised me. Only as we descended the porch did I notice the cardboard boxes in two stacks, shoulder high, by the porch swing. Those hadn't been there before we got trapped.

Up and down the street, other Jubilee residents stumbled from their homes, shielding their eyes from the bright summer sun.

"Jay! Jay!" Zeke called, crossing the street in a jog.

I exchanged a look with Mom and could tell she considered not letting go of me.

I said, "I'll be right back. Promise," then pried her fingers from my bruised tricep.

Zeke's dad caught up and clapped a hand on his son's shoulder before moving on to mumbling and perplexed conversations with Dad and other adult men who'd suddenly claimed my yard for their huddle. Mom, warily, skirted to the next yard, where women gathered. More kids drifted toward us. We knew them from the Academy, of course, but didn't really rock with them like that. No time for cliques now, though.

The questions and confirmations happened quickly. Yes, we'd all been stuck in our homes since Friday. Yes, our smart glass blocked out everything. It seemed it happened at different times of day depending on the household, though. Like, the moment everyone was home, their individual lockdown began.

"No one knew not to go home," Zeke said. "Perfect trap."

He leveled a stare at me. Resisting the urge to challenge the thought, I nodded. I was too happy to see him to start a fight. And he wasn't the only one making the whole thing sound more diabolical than it was. What was the point of Sandrina trapping us for a couple of days only to let us all go at once?

In the men's group, a neighbor got loud. "How dare they? I'm going directly—DIRECTLY—to Franklin Karloff over this!"

Some of them—Dad included—told dude to calm down until we knew more.

"No! I will not calm down. We were prisoners in our own homes. *Our. Homes.* Why?"

That question quieted everyone. Even him.

"What," Mom asked, pointing toward the Jubilee entrance, "is that?"

Only it wasn't the entrance exactly. Right direction, but too high. Her finger angled up.

It looked like a tiny smudge on a painting of a perfect sky. Absolutely still.

Parked.

"That's a drone," Zeke said. His dad nodded his agreement.

We moved like a herd toward the silent, hovering machine. Within twenty yards of it, the roving camera lens along its front glinted sunlight as it panned. Watching us watch it.

"Hey!" The angry man who would not calm down waved his fury finger at it. "Who's there? Who's controlling that thing? Do we need to come up to the Karloff house because we—"

He was struck silent by what we all saw beyond the drone. A dark, purposeful cloud approached quickly like that swarm of bees that chased Penny Pup in one of the more famous Karloff cartoons. More drones. They didn't form comical shapes—an accusatory pointing finger, a frowny face, a bow nocking an arrow—like in the cartoon. They zipped into place next to the first drone, sticking to a dedicated spot in the sky until they formed something like a net of suspended, floating eyes. Somehow it seemed less real than the classic animation.

Synchronous and terrifying, the familiar voice of our jailer, Sandrina, sounded from every drone's speaker: "Jubilee residents, apologies for any inconvenience you may have suffered over the last forty-eight hours. I'd ask you to return to your homes, but I can imagine you'd be wary. While I can assure you there will be no further malfunctions, I understand if you need time to trust me again. You have all been granted up to twelve hours of mental rest to do whatever you need to do."

An arm slipped over my shoulder—Mom. She pulled me into her, shaking.

The angry man stepped ahead of the crowd, stabbing his finger at the drones. "Mental rest? What is this? Someone answer me! Karloff, stop hiding behind your machines and come talk to us."

He was alone in his loud demands. Something like a toddler throwing a tantrum. Not that the things he said were unreasonable. But the lenses in each drone whined, focusing on him.

People closest to him took steps back.

He shut up then.

Dad joined Mom and me. He didn't hug us or hold our hands. He put himself between us and that angry man because we were all expecting something horrible to happen.

My father wasn't a big man. Mom often joked he lived on "one bean a day"—which only became mildly funny once we were Jubilee residents and it wasn't so close to the truth. I never thought much about him protecting us from anything before. Now . . . I wasn't sure he could.

Though angry man was silent, his finger was still aimed at a single drone among the dozens crowding the sky. Like someone in the presence of a rabid beast, afraid to look away.

It felt like an hour passed before the synchronous Sandrina voice said, "As a show of gratitude for your commitment to Karloff Country, you will find provisions at each of your homes as well as more information about necessary operational changes. This week's mental rest allotment begins now. Please take the time you need, but for your own safety and security, do not try to leave the resort. Service and joy, it's the Karloff way."

Mom's face creased. "Don't try to leave the resort?"

The first drone performed a precise 180-degree turn and zipped away. A few heartbeats later, most of the swarm did the same.

A dozen or so went elsewhere, aligning themselves in a low-altitude triangle.

Over Jubilee.

CHAPTER 15

The murmurs from before resumed but quieter, with more people glancing up at the nearest drones when they spoke.

Dad took Mom's hand and tugged her along; she pulled me. "Let's go to the house."

Zeke shot me a concerned look. I hit him with our crew nod. We'd talk later.

Dad had different plans.

At our lawn, he released Mom but kept moving toward the steps. She pressed her arm into my sternum so I couldn't follow him.

"You're not going back in there," she hissed.

Dad, flustered, said, "The car keys are inside."

Mom stiffened, getting it. My stomach fluttered.

"Meet me around back," he said.

He dipped inside, and I waited for the door to slam, sealing him in forever. Mom clutched the front of my shirt, and we circled the house. She'd maintained some sort of physical contact with me ever since the drones. Hand on my shoulder. Fingers around my wrist. Snatching at my shirttail if I strayed too far, like when I was little.

At the back of our house, anxious moments passed before our garage door slow-clanked up. I still didn't believe it would open all the way and imagined Dad stomping the gas to ram it if needed.

There was no interruption or obstruction. He backed our burgundy SUV into the alley. While we boarded, another neighbor I didn't know rocketed by us in their car, heading out of Jubilee at a less-than-safe speed. Dad's plan wasn't so original, then. Maybe not so well thought out either.

"Sandrina said we shouldn't try to leave, Dad."

It was like I hadn't said a word.

Dad drove us toward Karloff Country's main gate in silence. We tried the radio. Crunchy static across the dial except for the Karloff Country stations. KC Guest Info broadcast upbeat ads in cartoon voices for Wooly Martin's Burgers, followed by an ad for the Grand Virginian hotel. On the KC music station, a ballad—"The World Swims On"—from the latest Karloff animated film, *Drenched*. Dad twisted the power knob, and I welcomed road noise.

Several dozen cars packed the lanes before glowing brake lights forced Dad to stop. We weren't so far from the sealed gate. Maybe a tenth of a mile. Close enough to see the guards.

Dad rolled his window down, though nothing intelligible could be heard. Someone was yelling, but the men in Karloff Security vests seemed unbothered. They made jerky turn-around motions with long-bodied flashlights, and some cars complied. Those that didn't weren't so much the concern of the guys on the ground because other guards situated in freshly erected scaffolds aimed bullhorns at the more stubborn drivers from high ground.

"Phil?" Mom whispered.

Dad angled our SUV toward the median. It wasn't an official turn-around, but he used four-wheel drive to handle the curb and grass. He put us on the reverse lanes and took us back home more slowly than we'd come.

A faint ruckus sounded behind us. A scream, then a car horn sounding in a single, unbroken honk. Dad turned KC Music back on and cranked the volume.

●　●　●

We idled before the open garage door for nearly fifteen minutes, my parents arguing.

"Debating," said Dad when I asked them to stop yelling at each other. Every wrong and alarming thing came up but felt more like a recap than any progress or solutions.

Finally, Dad said, "We'll prop the exterior doors open so they can't close and lock. Then we'll see what we see."

"Jermaine stays outside," Mom said. Not a suggestion.

"Get out the car, son. We'll come get you when it's okay."

When was that going to be?

Circling to the front of the house, I found an empty street. I could've tried Zeke's without worrying my parents by straying too far, but I didn't want to tell him about the security at the exit. He'd latch on and take it too far, turn it into *The Hunger Games*, or one of those other extreme sci-fi movies.

My mind shifted to Chelle. Was she okay?

A pair of drones parked in the sky a few houses down. I went for our porch swing, hoping the awning gave me some cover from the hovering spies. Mom was in the process of wedging a red plastic cooler from the garage between the front door and its frame. She disappeared back into the house, never noticing the mysterious boxes stacked by the swing.

I looked them over closely. Brown. Plain. The only identifier was an address label featuring a barcode and the words *Butler Family, Jubilee—Members: 3.*

The tape sealing it tore away easily. Unfolding the flaps revealed an oversized envelope marked *Important Information.*

"Dad!"

Mom showed first and plucked the envelope from my hand. She

turned it over like she was looking for booby traps, then passed it to Dad, who worked his finger beneath the seal. While he did, I examined the other contents in the box.

"Wait," I said. "What?"

It was snacks.

But, like, the awesome kind.

Gourmet cookies. Fancy sour gummies from Europe that Dad once brought me after a business trip. Thick potato chips that looked like someone sliced and deep-fried them an hour ago. A ton of Karloff-brand chocolates in the green-and-purple wrappers that sold for, like, ninety dollars a box.

Mom seemed equally perplexed and bumped me aside with her hip so she could move the top box. She passed the second box to me while she worked the tape on box three. I forgot about Dad and the envelope.

Box two held containers of freshly chopped vegetables. Scallions, leeks. Dried spices and fruit. There was a recipe card for creamy soup.

Box three spewed mist when Mom popped the top. She removed cans of jumbo lump crab meat that had been packed in dry ice. There were duck breasts. A few thick steaks. Her face lit up at the sight of each delicacy—such an expensive rarity these days. I could see her forgetting how the day started, and my growling stomach could've triggered my own case of amnesia. What did *duck* taste like?

Dad flipped through pages he'd pulled from the envelope, his downturned face in shadow.

Mom said, "Phil, what's wrong? What are those papers?"

He said, "Our new work schedules."

PROPERTY-WIDE MANDATES
EFFECTIVE JULY 3 THROUGH JULY 10

Dear BUTLER FAMILY,

Something terrible has happened, and continues to happen, beyond the lauded gates of Karloff Country. Rest assured, all who reside on the property are safe. We may be among the few American citizens who can make such a claim in these devastating times.

However, to remain safe, it will require a concerted effort on the part of every Karloff Country Helper. The very good news is those efforts aren't different than what was required of you in better times. "Service and joy" have always been the Karloff way. You know it, and you embrace it. You're here within the safety of our divine walls because you are you! Rejoice in the fact that your unique and valuable talent, dedication, and work ethic have brought you here. Remember, those very same attributes will keep you here.

With this letter, you will find an ample stockpile of provisions to help ease your transition to our new Sandrina-controlled supply-chain process. We recognize there will be an adjustment period but know in time this will be like any new and improved process you've adapted. Provided we all do our parts, this change will be a smooth one.

Additionally, you will find updated work schedules for each Karloff Ambassador in your household. Review them carefully, and should you have questions or concerns, please direct them to your immediate supervisor when you report for your assigned shifts.

Thank you for your service. AND JOY!

Gratefully,

Franklin Karloff
CEO, Karloff Country

CHAPTER 16

Dad handed us our personalized schedules, then looked skyward at the nearest drones. Were they closer than before?

He said, "Let's go inside."

We were careful to leave all the stuff that kept the doors from closing in place.

"This is crazy. I . . ." Dad trailed off when the tip of the Sandrina pyramid on the coffee table lit to solid purple. That's the color when she's acknowledging commands. When she's listening.

Dad motioned us into the kitchen. The pyramid by the sink also flared purple.

I broke formation and ran upstairs to my room. A purple pyramid there too.

Mom passed my room on the way to hers. A moment later, she reappeared. Nodding grimly.

There was a spiral notebook on my desk, left over from the school year. I flipped it open and scribbled across a page with a dull pencil.

What do we do?

Mom took the pencil, touched the tip to the paper, and that was all. She never wrote a thing.

Dad spent an hour cycling through his go-to news channels, then the ones he hated, getting a black screen for each effort. The only channels that worked were the Karloff streamers. From our laptops, same situation. No real internet. Just Karloff sites. Our phones might as well have been decorative art.

Mom said, "Something's really wrong out there, Phil. Terribly wrong."

"I agree," Dad said. He spoke in slow, clipped phrases. The way he talked when he was thinking hard on how to deliver bad news in the best way possible. "But think. Maybe there's some comfort. To be had. In that."

Mom's head whipped from Dad, to the cartoons on our TV screen, back to Dad. "What possible comfort are you talking about?"

"Tish. We're safe. We have food. Shelter. If something bad's happening out there, it's *out there*."

Mom's mouth worked but produced no words.

I said, "I think Dad has a point."

Dad looked like he'd been thigh deep in quicksand and I'd tossed him a rope.

"Explain," Mom said.

"I think—" I stopped, trying to articulate thoughts I may have always had about our home. "I think Karloff Country was always meant to be something apart from the troubles of the world. Whatever bad thing is going on, we're protected. That's why we came here. It might look weird with the drones, and Sandrina locking us down, but we haven't been hurt, right?"

Dad rushed to the front door and motioned to the cartons on the other side. "Look at all this *food*."

As if that was the end of it.

And it was.

The sun set while our stomachs churned. We hadn't eaten much, and we'd gone through most of our food during our captivity. We brought our fresh provisions inside.

Mom made some incredible crab cakes while Sandrina played her favorite old songs by Chaka Khan, Anita Baker, and Mary J. Blige.

Dad removed the obstructions blocking our doors because it was a humid evening and Sandrina's environmentally conscious climate control system wouldn't turn on with the entryways open.

We filled our bellies, spoke very little other than to compliment the meal, and, despite the stress of the day, managed to go to our rooms and get some okay sleep while our Sandrina pyramids played soothing nature sounds.

Good thing too. We had work in the morning.

The prospect of leaving the house was more unnerving than being trapped in it. For the first time since whatever happened had happened, my parents and I were separating. It made me queasy, and finding Dad at the kitchen table while Mom made breakfast like a normal day didn't settle my stomach. According to the schedules that came with our provisions, Dad and I were heading to our usual jobs. Him at his business affairs office, me working a Helper shift at Enchantria. Mom's schedule was the outlier.

An industrial designer by trade, Mom had been on a project at the movie-themed Karloff Pictures park. It was a popular but small resort attraction. Maybe a quarter of Enchantria's size. The rides, eateries, and shops were fashioned after the hit films from the Karloff Entertainment catalog. And its most notable attraction, the Ferris Reel, a traditional Ferris wheel designed to resemble a film reel theaters would load onto their projectors back in the day.

Mom's focus ever since we moved to Jubilee had been the expansion based on the Serengeti Shadow films. The Shadow Lands was going to contain two new roller coasters, a water ride, and an amphitheater for a Serengeti Shadow stunt show. Half of the Shadow Lands was well into its construction while the other half was being excavated so they could pour the foundations. It had all been among the Karloff's highest priorities. Now . . . Mom was being ordered to the power plant—the energy source for the entire resort.

How she still made sure we were good and fed was beyond me. Wasn't she nervous?

Dad divided scrambled eggs and thick-cut bacon between our plates. I couldn't help myself—despite the purple glow from the pyramid between us, I asked, "Do you even know anything about the power plant?"

Mom's mouth was a thin line. "Basics. The system's a mix of wind turbines and solar panels with massive stored reserves if either of those sources run at a deficit."

Dad gawked. "Dang, look at you with casual knowledge of electrical engineering."

She rolled her eyes. "The Serengeti Shadow expansion was going to be a huge drain on the grid, so all the designers have a working knowledge of the resort's systems." She perked, seemed to direct the next part toward the Sandrina pyramid, saying, "Besides, I'm more than capable of learning whatever's necessary for my new role. It's the Karloff way."

My wristband vibrated briefly, as did my parents', alerting us to the hour. 8:00 a.m. Time to go.

We stood from the table, most of Mom's heavy breakfast untouched.

Our phones still didn't work. We weren't sure what, exactly, did work. Dad said perhaps the only thing he could say: "Find out any additional information you can and be careful today. This is all probably temporary, but learning more won't hurt."

Mom caught us before we broke for the door and did something we hadn't done in a long time. She pulled us into a group hug and prayed.

The shuttle ride to Enchantria was the same as always. Except for the silence. Broken only by short, mumbling conversations and the occasional cough. The driver was still Sandrina, and she was listening.

In the tunnels beneath the park, I changed into my uniform and approached our usual pre-shift staging area. Harry sat on the steps beneath ArcanaScape, his head cupped in his hands. His back heaving slightly. I called his name from twenty yards away, then slowed my stride by half. A courtesy so he had time to pull himself together.

He stood and mopped his cheeks with the heel of his hand before he greeted me. It didn't clear the tears, just made his whole face damp.

"Hey," I said.

"Are you okay, Jay? Your family?"

Before I answered, he pulled me into a hug. We'd never hugged before.

"We're as okay as everyone else, I guess. At least we're in the walls."

He pulled back, head cocked, appraising me. Then, "They give you a bunch of supplies you didn't ask for?"

"Yeah. You?"

He half laughed in a way that wasn't funny. "Ginger beer. They gave me a case of the stuff. High end. Only ever had it once, like, twenty years ago on a Caribbean cruise. Strong stuff, could never get it inland, so I always remembered it as the best ginger beer I ever had. Sort of resigned myself to never having it again."

He shook his head, and I said, "You don't seem too happy."

"When I was in the army, stationed in a bad, bad place, we once got this shipment of supplies we didn't request. Way better food and smokes than we were used to. The local government thanking us for our allyship. Within a couple of days of tearing into the stuff, our base was ambushed. Thought I was going to die that day. A bunch of my friends did. So, I guess you can say I'm a little wary of high-end surprises."

I asked, "You drink any of that ginger beer?"

He nodded. "It wasn't as good as I remembered."

More of the team joined us. When all thirty of our morning crew assembled, the entire group looked both lost and like Harry was a compass. Harry waved me to his side and addressed them. "Thank you all for showing up. I don't totally know how to begin."

"Begin with whatever happened on the outside. We were told we'd find out here." I didn't know who said it. Didn't really matter.

Grumbling murmurs spread through the group, and I felt compelled to regain some semblance of leadership since that's what I was being groomed for . . . before. "Everyone give Harry a second to get through what he has to say."

Please have something good to say, Harry.

He cleared his throat. "I've been told there was some sort of nuclear incident."

Carol, an older lady on our team, gasped and clapped a hand over her mouth.

Sal, one of our pricklier teammates, said, "That's bull. My neighbor's a team lead on the hospitality staff at the Grand Virginian, and he said we got invaded."

"Invaded by who?" someone else said, prompting even more questions. Order disintegrated.

Harry whistled shrilly, silencing them. "I promise you I'll get clarification. The thing that we know to be accurate is we're safe, here, inside the Karloff Country walls. Thank the Lord."

"Why we here, though?" a team member named Taryn asked.

"I think the Karloff Corporation saw something special in each of us. Our commitment to service and joy, our—"

"No," Taryn clarified, "why are we *here*? At work? Who's even in the park? My husband and I drove to the gates last night and got turned around by the security team. They got these concrete barriers up so no one can get in or out."

As far as that no-one-can-get-in part, Taryn hadn't been watching the sky on Friday.

"Maybe there are guests still on property," Harry said. "Mr. Karloff probably wants to give them a sense of normalcy?"

"After a nuke hit us?" Taryn pressed.

"It's an invasion!" someone countered angrily.

Someone else said, "I heard it has something to do with a virus."

"I'll get you answers!" Harry promised. "I will. Until I can, let's do what we do. If for no other reason, to think about something else."

They dipped into mayhem again. Talking at once, over each other, louder and more insistent that everyone else was wrong. It couldn't be like this here. I couldn't let it. Us at each other's throats was not the Karloff way.

Step up, Jay.

"Hey, everyone, I'm climbing these stairs and making sure my Dreamscape is cleaner than any other in this park. When it is, I'm going to brag about it. Unless someone else wants bragging rights and can do a better job than me."

Danni, one of our glass-half-full, always-down-for-friendly-competition team members, gently nudged their way through the crowd. They said, "I'll take that challenge. Somebody swing by PatriotScape later and see if you can't eat off the ground."

That prompted other challengers. Not many. But my team dispersed to their assigned Dreamscapes because what else were we going to do?

We were inside. We were safe. We were Helpers. To obsess over things outside the wall that *couldn't* be helped was wasted energy. Not the Karloff way.

The rest of them only needed time to see that too.

CHAPTER 17

I'd been in an empty Enchantria plenty of times. Before opening. After closing. All-night summer inventory. Never like this.

Not with the speakers blasting Karloff movie scores at a volume usually meant to compensate for the chatter of ten thousand families. With no one around, it stabbed my brain—probably loud enough to cause damage. Two hours into my shift, I'd already checked three supply closets for earplugs and radioed Harry to get the volume turned down. He said he'd sent a request to operations about it too. A bunch of Helpers had complained.

The theme from the movie about the Siren who couldn't sing faded into an upbeat version of "The Star-Spangled Banner," reminding me this was a holiday, Fourth of July, amplifying the strangeness of an empty park. It wasn't only my team either. The restaurants, the gift shops, the rides . . . all fully staffed like any normal day.

I tried remaining upbeat. Tried focusing on the execution of my duties. Yet, I couldn't stave off the occasional intrusive thought about the point of this. There had to be one.

"Yo, Jay!"

The sound of my name startled me. I tracked it to the entrance of the Sorcerer's Rapids ride, where Zeke stood in his engineering team coveralls, his tool bag resting at his feet.

I nearly ran to him like a lost toddler spotting his mother in a crowd but maintained some cool and strolled over. The scent of the ride's chemically treated water was harsh in my nose. In the absence of guests—no crowd sweat and BO—everything in this made-up world felt more extreme.

Zeke and I collapsed into a hug that we held way longer than we ever would've before. When we parted, my knee-jerk park training kicked in, warning me that he'd broken regulations. Engineers shouldn't be in the open in their grease-stained uniforms carrying dented toolboxes. It took away from the magical Karloff Country experience.

The obvious counter: *Whose* experience?

The Sorcerer's Rapids queue was designed to look like a cave. We were in shadows, and there were no cameras here. "The Star-Spangled Banner" faded to the ballad from the *Penny Pup for President* film, and no one was going to hear a word we said over it.

Zeke said, "Bro. What is happening? Seriously?"

"They said wild stuff at our team meeting this morning. Nukes. An invasion. But that can't be right."

His forehead crinkled. He exhaled long and deep, like he was prepping for some heavy lifting. "You don't think that's possible."

"No. I don't think somebody nuked America. If there was a nuclear apocalypse, we wouldn't be in Enchantria. We'd be underground in the tunnels or—" I stopped short of listing the alternatives because there weren't many and they weren't pleasant.

He said, "My dad thinks another big climate thing happened. He said tsunamis might've pushed the New Coast in even farther."

"That wouldn't affect Karloff Country, not at our elevation." I perked. "That would be good, then."

Zeke's expression was flat. "Not if you lived on the New Coast."

"I don't mean *good* good. I'm just saying."

"Hello? Is there anyone here?" somebody yelled.

We flinched. That the new voice was loud enough—insistent enough—to be heard over the movie themes was startling. And familiar. Only a guest could make questions feel like kicks.

Zeke snatched his toolbox as if to run. I held up a hand. "Hang back. I'll check."

Shielding my eyes against the sun, I emerged from the tunnel and assessed the loose group of backlit strangers.

"Oh, awesome. Someone is actually doing their job around here."

They looked like shadows missing a body, and my eyes hadn't adjusted enough to identify the yeller.

"Paige, this place is so kiddie, though," someone else in the group said. "Let's go to one of the water parks."

"Shut. Up." The yeller—Paige—snapped. Not banter among friends, but an order to a subordinate.

The one who wanted to swim didn't speak again.

Paige came closer. A white girl, about my age. Almost as tall as me, wearing denim shorts and a pink tank top with long, tanned limbs, blond hair falling across her peeling, sunburned shoulders. Expensive sunglasses hid her eyes. She said, "What time are the fireworks?"

Several things struck me at once. First, her accent, high and crisp. From the West for sure, maybe California. Second, her absurd question. I said, "Fireworks?"

She made an offensive show of slowing down her speech. "Fire. Works." To her group, Paige said, "Daddy told me not to expect much from these people right away, but Jesus."

Every time I thought I'd finally grown the rhino-thick skin Dad

146

said I needed to move up in this world, a guest insult disproved my immunity. *These people.*

My training was top notch. I held it together and focused on the question.

On a regular holiday, fireworks began around 9:00 p.m., once it was full dark. There was nothing regular about any of this. No way the park was doing a Fourth of July show *tonight*.

Guests like effort. They wanted to see you work even if the work was futile. Unclipping the radio on my belt, I said, "Let me check."

I thumbed the talk button. "Harry, this is Jay. Is there a fireworks show tonight? I have a guest right here who wants to know. Over."

The part about the guest being in earshot was a courtesy for Harry so he didn't respond with something crazy this Paige girl would overhear, like the *no fricking way* I was expecting.

The radio crackled, and Harry said, "Yes, at nine fifteen p.m. Please inform the guest that the best view's going to be in PatriotScape Square, and be sure to thank them for their trust in us. Over."

Wait.

What?

"Excuse me," Paige said, "are you having a stroke or something?"

She'd heard him, of course. But her hearing the same information I had wasn't the point. I stopped staring at the radio. "Fireworks are at nine fifteen and—"

"Oh my God," she interrupted, "I can barely hear myself think over this corny music."

Her crew chuckled unenthusiastically, like bad actors late for their cue.

Paige snatched a phone—a *working* phone—from her pocket and tapped her screen, then craned her neck toward the nearest blaring speaker. Maybe fifteen seconds passed while her crew and I looked where she looked.

The volume decreased to soothing background noise, no louder than elevator music.

What the other Helpers and I complained about for hours she'd fixed in seconds. Clearly, she was pleased too, judging by the grin on her face. That grin retracted when she spoke to me. "Well?"

"The fireworks are at nine fifteen tonight. You'll get the best view over in PatriotScape."

Her face remained flat and expectant.

"Is there something else I can help you with?"

"You're supposed to say it. The *trust* part."

Harry had said something about trust, but I'd forgotten it.

Paige huffed. "I so miss Calabasas. Lucia barely spoke English, and I didn't have to explain maid stuff to her. Listen, I'll say it slow. 'Thank you for your trust in me.' Go on."

Insufferable guests weren't new. Some people took joy in messing with Helpers because they knew we were bound to a motto of service and joy. We could be reprimanded or fired if we did anything but. Yet, the last few days had been *a lot*, and I felt my true feelings about this hateful girl bubbling in my throat.

Maybe she sensed it too. Because she did something that cooled my rage.

She lifted her phone like she wanted to take my picture, tapped something while flitting slightly panicked glances at me. As silly as it seemed, I wondered if she was about to turn down *my* volume?

Better sense took over. This girl wasn't worth whatever problems she could cause me. The phrase felt gross in my mouth, and the shame I felt executing her command even more so, but I said, "Thank you for your trust in me."

Her grin returned, small and spiteful. She lowered her phone. "You're welcome."

Paige left ArcanaScape and the others followed like they were trapped in her gravity.

With the coast clear, Zeke emerged from Sorcerer's Rapids. "Jay, what was that about?"

I had no idea.

CHAPTER 18

My recap of the Paige encounter left Zeke as confused as I was about who those people were and why they were here.

We probably could've spent all day speculating, but his radio squawked a new assignment that would take him to ExploraScape, leaving me to finish my shift with way more questions than when I started.

Before he left, he said, "If you can get out of your house tonight, meet me at the Treat around nine. I think the pavilion will shield us from the drones. We can talk more."

"No doubt." We slapped palms and hugged again.

Resuming my rounds, I stopped at various shops and restaurants, asking if any of my fellow Karloff Helpers had seen the blond girl. Some nodded with the enthusiasm reserved for spotting a celebrity, which happened often in normal times, though they had no more information about who she was than I did. Others who hadn't had the pleasure of Paige's company acted like I was describing Bigfoot.

Nobody had any insight on how that girl got into Enchantria when there seemed to be no other guests around. By five, I finally admitted that fake-cleaning the near-empty park in summer heat was misery and I'd nearly forgotten about that mean blond girl. I wanted to go home, take a nap, check in with my parents, and see Zeke at the Treat later.

Down in the tunnels, I swiped my wristband across the sensor that logged our in and out time. The sensor and my band flashed red.

I tried again. More red flashes, and this time I noticed the message in the little LED display. It said: SHIFT EXTENDED.

"Oh, come on."

Other team members lined up behind me, eager to leave for the day too. I stepped aside, mad.

Taryn swiped and got red. "What in the world?"

She looked to me, and I said, "Let Ronald try."

Our next teammate went, same thing.

I unclipped the radio from my belt and hailed Harry. "Hey, it's Jay down in the tunnels. We're having some issues with the time clock. A bunch of us getting a *Shift Extended* message. Over."

Harry came back immediately. "Ask the team to meet me in the cafeteria in five minutes. Over."

They heard him. Nobody liked it.

"What *now*?" Taryn groaned.

Our team gathered between four tables in the Helper cafeteria, an area that always seemed an insulting contrast to the colorful Karloff-branded world a hundred feet over our heads. Polished pea-green floors, white cinder-block walls sparsely decorated with motivational posters and corkboards for pinning company-approved flyers. The counters where we picked up food during breaks were shuttered with aluminum barriers now.

Harry stood before us, nervous. This time, I didn't stand by his side. I was tired and wanted answers like everyone else.

He said, "There's a fireworks show tonight. I know, I know. I'm as surprised as you. However, I've gotten word from operations that we need to institute a more traditional holiday schedule, meaning double shifts to best service the guests who'll be attending."

The backlash was immediate. The outburst echoed throughout the cavernous space.

"What guests?" Sal about screamed. "I was up there sweating my tail off all day and didn't see one person who don't work here."

"I saw someone," a Helper named Geoff said.

I perked, more than ready to cosign whatever story he told about mean-girl Paige.

Geoff said, "An old Black couple strolled through FuturaScape. She waved, but he didn't acknowledge me at all. That was about it."

"I saw them too," Eric confirmed. "Also ran into a super fit white lady. Or rather, she ran into me. She was jogging through my section, like, for exercise. It was so weird I thought I was hallucinating."

A few more told stories about the people already mentioned, or some different people, though no one described Paige and her group, so I kept them to myself because, I don't know, what did it matter?

There were guests. Multiple. That was the point. Yet the random one-off sightings felt stranger than no guests at all. When you were used to servicing upward of forty thousand people per day, serving none after a supposed crisis made more sense than serving, like, eight.

Harry was drowning in the team's frustration when there was clearly nothing he could do other than his job. *Our* job.

I had an idea. "Harry, if this is like the last two holidays, the bulk of the guests won't start showing until about two hours before the fireworks. It's a little after five o'clock. What if anyone who's really gassed from being up all day took a break now, while anyone who's not wiped goes back up for an hour or so?"

"A mini shift," Harry said, loud enough to see how the team reacted.

There was grumbling, but old, reliable Danni said, "I'll go back up for a while. I'm feeling okay."

More agreed to trudge on while making arrangements with a counterpart who would break now and work later. Harry and I exuded the same lead-by-example energy and left the cafeteria with big smiles on our faces. Walking billboards for the Karloff way.

When we were far enough from other Helpers that our conversation couldn't be heard, I asked my big question. "Who gave the order for double shifts today?"

"Came directly from Barnabus. He apologized, but he stressed that he needed us to do it. That it was beyond his control."

"Mr. Karloff?"

"I thought the same thing. I bucked a little and said Karloff needs to remember we're humans, not Sandrina." Harry slapped a hand to his neck, working the tension there. "Barnabus was like, 'There are other forces at play now.'"

"What does *that* mean?"

Thank you for your trust in me.

When Harry didn't answer my question, I asked another. "You get any more information about what's happening outside?"

A headshake. No.

We reached the stairs to ArcanaScape and climbed, him ahead of me. We emerged into afternoon heat and overcast skies, the smell of fresh cotton candy that would likely go uneaten sickeningly sweet in the air.

"I saw some guests today too," I said.

"Really."

The conversation I'd had with Zeke earlier and the many, many confusing thoughts I'd had during the long-isolated hours today were bubbling. "They didn't seem scared, Harry. I mean, if they're guests who were here before whatever happened, wouldn't they be scared that they can't leave? If they were on the outside when it happened, why would they come to an amusement park?"

"I don't know what you want me to say."

"Say *you're* scared. I know you can't say it down in the tunnels in front of the team, but if you are, say it to me. Because I am."

"I am," he said quickly, then clenched his jaw. "Let's go work. Less time for fear that way."

CHAPTER 19

The break I was supposed to eventually take . . . I didn't. No way would I be able to relax downstairs waiting for the inexplicable fireworks show. So I made my rounds, checked trash cans that hadn't be touched because there was no one around to touch them, and shortly before seven, when the ArcanaScape shops lowered their gates and started their closing procedures, I made the long walk to PatriotScape.

This section of Enchantria was a mash-up of American landmarks. The only place in the country where you could stand in one spot—the Square—and see scaled-down versions of the Washington Monument, the Liberty Bell, and Mount Rushmore at the same time. The Square was modeled after the Green, a town square in Dover, Delaware, where the residents voted to ratify the Constitution in 1787. A huge bronze plaque mounted to the side of the City Hall Gift Shop said so.

My familiarity with PatriotScape was minimal, thank God. Of all the sections in the park, this was my least favorite. It had the dullest rides—all slow-train history lessons, nothing thrilling. The worst food because, to be authentic to colonial times, things were mostly boiled or too salty. Mentioning the cuisine here used to get Connie going with the venom of a battle rapper.

I stopped like I'd run into a wall. It'd been a couple of days since I thought about her. Not how she inspired our attempted flight on the day Karloff Country went bonkers. Only her. The way I wanted to remember her. My food-snob friend.

The present snapped back around me when someone brushed past carrying a bucket of ice and I continued dissecting the "authenticity" of American history that didn't mention slavery, or what colonizers did to the Indigenous people who were here when they arrived. Things glossed over in a generously named "Hall of Remembrance" that dedicated an excessive amount of floor space to Betsy Ross's sewing.

The Square bustled with Enchantria staff I'd never seen in the same section. PatriotScape uniforms were a mix of tricorn hats, waistcoats, and gowns made from breathable material so summer heat didn't kill the wearer. They were present, of course. So were FuturaScape space suits, ExploraScape desert fatigues, ArcanaScape sorcerer robes, and the oddest uniforms: the dark dress slacks, vests, and neckties of event caterers.

The everyday Enchantria workers moved benches, and potted plants, and other mobile decorations from the Square to make more room for the waiters who arranged folding chairs—a lot of them—in neat rows along with tall round tables draped in white cloths. The jazz band that usually played welcome music at the park entrance was near the steps of city hall.

In two corners of the Square, bars had been set up, and the bartenders arranged their offerings—beer, wine, harder stuff. In the other two corners, longer tables with stainless-steel warming trays prepped for food.

"My man," a waitstaff boss with a thick New York accent yelled in my direction, waving me over. "We got a spill here. Could you help us out?"

His table was dedicated to snacks. The bulk retail boxes of individually packaged hard candies, gourmet jelly beans, Karloff chocolates.

The spill was a box of caramel corn that had somehow ruptured in transport. I did my thing, sweeping the loose kernels into my dustpan, and decided to ask, "Hey, who's all this for?"

He flinched like I'd faked a jab at his chin. "The Trustees."

The man skittered away, not to be delayed, and I heard Mean-Girl Paige in my head yet again.

You're supposed to say it. The trust *part.*

The first partygoers—the Trustees—trickled in. I knew it was them because they weren't us. They greeted each other like they'd been friends for years, engaging in long, celebratory handshakes and boisterous laughs.

The Trustees were a sight to see after two days of isolation, and most of today roaming the barren park. One of the men—middle-aged white dude, with thin gray hair and a soft round jaw—yelled, "We did it!" on his way to the closest bar.

Some were solo. Some were couples. Some were whole families with kids ranging from infants to my age. Like Mean-Girl Paige.

She entered the Square with two adults who looked like her elder clones. I assumed they were her parents. Her mom's hair was pulled tight into a bun, deep wrinkles etched the corners of her eyes and mouth, heavy makeup made her skin look as appealing as spoiled milk. A projection of what Paige would probably look like in middle age, and it wasn't kind.

Paige had swapped her shorts and tank top for a crimson party dress. She'd done her hair in a long braid that wrapped around her head. Another old white dude in a blue sports coat gripped Paige's dad's hand, ignored her mom completely, then zeroed in on Paige in a super cringey way. "Look at the pretty girl!"

To which everyone in the immediate vicinity—except Paige—laughed.

I might've felt bad for her, but I hadn't forgotten the way she spoke to me earlier, and I remembered something my mom liked to say. *Pretty ain't pretty if it's only an outside thing.*

I worked the perimeter and let that be.

There were plenty more Trustees to observe. Maybe if I did that long enough, and quiet enough, I might get answers no one had been willing to give.

That was the plan anyway. Quickly derailed when I spotted three new arrivals.

Franklin Karloff, in his trademark gray suit. Blythe Karloff, in white, as bright as a bride at her wedding.

And Seychelle.

CHAPTER 20

The Karloffs were swarmed by overly eager Trustees who wanted to touch the namesakes. In this rush, it struck me how the Trustees were mostly white, only a few people of color sprinkled in. Seychelle was a light brown buoy in a rough, pale sea.

Working Trustee phones were unsheathed for pics and selfies, and for a split second, I felt like everything was fine. This party, the rituals typically associated with parties, fooled me into thinking this was *Before* and not *After*. Seychelle was here, and she was okay.

She got crammed into a group photo with stuffy people draping their arms over her bare shoulders, her sleeveless silver party dress doing little to disguise her discomfort.

Barnabus had entered with the Karloffs but hung back, loitering around the edges of the bustle, looking as uncomfortable as the day I'd seen him at the jetport.

Cameras went off like silent bombs. Franklin Karloff stayed stiff and unreadable. Blythe basked in the attention, tugging more people into her space and calling for whoever had the longest arms to take a selfie. Seychelle shielded her eyes with one hand, looking away from the flashing cameras . . . to me.

We locked eyes for a hot second—I know we did. Yet, when I mouthed, "What is this?" she resumed her camera gaze, mimicking her mother and posing harder than she had before. When the photo barrage ended, she engaged in conversation with a young Trustee girl in the opposite direction as me.

Altering my spill-patrol route, I worked around the edge of the crowd attempting to get her attention. It became clear I already had it. Because with occasional glances over her shoulder, she saw me coming and moved. Seeking conversations in whatever area was farthest from me. Still, I chased her because . . .

Someone snapped their fingers inches from my face, stopping me cold. "Here. Take this."

A chunky Trustee with stubble over flaming cheeks held a plate littered with gnawed shrimp tails and used cocktail toothpicks.

But I was losing Seychelle, and there was a garbage can three feet away. I said, "The trash is right there, sir."

When I tried to move on, he smushed the plate into my chest, staining my uniform with red cocktail sauce. Shrimp tails and toothpicks littered the ground between us.

"I didn't *ask* you where the trash is. I *told* you to take my plate." He tipped back his beer, draining the bottle, then set it on his table with the other four empties he'd already downed. "Bring me another beer while you're at it."

A waitress—Juana by her name tag—saw it all and rushed to my rescue. She said, "What kind of beer would you like, sir?"

The very drunk Trustee said, "No. I told *him* to do it. Get me another beer. Now."

The jazz band continued to play, but no one in earshot of his order paid attention. The surrounding Trustees were flat-faced and curious. How was this going to play? How did they *want* it to play? I spotted Paige's shark grin among them.

My confusion over what had happened—the inappropriate demand, the assault because him crushing that plate into me was that—became anger. Behavior like his justified a park ejection, didn't

160

matter who he was supposed to be. I unclipped the radio from my belt to call security.

At the same time, he dug inside his sports jacket and retrieved his phone.

Something electric buzzed through the crowd, the sadistic glee of kids witnessing the moment before a playground fight.

A hand fell on my shoulder. Harry. He said, "Sir, I'm sorry about any inconvenience here. We'll bring you two beers."

"What?" I said. "Did you see what he did?"

Harry's hard gaze said: *Shut up, Jay.*

The band ceased playing, and feedback whined through the speakers, followed by two thumps on a microphone.

"Attention, everyone," Blythe Karloff's voice bellowed in surround sound. "The fireworks display will begin momentarily, but before it does, I'd like to say a few words of comfort on behalf of the man who made this all possible, my father, Franklin Karloff."

She motioned to a seated Mr. Karloff, who nodded stiffly. Uproarious applause followed.

Distracted by the announcement, the drunk accosting me did a wobbly half turn toward the mic, and Harry dragged me to the back of the gathering, where we talked in panicked whispers.

"What was that, Harry? I'm getting that guy thrown out."

Now both hands were on my shoulders, reasoning. "It's not an option."

"What does that *mean?* What does *any of this* mean?"

Instead of answering, he let Blythe speak.

"Tonight is a night of inevitability. One my dad saw coming long ago. As did you. You've invested your vast resources, maintained faith in my father's vision, and now in a dire time, you've helped execute our plans—*your* plans—to perfection."

"Our time! Our world!" Paige's father shouted, thrusting his sloshing drink skyward.

The call and response caught on. Most of the Trustees followed his lead, pumping their fists in the air. "Our time! Our world!"

Seychelle stood at the foot of the dais, quiet. She looked wary, nauseated. It was the only comfort I found in this moment.

Blythe continued speaking over the Trustees, eventually regaining control of the proceedings. "Everyone here saw the world speeding toward disaster. And, in the way true innovators do, you didn't decry the mistakes of the past, or try to stomp the brakes for some futile effort to wrench the gears of fate into reverse. As the masses raced to the brink, we said"—she leaned into the mic, smirking and proud—"*speed up.*"

More cheers from the Trustees. Raucous table pounding. Playful mosh-pit shoving.

And every Helper in attendance looked the way you might if the tiger enclosure at the zoo cracked from the force of incensed rabid predators suddenly throwing themselves at you.

Blythe said, "Phase one of the plan continues, and the sporadic reports we're receiving indicate a progressive crumbling of current societal systems, as expected. Rest assured, we have people in place at every major power center. When the dust clears, those who represent our interests and wisdom for the future will be positioned to lead the finest thinkers, fighters, and doers—"

"Gotta love a little forced Darwinism! Clear out the riffraff!" a woman shouted to bemused chuckles.

Blythe kept going like she hadn't noticed the interjection. "While the masses succumb to fear and weakness, we remain brave and strong inside Karloff Country. It's appropriate we celebrate our nation's birth on the eve of its rebirth. Whatever remnants of old ways persist, the great minds here have already paved the road to our future. The world outside might weep and gnash its teeth, but I want to personally guarantee that your investment in the level of comfort and care Karloff Country has provided for decades will not change throughout your stay. For the duration of the world's metamorphosis, you will live, as promised, with the award-winning, five-star service and joy you've come to expect within our walls. It's the Karloff way. Cheers."

Blythe raised a glass, and everyone with a drink did the same before cheering and gulping greedily.

Seychelle stood apart from her family. Her arms crossed, her face tight.

The band started a rendition of "The Star-Spangled Banner" timed to the first, second, and third explosion in the sky. Starbursts of red, white, and blue. I looked to the spot where Seychelle had been standing. She'd vanished.

For twenty minutes, fireworks doused the crowd in spectacular colors while they oohed and aahed. The rapid, booming finale began, when the drunk from before lurched our way.

Harry said, "Let me handle this. Sir—"

"Shut your mouth," the man began. "Didn't you hear you boss's speech? I didn't pay top dollar for bottom basement service. You people should be grateful we're allowing you to remain here. You enjoy a lot of privilege on my dime, and I can't even get a beer? Or a thank-you?"

"For what?" I barked, at my breaking point.

Harry stepped between me and the man. "Sir, I apologize. I'm getting your beer right now."

But it was like dude didn't want to hear Harry. "Karloff! What happened to all that service and joy crap? I'm not feeling the love over here."

His crazy rant would've gone unheard beneath the thunderous fireworks if he'd started thirty seconds ago. But the fireworks were over. Whether his complaint made it all the way to the Karloffs, I never found out. It was Paige who took it upon herself to address it, that phone of hers held at arm's length, as if recording the moment.

She said, "Oh my God. Stop coddling them."

She aimed her phone at Harry and tapped the screen.

Harry's wristband lit up a dancing red, the light array inside the accessory circling his wrist faster and faster, until crooked fingers of blue electricity snapped from the band to his flesh, sending him into a shrieking spasm.

His scream was so sudden and shrill, I scrambled backward, halfway expecting him to explode like the fireworks.

His left hand snapped to his right wrist, attempted to shove the band off, but it was too tight to clear the flare of his wrist. He collapsed to his knees, then toppled to his side, his legs kicking in a futile jig.

I rushed to him, kneeling. "Harry, Harry!" Instinct warned me not to touch him, a sense that wouldn't have been stronger if he was on fire with flames leaping to everyone in spitting distance.

Blood streamed from his nose, and he'd stopped screaming. His eyelids fluttered. Only the whites beneath visible.

"Somebody help!" I yelled. My training kicked in, and I snatched my radio off my belt. "Need an Alpha Unit in PatriotScape immediately. Not a drill. Not a drill. Over."

All around Trustees watched my boss—my friend—convulse and drool. Like children watching a mildly amusing puppet show.

Paige kept her phone aimed at him.

"What did you do?" I yelled in a manner unbefitting of a Karloff Country Helper addressing a guest. I didn't care.

Paige cared though. "What I should've done earlier."

She pointed her phone at me. Pressed her thumb down hard.

The servos in my band clenched my wrist like gnawing teeth. Red light shot the circumference once, twice.

A new sound filled the night. More screams. Mine.

A thousand needles stabbed my wrist. Then my brain. Then my lungs. Maybe my heart. My entire body cramped, and then concrete smacked my cheek as I tipped sideways. The ground was still warm from the day's heat and sticky from some spilled drink I wouldn't be cleaning up. Then it was the stabbing, all over my body to the point my brain wouldn't process anymore.

The pain only subsided when Paige's phone was snatched from her hand by her irritated father.

"What?" she said. "What's the point of having these if we're not going to use them?"

I didn't hear his response.

Blackness consumed me. Party over.

165

NOW AVAILABLE THROUGHOUT THE RESORT, WIRELESS CHARGING!

Utilizing the latest in KolAC+ Technology, your compatible devices will never run low when snapping that perfect picture, shooting that treasured video, or taking that important call.

Karloff Country will keep you powered up through all the fantastic days and stellar nights of your stay!

CHAPTER 21

My eyelids fluttered, and the gentle motion felt like kettlebells slamming into my temples. The initial pain so bad hot acid splashed the back of my throat, triggering convulsive, agonizing coughs.

"Don't move, baby." Mom sat next to me, rubbing and patting my chest in succession. "You're fine."

That was a lie. Because everything hurt. Like a whole body bruise being poked by a giant, invisible thumb. I managed to get my eyes somewhat open so I could see her, and the pain from before tapered. Thankfully, the fluorescents overhead were dim, and it was still nighttime beyond the window. My hazy vision adjusted quickly. The med center, then.

"What," I croaked, "happened?"

"You're fine. You are."

I wanted to yell *stop lying*; but instead I managed a single word. "Dad?"

"He was here for a while but had to step away. There are a lot of . . . meetings right now."

Something wrong with that too. Because there were other people in the room.

I detected at least two standing along the back wall where the shadows lingered. One stepped forward, and when the figure emerged in the light, I wondered if maybe I was still asleep and dreaming all of this.

"Hi, Jay," Chelle said. "If you're up to it, we should talk."

My head throbbed, suggesting not-a-dream. The figure who'd been next to her stepped beneath a fluorescent. Mom's book club friend,

167

DeeDee, a nurse here. She crossed the room, joining Mom. Like a united front. The unmistakable posture of protection. From what?

Fuzzy memories of Chelle at a party came back to me, but she'd been in a dress; she now wore jeans, a plain blue hoodie jacket, and a fitted cap low on her brow.

I flashed on her at the party, that silver dress. The rest came back. Harry shrieking. Paige's phone. Pain like I'd never experienced.

"How long have I been here, Mom?"

"A little over a day, baby."

It wasn't even the *same night*?

"My mom and grandfather don't know I'm here," Chelle said for reasons I didn't understand.

Mom said, "If they find out, is that going to be a problem for us?"

"They won't find out. They have bigger concerns than me. Always."

The bed controls were in the safety rail. I thumbed the elevate button for a better view. "Let her talk, Mom. Go on, Chelle."

"Do you—any of you—know what's happening outside the walls?"

Nurse DeeDee said, "Folks around the med center have been saying a massive hack of the electrical grid has blacked out half the country. Or something."

Chelle's shoulders slumped. She motioned to a chair no one was using. "May I sit?"

Mom nodded, and Chelle about collapsed in the seat, her eyes on the window.

"I can't say with certainty there hasn't been some power hack. Those happen often. Thing is, if that's true, it would be like the fourth- or fifth-worst thing going on outside of Karloff Country. Y'all might want to sit down too."

168

"I'm fine." Mom clutched my shoulder.

Nurse DeeDee remained standing as well. Though she looked wobbly.

Chelle said, "There has been fighting at the Capitol. Bad fighting."

Mom said. "With who? What country?"

"Ours."

"Another insurrection?"

We talked about them in civics class. Over the years, there had been repeated attempts to overthrow the Capitol building in Washington, DC. Everything from ridiculous lone wolves who were stopped within thirty seconds, to protests escalating too far, to tactical breaches by mercenaries who left lawmakers dead in their wake. Our teachers always framed them as flukes, though. Futile disruptions. One teacher I had when we still lived outside the walls told us they were fake.

Chelle kept staring beyond the window. "It was over the food shortages. Thousands of hungry people stormed the Capitol while Congress was in an emergency session."

DeeDee said, "What about the National Guard? The police?"

"They helped the mob, maybe even led them." Her voice hitched. "It was all very coordinated. And it's happening in other countries. Folks have stormed Parliament. The Rashtrapati Bhavan. The Kremlin. Anywhere people are hungry, they've been"—she hesitated, the corners of her mouth turned down in disgust—"*motivated* to blame their leaders and fight back."

People were hungry everywhere. Climate change, the rice and potato famines, those mosquitoes infecting livestock with deadly viruses. We talked about all of that in school too. It was always elsewhere, and someone else's concern. As abstract as those math problems about two trains leaving the station at different times and speeds.

Chelle said, "Society's been on the brink for a long time. My grandfather, and his friends, gave it a kick."

"What's that got to do with my baby being in this hospital bed?" Mom said sharply.

"Apparently"—Chelle's voice cracked again—"the Karloffs and their investors orchestrated this moment in time. They used their power and influence to create a nexus point when all the world's problems intersected in just the wrong way. They also created a haven from their own horrors. Here. The walls will protect them from any unwanted forces that drift this way. The supplies they've hoarded will stave off what's inevitable for those on the outside."

"They?" Mom closed the distance between her and Chelle like she might slap my friend. *"Them?"* She stopped just shy and hissed, "What's that got to do with us, Seychelle *Karloff*?"

Chelle wasn't rattled. For some reason, that frightened me. "The people behind the current situation didn't only invest in food and shelter. They invested in service. The same service they'd have gotten if the world wasn't burning. Anticipating some resistance, they created safeguards." She glanced at my wrist.

New pain prickled there. I lifted my arm and gasped at a nasty burn beneath my charging resident band. It was slathered with ointment but not bandaged.

Stop coddling them.

Oh God. No. No way.

Mom backed away from Chelle as if she'd flashed vampire fangs, then looked at the glowing orange band on her own wrist. Nurse DeeDee raised her band to eye level. Sneering and angry, DeeDee worked her fingers beneath her band, trying to slide it over her hand, then resorted to yanking it. The orange charging light flashed, shifting to rapid red.

"I wouldn't," Chelle said. "They've planned for that too."

Nurse DeeDee stopped meddling with the band, and the red became orange again.

"How do we get them off?" Mom said, her voice weak, lacking conviction. Like maybe she knew the answer wasn't in this room.

Chelle only said, "The world we remember is gone. There's always been a plan for this inevitability. We're all part of it. We just had no clue. I thought I should tell you."

She stared at me like we were the only ones here. My stomach lurched, and I raised my bed higher even though it made the room slow spin. "Mom, can I talk to Chelle alone?"

Mom tensed, but Nurse DeeDee said, "No one's going to hurt him here."

Mom relented. "I'll be in the hall. Right outside."

Nurse DeeDee led Mom away and closed the door behind them. Chelle dragged her chair to my bedside, and said, "Do you understand everything I'm saying?"

"No. Do you?"

"Not at all. For a long time, I told myself it was some weird, sick joke, until—" She motioned to my arm.

"I was tortured at a party for your family's rich friends. Now what? What am I supposed to do with this information?"

Quietly, she said, "I don't know."

"If we don't want to be here, me and my family, can we leave?"

She stared.

"Chelle!"

"There may not be anywhere to go."

"You're making it sound like the world ended."

She stood, frustration boiling over. "You haven't been paying attention. You never do! The world has been ending since before we were born. The plagues. Starvation. Droughts. This isn't a hiccup. It's not going away. The people who made this possible aren't looking backward at laws and decency. They made a desert and an oasis. They are going to have their way."

I said, "You."

"Huh?"

"Not *they*." I lifted my burnt arm with my glowing band. "You don't have one of these, so it's not *they*, it's *you*. This place that you're telling me is a doomsday prison has your actual name on it."

"That's not fair."

"Wasn't that your point?"

She slid her chair back until it bumped the wall. Done. "I wanted to make sure you were all right and explain things. I don't know when I'll be able to reach you again. So be careful. Everyone won't have the information you do, and many of the Trustees aren't the kind for gentle lessons."

"That's it? 'Jay, welcome to Apocalypse Resort, I'm out.'"

"No. I'm going to learn more. See what I can do to make whatever's coming tolerable. I'll be in touch." She took steps toward the door, then reversed course, leaned over my bed rail, and kissed my cheek.

It burned.

172

ZEKE

Jay. Bro.

Everybody was talking crazy. Some people said a Trustee had, like, a ray gun and shot Jay and his boss, Harry, with it. I knew that was stupid and not true. Something bad happened, though. Nobody was lying about that.

The word spread like germs. From the waitstaff up top, to the janitorial staff dipping into the tunnels afraid they'd be next. The bosses told us to go home, and that felt as scary as Trustee ray guns. Dad ain't been doing so good ever since Sandrina locked us in the house, and I ain't been doing so good with him.

Where else was I going, though?

On the shuttle, I heard some say Jay and Harry got rushed to the med center. I could've maybe switched shuttles at Jubilee and gone to see for myself, but the med center sounded worse than going home with Dad. Clinics, med centers, hospitals. I never wanted to go in one again after Mom died back before we made it inside the walls.

She'd suffocated on her own snot in a crowded hospital hallway because that's what it was then. Too many sick people. Not enough doctors, or medicine, or rooms, or even cots so people didn't have to die on the floor.

So, no med center visit. Which left only my house.

Dad worked with an engineering crew at the Grand Virginian hotel. There were only minor tasks there, though, and we'd received notice he'd likely be reassigned to the Vertical Farms, so it wasn't surprising he'd beaten me home.

Ghostly blue light flickered in Dad's man cave. The sour tang that was the result of little cleaning and even less showers pricked my nose. I found him doing what he'd been doing for days. Sitting silent and listening to the chatter on his CB radio. The only form of communication still available.

"—stay off Interstate Sixty-Six. The pileups are traps. Armed men are taking anyone trying to get in or out of DC."

I said, "Dad?"

"All of the attention is on the Capitol. That's good."

"Something bad happened tonight," I said.

He lowered the volume on his broadcast. Not all the way. He didn't face me. "Are you all right?"

"I am. Jay got hurt. Harry from Enchantria janitorial too. The Trustees hurt them."

Dad faced me then, his concern apparent. Maybe I'd finally gotten through to him.

Then he said, "Well, what did Jay and Harry do?"

"I don't think they did anything."

"If the Trustees hurt them, that means they did something."

"I—" I didn't know how to respond to that. Those words sounded as logical as Trustee ray guns.

He got up and grabbed me by the shoulders. "Ezekiel, the Trustees saved us. Being here, in Karloff Country, is a blessing. Don't believe me? Listen to the things I've been hearing on the CB. They've lost their minds outside the walls."

"They?"

"We're in a refuge. No one's even talking about Karloff Country on the channels. The Trustees have kept us invisible. So your friend

174

probably did something dangerous. Something to jeopardize their preparations."

Dad let me go and returned to his radio like we'd come to an agreement.

I left him there as I had the last few nights and closed myself in my room, the soft purple glow of my Sandrina pyramid acting as a night-light.

Okay. I had a shift tomorrow. I'd ask if anyone had any more info on Jay. Maybe he'd be home by then, and I'd be able to—

A soft buzzing drew my attention to my desk, where my useless phone had sat for days, bricked. Now its screen was lit.

I grabbed it, thinking maybe it was some random surge, or it was resetting itself.

There was a message.

Unknown Number
Our friends are in trouble. Bigger trouble's coming.

Unknown Number
Don't you think we should help?

CHAPTER 22

It was another four days before I was allowed to go home due to a continued tingling in my toes and queasiness I couldn't shake. My diet of broth, saltines, and ginger ale left me feeling hollow, and in that time, the med center went from unnervingly quiet to alarmingly loud. I tried not to think too much about what that meant.

My parents sat with me in shifts, a schedule allowed by whatever bosses made decisions now. Dad explained his "meetings" weren't the usual marketing and profit things he specialized in—what was the need? He'd been reassigned to the Karloff Country Vertical Farms. Managing workers maintaining our food supply. He relayed this to us in his most upbeat tone, so I knew he was trying extra hard. "At least I'm working crops. I hear the livestock tower's a little gruesome but also largely automated. Thank goodness."

Nurse DeeDee let me know Harry was recovering well, just a little slower than me. Mom said youth was on my side here, but I remembered the way Paige had strung out Harry's punishment, delighting in it, before turning her attention to me. I'm almost certain whatever jolt I got was half of his. What if her dad hadn't intervened when he did?

Neither of my parents discussed how they felt—how we *should* feel—about our circumstances. At least not with me. Whenever I brought up what Chelle said, they told me to rest.

On day three, Nurse DeeDee guided Harry into my room in a wheelchair, and I about fell from my bed in a rush to hug him, trying not to stare at the way the left side of his body seemed to slouch. We spent most of the day together, with several Enchantria teammates dropping in to visit. Nothing but well wishes and encouragement. Almost like they were afraid to express anything else.

Still, I was glad to see them. Their presence helped ease my true desire during those long days of healing: that Chelle would come back or that Zeke would come even once.

On the day of my release, both of my parents were allowed to see me home. We sat together waiting for the doctor to give me the green light. He stepped into my room before noon, his resident band partially concealed by the sleeve of his white coat. It was a short evaluation, ending with him saying, "Be careful with your attitude and mind the new curfew. Would hate to see you back here again."

Dad swiped his band over the lock at the house, pushed our front door open, and stiffened.

Mom slid in front of me like a human shield, though the crown of her head stopped at my chin, so anyone who meant me harm only needed to aim high, but that wasn't what this was. I saw what had changed since I was last home.

Boxes of provisions were stacked in our living room. Easily a dozen cartons of pantry staples, premium meats, and expensive snacks. Much more than we'd been allotted after the Sandrina lockdown.

Dad delved inside. Mom followed and tugged me along. We sorted through the supplies together.

My reaction was neutral, recognizing this as some sort of trade-off for my . . . ordeal. Some carrot-and-stick version of Pup Points. My parents' reaction was abject terror, though. I didn't know why.

"What's wrong, Mom?"

She asked Dad a question instead of answering mine. "Did you bring this stuff inside before you came to the hospital?"

Dad shook his head, and suddenly I got it.

Not only was Sandrina listening all the time here, but strangers could enter at will, without permission. This time they were Santas sneaking down the chimney with gifts. What if they came back, in the middle of the night, for something less generous?

Worse, what could we do to stop them?

The extra provisions came with an adjusted work schedule. I'd been granted an additional week off to continue my recovery, along with a message.

"Duty updates coming soon." Dad read that part aloud.

Conscious of the electronic ears in the room, I mouthed, "What does that mean?"

Dad shook his head, because how could he possibly know? Mom squeezed my thigh, but if she had further thoughts on the matter, she kept them to herself.

While I got to stay home for now, they got the opposite. Their schedules were changed to account for the time they'd been allowed to sit with me. Double shifts at their respective gigs, keeping the power and food in tip-top shape for the real bosses. Starting that afternoon.

Mom really tried to convince me staying in bed all day was the move, but come on. I could barely sleep, let alone lie there. At first, I tried firing up the PS6. Most of my games required a network connection, though. The ones that didn't weren't fun enough to distract me from Sandrina glowing purple, always on.

After a day, I found myself on the porch, digging into novels Mom had left in the little table/chest that sat next to the swing. *Kindred* by Octavia E. Butler, I flew through in a sitting. *The Good House* by Tananarive Due took me two days. They were great but not exactly comforting under the circumstances. I tried Zeke's house, of course, but his shifts must've been long ones because he and his dad weren't ever home. I peered through their windows checking for furniture, made sure they hadn't disappeared like Connie.

Past the midpoint of my off week, I started walking the neighborhood. Like obsessively. I didn't want to be inside at all, so I loaded up a water bottle and did slow laps. Jubilee was big, miles and miles to cover on foot. I walked so long that I returned home sweat soaked, smelling like something cooked, with blisters on my heels. I'd been trying to outpace the closest patrolling drones.

Day six was different. Mom and Dad left; I was on the verge of panic knowing that another long walk wasn't an option—my feet hurt—but I couldn't do the isolation of my house either. I even wondered if I could still get into Enchantria for free. It was that bad.

Another book from Mom's chest, *The City We Became*, was how I'd planned to spend a day on the porch, but the novel slipped from my grasp when I found a surprise guest in my seat.

"Zeke."

He left the porch swing and threw himself at me for a hug. Not some bro-hug, half-in sideways stuff either. Chest to chest, squeezing-squeezing-*squeezing*.

"I'm sorry for not coming to the med center. I—"

"I know why. You don't have to be sorry." If I lost my mom the way he did, I wouldn't set foot in a hospital willingly either.

He pried away, dragging his forearm across his eyes, sniffling. "Heard you were okay. It hits different seeing you, though. I was scared for you even though my dad said I shouldn't be. I don't know how much I believe the parents about anything anymore."

From that angle, beneath the porch's awning, I couldn't spot any drones, and I got angry I thought of those machines first before I said, "Thanks, bro."

"How you *feel* feel, though? You good?"

"Now I feel super normal. The first few days, though . . ." I eyed the fully charged bands on my wrist and his. "Has anyone told you about what they did to us? All of us?"

"Word got around quick."

"Because of Harry and me?" Somehow I knew I was exaggerating our notoriety in Karloff Country.

Zeke shook his head. "You know the housekeepers at the Grand Virginian? Ain't no need for hotels anymore, so they got ordered to strip rooms for supplies that the Trustees can either use now or stockpile for later. From the peanuts in the minibar to the toilet paper. Well, a few people bucked and got zapped for it."

"No."

"Someone taking tickets at the Downtown Karloff theater caught a bad one because they'd directed a Trustee to the wrong auditorium. One of the performers in the *Drenched* Stanley Squid costumes at the Karloff Pictures park got zapped because his costume scared some Trustee's little kid."

His face got cloudy, though bright sunlight beamed on us.

I said, "What?"

"Those costumes, you know how much they suck. Especially on

180

a hot day. When dude collapsed, and they were waiting on an Alpha Unit and medics, no one took his costume head off. The Enchantment Code was still in effect."

The Enchantment Code was company speak for "always maintain the illusion." Never break character in front of the guests.

Zeke said, "Dude died right there."

I almost said I thought no one ever died in Karloff Country, but that was wrong and bitter. "Did—did we know him? The guy in the suit."

Zeke shook his head. "He was older than us. Lived with his partner. No kids."

"What did people do?" By people, I meant those like us. Employees. Residents. The families that made Karloff Country work. I'd already started thinking of the Trustees as something else. Un-people.

"Yelled. Cried. Spoke to their supervisors. The Trustees were happy because they thought there'd be more of a dustup over it. They really pushed the managers to stress how dude had a heart problem already, and how that's what killed him."

"*Did* he have a heart problem?"

"Does it matter?"

My rage and terror thumped in my throat. Yet, something struck me. "How do you know what the Trustees were happy about?"

"Let's walk to the Treat." Zeke stood, grabbing the strap of a bulging backpack he'd tucked under the swing.

On the walk, I noted three drones parked at a distance. They didn't seem interested in us. Yet.

We didn't talk on the way, and when we sat at our table, he fished out things that reminded me of the school year. Notebooks, his laptop, a phone, which surprised me because they were only good for the Trustees now. "What are we doing?"

He opened an audio program on his computer. "Yo, check the scratch tracks for my musical."

My confusion nearly knocked me over. "*DeVos?* You're still working on that? And you made . . . *scratch tracks?*"

A tap of his space bar started a drumbeat intro, followed by Zeke's voice:

"How does a debutante, heiress, child of a tycoon
Buy a path through politics to oversee your classroom . . ."

The verse continued. Zeke pointed at his phone, leaned across the table, whispering, "The drones aren't in range, and their microphones ain't really that good, but I didn't want to take any chances. If they pick up anything, it'll be the music. Now look."

The phone screen was lit, fully functioning

There were a lot of messages. Zeke and whoever had a lengthy convo going. The name of the mystery texter and the last two messages drew my attention.

Panopticon
The Trustees are afraid of
blowback. Now more than ever.
It may be time to move soon.

Panopticon
But we need more fighters.
There's no rebellion without them.

Panopticon

We doing this?

Zeke

I'm in.

He stared across the table at me, the most serious I'd ever seen him. He asked: "Are you?"

CHAPTER 23

"What is all of this? *How* does your phone work?"

Zeke turned the phone screen back to himself, scrolling. "Not everything works. No calls or internet. Nothing from the outside. It had been sitting on my charger, and I'd forgotten about it, really. The night you went down, it lit up with a message." He showed me.

> **Panopticon**
> Our friends are in trouble. Bigger trouble's coming.

> **Panopticon**
> Don't you think we should help?

I sucked in a breath so fast, I choked, triggered a coughing fit. Between the hacking, I managed, "Chelle came to see me in the hospital," I said. "It has to be her."

He frowned. "Chelle told you she had a way to contact me? So we could fight back?"

"Not exactly. She was sneaking and being careful."

"But she wanted to fight back?"

"She said . . ." I trailed off. What she said was *tolerable*. She'd do what she could to make things *more tolerable*.

"Jay?"

"Who else considers us both friends? Who else would call themselves that stupid name if they didn't know you followed that message board?"

"She didn't know I was on Panopticon. Unless you told her." His voice deepened with the accusation.

"I didn't."

"So it ain't her. These messages don't really sound like the way she text."

"What if she's being smart? I mean, what if she used Panopticon because she knew no one would think it was her."

"That's a lot of what-ifs. Look. Whoever it is has *access*. They've sent me all kinds of text transcripts between the Trustees and tech specs for stuff I haven't seen before. Like the drones. That's how I know we're probably good to talk like this, because they don't have sophisticated directional mics or audio isolation software."

"All information Chelle could get. Same way she could book a private flight on a chartered plane with her mom's passwords."

Zeke said, "You really think it's her, huh?"

He opened a thick binder he'd brought along, all stuff he'd gotten from Panopticon, I figured. He flipped to a page he'd marked with a pastel tab. Then spun the book around so I wasn't reading upside down.

It was scaled-down blueprint of Karloff Manor.

The house, the structures beneath it. A tunnel system like what ran beneath Enchantria. Zeke flipped the page and showed me the rest. A map. Instructions. A door code.

He said, "Let's go ask."

We'd never been to Karloff Manor. Three years of friendship with Chelle. She never invited us, and we never asked. I always imagined it as a mini Karloff Country. Its own world behind its own wall. There was an unspoken understanding that some part of our friendship hinged on her spending as much time as possible away from that place. Though we'd never asked to go to her house, we sensed enough about her household to know the progressive, down-for-her-Black-daughter Blythe we saw on Juneteenth might be something different away from prying eyes and rolling cameras. What I saw at the Trustees' Independence Day party was final confirmation.

Going up the mountain to that big house behind that big wall . . . I wasn't into it. Especially not sneaking through some secret tunnel. I was slow answering Zeke's proposal.

His eyes rolled to the sky. "Bro! Don't act like you don't want to see her."

"She's gonna *love* us breaking into her house."

"Their wall. Not the house. We're getting onto the grounds to see what we see. That's it."

"Unless we get caught."

The weight of that fell on us like a chunk of sky had broken loose.

The note I left (*Out with Zeke, be back by curfew*) was going to get me in a lot of trouble with my parents. The unexpected bonus of not having a working phone was their inability to call/text/track me. But Mom was going to be terrified, and Dad would pretend he wasn't terrified, which would translate to rage. So, I was 100 percent going to feel some pain. Necessary pain. I did want to see her again.

The sun didn't set until late, and we agreed it best to make our approach with visibility as low as possible. That meant we had to roam. Kill time. We caught an empty shuttle to Downtown Karloff.

Wide cobblestone walkways ran like drought-dry rivers between Karloff-character-themed restaurants, bars, the movie theater with the digital marquee displaying more showtimes than there were visible people.

We walked the lanes but weren't completely alone. Trustees were scattered about. All white people this time, not even the few people of color from their party—if you didn't count everyone working. Like Enchantria, every attraction was open and staffed. Unlike Enchantria, any Trustee who noticed us met us with suspicious glances and hushed whispers to their nearest companion.

"Guess we're not blending in too well," Zeke said.

A Sikh man with a streaky gray beard and a dark turban pushed a Penny's Popsicle cart. Slowly, though, because one of his arms was injured. It was heavily bandaged and in a sling.

There was an East Asian woman running a Monte FISHto's stand we'd passed. Two Cuban boys I recognized from the Academy were in the movie theater ticket booth, and Zeke's tragic crush, Ramona, worked her T-shirt stand. She waved.

Zeke waved back, no hard feelings from the night things didn't go his way. She stretched her eyes wide, jutted her chin slightly, then dropped her gaze. The hairs on the back of my neck pricked. A quick glance over my shoulder and I saw what she was warning us about.

A group of male Trustees stared from a fancy restaurant patio; Zeke and I were more interesting than their bloody steaks and dozen empty martini glasses.

I *felt* them evaluating us. Felt them determining if something needed to be done about us existing in their space.

A group of Trustee girls younger than us erupted from the arcade, doubled over and giddy-laughing, drawing the attention of the steakhouse gang, and a lone boy devouring the Cra-burger he'd gotten from the FISHto's stand.

One girl pointed at the boy, whispered something to another, then that girl said something to the rest of their group. The bunch of them were cackling again. A new inside joke, and the boy was the obvious punch line.

The woman working the FISHto's stand chuckled too.

She shouldn't have.

The girls disappeared around a corner, but the boy, so bright red in the face his brown hair seemed like it was growing out of a lit match, dropped his burger, pawed a phone from his back pocket, and aimed. The woman seized, then toppled sideways convulsing on the ground.

Phantom pain seared my entire body. I saw *her* but remembered *me*.

The boy thrust the phone toward her in a stabbing motion, never letting his thumb off the phone screen. He'd lost it. No intent of ending the torture.

Shouting, enraged, the Sikh man ran his cart at the boy, slowing enough to soften the impact—a mercy the boy didn't deserve. The cart clipped the boy's shoulder, knocking him down, his phone skipping from his hand.

The woman he'd zapped went limp. Groaning, but alive.

The Steakhouse Bros sprang from their seats, hopping over the patio fencing with purpose. Each drew their phones and aimed at the Popsicle Man, intending to put him down.

"No more!" the Popsicle Man shouted. "Never again!"

The Steakhouse Bros looked to their phones, to the Popsicle Man defying them, back to their phones, and became afraid. The attempted zapping hadn't worked.

The Popsicle Man used his good arm to rummage around his sling, grimacing in pain. The bandages covering his hand were wet and red. He pulled a long-handled wrench free of the sling, unraveling some of the protective dressing, exposing raw, scarred flesh.

One Steakhouse Bro yelled, "He doesn't have a band. There are children here, and he doesn't have a band!"

True. But to accomplish that feat, the man had somehow, some way, removed his own hand.

He lunged in their direction, swinging his wrench and dribbling blood on his own shoes. Even with ten yards between them, the Steakhouse Bros flinched like he'd pressed a sword to their throats.

The boy who'd started this pulled his knees to his chest, sniveling within the Popsicle Man's striking range. He sobbed when the Popsicle Man raised his wrench high.

The wrench fell and landed with a dull crunch. On the boy's phone. Sending glass and plastic shards flying.

Zeke and I were rooted to our spots. I was afraid to take a breath, knowing my resident band was still intact. Knowing I could easily draw some terrified Trustee's attention.

The Popsicle Man pointed his wrench at the Steakhouse Bros, warning them to keep their distance, then tended to the woman who'd been zapped. He knelt by her side, shouting at the men he'd defied. "Call for help. She needs a doctor."

Those Trustees *weren't* the only ones with working phones. Zeke's hand snaked to his back pocket. I grabbed his wrist and shook my head.

The Popsicle Man screamed more but stopped abruptly. His eyes on the sky.

A grouping of black wedges—drones—flew closer. Eight of them.

They slowed their approach, then parked in the sky, thirty yards off the ground, their cameras keying on the Popsicle Man.

He rose. I waited for him to point his wrench at the swarm, taunting them or whoever might be watching the security feeds. But when tiny glass eyes in the black teeth of any invisible monster stared at you and only you, maybe it was impossible to be brave.

Four drones plunged from their parked positions, arcing like darts flung by an unseen hand.

The Popsicle Man managed a half-turn retreat that did nothing but offer his thigh, ribs, and shoulder to their sharp beaks. The piercing impact pinned him to the ground, where he shrieked, blood blooming into pools beneath his uniform. He crawled, smearing a trail along the concrete, whimpering. Two more drones fell. They struck his throat and forehead, stilling him.

This wasn't real. No one died in Karloff Country. The body was fake. A prop for some new stunt show, and I wanted nothing to do with any of this . . . oh God.

Worse than the Popsicle Man's screams was the sudden, utter silence that followed. Nothing should be so quiet.

Then quiet was broken by the Trustees' applause.

Two drones remained in the sky, observing the scene. Zeke punched my shoulder twice, knocking me from a daze, and he ran for the nearest alley, between a seafood restaurant and more shops. I chased, catching one of the drones rotating toward us just as I made the corner.

We kept running. Sprinting longer and harder than our bodies were used to, snatching glances over our shoulders every few seconds.

When we stopped, gasping, willing away cramps in our calves and thighs, we lay in manicured grass next to a churning koi pond far outside of Downtown Karloff. That it was so beautiful seemed an exclamation point on what we'd witnessed. Everything was insane now.

Pumpkin-colored fish zipped beneath the surface thinking fish thoughts. My view of them blurred by tears I couldn't hold in. Zeke was somewhere behind me. His occasional hiccup-like sob stood out among the low sounds of nature.

"Could we have helped the man?" Zeke managed to say. "Should we have tried?"

"We could've tried, but we'd—we'd still be there with him."

It was true. But knowing it didn't make any of this better.

We walked for an hour, with another hour to go before sunset. Not aimlessly, but in the general direction of tonight's destination. Up the mountain.

The hiking trails angling toward Karloff Manor were a hard climb, made more difficult by a persistent need to check the sky for drones. I found focusing on my burning muscles and shallow breathing was an antidote for the clawing anxiety. So, of course Zeke had to ruin it by saying, "I've been thinking about Connie."

Don't, I would've said, but I was short on air.

"What if it went down like your dad said? What if Mr. Chambers got her somewhere safe before all this happened?"

I managed an "Okay."

"Maybe she's the lucky one."

Gasping, I asked, "Do you really believe that?"

"I want to."

So did I. We kept climbing.

The sun set at 8:16 p.m., and we were still hiking up the south-eastern slope of the hill Karloff Manor rested on. The western side was the main entrance, walled off with a guarded wrought-iron gate. The south side was for deliveries, maintenance workers, and domestic staff. The path we took was an escape route.

According to "Panopticon," there were secret ways in and out of the estate because, I guess, that's what stupidly rich people build in their houses? If our intel was correct, we'd be accessing a tunnel that ran a quarter mile into the mountain, then brought us up inside the groundskeeper's hut.

How Zeke couldn't deduce this type of detail had to come from a Karloff—Seychelle—I didn't know.

Our hill was thick with ancient trees, the leafy canopy leaking patchy moonlight. Zeke produced two flashlights he'd gotten from his dad. They were the army kind that shined red and made me feel like we were in a video game. A scary one.

"Are you sure we're going in the right direction?" I asked. "We don't have a compass or anything."

"Panopticon said keep along the estate's eastern wall. We know the main entrance is north, and we're to the right of that. Now we're look-ing for— There!"

Zeke flicked his light at an outcropping of boulders on a hill of mostly dirt and trees. We hiked that way and found the rocks rimming a cave entrance. Our flashlights did little to beat back the dark inside.

"Dude, there could be cameras in there, or"—I flashed so hard and fast on the Popsicle Man in a pool of blood that I flinched—"drones."

"There're no drones. Panopticon says Trustees don't surveil things *they* want hidden." Zeke stepped in, lighting a path. I followed. A few yards beyond the mouth of the cave was a steel-riveted door with a keypad set in the jamb.

Zeke scrolled through Panopticon's messages. "Read that to me."

It was a mix of numbers and letters, fourteen characters total. I read them off, while Zeke pressed the buttons. I halfway expected an alarm to blare and armed men to corner us in the cave. Instead, the pad gave a cheery chirp and the door unlatched.

The tunnel beyond was lit like mineshafts in movies. Shaded bulbs dangling from cables all the way to the vanishing point. Summer heat didn't reach this depth; spontaneous moisture made the rocky walls and ceiling slimy, like they were coated with phlegm. Zeke hadn't turned off his red flashlight, so whatever the cone touched became a sickly pink, and I suppressed the sensation that we were traveling down a throat.

"How far?" I said. A short sentence because you could taste the humidity and I didn't want to keep doing that.

"It's like doing a lap around the track at school. If we hurry, less than five minutes."

We didn't hurry, though, because the trade-off for extra exertion was taking in more of the swampy air. We reached a concrete staircase seven minutes later.

At the top of the two-story climb was another door and another keypad. Zeke punched us in, and we emerged in darkness. Zeke closed the tunnel door behind us gently. From this side, it looked like a supply closet, a Do Not Enter sign mounted at eye level. Someone shrieked with glee, followed by a splash.

"We'll have to be extra careful from this point on," Zeke whispered. "Panopticon suggests sticking to hedge shadows and we should be fine. Still."

He didn't need to elaborate. I understood the consequences for getting caught by anybody but Seychelle were different—and deadlier—than what we thought when we left Jubilee. We probably should've aborted the mission after what we witnessed in Downtown Karloff. I didn't suggest it because I wanted to see Seychelle that bad. I knew *my* reason for wanting to see this through even after the Popsicle Man.

What was Zeke's?

The question settled in the back of my mind like an itch I couldn't reach.

Nudging the shed door open, Zeke scanned the surrounding area, then waved me along. We darted to the nearest bushes in a crouch, not with any skill or stealth, only imitating video game soldiers in the shooters we played. From our concealed position, the peaking roofline of the Karloff mansion was visible. Eaves and gables that stretched nearly the length of the nine houses that lined my side of the street in Jubilee.

The giddy sounds, scored by angry hip-hop, were louder. Sharp chlorine seasoned the air. A pool party. I didn't like parties so much anymore.

A concrete pathway broke through the hedge wall, and xenon landscaping lights made that way daytime bright. Checking that he was clear, Zeke darted across the path to where the hedge wall continued. In the single breath and heartbeat when he was exposed, I imagined him collapsing to the concrete in writhing pain, dying before my eyes.

He made it, though. Positioned himself so he faced me, then cut his eyes toward the pool.

I scooted to the edge of my cover and peeked around. A wide patio separated us from the festivities, and because this was all still the side of a mountain, level changes meant I didn't have a straight-on view of the guests here, only glimpses. The top of someone's head as they bounced on a diving board. Someone blond jogging poolside.

Zipping across the path to Zeke, I settled into the shadows. He made a circular motion with his index finger, indicating he'd clocked the same thing I did. If we went all the way around, we'd get a better look. He started that way, but I grabbed his backpack, halting him.

"Text Panopticon. Say we're here."

His eyes narrowed. "They sent me these plans in a data dump. I don't want anyone knowing we're here *right now*."

"*She* should know."

He let out an exasperated breath. "It's not her, Jay."

"Just do it."

He fished his phone from his pocket and sent a cautious message while I peered over his shoulder.

Zeke

We're close to you right now.

"Happy?" He pocketed the phone, and we continued creeping along the hedge wall.

A few minutes later, we were poolside. This close, with only foliage separating us from the swimmers, we heard everything and could make out a few faces through gaps in the leaves.

Paige was here.

She hoisted herself from the pool, her blond hair slicked down her back, and she scampered toward an impressive waterslide in her pink-and-purple polka-dot bikini. A couple of boys hooted from the water, and some other girls groaned from deck chairs.

Among them, Seychelle. Grinning. Looking like a model in a generic ad for "fun."

Her phone was on a table by her chair, next to a frothy pink drink. If she'd gotten a text about her suffering best friends being nearby thanks to the clandestine data dump she'd provided, she played it off well.

CHAPTER 24

Paige took the curving slide down to the water, squealing until she splashed and sank. She shot beneath the surface like an eel, popping up close to Seychelle and the other girls to chatter about something or other.

The music was louder where we'd come from, no thumping high-end speakers on this side of the pool. We caught snippets of the girls' conversations.

"Did you see that speed? That stroke?" Paige said. "I could've gone to the Olympics, you know."

"As a spectator?" a dark-haired girl said.

Paige didn't clap back. Maybe didn't recognize the jab at all. She sounded sad. "No. Like, I was really good for a long time. But Daddy knew what was coming, and there was no reason to focus on training after a certain point."

A heavy silence fell over the group. Before it stretched too long, a redhead in a lounger next to Seychelle slurped something icy through a straw and said, "I can draw. I wanted to do comic books or story-boards for movies. Anybody else into art?"

Shrugs and low grumbles.

The redhead wasn't deterred. She turned sideways, fully facing Seychelle. "Sey-Sey? I even thought about doing character designs for some of your grandfather's movies. Can you make that happen when everything's back to normal?"

Zeke sneered and mouthed, "Sey-Sey?"

Paige shouldered herself from the pool, dripping water and

disdain. "What kind of dumb question is that, Ames? Nothing's ever going back to normal."

The redhead—Ames—turned vicious. "About as dumb as your dye job. The pool's going to be blond now."

Paige grabbed a phone off the table and aimed it at Ames.

I flinched, waiting on the zap, but realized almost instantly it was an empty threat.

Ames rolled her eyes, unbothered. "I know, I know. You *love* your little torture button. Take it out on your Concierge later, boo. I'm not the one."

Was *Take it out on your Concierge* a rich people expression? I didn't know what that meant.

Paige lowered the phone and opted for an obscene hand gesture before flopping on a deck chair.

Ames said, "Sey-Sey, what are you doing when things go back to normal?"

Seychelle said, "Hopefully never seeing you again. So, I probably won't be helping you get an internship."

Her words were as sharp as I'd ever heard them. Mean in a way I wasn't used to from her. A way I didn't know she was capable of. Though directed at Ames, I felt the sting.

Then Seychelle laughed, and they laughed. Mean was funny to this crew.

One of the Dude Bros splashed to the pool's edge, breaking up the tension. "Anybody down for something stronger than drinks?"

Paige said, "If it'll make Sey-Sey be less of a butt, sure."

The boy thrust himself from the water and went for a bag on an empty chair. He yanked the zipper and poured a few shiny morsels onto a table. They looked like Karloff chocolates, but in prismatic wrappers that combined the usual Karloff candies' purple and red with splashes of yellow and green, giving them the look of psychedelic diamonds.

Seychelle sat up, shifting from cruelly aloof to concerned. "Where did you get those, Brett?"

Dude Bro Brett said, "Jacked my parents' safe. The code's their wedding anniversary."

"Only three?" Ames said, disappointed.

Another of the Dude Bros sprinted up and snatched one. "Dibs!"

"Jensen!" Brett shouted. But the candy thief already tossed the wrapper and was munching.

Seychelle scrambled from her chair. "Don't, okay! Those aren't to be played with."

Jensen's grin was stained chocolate. And, this was the weird part, probably a trick of the light, or our bad angle behind the hedges, but that grin seemed speckled with golden flecks that twinkled like fireflies.

He swallowed, then said, "How long's it supposed to take?"

"Fifteen, twenty seconds. You don't feel anything?"

"I mean—" Jensen collapsed to his knees, clutching his stomach and grimacing.

All the Trustee kids stood. Seychelle backed up a step, almost to the hedges. Almost close enough to touch.

Jensen lifted his head, his grin wider and scarier than before. Veins bulged along his temples and forehead. His eyes stretched like he'd lost the ability to blink. "This feels wild!"

More veins emerged like snakes beneath thin flesh. He flexed his fingers and rolled his shoulders. He stood near a beast of a grill, its stainless-steel hull partially visible beneath its tarp cover. For kicks, he dropped his fist on it like a hammer. It dented like he'd hit it with a car.

Zeke grabbed my bicep and squeezed, terrified. It may have been the only thing that kept me from running.

Jensen said, "Everything feels different. I want to move. I want to fight. Ohhhhhh!" He howled at the sky.

On that endorsement, Brett took one of the remaining candies and Paige beat Ames to the last one.

"Guys," Seychelle said weakly, like someone trying to talk a train off its track.

Brett and Paige followed Jensen's lead, and within thirty seconds, they'd surpassed their initial pained reactions and were hooting, hollering, and tossing heavy things into the pool with ease. Ames and the others bemoaned not being able to partake. Paige grabbed Ames by the ankle and whipped her into the deep end like a doll she'd outgrown.

Seychelle said nothing.

She returned to her lounger, seeming to make herself smaller. Less noticeable. Like maybe she didn't want to tempt these juiced-up bullies into testing their new strength on her.

Understandable.

Zeke jerked his head in the direction we came.

He started that way, not bothering to wait on me.

We took the slow stealth route back to the secret exit off the Karloff property. Inside the shed, we'd barely gotten our flashlights out when the fluorescent bars in the ceiling flared on, erasing the shadows concealing us.

Seychelle stood there, a dangling cord in her grasp, terror etched into her face. "You can't be here! What were you thinking?"

The mild heart attack I suffered stunned me silent. Zeke had the opposite reaction. "You gonna zap us with your phone, or call your 'roided-out besties to drown us in the pool?"

Visible contempt washed over her. She stepped to him. Then she embraced him. He squeezed back, awkward.

Seychelle released him and turned to me. A breath passed between us. She planted her palms on the sides of my face and pulled my lips to hers.

Our kiss was a greedy one. Maybe the best kiss we'd—*I'd*—ever had. It also felt like a last kiss.

She shoved me. "You can't be here. I don't know how you got in, but you better thank God it was me who saw your little fake ninja routine and not them." She waved a hand in the direction of the pool party.

Zeke said, "We watched someone die today, Chelle. Murdered."

Seychelle flinched. "What? No."

It was a weak denial; she didn't sound like she believed herself.

"Sey-Sey!" a Trustee called. "Where are you? Paige, Brett, and Jensen are crashing. We'll probably have to carry them home."

Low murmurs cosigned the sentiment. Seychelle reached into her bikini top and produced a brass key. "My wing is on the west side and private. Grandfather only keeps two guards on property, for him, on the north side—I'm going to call them to help escort my guests off the estate. So if you swing south, as close to the wall as possible, you should be able to get there, no issues. Use this key, and leave the door unlocked. I'll be there soon."

"How soon?" Zeke said.

"When I can! You decided to come here despite the trouble that could mean for all of us. You want to talk? You'll wait until I think it's safe. Hate me all you want, Ezekiel, but I didn't ask for any of this either."

She headed back to the sun-bright patio under that starless sky, and it occurred to me that if you were rich enough, even day and night bent to your will.

The path to Chelle's "wing" was as she said. We didn't encounter any resistance and found a shadowy walkway leading to a set of french doors. The lock turned smoothly, and when I tugged one side of the doors wide enough to slip in, Zeke pushed through the drapes like they were the veil of reality separating us from some other world.

The wing opened into a grand space my whole house could fit in. It was a combination of a study, living room, library—or maybe none of those things. For all I knew, the super wealthy had different names for stuff. There were plush chairs. And walls filled with books. And a wall-mounted TV that Zeke gravitated to immediately.

I went the other way, toward a staircase that led to an area that was, I don't know, *a loft*? My flashlight beam didn't reach the upper level, but I imagined that's where Chelle slept.

I was tempted to explore more, but Zeke's rummaging through items on a coffee table alarmed me. He'd found the remote control next to a full bowl of Karloff candy.

"What are you doing?" I hissed.

"They might get outside news."

I'd gotten so used to nothing but Karloff channels, it didn't occur to me the actual Karloffs might have access to more.

Zeke thumbed the power button. NO SIGNAL popped in the bottom-left corner of the screen. The routine repeated a few times until Zeke landed on the same Karloff streaming options that were available in our homes. He powered the TV down.

"Now what?" I asked.

"We wait." He sat on the couch. I took the other end. The cushions were clouds, and I didn't know furniture could be that way. I don't know who dozed off first, but it was the best sleep I ever had. Until it wasn't.

A hand rocked my shoulder, and I blinked awake, mumbling, "Chill, Chelle."

It wasn't Seychelle, though.

It was Franklin Karloff.

CHITCHAT WITH UNCLE FRANK

A Karloff Entertainment Weekly Address

[Insert Karloff Magic Intro, v. 16.9, Blue Color Key]

Midshot on Franklin at the Cartoon Desk

Director: Counting Franklin in five . . . four . . . three . . . two . . . annnd

Franklin: I . . . where? My glasses. I need my glasses.

Director: Cut. Everybody back to one. Frank, they're on the desk, by your right hand.

Franklin: Oh, I . . .

Director: Your *right* hand.

Blythe: Danny, Dad's going to go back to his dressing room for a second. He's had a bad sinus infection this week, and the medicine's made him foggy.

Director: Sure. We'll, um, figure something to do in the meantime.

Blythe: Come on, Dad. We'll get you some water.

Franklin: My glasses.

Blythe: I've got them.

[Forty-five minutes later, the entire crew was dismissed for the day without explanation.]

CHAPTER 25

Franklin loomed over us, recognizable from when my whole family used to watch those *Chitchat with Uncle Frank* updates on Karloff Streaming, and from the rare times we'd crossed paths with him in person, like at the jetport. At the same time, I wondered if I made myself think that because I was in his house and who else could it be? Honestly, he didn't look like anything I was used to.

He wore a bathrobe, sloppily tied, so I made out a stained white T-shirt underneath and some blue pin-striped boxers stretched around one exposed thigh. His white hair was tussled, and he didn't have his trademark glasses. He did have a walking stick, the kind that split into a four-pronged base for extra stability. I'd often seen elderly guests around Enchantria use them. How old was Franklin Karloff? Did it matter now that he'd caught us trespassing in his home?

I glanced to Zeke, who looked as terrified as I felt.

The tension ballooned, and my resident band's orange glow felt as bright as a star.

Franklin finally spoke. "Titus, Abel, where's Mama?"

Titus and Abel? Huh?

Franklin did a half turn toward the doors. He stared at the moonlight beaming through the high windows. "Mama said we could go to the fair and see the fireworks."

Zeke mouthed, "What is happening?"

Franklin's back heaved. He began crying like a child. "Where's Mama?"

The french doors parted, and Seychelle stepped inside, freezing when she saw her grandfather.

He wiped tears away with the back of his hand. "Ethyl, do you know where Mama is?"

Seychelle seemed to shrink three inches. She went to him, gripping his arm above the elbow, steering him toward other parts of the house. "I'm not Ethyl. I'm never going to answer to it. Come on, I'll get you back to bed."

Franklin shuffled, and she kept pace. Over her shoulder, she said, "Wait for me. I'll be as quick as I can."

For the next half hour, we waited. The entire time curfew—and how we weren't going to beat it—was on my mind. We couldn't leave with so many questions.

Zeke paced the richly decorated cavern, neck craning like every time he blinked it all became new again. We heard Seychelle return before we saw her. "Sandrina, relax."

We'd still been sitting in the dark, our eyes used to it. Seychelle's command turned up the lights to a soothing amber glow. She'd traded her bikini for sweatpants and a tank top and flopped on the couch next to me, looking exhausted. "So now you know the Karloff family's dirty secret."

Zeke said, "Alzheimer's?"

She nodded. "Been a while now."

"But"—I tried working through it—"he does those investor dinners. He seemed fine at the jetport. Even at that Trustee party."

"There's medicine that helps if the dosages are timed right. That's getting riskier, though, because the supply is running low."

My mind raced. A lot of questions. A lot of implications. Zeke derailed all that with "Who are Titus, Abel, and Ethyl?"

Seychelle said, "Driver, cook, and nanny respectively. They all worked for my great-grandpa and helped raise Grandfather. The only Black people he knew for most of his young life, and he only saw a need for more talent of color once he started dreaming up Karloff Country. So, ponder that all you want. Right now we've got bigger problems, if you haven't figured it out yet."

"No, Chelle," Zeke said, bubbling rage. "Because the biggest problem I *thought* we had were these shock bands on our wrists"—he lifted his for show—"but now we have *murder drones* and, apparently, candy that can turn your rich buddies into the Hulk. So, please, school us on the problems bigger than those."

Her face twisted for a clapback, but I jumped in. "Seriously, what was that at the pool?"

"What you saw them take was a batch of candies with the wholly original name Karloff's Special Reserve. You've actually heard about a version of it already."

Zeke said, "I think I'd remember your family making sugar 'roids, Chelle."

"Final presentations," she said through gritted teeth. "The one about enhanced athletic performance. My family's partnered with biotech companies for years as a diversified investment. You saw a product that was never going to get approved for any legitimate use but went into small-batch production anyway. It gives short, intense bursts of strength, speed, and stamina."

I said, "For what?"

She got cynical, almost snarling. "Come on, Zeke. I know you've got a theory."

He shook his head slowly. "In case the wristbands fail. In case they need to fight us."

As if things weren't bad enough.

"You have to keep what you saw tonight secret," said Seychelle, "No one can know about Grandfather. The Trustees think he's still running things. They think he's as ruthless as they are. Any signs of the contrary, no telling what they'd do."

Zeke said, "You know exactly what they'd do. Run up in here and take over. The way he looked, they wouldn't even need that Special Reserve stuff."

Seychelle remained quiet.

"If not your grandfather, who *is* in charge, then?" I asked.

"Mom's putting up a smoke screen. She's making decisions and saying they're from him. She delegates stuff to Barnabus the way Grandfather would."

"That can't last forever."

"I know. That's why I'm spending so much time around Paige and the rest. I can't stand them, but they run their mouths. Sometimes I can get information they've gotten from their parents and pass it on to my mom. Grandfather only told her some of how this is supposed to work, and when he does have moments of clarity, we still don't know if his information's reliable. Sometimes he won't say anything if I'm in the room. He was raised not to let 'the Blacks' hear family business. Mighty big conflict there since I'm Black *and* family."

Did he actually say "the Blacks"? If he's flashing back to his childhood nanny, it's probably the *most* polite thing he's said in foggy moments.

Zeke said, "Well?"

"What?" Seychelle said.

"Information. You get any? Something we can use to keep our people alive and out of the med center?"

"I'm working on it."

"Sure. Okay. My mind's at ease now."

"What's the end game?" I asked her. "How far does this go?"

"Far. You heard what I heard at the Trustee party. They've got people in place to take over whatever's left in all the world's major power centers. They're sheltering here until the fallout blows over. Then, I guess, they go wherever."

"But . . ." I didn't know how to say what I was thinking.

"What, man?" Zeke said.

"How are they just going to leave after, like, holding us hostage?"

"You want them to stay?"

"No. I mean, you don't gotta be a genius to know this is illegal, go-to-jail-for-the-rest-of-your-life stuff."

Seychelle said, "These aren't people who go to jail. If they ever do, it's the kind with tennis courts and no fences."

I'd heard things like that about the rich and powerful my whole life. The worst people faced the least consequences for wrongdoing. But that couldn't be the case here, for this? Could it? When I spoke, my voice sounded whiny to my own ears. "But they've tortured and killed people."

Zeke said, "You act like that's different from anything before." Then, to Seychelle, "Waiting for Trustees to get bored and move along doesn't sound like an A-plus plan to me."

"This is a *pit stop* for the Trustees," she said. "The way to keep the most people from getting hurt is by letting them have their time here, then letting them move on. I know you don't like it. I don't either. But it's the best plan. At least for now."

Zeke didn't agree or disagree.

Seychelle's eyes narrowed. "How'd you know about the tunnel to the groundskeeper shed anyway? I barely remembered it was there."

My stomach lurched from disappointment and Zeke's inevitable *I told you so*. If she was Panopticon, she wouldn't have asked.

Zeke said, "At work, there was a small coolant leak in the tunnels my team couldn't trace. They sent me to the engineering archives for Enchantria tunnel specs, and I found some cross-references to your house. Total accident."

"Oh."

I followed his lie with truth. "We gotta get home. We're already past curfew, and it's going to take almost an hour to get back."

Seychelle didn't protest the loss of our company. She escorted us to the door.

Zeke crossed the threshold and said, "Chelle, do you know if there's any way to deactivate the bands, or disable the defensive charge so we have time to cut through them?"

She shook her head. "I don't. Like I said, I have to be delicate with info gathering."

Zeke gave no indication if that satisfied his curiosity. He stepped away to give me and her a moment.

She said, "How are you feeling?"

"No pain anymore. That's something."

"I'm still working to make things better."

Better or tolerable? Because *tolerable* is what she said before.

And for who?

I pushed those questions away. She was doing what she could.

Wasn't her fault she was born into a class of horrible people. Wasn't her fault her efforts didn't feel like enough *to me.*

Right?

I did ask, "How did you make it growing up in a place like this?"

"I don't know if I would've if I hadn't met you all."

Wrapping my arms around her, I wished so hard that things were what they used to be. Me, her, Connie, and Zeke at the Treat. That was the best it'd ever been. I said, "I don't know when I'll see you again."

"Leave that to me."

I pulled away slightly. Worried.

"Be patient. Trust me." She leaned in for a quick, soft kiss. I kissed her back.

I joined Zeke in the night, and Seychelle whispered, "Be safe."

Thing was, if we weren't, would she even know?

We were down the mountain and halfway home before Zeke said a word. I hadn't been looking forward to it.

To my surprise, it wasn't a dig at Chelle. No *I told you so.* It was worse.

"Panopticon is legit, bro. That tunnel, the interior design of the Karloff house. One hundred percent."

That's what he was doing when he was pacing Chelle's wing? Comparing it to his intel? I thought he was being dramatic.

"So what?" I said.

"That means they're right about the rest. We can fight back."

CHAPTER 26

The trip back to Jubilee was quicker than expected. Zeke was energized, double-timing it, and I had no choice but to keep up despite
my screaming lungs and jelly legs. With home in sight, we slowed,
checking for drones.

It was after midnight when we arrived at the woods surrounding
the Treat, then back on our street. Creeping, we tiptoed on asphalt
and almost made it undetected.

A flashlight clicked on a hundred yards ahead. The glowing bulb
grew larger and drew closer, propelled by a golf cart motor. Fletcher
and Burke, the Jubilee Residents' Association officers who'd rolled up
on us at Connie's house weeks ago, swung the cart sideways to block
our path.

Burke leapt out, the awkward gear on his new belt clanking. A
baton, zip-tie cuffs, and a stun gun. "Curfew was an hour ago! Don't
you know that?"

Zeke said, "We're going home now."

We attempted to sidestep the cart.

Fletcher jumped from the driver's seat and shoved Zeke hard in
the chest, scanning the sky. "We're responsible for enforcing the new
regulations. That's our job."

A familiar whining drew near, and my fear doubled. A drone hovered above us. Observing.

"Where are you coming from?" Burke asked, a twitchy hand set-
tling on his baton.

"Walking," I said. "We got tired of Jubilee and walked."

Burke got nose-to-nose with me. "Tired of Jubilee? You should be thanking God you have a place here." His voice was louder than it needed to be, a show for the drone. "Praise Him and the Trustees you're among the chosen!"

"Praise who?" Zeke said.

"Shut your mouth." Fletcher slapped him. His palm on Zeke's cheek was loud enough to break neighborhood sound ordinances.

Zeke stumbled. When he stood straight again, the rage burning in him was apparent. Fletcher's hand slid from his baton to the stun gun.

"Dad!" I shouted, my house a couple of yards down. "Dad, help!"

I screamed it over and over. Burke and Fletcher recoiled, startled. The drone remained parked.

Dark houses lit up, and silhouettes filled windows. No one came to help at first, but then my door opened. Mom and Dad rushed off the porch, crossing the lawn at a speed I didn't know they were capable of. Zeke's dad followed them. Nothing about that was strange because of course he would've been at my house worrying right along with my parents.

There was a fourth person, though. One cloaked in the shadows of my home, who ducked out of sight the second I glimpsed them.

"Hey!" Dad shouted. "Get away from my son."

Burke faced Dad, unsnapping the stun gun's holster. I forgot how to breathe.

Mom pawed at Dad's arm, trying to calm him down. Fletcher seemed confused, like slapping a kid wasn't supposed to result in all this and could we start over?

It was Mr. Johnson, Zeke's dad, who said, "Relax, everyone. Breathe."

Mom moved beyond Dad to me, placing herself between me and Burke while grabbing Zeke's sleeve. "Boys, come on. This was a mistake, and it won't happen again."

She was speaking to the drones. A second one had joined us.

Mr. Johnson draped his arm over Zeke's shoulder, directing him away from the confrontation. My dad paced Mr. Johnson, hug-walking Mom and me toward our house. The Jubilee Residents' Association officers made no effort to stop us, instead angling their eyes toward the drones. Perhaps hoping whatever pilot evaluating the incident would see they tried to uphold the new way of things.

Once we were inside my house with the door closed and locked, Dad peeked outside. "Everyone's leaving began, but I can't tell if the drones are still there."

"They shouldn't be a problem," an unexpected voice said.

The owner of the silhouette I'd peeped earlier stood in the dim lights of our kitchen, his face tense.

"Now that we're all here," Barnabus said, "I guess we should have a sit-down."

Barnabus. Here? In my house?

As these questions bounced around my head, Mom bombarded me with her own interrogation. "Where were you? Have you lost your mind? Do you know what could've happened to you?"

Mr. Johnson pulled Zeke aside and hit him with essentially the same scolding, with less words and more *gruff*, their tough-guy way of communicating.

"Are you hurt?" Mr. Johnson asked, squeezing his son's shoulders as if that was the proper way to get a diagnostic reading from a boy.

"I'm fine," Zeke insisted.

Mom kept hitting me with question after question. Did I run into any Trustees? Was I in trouble?

Zeke interrupted, a gamble on his part. "Mrs. Butler, we walked. Like we told Burke and Fletcher. Lost track of time."

Mom's head cocked, skeptical.

I said, "It's not a problem to walk around the place we live. Is it?"

"If someone has to answer that question for you, you haven't been paying attention," Dad said.

Barnabus showed his palms, a gesture of peace. "Please, everyone, let's turn the temperature down a bit. I'll leave shortly, and you can tend to the boys how you see fit, but since I'm here, we need to discuss this new paradigm we're living under. For all our sakes."

Mom threw up her hands but shot me a pointed look. We weren't done.

She motioned to the couch, and we all found seats.

Surprisingly, Zeke spoke first. "Mr. Barnabus . . . why you in Jay's house?"

"Boy," Mr. Johnson warned. A whole lecture in a word.

"It's a valid question," Barnabus said.

I stared at the Sandrina pyramid mounted to the coffee table, the glowing tip indicating she was listening too. Barnabus saw me watching.

"You don't have to worry, Jermaine." He produced something from his pocket that looked like a car fob, glowing with the same soft purple light as Sandrina. "It's safe for us to talk as long as one of these is active and in the room."

Zeke looked ravenous. "You got any extras?"

His dad nudged him to shut up. Barnabus grinned like he'd met his new best friend and patted a satchel next to his chair. "I came bearing gifts. I'll leave you some goodies before I go."

"Why *are* you here?" I asked him, feeling the same inspector-shows-up-early vibe from the last time I had an up-close-and-personal with him.

"*We* contacted Mr. Barnabus," said Mom. "When we couldn't find you."

The unspoken *see what you made us do* rang in my head like a bell.

"I was going to have to speak to you and your parents soon anyhow," Barnabus said to me, then to Mom, "but I was surprised to hear from you first. Been a lot of surprises lately."

Dad, angry, said, "Imagine *my* surprise over us being on your to-do list since I work in the produce department now."

"Phil, I wish I knew how to make right what's gone so wrong. I wish that was in my power. Nothing that's happened has been my call."

Nothing? At all?

I supposed that could be true. Barnabus still believed he worked for Franklin Karloff even if the orders were really coming from Blythe. I doubted Blythe would be okay with him having secret talks about whatever in my house. So he wasn't a total Trustee lackey.

Barnabus addressed me and Zeke. "Your parents were rightfully worried when they couldn't locate you. We're still working on the logistics of emergency services in this new iteration of Karloff Country. It's pretty clear cut when it comes to the Trustees—something goes wrong, it's every non-Trustee's business to fix it."

Zeke said, "So same as the old days."

Mr. Johnson stared murder.

"You're not far off," Barnabus admitted. "I was in the process of gathering some of the security detail I still trust to help find you, but you showed up, and that solves tonight's problem. Tomorrow's is what we still need to discuss."

It was hard tracking everything he was saying. That *I still trust* reference to Karloff Country security was doing a lot of work in my brain. The *tomorrow problem* was working harder because he looked directly at me when he said that.

Mom hugged herself, and Dad's arm slipped over her shoulder as part comfort and maybe part restraint. She exuded big claw-your-eyes-out energy toward Barnabus.

He said, "Jermaine, after what happened at the Independence Day celebration, it's been decided that it's in everyone's best interest if you don't return to your post at Enchantria."

"Decided," I said. "Not by you."

"No. Not by me. All of the Trustees saw what happened, and they wouldn't necessarily feel comfortable with someone who'd 'suffered such a terrible accident' having to return to such a potentially trigger-ing place."

Mom said, "Accident. An *accident*?"

I said, "They don't want to be reminded of me flopping on the ground in agony while they're enjoying cotton candy and bum-per cars."

He moved on. "There's been a request for your services."

Mom leaned forward, her fingernails hooking into her knees. "We really can't say no?"

"Tish," said Dad.

"Don't 'Tish' me. He doesn't have children. No one who did could be this calm about it."

Mom was scared. I wouldn't make it worse by letting on I was scared too. What had been decided about me?

Barnabus said, "I've looked into them. They're not bad people."

Tired of being talked around, I said, "Just tell me!"

"A Concierge Package Trustee has offered to take you."

"A what?" I said, terrified. "Take me where?"

The next day, I discovered a section of Karloff Country I wasn't sure existed. I'd heard the rumors of new housing for new Helpers, but even the drive over made it clear this was never meant for residents as lowly as us.

It was situated along the resort's eastern perimeter, far away from Jubilee, hidden by thick bands of forest, and accessible by streets I would've never known to look for. The foliage canopy covering the road to this secluded section eventually opened wide on a slate-gray sky and brought us to a wrought-iron gate guarded by men wearing resident bands. My driver—who'd yet to speak to me—got jolly with the closest guard and was granted access. That gate swung open into a sprawling green space occasionally broken by homes that made our "luxury" Jubilee houses seem like aluminum shacks.

After passing Trustee mansion after Trustee mansion, we pulled into the driveway of a home that seemed more suited for some tropical island than the Virginia mountains. The pastel-pink stucco and clay shingles were a little wrong in this part of the world.

"This is it, buddy," said the driver.

I climbed from the SUV with my duffel bag, trying not to think of Mom sobbing and pounding her fists into Dad's chest. Him saying, "It's just during the week. He'll be home this weekend."

The weekend, I pictured it like a goalpost in the distance and prayed it wouldn't move.

The guard who'd ridden in the back seat with me trailed me to the front door. When I rang the doorbell, the sound on the other side was as grand and sacred as church bells.

The door swung inward, and a couple—her dark-haired, in khaki shorts, a short-sleeved blouse, and a lavender sweater draped over her shoulders with the sleeves looped into a loose knot; him lanky and tall, in faded jeans, button-down plaid, and wire-rimmed glasses—greeted me with warm, welcoming smiles.

"Oh, Jermaine." The woman came forward, embracing me. "Let me show you to your room!"

Of all the things I'd thought I was prepared for, I wondered why no one warned me of the one thing I did not see coming.

This couple was Black.

KARLOFF COUNTRY CARES

We stand in solidarity with our Black colleagues
and guests against the long history of oppression, violence,
and injustice that has plagued the Black community.
Acts of racism and intolerance will never be condoned
within the borders of Karloff Country.

We care, and we show it.

[KC Cares Social Media Asset_V12.6.jpg, 600 x 335 pixels, 72ppi.

Approved by KC Corp Comm.]

CHAPTER 27

The timing felt horror-movie ominous when the sky burst and rain hit the pavement like a weighted blanket, drenching my escort. I thought he might join me under the awning, but coming too close must've been against orders. He remained a human sponge until the woman—Mrs. Greer, I'd been told—dismissed him with a wave. "That'll be all. Thank you!"

She grabbed me gently by the arm and tugged me inside. "Lord, it's nasty out there. Did you know it was going to rain?" she said to her husband.

Mr. Greer said, "Had no clue."

"If there's one thing I miss about the outside, it's a reliable weather report."

That's the one thing, huh?

"Clinton." The man extended his hand, and I shook, making sure to get a good grip like Dad taught me.

"I'm Bettina," said the woman, taking my duffel bag by the strap. "Everyone calls me Bette."

"Hi." I didn't know what else to say or do. No one could help me now.

Bette delved deeper into the residence with my bag, and Clinton hovered over my shoulder. I was supposed to follow her, but I was still a little slow processing it all. This house was amazing. Everything from the flooring, to the paintings on the wall, to the freaking door-knobs . . . It all had weight you could see, and feel, and smell. It was like that one Karloff animated movie about the house where all the inanimate objects—the toaster, the throw rug, and the recliner—came to life when the owners left for the day, except if the stuff in this house were alive, it would all scream, *You are beneath us.*

Then there were the Greers. So nice and welcoming with the obvious rectangular bulges in their hip pockets. Phones. As noticeable now as holstered guns.

When Barnabus explained my new role as a Concierge, how I was expected to stay with the Greers and perform vague "services" throughout the week, Mom raged. It was modern slavery! What about our civil rights? How did we know I wouldn't be harmed?

Barnabus promised my safety, of course, but in no way prepared me for anything other than some white, Southern-drawl plantation owner asking me to fetch well water. The kind of money and access I assumed you needed to be a Trustee, I didn't know there were Black people who had it like that, despite seeing a speckling of color at the Trustees' Independence Day party.

Now here we were . . .

Bette stayed close as she gave a tour of the house, pausing her description of each room to remind me, "You can relax. We've got you."

She took me through a living room Zeke and I could throw Hail Mary passes in, a restaurant-worthy kitchen, a sunroom that overlooked a pool whose surface was being violently peppered by the downpour, then finally up a back staircase to a bedroom that looked more like the picture of a bedroom than something anyone would sleep in.

"This is yours," Bette announced.

Bette sat my duffel on the bed. Clinton filled the doorway behind me. Mom's grim, tear-filled warning sounded in my head. *If anyone tries to hurt you, fight as much as you can. Fight more than they want.*

Bette parted the curtains for a view of the storm and did a little showy stomp, like a kid's tantrum. "Dang it! I thought rain this hard didn't last very long. You ever hear that, Clint?"

"I have," he said.

"I suppose we can still go to the parks with umbrellas. Jermaine, it won't spoil your fun if we have to use umbrellas, will it?"

"I—" What?

Bette's eyes were wide and hopeful.

Confused, I spoke slowly, carefully crafting the answer I thought she wanted. "I've been in the parks through all kinds of weather, so rain won't bother me."

It wouldn't be fun for me either, but I sensed I should keep that to myself.

"Wonderful! I'll arrange for an eleven a.m. pickup." She did a cheery little clap and trotted away with Clint following.

The rain didn't let up, but Bette was not discouraged. Another black SUV arrived on time, and we were shuttled toward the parts of Karloff Country I was most familiar with. I'd hoped she might be interested in the Karloff Pictures park, or even the nature-themed Karloff Wilds, but she wanted Enchantria first. Everyone wanted Enchantria first.

Now, walking the familiar deserted paths, Bette was grins and giggles and Clinton seemed happy she was happy. Bette said, "Jermaine, come. Let's get a picture in front of the palace."

It was the ridiculously cliché pose every family copped on their first, or fifty-first, trip to the park. The one in Karloff Country commercials when commercials were still a thing. I'd snapped this pic about a billion times being the helpful Helper I was. Given my "Concierge" role with the Greers, I assumed Bette wanted me to take a picture of her and Clinton.

"I need your camera," I said, on autopilot.

"Don't be daft." Bette looked past me, waving. "Excuse me, excuse me."

Several yards away was one of my former teammates. Sal. In the uniform I'd probably never wear again. He approached skittish and made sure not to stare at me directly. No one wanted to look a ghost in the eye.

He said, "How can I be of service, ma'am?"

"We'd like a family photo. Would you mind taking it?"

A *family* photo?

I forced my face still, because yes, it was creepy weird, and yes, I immediately envisioned being locked forever in that picturesque bedroom Bette declared "mine." But . . .

This is a pit stop for the Trustees.

It was only a photo.

Right?

Bette unlocked her phone and offered it to Sal. The same kind of phone Paige had used to torture me and Harry. Sal hesitated.

Clinton stepped in, alarmed. "No, Bette. Let him use the camera in your purse. The picture will be better."

"Of course." She made a show of slapping her forehead. "Silly goose." She swapped the phone with a slim camera from her bag.

Sal went through the motions. "Everyone, squeeze in."

Bette was in the center. Clinton to her right. I stood on her left, and when Sal said "squeeze," she snaked an arm around my waist and pulled me closer.

"On three . . ." she said.

There was a flash, then Bette retrieved her camera and showed the picture to Clinton, who nodded his approval. When Bette showed me, I gave my best, most practiced Helper smile while my skin crawled.

A family photo. How else might I be of service to the Greers?

CHAPTER 28

It was late afternoon when our SUV took the winding road back to the Greers' place. On the way was a mansion that looked more ultra modern than the others. The exterior had the same metallic sheen as stainless-steel appliances and dark mirror windows, giving no hints of what was inside. There was a covered porch where a man and woman sat, him swiping at a tablet and her . . . just there.

"Ted's out," Clinton said. He tapped the driver on the shoulder. "Swing into the driveway for a sec. I want to chat with my buddy."

"Yes, sir."

Bette sucked her teeth. "Really, Clint? I don't like that man."

"I'll only be a moment." He turned his attention to me and said, "Jermaine, are you familiar with Ted Cole?"

"No, sir?"

"Founder of Genuity, one of the most valuable technology companies on the planet. The man's been to space."

I couldn't fake recognition.

Clinton shook his head like he pitied me. "What are they teaching kids in school these days?"

The SUV pulled up to the steel house. Ted set his tablet aside and came down the steps, greeting Clinton warmly. The woman Ted left behind didn't budge.

I recognized her.

We'd only met for a few minutes. She'd worked the lounge at the Karloff Country jetport. Brought me orange juice.

Clinton talked up Ted. Their conversation was animated. Big laughs. Ted spoke with his hands.

Bette said, "I don't know what Clinton enjoys about that pervert's company."

"Pervert?" I probably shouldn't have said it. I couldn't have *not* said it.

Bette patted my knee. "Not every Concierge gets as lucky as you, sweetie."

Oh God.

Ted looked like the happiest man on earth. The woman from the lounge was emotionless, her face as still as a mannequin's.

Her outfit was a variation on the professional blouse/blazer/skirt she wore the last time I'd seen her, but smaller by degrees. Less fabric covering her chest, a much shorter hem on the skirt, ridiculous heels she'd kicked off under the table. Long sleeves, though. And her right arm where her resident band dangled on her wrist, was cradled limp in her lap.

Farah. She was Farah.

Remembering her name felt like minor decency. Literally the least I could do.

Bette rolled down her window. "We're tired, honey. We'll need some rest if we want to still do game night."

Clinton nodded. "Yes, dear. Right away."

The men wrapped up the conversation, and Clinton rejoined us, looking energized. "That's a whip-smart guy, I tell you. Whip smart."

Clinton didn't elaborate, and given what Bette implied about Ted, I didn't want him to. Though I had new worries. If such a horrible man perked Clinton up like this, what other horrible things energized him?

227

· · ·

For game night that evening, Bette picked Monopoly. Every bad turn on my part earned me a mini lecture from Clinton. "Proper stewardship over the physical and financial blessings God grants is a valuable lesson that most of *us* never learn."

The emphasis on *us* was supposed to mean Black people, but somehow I had a hard time believing he considered other Black people as part of any group *he* belonged to. My internal Mom uttered an old-timey saying: *All skinfolk ain't kinfolk.*

Also, he was cheating. He'd palmed an extra five-hundred-dollar bill from the bank when the game started, but whatever.

He said, "So many of *us* spend time bemoaning 'the system' and crying 'racism' when ample opportunity would present itself in the wake of better decision making. Now please pay me the rent you owe on St. Charles."

I could've played better, maybe won. But I couldn't stop thinking of Farah, her staring at nothing.

Losing felt safer.

The rest of the week was all good weather and had us visiting other Karloff Country attractions. We rode the Ferris Reel in Karloff Pictures with Bette patting my shoulder at the height of the first rotation and saying, "There, there, no need to be afraid of heights. And look at that view."

I wasn't afraid of heights, but I nodded and focused on the tops of the Vertical Farms towers poking over distant treetops during each rotation.

We did Splash Zone, and she insisted I wear a life vest even though I could swim and the deepest pool only came to my collarbone. By the day she wanted to do Karloff Wilds, Clinton bowed out, citing a "necessary community meeting," leaving me alone with Bette for the first time.

On the Safari Tram, Bette clenched my hand at the sight of a drowsy lioness and said, "Don't be afraid, CJ. That cat can't hurt you."

Though I'd suspected the true motives behind the Greers' particular Concierge arrangement, that's when I understood, for real, what this was.

CJ. Clinton Jr., I assumed.

The speed with which I processed it, then compartmentalized it, never letting on that Bette had slipped—if it was a slip—was alarming in its own way. So many horrible things had happened since Connie disappeared, and I managed to keep it moving. Cataloging each new violation, atrocity, or mild inconvenience the same.

Because this couldn't last.

Even if there were no consequences for the Trustees outside after the world stopped burning, they'd move on. There'd be no reason for them to stay here. No reason us in Jubilee couldn't go back to the way things were.

Me and my friends and family only needed to wait a while longer.

Three months later, we were still waiting.

AFTER HOURS

Blythe: Happy birthday, sweetie.

Seychelle: It's a necklace. I wanted a new MacBook, Mom.

Blythe: You can get a computer anytime. Diamonds are for special occa-
sions. Twelve karats for twelve years.

Seychelle: I don't like wearing jewelry. It's shiny rocks.

Blythe: Like them or not, those shiny rocks make clear your place in the
world. They tell people who you are, and more importantly, who
they're not. Get a few more birthdays—and karats—under your
belt, and you'll understand. Now put it on.

ZEKE

Panopticon
What did you do last night?

The text woke me, but memories of the night before had me smiling between yawns.

It wasn't the first time Panopticon reached out after one of my squad's outings.

At first, it was only me and a few dudes from the Academy football team. A little tagging with spray paint I lifted from the engineering supply closet. Then some bricks through a few Downtown Karloff shopwindows. Then more people got fed up, and with greater numbers, the destruction escalated. Slashed tires on Trustee transport SUVs. Shooting some drones down with improvised slingshots. That sort of thing.

Word got back to Panopticon early on, and they warned us not to get too bold until their slowly budding rebel force was better organized. They never got into too much detail about what that looked like, though, and my peeps were mad impatient when it came to the Trustees. And lately, mad creative. Last night was chef's kiss—shout-out to Connie.

I knew what the next message would be. The text version of a slap on the wrist. Like those times back when Dad was still Dad, and he'd tell me that violence was wrong while lovingly squeezing my shoulders for handling that week's bully.

234

Panopticon

WHAT DID YOU DO?? HAVE YOU
LOST YOUR MIND??

Okay. Maybe a *slap on the wrist* was a little too hopeful on my part. But it was still just a text, so whatever.

My boy Mitch brought those alcohol-filled bottles with dirty rags flapping from the necks. Had no clue those fancy metal lighters with the flip-up tops were real outside the movies, but Mitch brought one of those too. We tagged messages of *Don't Trust Trustees* and *Karloff Country Is for the Real People* as usual. Then Mitch, me, and the others lit those rags and tossed those bottles through the window of the steakhouse in Downtown Karloff. Watching the flames dance through the place felt like tiny justice.

Not gonna lie, I knew Panopticon would be mad, so I played with ignoring the messages until they cooled off. Not like they were gonna come to check me in person.

Panopticon

I told you no violence! Not yet!

Panopticon

Do you think there won't be
consequence?

That made me sit up.

Me

What you mean violence?

Then it occurred to me . . . We didn't check the restaurant. Didn't make sure no one was in the back, or hiding under a table because they saw us outside tagging stuff with the paint. Jesus. What if . . .

Panopticon
Attacking a Trustee convoy directly. Taking
their phones. What you did to their hands.
How did you think that was going to go over?
I'm trying to help and you don't listen.
Whatever happens next is on you.

A convoy?

Me

Dude, I'm totally lost.

The dancing dots of an incoming message appeared, then disappeared. Appeared. Disappeared again. Finally.

Panopticon
You and your crew didn't attack
three Trustee transports last night?
Don't you dare lie to me.

I swear I don't know what
you're talking about.

Panopticon

Then we have bigger problems
than I thought.

Panopticon

Stay away from Splash Zone
today if you can. Tell anyone you
care about the same.

Me

Why? Ain't Splash Zone closed
for the season?

No dancing dots. After ten minutes, no new messages.

That *stay away from Splash Zone* and *tell anyone you care about* stuff, I didn't like the sound of. Dad was downstairs getting ready for a Vertical Farms shift. He'd be nowhere near the water park. I didn't have a shift today, and the rest of our squad always knew to keep it low the day after our outings. None of them had reason to be near Splash Zone, so we were all good there. Tell anyone I care about.

I would if I could, but any other people I cared about hadn't been around in a while.

237

CHAPTER 29

The Concierge arrangement had been everything my family and I were promised. Clinton and Bette contracted my services on weekdays, and I was released home on weekends. Our provision allotments were larger because of my specialized work, and we were given an additional Pup Points stipend—the only currency accepted if you needed to purchase items outside your weekly provisions from the Karloff Country vendors. Didn't exactly make us popular among other Jubilee residents whose allotments and pay stayed the same, but I put in the time and *earned* those benefits, so was I wrong for expecting a little more when I went home on the weekends? All things considered.

Bette's "CJ" slips got more frequent. In my second month, she did it in front of Clinton and there was an electric moment when he'd pinned her with a hard glare, and I thought he'd shut it down. But his brow softened, he gave one of his customary whatever-makes-you-happy-dear nods, then excused himself to Ted's, where he'd been spending more and more time.

Being alone with Bette felt like more of a chore than it should. Like this weird reverse babysitting. She was still clearly the adult here, but she called me from a different room and different chore for the simplest tasks like a kid would. I passed her a glass of water that was two steps from where she sat. Surfed between the three working streaming channels with a simple remote she claimed befuddled her. She copped to the truth of these tedious summonings one afternoon when she'd dipped into the liquor cabinet.

"I don't like not seeing your face," she slurred. "There were too many years of not seeing your face, CJ."

Her insistence on calling me by her dead son's name was uncomfortable, but I was still one of the luckier Concierges.

A couple of houses down was a beefy man who used to run a mixed martial arts association. His Concierge was one of my old Academy classmates, kid named Barrett. Whenever I saw him, his face was bruised. His knuckles scraped and swollen. On a grocery trip to the merchant section of Downtown Karloff, Clinton and the MMA guy got chatty, so Barrett and I had a chance to talk too. Wincing through the pain of recently having a tooth knocked out, he told me Mr. MMA used him as a sparring partner, except dude never taught Barrett any moves.

We both knew it could be worse.

A few streets over, in a house with a rough brick facade resembling an old castle, lived a surgeon, Dr. Mask. That wasn't her real name, just what Trustees whispered behind her back because her Concierge was never without the porcelain-doll face mask she forced them to wear. I'd seen the pair walking the neighborhood. I'd seen blood seeping from beneath that mask.

And yet . . . it could be worse.

I never saw Clinton's buddy Ted and the former jetport agent Farah beyond his sleek home's porch. Whenever I strolled by on evening walks with Bette, Farah was often there with Ted, him on his tablet, her staring into another world. She always wore long sleeves, even on hot days, and her right hand was increasingly swollen and discolored. I walked faster passing Ted's.

Almost every Concierge interaction had me returning to Clinton and Bette's feeling somewhat grateful. I hated that. Why were they still here? When was this going to end?

Sometimes I cried myself to sleep out of disgust for that feeling.

But my tears weren't driven by pain. Or fear.

So, still. It could be worse.

Then, one morning in October, I awoke to wrongness. Bette seemed distant—which was totally fine by me—when Clinton said, "Get ready. We're going out."

"Where we headed?" I asked.

Bette shot an angry glance at Clinton, who wasn't emitting his usual happy-wife-happy-life vibes. He said, "Splash Zone."

The day warmed fast, so I didn't think much about how Splash Zone's season typically ran April to September. If they'd kept the place open longer at a Trustee's request, it wouldn't have been different from all the other concessions we'd made for them. The trip over was weird, though.

Like, I assumed Bette had packed swimwear that we'd change into once there, but when I glanced over my seat into the SUV's cargo area, it was empty.

Also, Clinton was with us.

He'd started backing out of the park trips sporadically weeks ago, then stopped going altogether. Yet, here he was, riding shotgun and looking fidgety.

At the drop-off loop, there was an unusual number of black SUVs transporting Trustees. No park we'd visited since they arrived ever hosted this many at once. No one was dressed for swimming.

"What are we supposed to do?" Bette asked.

"Show solidarity," Clinton said. "Watch."

Watch . . . what?

We filed through the gates and passed empty, covered pools. The unattended waterslides with their cartoon-colored coils and loops looked wrong dry, like the diagrams of guts in a science book.

The bulk of the crowd gathered around the only attraction with water: Devil's Race, Splash Zone's most popular ride.

It was a waterslide. Really, two slides. Both a hundred fifty feet down, and you hit speeds over fifty miles per hour, the idea being two people—one on each slide—go at the same time; a race to the bottom. I rode it with Zeke once and thought I'd left my heart on the drop deck at the top.

The slides were red with orange-and-yellow trim painted like flames. They were slick with water, misty rainbows wavering, and the five-foot-deep receiving pool was freshly filled, a brackish gray instead of the chemically treated blue typical of the place. People crowded the drop deck. I assumed it was the batch of lifeguards acting as ride operators and safety police so people didn't try something dumb like going down three at a time. Until I saw Seychelle and her mom among them.

So many more questions filled my head, but they all vanished when two people—one on each slide—were forced kicking and screaming to the drop zone with nooses around their necks.

Now I knew what we came to watch.

SEYCHELLE

When Mom and I first climbed the plank steps to the top of Devil's Race, we met a group of seven Trustees. The only one I knew was Paige's dad, who'd been present at most meetings I'd attended with Mom. His right hand was in a cast, and his left eye had a purple pouch swelling beneath it. Most of the Trustees here had their right hands in casts.

However he'd been injured, it hadn't sapped Mr. Radford's energy. He still spoke fast, with all his teeth showing. He introduced another old white guy as Judge Finn, who apparently came up with a "fair system for today."

I didn't know what system the judge came up with, or why, but when four security guards muscled the two workers to the deck with us, I got queasy. One worker was short, Black, with gray roots ratting on her dyed hair. She wore khakis and a Splash Zone Polo and her name tag said PAM. The other was a tall, slim Mexican man with brown hair. He wore red lifeguard shorts with GERARDO stenciled over a Penny Pup logo on the left hem, and a stretched T-shirt that simply said LIFE'S A BEACH.

Bulging duffel bags rested at the Trustees' feet like sleeping dogs. The judge unzipped one and removed a roll of duct tape he looped around their feet. Pam bucked, and a Trustee woman rushed forward, slamming her new cast into the woman's nose. "You animals think you can get away with what you did to us?"

I stepped forward to—I don't know why. Mom grabbed my elbow and dug her nails in. That wasn't enough to stop me. The lengths of rope Mr. Radford uncoiled from the bags, with ends already fashioned into nooses, froze me, though.

Pam and Gerardo saw what I saw and became absolute brawlers. Except their hands had been bound in tape, so any blows they attempted to land were ineffective.

"Mom, what is this?" I panicked quietly.

The ends of the ropes were secured to support beams, while those nooses got slipped over Pam's and Gerardo's necks and cinched snug.

Unable to hold back, I hissed at my mom. "You didn't tell me this is what we're here for! You didn't say anyone was going to be hurt!" My throat felt raw. I'd cried so much over what my family's done.

The Trustees had plans to do so much more.

In the duffel bags were a pair of twenty-five-pound kettlebells from one of the property's fitness centers. More tape was used to secure the weights to Pam's and Gerardo's leg bindings.

I turned to the safety railing. The open air beyond it. And I wondered, *What would it take to fly, if only for a moment?*

Mom snatched me back to this . . . damnation in action. She leaned close and whispered in my ear with the urgency of a priest praying for strength against demons. "Don't make us look weak in front of these people. Or we could be taking this ride one day."

Mr. Radford raised a bullhorn from beneath the operator's panel and approached the rail overlooking the crowd while the judge and his crony loaded Pam in the drop chute of one slide and Gerardo in the other.

Squawking through the bullhorn, Mr. Radford said, "All present, understand that last night mine and two other Trustee families were ambushed on our way home from dinner. Our phones were smashed and our right hands broken. Slowly and gleefully. By the very people we've worked hard to protect inside this enclave we've built. So, examples must be made.

"We do not know who our attackers were other than they were not Trustees, evident by the resident bands they wore. Without the actual culprits here to pay for their crimes, what you're about to witness is as fair as we could manage. The judged were chosen at random to fulfill the God-given promise of an eye for an eye. I want you—Trustees and any Helpers on-site—to tell this tale far and wide. There are grave consequences for betraying us."

Eye for an eye? No Trustee was killed. How could this be justified?

Like everything else in Karloff Country since the Trustees arrived. Because that's what they wanted.

He lowered his bullhorn, then pressed the green go button on the console.

A klaxon sounded, the chutes dropped, and the workers screamed as gravity took them and their hanging ropes snapped repulsively taut, aided by the additional weight secured to their ankles.

Except the second rope—Pam's rope—had been secured with a bad knot. The force undid it almost instantly, and the rope went whipping down the slide, chasing Pam into the water. Mr. Radford rushed to the safety railing, befuddled.

I joined him at the rail, my disgust for his entire family forgotten momentarily as I peered into the pool below, willing myself not to glance at Gerardo's dangling lifeless body on the far slide, jostling back and forth. Instead, I focused on the writhing shape beneath the water's surface. Pam. That twenty-five-pound kettlebell dragging her to the bottom like an anchor.

Gasps from the audience on the ground. A few shocked screams. Mostly . . . applause. Some pointed and snapped flashing photos of Gerardo. Others leaned over the pool, making a show of extending an arm and tapping their wristwatches as if betting on how long it'd take Pam to drown.

It was a long way down. Not easy to distinguish faces. But while most gawked over a drowning woman, one looked up. At me.

"Jay?" I whispered.

Then all of our attention was snatched to the pool, when Pam exploded to the surface, having somehow separated from the kettlebell.

My heart lifted. The elderly Black woman survived this brutality devised by despicable men. I might've cheered if not for the danger those same men posed to Mom and me.

Only one life lost in this horror, I thought, relieved and ashamed at once.

Also, I should've known better.

CHAPTER 30

Dad had told me stories and showed me evidence of white mobs destroying Black lives and communities. There was the brutal murder of fourteen-year-old Emmett Till at the hands of white men for supposedly flirting with a white woman. We looked at photos of the postcards white people once sent depicting their smiling families posed before a hanged Black man after a lynching. Watched documentaries on the destruction of Tulsa, Oklahoma—hundreds of Black people killed during a days-long massacre. Dad made me memorize names like Trayvon Martin and Sandra Bland and George Floyd.

His reasoning: If we didn't know our history, we'd be doomed to repeat it.

I knew the history, and still . . .

Me, Clinton, and Bette, the murdered man dangling in the slide chute, and the woman who splashed into the pool. We were the only brown faces here. Us and Seychelle. No one else seemed even a little sympathetic to the trauma. Someone gasped, someone else screamed, but the same gasps and screams you'd hear from a packed house at a horror movie.

No film with their makeup effects or CGI monster could ever capture the horrific sight of a real body whipping about on the end of a rope. His shoulders batting the sides of the slide with discordant thuds like a drummer who'd dropped one stick.

History wasn't repeating. It was now. And the Trustees were proud.

The older Black woman, who miraculously escaped the noose, emerged from the water, gasping with the loose rope snaking from her neck. In one hand, she held a small pocketknife. A blade she must've used to cut loose the weights on her ankles, then the tape on her wrists. She swam to the edge of the pool, eyes bulging. "Help! Someone help!"

The Trustees closest—some with small kids they'd brought to observe the lynching—scuttled back like the woman was some devil come to claim them. While they panicked, other Trustees jeered. They hadn't come here to see her *live*.

Some Trustee, stupidly arrogant in a way only they were capable of, pointed his phone at the woman as she planted a hand to lift herself from the pool. Her resident band still jostled on her wrist, and when the Trustee triggered it, the electrical current seized not only her but several Trustees and their kids standing in a poolside puddle.

"Stop it!" someone shouted. "The babies!"

Whether it was simply slow reaction, malfunction due to the wet conditions, or a bloodlust fueled delay in reflexes, the zapping wasn't stopped soon enough.

The woman who'd almost made it slumped and sank lifeless to the bottom of the pool. The four Trustees who got a taste of her punishment were still too.

When the panic began to spread, Bette looped her elbow in mine and tugged Clinton along with her other hand, recognizing, maybe, this was no place for us. She said, "We have to get CJ out of here."

"We?" Clinton said, as absorbed by the violence as the other ravenous Trustees.

Bette tugged his sleeve harder, exuding her quiet dominance and breaking his trance. His shoulders slumped like a child called away from play because the streetlights flared on.

247

Clinton nudged us a path to our car as the shouts for "Payback! Payback!" began. As if payback hadn't started this nightmare. As if payback could ever make it right. I pressed my hands into my thighs, hard, until the muscles ached, only moderately succeeding in controlling the shakes.

Their shouts chased our car away, but even when we were out of earshot, I heard them. I might always hear them. This wasn't going to end until the worst of them were satisfied.

This wasn't going to end for a long time.

KARLOFF COUNTRY'S COMMITMENT TO SAFETY

We are deeply committed to your well-being when you visit our resort. It starts with our Helpers, who receive the most-up-to-date training on how to keep you safe and secure inside the resort walls, and ends with your adherence to best practices within your own travel party and when interacting with fellow resort guests.

PROHIBITED ACTIVITIES INCLUDE:

- Unauthorized access to areas designated as Helpers Only.
- Unauthorized events, speeches, or other disruptions that might be construed as a demonstration over personal grievances.
- Obstructing walkways, entrances, patios.
- Engaging in photography, videography, or recording of any kind for unapproved commercial purposes.
- Hanging any clothing, towels, bedding, or other similar items over balconies or safety railings anywhere within the resort perimeter.
- Engaging in any unsafe act that might impede the normal operations of the Karloff Country Resort.

PROHIBITED ITEMS INCLUDE:

- Firearms, ammunition, knives, and weapons of any kind.
- Fireworks or other similarly explosive objects.
- Recreational devices such as drones, remote-control toys, skateboards, scooters, in-line skates, or shoes with built-in wheels.
- Self-defense or restraining devices.
- Horns, whistles, and large megaphones.
- Plastic straws.

CHAPTER 31

We didn't discuss it on the ride home, and the Greers never mentioned it again. At least not directly. Bette proclaimed we'd all had a tiring day, and she allowed me to eat alone in my room, where I cried until I dozed off wondering what the "Payback! Payback!" Mob got up to after we escaped Splash Zone. My nightmares presented vivid possibilities.

The next day, it was back to chores and watching clocks that felt broken.

That evening when we resumed our usual dinner routine in the formal dining room, Clinton abandoned a bloody, half-eaten sirloin for one of his rants about "bad choices and poor preparation often having undesirable consequences." He was talking about Splash Zone, I knew. But, even after months of his bigoted assessments of Black people—or any people—who weren't him, I couldn't figure how he made the lynching we witnessed anyone's fault other than the Trustees who committed the act. Maybe I'd gotten too comfortable or too fed up since I only saw dangling nooses whenever I closed my eyes now. I couldn't let it go.

I said, "Like what?"

"Excuse me?"

"What kinds of choices could I make right now to avoid undesirable consequences tomorrow? Or next week. Or when I'm old, like you."

Bette sat between us and tried to thin the tension. "Oh, Clint. If you're done with your meal, maybe we can have ice cream. There's a little mint chocolate chip in the freezer."

"I don't want any ice cream," he said to her. To me, "That's a different path for every person. My choices wouldn't necessarily be yours. It's incumbent upon the individual to carve their path."

"So it's luck."

"No."

"If you can't, like, lay out steps that can be reproduced, and it's all individual whatever, that means some people get lucky and some people win the bad consequence lottery."

Clinton removed the napkin from his lap and tossed it onto his plate, where it soaked up the juice from his meat. "If it makes you comfortable to favor fate over personal responsibility, I'm afraid you've benefited very little from the knowledge I've tried to impart upon you."

"I'm saying it's lucky you have money, and I'm lucky you picked me as your Concierge, and we're all lucky your friends decided to string up and electrocute some random Splash Zone Helpers instead of us."

"Enough!" Clinton roared, viciously jabbing his fork in my direction. "Shut your fool mouth before I shut it for you!"

He stood, dropping his fork, and yanked his phone from his pocket. I don't know if I'd meant to push him this far, but the terror I felt was halved by the relief that we'd finally gotten to this part. Because I'd known in the pit of my stomach and the depths of my soul I'd eventually displease him, and it wasn't like all he said was garbage. There was power in making the choice myself.

But Clinton was so mad he fumbled the phone onto the table. When he attempted to retrieve it, Bette slapped his knuckles with a spoon. He snatched his hand to his chest, massaging the sting. She chastised him with a look, and whatever rage beast had jerked its chain he reeled in as if he knew it couldn't protect him from the biggest dog in the room.

"Sit down," Bette said.

Clinton sat.

"Jermaine, go get that ice cream. It's time for something sweet now."

I did as told, and when I returned with the carton and three bowls, the momentary glare Clinton shot my way made clear there'd be no sweetness between me and him. Not ever again.

Perhaps I'd pushed my luck too far.

Clinton barely spoke to me the following day other than issuing the chore of tending to the violas in the backyard garden. I was wrist deep in potting soil when the grand gongs of the doorbell sounded. I'd assumed it was a provisions delivery guy.

Bette appeared on the patio, gushingly nervous. "Hey, sweetie, come inside. We have a guest."

I wiped sweat off my brow with a handkerchief and set aside my trowel. Why she wanted me inside for one of their guests I didn't know. Stomping garden dirt on the doormat, I followed Bette through the kitchen and into a flowery scent that was better than anything Clint's garden would ever yield. That perfume . . .

Seychelle.

On the couch. Next to Clinton.

My world hit a level of bizarre I didn't know possible.

Had she come to take me to the Devil's Race?

Clinton stood when I entered, exuding thirsty energy. His face might rip from his unnaturally wide smile. "Jermaine, you've been keeping secrets! You didn't tell me you know the one and only Seychelle Karloff."

Seychelle stood too. "Hey, Jermaine. I was telling the Greers how we were classmates at the Academy, and we'd been partnered together on group projects. One of my ongoing responsibilities in Karloff Country will be student liaison to the Board of Trustees. Given the school year will start way later than expected and the recent events around the property, I was hoping to chat with you about changes that might benefit students from Jubilee."

What was she talking about?

The thing I got completely: When she said *given recent events*, Clinton stopped that goofy grinning.

Seychelle addressed Bette. "May Jermaine and I take a walk around the neighborhood?"

Bette was taken aback. "I don't— Clint, can we—"

The next thing out of Seychelle's mouth chilled me.

"Don't worry, my guards will be present the whole time."

We left the Greers' with Seychelle rambling about "curriculum shifts" and "focus on practical vocational skills." I still hadn't said a word. We'd rounded a corner, en route to the lake at the center of the neighborhood when she dropped all the student liaison garbage and told the two burly men with resident bands who'd been accompanying us, "Take a break."

They were obedient and took seats on a bench while she led us closer to the water.

At the shore, four turtles lumbered about hoping to be fed. I wished

I'd brought some bread crumbs for them just to have something to do with my hands.

Away from Clinton and Bette, with her guards left behind, she dropped her girl boss act and looked . . . *haunted*. I probably did too. "Why'd you drag me here?"

"I know this is unexpected. And I'm sorry."

"For what? Not making contact in months? Not doing anything to stop—" I meant Splash Zone, but I couldn't say it, so I motioned toward anything and everything. "What are you sorry for? Be specific."

She didn't respond.

"The list is that long, huh?"

"I understand why you're mad," she said. "But I needed to see you, okay?"

"You saw me the other day. Right? I saw you."

She squeezed her eyes shut and turned away slightly. "I didn't know what was going to happen."

"If you did know, could you have stopped it?"

"No."

"Why you here, Chelle?"

"The way you're talking to me, I doubt you'd believe it."

"Many unbelievable things have become acceptable lately."

She nudged a rock with her sneaker. "I miss you."

There were bags under her eyes. A dull braid flaky with dandruff fell over her shoulder. Baggy gray hoodie. Loose jeans. An unremarkable outfit that looked as good as when she'd come to do homework in an evening gown. Truth: I missed her too.

Didn't mean I believed her. "There's more. Isn't there?"

"I knew you were in the Concierge program, but I became more concerned after Splash Zone. There have been some disturbing rumors about other participants in this program, and I now know there's no cruelty too great for Trustees."

"Those aren't rumors."

She nodded slowly. "But you're with the Greers, so I figured you'd be okay. Plus, since the Board of Trustees was announced, and the Greers weren't on it, they've been low-key hinting for more access. Easy in for me to come see you."

"It's real sexy how you're using that supervillain mastermind of yours to get some quality time with me. No far-reaching implications there at all."

"You're being mean."

"You lied to me, Chelle. You said all of this would be over soon."

"If you want me to leave, I will."

I didn't. "Is any of the school liaison stuff true?"

"Somewhat. The Board of Trustees agrees that we'll need school reform. But they won't be sending any of their kids to school with any non-Trustees. Things are getting tense. That's another reason I wanted to talk to you. I'm hoping you can help me here."

She let that dangle for a second. I bit. "Go on."

"The Trustees thought Splash Zone would put an end to any resistance, but there was another incident last night. A fueling station for Trustee transport vehicles was blown up. No one was harmed this time, but the Trustees won't care. There are going to be more consequences."

"More lynchings," I corrected.

She produced a phone from her hoodie pouch and showed me a

photo of a message scrawled on concrete in neon yellow spray paint: *For Connie.*

Seychelle said, "Tell Zeke he can't keep going. Tell him to tell whoever he's working with they have to stop!"

It took a lot not to react, and my words felt idiotic crossing my lips. "This doesn't mean it's our Connie. This picture doesn't prove Zeke did anything."

"Did you see anyone present evidence at Splash Zone? None of that matters anymore. Tell. Him."

"I understand," I said.

She nodded but seemed to have exhausted most of her words.

"Should I expect more of you visiting me here?"

"No." It was quick. Unshakable.

"Figures." The anger hit me fast, but I didn't say more. She knew me well enough to feel it.

"If I come here," she said, "I have to bring the guards. I was hoping, maybe, you could come to me."

My head whipped so fast it cracked my neck. "How's *that* supposed to work?"

"We could meet Friday night. Just us. At the mountain entrance to the tunnel you and Zeke used."

"How am I supposed to get out of Jubilee after curfew, Chelle?"

"The drones have set rotations. After ten thirty, go to the Treat and follow the bike trails. Use the trees for cover and you'll be fine."

"You *know* that'll work?"

"I already tried it. You haven't been home." While still gazing across the lake, her hand drifted to mine. Her pinkie grazed my pinkie. "I'll wait until midnight. If you don't come, I won't bother you again."

She turned abruptly, waving for her guards. They approached, and before they were within earshot, I said, "We left Splash Zone when the crowd got heated. What happened after?"

She flinched. "Please come on Friday."

Then our chaperones were back, and I knew to keep my mouth shut.

When I arrived home for the weekend, it was to an empty house, and a wave of panic crashed over me. Before I ran through each room screaming my parents' names, I spotted the note scrawled on the magnetized whiteboard clinging to our fridge.

Dad and I have evening shifts. Prep work's picking up. See you later tonight. Service and joy. ~Mom

The calmness of the note betrayed the events of the week. I glanced left and right, catching the ever-present purple glow of our Sandrina pyramids. Had the AI developed the ability to read Mom's handwriting?

Last weekend, she mentioned their workloads picking up as the power plant and the Vertical Farms prepared for the demands of the winter. I dropped my duffel bag in our laundry room, grabbed the muting fob Mr. Barnabus gifted me from my desk, then left Sandrina for some fresh air.

The sun was already down, and Zeke's bedroom light was a beacon across the street. When he opened the door, his face was unreadable.

"Hey?" I said.

He waved me inside, and I followed him upstairs. He moved with urgency and still hadn't spoken. So I said, "You good?"

Holding up a halting finger, he rooted in the pocket of jeans slung across his desk chair, produced his own muting fob, and clicked it on. "You hear about the water park?"

I didn't think this *wouldn't* come up, but I'd hoped for, I don't know, something that made returning to Jubilee feel different than my Concierge time, for a little bit anyway. More and more that separation was hard to maintain. "I . . . was there."

His fists clenched.

"How . . ." he finally said, then struggled going on. "How could you have been there?"

"I'm a Concierge. My hosts wanted to go. I didn't have a choice." It sounded more defensive than I wanted.

Zeke pinched the bridge of his nose as if staving off a headache. Like I was giving him a headache.

"There wasn't anything I could do, man. I didn't even know why we were there until two people came down the slides. When that lady tried to get out the pool, the mob got wild, and the Greers dragged me— What?"

"You don't know." He grabbed the phone he still used to communicate with Panopticon. Showed me the photos on-screen.

Bodies.

So many bodies.

"Who are they?"

Zeke said, "Every Helper who worked at Splash Zone. The Trustees killed them all."

CHAPTER 32

It felt like I was outside of myself, watching some other entity work my hands. That other me pushed Zeke's phone away. "Where'd those pictures come from?"

"I took them. The bodies are in Downtown Karloff. For everyone to see."

That shook me. "Nobody saw you with a working phone?"

"I went last night. After curfew."

They. Killed. Everyone. Left their bodies in the street. To rot.

Zeke drew me out of my head with his next words. "It's time to go harder, bro. Get some payback."

A raging Trustee mob cried in my head: *Payback! Payback!*

"Harder than blowing up a fueling station? Chelle came to see me. She knows what you've been up to. Said you should stop."

He sat up straighter, the tough-guy, get-some-payback posturing gone. "She tell anybody else?"

"Would we be having this conversation if she had?"

His eyes narrowed.

"Splash Zone happened after someone attacked a Trustee convoy. Broke their hands. Was that you?" I said.

"No."

"No point lying to me, man."

"I ain't lying. That wasn't us! But it sounds like you're saying what the Trustees did was somebody else's fault. Nothing justifies what they did."

I felt I was on my heels again, defending myself. "All I'm asking is who?"

"I don't know," he said real fast. "But why are you acting surprised by anything happening now? You thought folks was gonna sit back and be service puppets for people who'd just as soon fry us as look at us? The only people who seem to be okay with that go-along-to-get-along mess is—"

Shaking his head, he spun his desk chair away. I grabbed his shoulder and spun him back. "Who?"

"*Your* people, bro. *You!* Go Along to Get Along Jay, unbothered again."

My insides bucked. "Don't call me that. I'm not *unbothered*. You don't know what you're talking about."

"I don't? We be dunking stale bread in onion soup, but the provisions to the Butler house ain't slowed down, have they?"

"What?"

His face brightened, and his tone mocked. "*I suppose you and your cohort aren't aware of how the commonfolk live.* Food been slowing down. You try to buy more, the Pup Points they take are crazy. Let me stop burdening you, though. I can imagine how stressful it is at the Concierge suite or wherever."

Rage and denial and confusion swirled in me. Zeke was way out of line, going hard in a way he'd never done before. His words felt like an assault, and what else was there to say anyway? The dead Splash Zone Helpers were a whole conversation to be had, but not with him. "I'm going to go."

"Go where?"

"Home," I lied.

Zeke scratched at his eyebrow with his pinkie nail, his head tilted slightly. Scrutinizing. "Lock the door on your way out."

. . .

I showered and changed. I scribbled my own sketchy note to Mom on the whiteboard, nonsense about hanging with some other "Concierge kids" and how our special status gave us nonexistent "curfew passes," then set out for Karloff Manor a full hour earlier than I was told, hoping my eyes were good enough to spot any drones before they spotted me.

Best I could tell the sky was clear. Entering the Treat and passing my crew's pavilion I read the literal writing on the wall. A graffiti message tagged on the side of the public restrooms.

34 Missing Since the Trustees Came
15 Dead Since the Trustees Came
0 REAL Consequences

It froze me.

When was this painted? Fifteen? Did that include the Splash Zone Helpers?

The paint wasn't new, already flaking in places, so probably not.

I got moving again, faster. I wanted to be in that cave before Chelle arrived. It was time for me to surprise her for a change.

It was ten minutes to midnight when the tunnel door creaked open. Chelle stepped through with a bulging backpack cinched tight on her shoulders and a couple of thick comforters cradled in her arms. She resealed the door before I emerged from the shadows, startling her. As intended.

She shrieked, dropped the comforters, and backed into the cave wall. "Creep!"

My dirt-caked shoes ground mud into the linen when I got in her face. "Why didn't you tell me the rest about Splash Zone?"

"What was I supposed to say?" She sniffed. "I was already taking a risk to see you, and if I'd brought it up"—her chest hitched—"I might've broken down, and I can't be seen that way by my guards, the Greers, or anyone else who might've been watching. You understand that, don't you?"

"No, Chelle. I don't understand. How do you move between seeming like a decent person with me and playing *Game of Thrones* with your family and their psycho rich friends? Did you watch all those people get murdered? Did you come home and sleep it off like 'Hey, we had a rough one but tomorrow's a new day'?"

She shoved past me. "Things have gotten so bad, and I don't know how to make them better. No, I don't wake up thinking tomorrow's a new day. I wake up thinking, *Is this the end? Will the Trustees finally see through the smoke screen and come for me and my mom?* Every day that doesn't happen, I'm halfway disappointed because the terror starts all over. I've got the biggest, best room in a burning house, Jay. I'd hoped I could escape it for one night."

She snatched the blankets off the ground and punched her long code in the doorjamb keypad. "I'm sorry I bothered you. I'm sorry about all of it."

The lock clacked, but when she tugged the handle, I pushed it closed again. "Wait. Don't go yet."

"I can't be here if you're going to keep coming for me."

"I know. I won't." My hand slipped off the door to her wrist, and I gently tugged her closer in an embrace, where she cried softly into my shoulder.

An escape for one night. Why not?

The fire would still be hot in the morning.

ZEKE

Jay, Connie, Chelle, and me played spades together. Once.

It sounded like a good idea when Connie suggested it because she immediately claimed Chelle as her partner and I assumed the rich girl would be the weak link. But, I don't know, she probably trained with, like, the best spades player in the world or something.

My mom taught me to play when I was five, and she imparted on me how messing up a spades game could crush friendships, break up families, and start wars. If you know, you know. Anyway.

I figured me and Jay would crush the girls every hand. And we might've . . . if not for Jay. My dude *sucked*.

He miscounted his books in the opening bids. He reneged like three hands in a row. And his face don't hide nothing, so Connie and Chelle read his plays before and better than he did. Jay didn't play his cards close to the chest. Never has, maybe never will.

So, him talking that *home* stuff and looking like he was going anywhere but . . . got me curious. What did a Concierge get up to in their time off, when they thought no one was watching?

I should've guessed.

My watch read 12:05. He'd been in that cave awhile, quiet, but that was definitely Chelle's voice in there now. My suspicions confirmed.

Backtracking down the hill, I sent a text.

Me
He's with her. I don't think they're
going anywhere anytime soon.

Panopticon

Get to a road and
send me your 20.

Panopticon

It's time we met face-to-face.

Panopticon

You've earned it.

CHAPTER 33

The cricket song—or lack of it—woke me. They weren't so noisy at sunrise.

"Chelle!" We'd fallen asleep. My back wedged in a half-comfortable nook in the cave wall, her slumped in my arms after retrieving the soiled comforter for warmth sometime in the night.

Ultra awake, checking my watch—6:47—I scrambled from beneath the blanket. She roused, fingering the crust of dried tears from her eyes, catching some of my panic. "Are you going to be okay getting home?"

"I'm not sure."

"I—I can . . ." She didn't finish because we already knew how powerless she was in our new world. She couldn't drive me home. Couldn't come up with anything that justified us spending a night together. The only thing I had going for me was daylight. There were no rules for how I could move or where I could go when the sun was up. Not yet.

She said, "Can you come back tonight?"

"What? I don't know. Probably not." It was a ridiculous request.

"Because I won't know you're okay. I don't have a way to reach you."

"There's nothing I can do about that."

She negotiated. "Next Friday, then? Same time?"

"If I can." I was legit worried about even being around next Friday. My parents would be going crazy.

She rose and kissed me so hard it almost pushed me from the cave into the light.

"I gotta go," I said, prying myself from her embrace. "Next week."

"Promise?"

I didn't.

The trek down the hill was so much easier in daylight. On level ground, I cut back toward the Jubilee bike trails ready to sprint but came to a stop. Zeke blocked my way.

His face was tight, and I could see him clenching his teeth. He said, "You're lucky it's me."

Didn't feel so lucky. "You followed me."

"Yep. Wasn't hard either. You were so busy watching the sky you never looked behind you."

"You sat out here all night?"

"No." He seemed twitchy, looking over his shoulder. "Once I knew where you were, I had to go talk to the man. You'll see."

He motioned in a direction I hadn't planned on going.

"Bro, I gotta get home. My parents—"

"It's handled. Come on." He closed the gap between us and clamped down on my elbow.

I snatched away. "I'm not going anywhere."

A couple of dark shapes emerged from the tree line like forest spirits. Karloff Country Security. The same class of officer responsible for driving me to and from my Concierge duties each week. Each with a glowing resident band dangling on their wrists. Typical. Each with a black rifle dangling from a strap strung across their chests.

That was new.

"Change of plans," Zeke said. "Sorry."

His disgusted little head shake suggested the apology maybe wasn't genuine.

•   •   •

It was a trip along familiar streets with no other traffic, yet I didn't know where I was anymore. I felt I was in a foreign land with guides who spoke a different language even though my best friend was in the seat next to me.

I'd been staring at him. He stared back, unblinking. What I read in that expression scared me more than waking up in Chelle's cave this morning. I'd been trying to understand how Zeke could do this to me, but what I saw in his face was absolute conviction. I imagined him thinking, *How could I* not?

Our destination was obvious before we passed the bright, cartoony sign shaped like a film projector. The employee-access road cut to the back of the Karloff Pictures park.

Zeke and his goons walked me to the Director's Diner—a restaurant that sat in the morning shadow of the Ferris Reel ride Bette loved so much, its walls overwhelmed with grids of Karloff film memorabilia. Framed photos of starlets from the black-and-white days, one-sheets of Technicolor classics, and all versions of Penny Pup and friends from their original character sketches to modern marketing-approved redesigns. A few armed, older white guys occupied random booths. I recognized a couple from the bring-your-family parties my parents dragged me to during the holidays in prior years. These were my dad's old coworkers, and they regarded me with interest they never had before.

The salty scent of savory eggs and bacon was thick, though the person working the grill made it the most surreal diner meal I'd ever experienced.

Barnabus divided the scrambled eggs and meat onto a couple of plates as some scorched bread ejected from a nearby toaster. Zeke motioned to a stool.

I waited for Barnabus to do something dramatic and corny like pop the little bell on the pickup counter and shout some ridiculous cook jargon. Instead, he brought the two plates through the swinging door between the kitchen and counter and placed them before Zeke and me.

"I imagine you boys are hungry," he said.

Zeke gripped the fork and shoved food into his mouth. My stomach gave a compulsive twist, and I couldn't resist. The eggs were amazing.

"Cornstarch slurry and a lot of butter," Barnabus said.

"Huh?" I spoke through the food. Rude, if you let Mom tell it.

"It's how I get the eggs so creamy. I could see the wonder in your eyes."

I disliked him a little for his keen perception.

"You should try the bacon. No secret there. Only good, quality meat from the Vertical Farms." He leaned forward, waiting. I didn't like the vibe enough to give in again. I changed the subject to a topic of greater concern ever since I stepped into the restaurant.

"Why those dudes got guns? I didn't even know guns were allowed in Karloff Country."

"Mostly that's true." He snatched a strip of my bacon and chomped down. "For guests, absolutely no guns allowed. But there's always been a small armory for those with the proper access."

"Do the Trustees have access?"

"They're pretty well armed as is, I think." He raised his resident band. "No need to burden them with more responsibility."

I glanced from Zeke to the guards, back to the man driving all this mysterious nonsense. "What do you want from me, Mr. Barnabus?"

"I'll tell you, but you'll probably fill in some of the blanks yourself if you know my other name." He stole another piece of bacon and crammed it into his mouth. "These days I prefer Panopticon."

CHAPTER 34

"*You're* Panopticon?" I twisted on my stool and asked Zeke, "The dude who's been texting you?"

Neither responded. Letting me work it out on my own.

I aimed my fork at Barnabus. "The Karloff conspiracy message board from before the Trustees came. Was that you too?"

He nodded.

"Why? You work for Franklin Karloff. You're, like, his right-hand guy."

"The site was supposed to be a place for Helpers to air grievances anonymously. In my public role, there was only so much interaction with subordinates I could engage in. There, I could hear from the real people who kept the place running. In some cases, that bit of subterfuge allowed me to institute necessary change without someone with more to lose putting themselves at risk. I never intended for the conspiracies about the Karloff family to take off the way they did."

He rubbed his eyes, the dark half circles beneath them standing out against the pale flesh of his fingers. "And I never meant to inspire the more radical factions that align against them."

"Radical factions?" I said

Zeke said, "The people who broke those Trustees' hands. Though that's nothing compared to what's probably coming after the Splash Zone retaliation."

Barnabus didn't add anything. He didn't contradict Zeke either. Instead, he said, "Nothing is like what any of us expected when we came to Karloff Country. Not for me. Not for you. We all thought we were escaping the degradation of the outside world. Now we're no more than pets with shock collars. What kind of life is that?"

"Tell him," Zeke blurted.

Barnabus held up his hand, a request for patience.

I said, "Tell me what?"

Zeke said, "Two more of us were killed last night while you were booed up with Chelle!"

"Ezekiel," Barnabus said, stern. "We can't terrorize him into our point of view. Nobody can be a part of this simply out of fear. Or retribution."

Zeke shoved away from the counter and paced.

Barnabus said, "Is what Zeke's told me true? You have a close relationship with Seychelle Karloff?"

What Zeke told. My back was to him, but I sensed him pass and resisted the urge to spin on my stool and kick him in the stomach.

Barnabus continued like I'd answered. "So many times in history it's the youth who see the clearest and can save the day. Like Zeke said, two more people—our people—died in the night. The Trustees cannot stay in power. Access to a Karloff might be the key to overthrowing them."

"*You* have access to a Karloff! You're always around Chelle's granddad."

"Not anymore. The old man's, I don't know, grown paranoid now. The family has walled themselves off in that estate. Everything goes through Blythe."

He seemed especially bothered by this change in circumstance. But Zeke couldn't have told him *everything* about the Karloffs, or Barnabus would know it was Franklin's dementia—not paranoia—that had Blythe running things.

Barnabus said, "Their 24/7 security is a problem. If we attempted some kind of assault—"

"Wait, what?"

Barnabus waved me off. Offered a smile. Two old friends having a chat. "Hypothetically speaking. *If* that were an option, and it's not, they'd trigger our bands as soon as we got close. We'd be incapacitated or killed as fast as they could move their thumbs. Wouldn't you agree?"

Everything he said sounded crazy. I waited for him to get to the point of all this. Really, I wanted to know if I'd be allowed to leave. I had doubts.

"What do you think me knowing Seychelle can do, Mr. Barnabus?"

He leaned back in his chair. "Give us Sandrina. Then the whole thing topples."

"I don't understand."

"There aren't any satellites, or cell towers, or anything like that anymore. Those things likely still exist, but this Karloff Country cage we're in was built independent of all that. So how do the Trustees communicate with each other? How do they control the surveillance? How do they trigger our bands? Internal, dedicated systems. Sandrina."

"You think I can convince Seychelle to hand over access to Sandrina. Like a password or some codes?"

"I doubt *she* has the access we need."

"What, then?"

He resorted to his favorite word. "If"—he stopped short, spoke carefully—"*if* we could *separate* Seychelle from her guards for an extended period, that would give the old man incentive to relinquish control of all the Trustees' oppressive protocols. That's shutting down surveillance, taking over the Vertical Farms, deactivating our bands. That's our liberation, Jermaine."

I was still stuck on *separate Seychelle from her guards for an extended period.*

"No." They couldn't force me to do anything. I wouldn't let them. "I won't be able to help you."

Zeke slammed his palms on the counter and looked me dead in the eye. "We could've taken her this morning, Jay. You get that, don't you? This is a chance for you to help us do it right. So nobody gets hurt."

Barnabus said, "I know we're asking something very difficult of you. If she leaves the guards behind willingly, nothing gets messy. If you're with her, she'll be comfortable and open to reason. This is a chess move, not a boxing match."

I stood. Carefully, to see how they reacted. Everyone in the booths remained cool. "Can I go home?"

Barnabus ran a hand over his face, as if to wipe away his exhaustion. "Yes. Of course. Me thrusting this upon you isn't fair. We don't have the luxury of fairness when people are dying simply to fulfill the gluttony of those who rose to the top of a society *they* let crumble. I'll ask that you take some time to consider our proposal. I'll also ask you keep this to yourself."

"My dad doesn't know his old boss is a secret rebel leader, then?"

"No. You're smart. Tell me why."

It felt like that day in Enchantria a million years ago. His quizzes on supplies and restocking.

"If things go wrong, all the trouble falls on you. You're the bad influence who corrupted some kids."

"My life for the fight," Barnabus said. "No one else's. Your father's always been a good and diligent worker whose reassignment to the Vertical Farms guarantees his safety."

"What about them?" I motioned to the other guys Mr. Barnabus recruited while he made Dad's safety a priority.

Barnabus leaned into me and offered a tight smile. "What can I say? Ten of those guys aren't worth one of your dad. They're lesser men. Am I right?" Then, to Zeke and the guards, he said, "Take him home. He's got a lot to think about."

He released me. A man of his word.

When Zeke walked me outside, I caught a glimpse of men leaving their booths and taking counter seats shoulder to shoulder. Barnabus was about to hold court, and his audience looked more like loyal Knights of the Round Table than the "lesser men" he claimed. The diner door swung shut, and I was ushered away.

I didn't speak to Zeke the whole ride home. I couldn't. Not after Go Along to Get Along Jay. Not after he led armed men to me. My words might become fists real quick.

How was he was on board with whatever his bootleg resistance had planned for Chelle? We're supposed to be crew!

Could we ever get back to what we were before? If not, could anything ever be what it was?

At my house, Mom and Dad met me on the lawn with grateful hugs. The cover story they'd been given involved Barnabus needing some assistance at Enchantria. Late-night park maintenance had become commonplace at the behest of the Trustees. We'd all gotten so used to their whims, my parents barely asked questions—they were simply happy I was safe. They trusted Barnabus to keep me that way.

My remaining time in Jubilee I spent in my head. Barnabus was wrong, though. There wasn't much to think about.

The only thing on my mind was how to best warn Chelle trouble was coming.

CHAPTER 35

At the Greers', Bette got pouty when I bypassed her in the foyer and sought Clinton in his office.

He looked up from whatever thick volume he'd been reading and peered over the rims of his glasses, big displeased-teacher energy. "Can I help you?"

"I hope so."

Bette lingered in the hallway behind me, quiet and nosy.

Stepping deeper into the office, I produced a creased sheet of notebook paper covered in scribblings. "I was thinking about Seychelle Karloff's education reform initiatives and wrote down some notes she might find interesting. Of course, I don't have any way to get them to her, and she might like some time to review them before we meet again."

Before the first syllable of *Karloff* cleared my lips he perked, like I'd been counting on.

"Let me see what you have there." He reviewed the sheet. Seven or eight bullet points I'd plagiarized from the introductions of several design textbooks Mom kept from her college days. Jumbled things about *learning objectives* and *desired outcomes*. He nodded while he read, trying to pretend it made sense, then peered over his glasses, impressed.

"I can certainly make sure this gets up the mountain." He refolded the paper with nimble fingers and slipped it into his breast pocket.

"Thank you, sir."

If he actually did it, and if Seychelle understood me writing up a bunch of nonsense was me pulling the emergency alarm, I might see her before Friday and warn her to keep those guards around at all times.

Bette, impatient and vibrating with manic energy, linked her elbow with mine, reclaiming me. "I have an incredible week planned for us. First up, Enchantria! Your favorite. Get ready. Quick."

We spent most of the day in the park, and I was told to expect a trip to the Karloff Wilds on Tuesday. But when I came down the next morning, Bette and Clinton were in an argument.

He said, "I need him tonight."

"There's a pottery-making workshop in Downtown Karloff this evening," she whined. "I thought we'd all go and grab a bite after."

"I don't really care what you thought, Bettina! I need him."

"For what?"

That's the part I wanted to know too. But he noticed me and issued an order instead of an answer. "You're accompanying me tonight. End of discussion."

Bette huffed, *mad* mad. "Is it now?"

Clinton swept a dismissive wave her way and stomped off to his office, uttering his final instructions on the way. "Have yourself cleaned up and ready to go by six. Do not keep me waiting."

As if I had a choice.

I only saw Bette once before we left. In a bathrobe, shuffling into my room to kiss me on the cheek and wish me a good time. She seemed much less Bette than I was used to, and that scared me. A good time doing what and where? A Trustee's good time was rarely the same as a Helper's. Then it was six and Clinton wanted to get going.

No driver tonight. It was humid, the air thick as stew, but Clinton insisted a brisk walk was good for the heart. That's when I figured we were going to Ted's. Ted's was the only place Clinton ever walked.

It was a little under a mile to the mansion, and we were sweating rivers within thirty seconds, yet he was chattier than he'd ever been.

"I sent that message up the mountain via courier yesterday. I'll be sure to let you know if the Karloffs get back to me about it."

"Thank you." My pulse doubled. I tried not to sound too grateful.

"Has it been nice seeing your family on the weekends?"

"Yes, sir."

"None of that *sir* stuff for tonight. Clint's fine. United front around these white boys." He laughed and extended his hand palm up. I hesitated because this we-got-to-stick-together-against-the-man stuff was way different from how he usually looked down his nose at me. Especially since our blowup last week.

Clinton was scared.

As much as he needed to be Ted's buddy, or equal, or maybe superior on a normal Trustee day, he was frightened about whatever we were walking into. That made me more nervous. I slapped his palm like he wanted me to. He said, "Right on, homeboy!"

How old was this guy?

"There'll be some real sharks there tonight," he said. "Hang by my hip. I won't let anything happen to you."

"Anything like what?"

He got shifty. "I mean nobody'll bother you if you're with me. So, your family. How were you brought up?"

I tried to interpret it in a way that made sense. He'd never asked about my family because he clearly never cared before. Probably still

277

didn't care, but he was an anxious talker. "My dad's a business guy. Mom's a designer. Or they were. Now she's in the power plant and he's at the Vertical Farms."

"The farms?" He seemed taken aback. "What tower?"

"Produce."

"Oh. Yes. Makes sense. We're grateful for that crew."

"Um. I guess." I've barely seen Clinton eat a vegetable, but okay.

"You come from educated people. I suspected as much from the way you speak. So don't say *um*; you're better than that."

Nice to have the old Clinton back.

He kept on. "A couple of better breaks out in the world, a little more time before things went to pot, and your folks could've very well ended up in a position like Bette and me. I don't discount your point about luck in all this. The harder you work, the luckier you are."

My point about luck. He hadn't forgotten our blowup. Had he *gotten over it*, though? That felt important.

"What is it that you and Bette do? Or did?" We'd never talked about this either. It never seemed to matter.

"I'm an architect, like my father. I ran our family's firm. Designed and built high-capacity venues. Football stadiums and the like. Even did a portion of the Olympic Village for the Milan games back in '24. Bette was a therapist to the stars, if you can believe it. Big '*self-help guru.*'"

By the way he described Bette's work, he didn't respect it much. It's sort of like when Connie, Chelle, and I called Zeke a "genius playwright" with the air quotes. I said, "Your father started the firm?"

"He did. I turned it into the international juggernaut it eventually became."

"You always liked building stuff?"

"Not as much as blowing things up. The day my father let me activate the charges on this casino hotel demo . . . let me tell you. The only thing more fun than building them up is knocking them down. Not as much money in that side of it, though." He chuckled, in a genuinely good mood.

A fuzzy pattern was beginning to form. Maybe wealth wasn't enough to make it into this version of Karloff Country. There had to be other contributions. An architect would've been useful in building this neighborhood. I said, "Did you design something here in Karloff Country?"

"Where do you think the walls came from? The Vertical Farms? Greer Design and Fabrication has been meeting Franklin Karloff's custom construction needs for decades. Ah, here we are."

We'd made it to Ted's, and a Trustee stepped off the porch, a glass of something murky in his hand. "Clint, you really brought your boy. Excellent!"

I looked to Clinton. He would not meet my gaze.

Guess we weren't homeboys anymore. And that terrified me.

He placed his hand on my back and nudged me inside.

CHAPTER 36

More old men occupied the porch. Inside, the murmurs and soft music of the get-together beckoned. Low amber lighting gave each room a honey glow while everyone drank and laughed, until they saw us. We passed through the various chambers—because now that I was inside it all felt more grand and ominous than regular rooms—and Trustees quieted, waving away hazy cigar smoke. Clinton greeted some with nods and handshakes while I trailed like a minion.

We eventually reached Ted's spacious home office, where he held court. There were two couches—both filled—some desk chairs that were also occupied, and Ted stood in the center speaking passionately.

Farah, the only other Concierge I'd seen since entering the home, lurked in a corner behind Ted. She tugged at a sleeve partially covering a hand that had become a blackened curled thing, like a shrimp that fell through a grill grate.

Her face was still, and she stared at nothing.

". . . with the unforeseen failures in the grand coup, sooner than later," Ted said, "we'll need a reliable guard."

Clinton dived into a conversation he was obviously familiar with, one that had been had many times. "As a *secondary* defense. The wall will hold, Ted. Don't worry your pretty little head."

"Here comes Greer boasting about his *big* construction prowess." Ted waggled a finger in our direction. "It's my business to worry, and you're going to thank me for it."

A familiar man spoke next. The last time I saw him he'd been officiating a lynching by waterslide.

Mr. Radford held his drink in his good hand and said, "Jesus, Greer, wasn't sure you'd join us since there's no poker for you to cheat at tonight!"

A bunch of knowing laughs around the room.

Radford said, "Seriously, I thought you'd chucked that habit you people have for being late. What's it called?" He switched to a high-pitched mocking voice that, I guessed, was supposed to be a Black person. *"That CPT? Colored people's time?"*

Every white man in the room cracked up. Funniest thing they'd heard in a life.

Clinton didn't even look uncomfortable. "Oh, come on, Preston. I'm *fashionably* late. There is a difference."

I don't know if I ever hated Clinton more than in that moment.

Ted said, "Settle down, everyone. Now that Greer's in the building, I can show you what I've been working on. I think you'll be impressed."

Another old white man, who'd been quiet but stared at me nonstop since I stepped into the room, said, "Should we be discussing any of this in front of Greer's boy?"

Clinton put him at ease. "This is all over his head. Plus, if Ted's really done what he's claimed, what's it matter?"

The over-my-head comment stung because it was true—I *didn't* know what they were talking about. Also, the sting was in the unspoken insult.

Clinton thought he was smarter and better than me, no secret there. Yet he still didn't want to be the only brown face in the room. If he was so smart, why didn't he realize whatever he thought about me, they thought about him too?

"That's a big *if*," said yet another white man. I was starting to lose track of who was who.

Ted shut the whole thing down by tapping something on his phone screen. "Not *if*. It's already done."

The room went quiet. Except for the chirps.

Each man tugged phones from pockets, checking the newly lit displays.

Ted said, "I pushed an update to your devices. You're beta testers."

Farah's head jerked up, taking in the room, attentive now.

"Farah. Here!" Ted was louder than necessary—she was *right there*. She shuffled forward quickly. The pace of someone who'd learned not to lag.

Ted focused on his phone. Tapping. Swiping. "I've been working on recalibration, intensity, really coming to the conclusion that the resident bands were overclocked." Ted kept fumbling with his touch screen. "It's still a little tricky, but if you know what you're doing . . ."

A final tap, and Farah shrieked.

Sudden. Soul scarring. One startled man dropped his glass; it shattered between his feet.

Farah's knees bent, her spine arched, her chin tipped to the ceiling while she wailed continuously. Her good hand gripped the wrist above her disfigured one, jostling her sleeve and revealing the pulsing red resident band shocking her. *Cooking* her. Smoke sizzled off her flesh.

Ted talked over her screaming. "The initial electrical jolt was similar to a stun gun. Great as a behavioral deterrent, but it put the individual wearing it out of commission for an extended period."

"Sometimes permanently," a whiskey-drinking man said before

taking a sip. "I lost a Concierge because I accidentally dropped my phone under the couch before I could deactivate the band. That skin-flint Karloff wouldn't provide me another either."

Some grumbled their solidarity over his inconvenience.

Ted continued. "We'd completely underestimated the bands effectiveness as a heat conductor. Reducing voltage and turning up the temperature creates a more *motivating* stimuli."

"Please stop. Please stop. Please stop," Farah pleaded.

Ted tapped his screen, and her band deactivated, though the redness of residual heat remained. She was on her knees, her eyes squeezed shut, the flesh beneath her band raw.

Clinton spoke up. Not to defend Farah as I wanted to do. Not to demand Ted stop abusing the third brown face in the room. He said, "How much usage are we talking? Heating and cooling the band over and over can't be great for the equipment."

Ted grinned. "I've managed nine tests of varying degrees. Very little degradation that I can tell. Your updated apps allow for sliders now. Temps. Amperage. Duration. You'll be able to play with whatever settings you like."

Mumbling and pleased nods all around.

Radford said, "Brass tacks, Ted. If push comes to shove, will this allow for the creation of a controllable defensive force? Will they fight for us?"

Fight? As lost as I was in all this, I couldn't shake the weight of the word. Fight *who*?

"Oh yes," said Ted. "Given the choice between enduring the band or charging some militia trespasser, they'll take a bullet for you."

Radford killed his drink, then eyed Clinton. "Now I see why you brought your boy. You want to see this thing in action before the rest of us, huh, Greer?"

Clinton beamed. "If another test is needed, I'm game."

My stomach turned loose and swishy. All eyes fell on me.

Clinton checked his phone. "My update's only at sixty-eight percent."

Ted swiped at the air, no big deal. "It's a big file. I can give Farah another low jolt if you want to see the slider functionality while we wait. How's that sound?"

Radford pumped his fist. "One more go!"

It became a group chant. These people loved shouting their cruelty. "One more go! One more go!"

Farah shook her head pitifully. "No. Don't."

Run! The thought came suddenly, slippery. *If Ted zaps her again, they'll be distracted and you can run.*

Except how far would I get? Someone would zap me before I cleared the room. Even if I made it outside. Where would I go then? What kind of person would I be using Farah's torture for cover? I stayed rooted, awaiting my fate and telling myself the lie that I wouldn't scream.

Ted fiddled with his phone screen again. Lifted his finger high above his head to build anticipation, then dropped it to the screen with the flair of a stage magician working a saw across his assistant's boxed-up body.

Farah braced for her pain. As did I.

It didn't come.

Flustered, Ted tapped his screen again. And again. Still nothing. Ted's audience turned on him playfully. Lighthearted boos and corny jokes about his "equipment not working."

None of them noticed Farah rise and grip the fireplace poker with her good hand.

Ted maintained his master-of-ceremonies bravado. "Settle down, settle down. There are still some bugs, but I promised you a quick device reset will—"

With an almost-lazy swing, Farah buried the poker's curved hook into the top of his skull—*SPLUNK!*

Ted's eyes rolled to the whites. A streamer of blood dribbled from the crown of his head and collected in his left eyebrow before he toppled over. Farah's wide-eyed, ecstatic gaze swept over the men who'd been boisterously cheering her abuse a moment before.

Someone near the door had his phone to his ear, speaking as he left the scene. "We need security now. We have a violent Helper with a malfunctioning band."

Farah yanked the poker from Ted's head with some effort and took half-hearted swings at the Trustees closest to her, discouraging any "heroes." Those terrified men didn't dare take her on.

Was she going to break for the exit? I remembered the Popsicle Man. The drones that took him down. If she made it outside, she wouldn't make it far.

But she didn't run.

Then armored guards were in the room, three burly men with their resident bands dangling on their wrists. They shoved Trustees aside, fanning out with cattle prods that crackled with blue sparks at the tip.

Farah pressed her back against the shelves.

"Take her alive!" a Trustee shouted.

Farah had a different plan. One last act of defiance in her.

285

She turned the sharp end of the poker to her throat so her flesh dimpled around the point. Then she threw herself to the floor with force. The poker's handle wedged into the throw rug like a strut and the tip tore through the back of her neck, wet and glistening.

Her last gurgling breaths sounded like she was laughing.

My homeboy Clinton didn't say a word to me the entire walk home.

CHAPTER 37

That night, the bass and the highs of Clinton's voice seeped through the walls. Recapping the horror at Ted's, I assumed. Eventually Clinton quieted, and maybe him and Bette slept. I couldn't get there because when I closed my eyes I kept replaying Farah's revenge, that *SPLUNK* as loud and frequent as my heartbeat.

The next day, the Greers didn't want much to do with me. No park trips or chores. I retreated voluntarily to Clinton's garden because outside was better than being inside with them. During an afternoon break, I returned to my room and dozed. Farah showed up in a nightmare confirming my orange juice order before filling the glass with *red* juice spurting from her throat. I awoke with a hand pressed to my mouth, sealing in a scream.

By evening, Bette had warmed to me again and insisted we catch a movie in Downtown Karloff even though they'd been playing the same eight films since the Trustees arrived. After, she wanted ice cream and a smoked turkey leg. The ice cream wasn't a problem, but she expressed great disappointment over the lack of meat. The vendor, terrified, swore they'd been sold out since midmorning. Thankfully, Bette let it go. "Sticks in my teeth anyway."

In my dreams that night, I saw Farah on Ted's porch. I was in the car with the Greers. Clinton waved to his buddy. Ted waved back as Farah swung her poker side-armed and knocked Ted's head rolling across the lawn.

I sprang upright in this bed that wasn't mine drenched in sweat that was.

Thursday, Seychelle showed up unannounced.

She was with the same pair of guards and played her part in front of the Greers. "You want to walk and talk about the school year?"

I'd planned to warn her of Barnabus's intentions. But Farah was a constant presence in my head and I had to consider if—maybe—Barnabus's plan had some merit. Again with the ifs.

What if he could end this?

I said, "Let's walk."

At the lake, with her guards seated on the bench, Seychelle said, "Hey, why'd you call me down here?"

Before Ted's party, this would've been easy. I would've said, "People are coming for you, Chelle. You have to be careful."

I remained quiet.

She pressed, "It wasn't easy for me to make this happen. What's wrong?"

We didn't necessarily have to do it Barnabus's way where her . . . *assistance* was a surprise, something that required comforting from me. Seychelle was an ally and smart, and maybe I could tell her straight up why she was needed and she'd probably help on her own. Get her mother to turn over whatever codes or access Barnabus needed because it would be better for everyone.

"Jay!"

I said, "What if the plane had taken off? Like, say we'd gotten in the air, all the way to Cleveland. Before everything changed. You ever think about that?"

I anticipated confusion. Questions.

She said, "All the time. I think about that. I think about Connie."

We stared over the lake. The last time turtles lumbered across the silty shore. Where were they? I wondered. Were they okay?

Chelle said, "Have you ever heard of a country called Qatar?"

"No."

"It's part of the Arabian Peninsula and hasn't suffered much from the creeping oceans. My mom took me there once when I was little. It was gorgeous. Some people say it's one of the safest countries on Earth."

I was careful going forward, afraid to hope. "What are you getting at?"

"I don't believe in the apocalypse, Jay. Not from God, not from men. Maybe there are *little* apocalypses every day. Like the world ends when you lose a parent, or a friend, but then it starts right back up the moment after because people go on.

"The plane is still in the hangar. Captain Lucio works in the power plant. I've checked on him. He's still polite to me, even though I scare him now."

My pulse quickened.

"If," she said carefully, quietly, "*if* leaving here, for good, were an option, would you?"

I began to state the obvious; she cut me off—

"Your parents too. Zeke and his dad. If."

She hadn't mentioned her mother or grandfather. I didn't dwell on it. "Is the place you're talking about an option?"

"I'm not sure what's happening beyond the wall. Everything I've heard and seen suggests it's bad out there. But, Jay, we're not good in here either."

No. Karloff Country, and the majority of the Karloffs, weren't good. She was the exception to that rule, and I couldn't give her up to Barnabus. Maybe that was selfish. I wanted to be selfish for her.

"Chelle, people are plotting against you. Zeke's got a working phone, and he's been getting texts from a rebel leader."

She leaned in, terrified, her concern for Zeke making her overlook the first part. "Zeke's phone works? They'll kill him if they find out. Maybe his dad too."

"He knows, but this goes deeper. Panopticon, that site with the wild conspiracy theories about your family, that's really—"

The air parted, a sharp whistling keen created by something crossing the lake. One of Chelle's guards gasped, a half yell. We turned to see the man closing the gap between us and him, reacting to some unseen threat. And then a chunk of his head was missing above his left eye socket. He toppled facedown on the lakeshore, giving us a view of his slick pink brain matter.

His partner didn't react for what felt like a year. When he did, he made the mistake of reaching for his radio instead seeking cover. There was another parting of the air, and a blood-mist halo crowned the second guard as he collapsed dead too.

"Chelle, come on!" I gripped her hand and ran in the only direction I could think to go. Back to the Greers'.

On the street, we sprinted between mansions. The Greer house was halfway up the block, but beyond, at the cross street, rugged safari-styled vehicles from the Karloff Wilds park rounded the corner. Big tires and camouflage with burly armed men in bandana masks hanging off the sides. This wasn't random, and I knew who these men likely wanted. I dragged Chelle up the porch steps while attempting to calculate how many seconds we had before they came for her.

Bursting through the Greers' front door, I found Clinton awkwardly wielding a knife with one hand while pressing his phone to his ear with the other. "Pick up! Pick up!"

Bette stood on the stairs, a fist pressed into her sternum, crying until she saw me. "CJ!"

She rushed to me and knocked Chelle's hand from mine. Then she grabbed my wrist, leading me deeper in the house.

Chelle trailed, raising her own phone to her ear, and in the moment she looked more like the cruelest Trustees than my friend.

Her voice quaked. "No signal."

"This is it," Bette said. "We knew this day might come."

We stopped in her study, where she opened a center desk drawer and removed a polished wood box. I expected her to produce some sort of weapon, but when she opened the clasp, the only thing inside were Karloff candies. Two pieces.

They had the same red-purple-green-and-yellow wrappers we'd seen the Trustee kids use poolside the night Zeke and I snuck onto the Karloff Manor. The performance enhancers. Karloff's Special Reserves.

Bette unwrapped one piece and crammed it into her mouth, then did the same for the second, puffing out her cheeks like a chipmunk with a sweet tooth. Gold-flecked chocolate spittle wet her lips.

"Oh no," Chelle said, putting a few extra steps between her and Bette while beckoning me to do the same.

There was a *crash-boom* that had to be the front door being knocked near off the hinges. Heavy footfalls shook the house.

Clinton rounded the corner in the study, going for the desk as Bette had, but stopped short when he spotted two discarded candy wrappers. His fury was instant, aimed at Bette. "You took mine?"

Whatever processes those candies sparked in the body burned hot in Bette. She doubled over, clutching her stomach and biting back a scream.

Three men with guns and cattle prods spilled inside. One yelled over his shoulder, "Here!"

Clinton, braver than I expected, charged the closest trespasser with his knife. His slicing attack was easily deflected, though, and a cattle prod to the jaw left him a convulsing heap on the floor.

I nudged Chelle behind me, backed us both into a corner.

The man who'd subdued Clint eyed me and shook his head, disgusted. He started toward us unconcerned, his cattle prod limp at his side because what kind of threat was I really?

I'd forgotten about Bette, who'd gone quiet and looked small in her pill bug pose on the floor.

As the man skirted by her, she grabbed his leg with animal speed and drove a fist into his lower abdomen. The air gusted out of him, but even then, Bette was moving, shoving the man backward, using him as a battering ram she slammed into his companions. The whole time she roared like a lioness. Or maybe she was laughing. In this context, neither was less terrifying.

Off balance, unprepared bodies tangled on the floor. Mr. Cattle Prod tried kicking Bette off, but she used the grip she had on his leg for better purchase to climb the length of his body like a ladder, then bash his head into the doorframe. There was a wet crack, and the man went limp, blood pooling under his broken skull.

His dead weight kept the second intruder pinned, and the third, armed with a short-barreled rifle, hesitated squeezing the trigger, perhaps fearing he'd hit his friends. It was a mistake.

Bette ripped the gun from his hands and turned it on him. The gun barked twice, and that man was writhing on the floor with holes in his gut. Bette then turned the rifle on the one pinned beneath Mr. Cattle Prod and ended him.

The speed and brutality of it was insane. Sure, those candies were fuel, but what of the engine? Bette stood over the men she killed, her chest heaving, and radiated pure joy. Bette's gaze panned to Chelle and me, her eyes bulging yellow, and my bladder nearly released. Chelle dug her nails into my side, shaking behind me.

Bette said, "CJ, come to your mother. Right now."

Another gunshot then, and the contents of Bette's skull were jettisoned through a new hole on the side of her head. The force of the bullet toppled her sideways, making her the newest lifeless mound on the floor. Her murderer entered the room and greeted me warmly.

"Jay," Barnabus said, wispy smoke trailing from the pistol in his hand. "Thank goodness we got to you in time!"

New lackeys followed him in, coming for Chelle, reaching around me and grabbing her by the wrists. I attempted to pry one of them off her while she bucked and screamed, "Let me go!"

They were grown men, strong and practiced in controlling the unruly. I was brushed aside easily, and plastic zip ties secured Chelle's hands behind her back.

They dragged her away despite her struggles. My intervention interrupted by Barnabus extending his hand to shake. "Thank you, Jay. We couldn't have have drawn her away from the estate without you."

Chelle stopped fighting then. My implied betrayal defeating her in a way her captors couldn't.

"No," I said, a useless word. It didn't stop them from taking her, and it didn't expose Barnabus's lie. Chelle was gone, thinking I'd sold her out.

"No," I said again, weaker than before. Because the more I thought about it, I wasn't entirely sure she'd been wrong.

CHAPTER 38

Barnabus lowered his hand, unconcerned with my rudeness. Maybe he'd never been concerned with the handshake and only wanted to twist the knife for Chelle. And me.

He turned his attention to his closest subordinate. "How are we looking with the other Trustees in the neighborhood?"

"Good reports from the other teams. Only a few losses."

The muffled gunfire and screams in the distance barely registered for me. I grabbed his arm. "Where are you taking her?"

He flashed his thousand-watt smile. "She won't be harmed. We're going to sit her down, reason with her. That's all."

More gunfire outside. Closer this time.

"Let me go with her, then! That's what you wanted me for. Make her feel comfortable. That's what you said."

"You're trying my patience." His smile slipped away like a thing he'd gotten tired of holding. "We'll discuss later."

He started to walk away, but my rage about Chelle overrode my common sense, and I shouldered past his guards to shove him. "Keep your word!"

He lost his balance, and his knee slammed into the hardwood floor, eliciting a yelp. The pure violence radiating off him, the way he sneered like a mad dog, I understood that I was meeting the true Barnabus for the first time.

Gathering himself, not bothering to fake camaraderie anymore, he said, "Fine. You want to go where she's going?" He turned to someone behind me. "Grant his wish."

The butt of a rifle turned my day into a long, dark night.

With consciousness came a retching gag, me reeling from the blow I'd taken while recognizing the foul air I was breathing. My time in janitorial had me sorting smells. Mold, body odor, human waste. Someone nudged my shoulder.

"Wake up," my companion in the dark said. "I need to see how messed up you are."

Initial assessment: *very*. The cot beneath me did a turntable spin, and hot iron shards stabbed me in the face.

"Your jaw is swollen, but I don't think it's broken. If milkshakes are ever a thing again, we will partake."

Through the pain, I forced my eyes open. "Connie?"

She leaned fully into the light. Here. Alive.

"Hi, Jay. You survived. I hope you don't come to regret it, but my hopes aren't high."

EXCUSE OUR MESS WHILE
WE ENHANCE YOUR
EXPERIENCE

KARLOFF COUNTRY: A STOP ON THE FOOD CHAIN

by Heather Beachum

One thing Shenandoah Valley residents can't get enough of is fun facts about the resort wonders just a ways up the mountain. We tend to think of Karloff Country as simply a vacation destination, but Chief Operations Officer Ben Barnabus dispels the notion. "We're really a city, with all the things a city needs. Power plant. Wastewater treatment. Full-time residents. We're so much more than what you see on the surface. I promise, the more people learn about the amenities and efficiency of our little corner on the mountain, the more they're going to want to be a part of it. Particularly when it comes to the way we feed our guests."

Aside from the utilities and staff Barnabus describes, there's a unique aspect to his facility that not even competitors like the Disney Parks, Universal Studios, Busch Gardens, or Six Flags can boast: a farm-to-table food production system that provides over 60 percent of Karloff Country's edible goods.

"Of course we still have contracts with outside food suppliers and international brands to make sure guests can have a Coca-Cola or their favorite Cra-burger from Monte FISHtos," said Barnabus. "But our goal is to be superior global citizens, so we limit the carbon footprint associated with such shipping and receiving. That's where our Vertical Farms towers come in."

The towers he speaks of are modern marvels. The stout buildings, each standing about five stories, feature sleek exteriors and top secret interiors. "I can't provide details about the proprietary systems in the towers," Barnabus says, "but I can tell you there's a balance between workers and automated systems that ensures a safe environment."

Asked about rumors of inhumane conditions in the livestock towers, Barnabus says, "No one's complained about the freshness of our on-property meats and produce. Our most popular restaurants are stocked exclusively from our Vertical Farms, and the test kitchens within each VF tower are constantly innovating recipes, so you know when you're eating at Karloff Country, you're eating its best."

SEYCHELLE

There's a thing I've learned about mortal fear.

It levels off when the danger stretches. There's only so much adrenaline to spike, and if I was being honest, being in a transport, bound by these people my family recruited for our heinous social experiment, was something of a relief. I'd had the sick sense, for a long time, that this was exactly what I had coming. Now the wait was over.

There were still guards at the estate. Maybe they'd remain loyal. But Barnabus, who I never liked—there was always something slithery underneath the smile, the pressed shirts, and the practiced charm—was still an excellent negotiator. He knew how to talk to people. And it didn't take much when they wanted what you had. Grandfather had a saying: *It's not difficult selling sugar to a candy shop.*

My captor's convoy approached the gate at my home leisurely, like an invited guest. Barnabus rolled down his window and addressed the guard on duty.

"Listen," he said, "we've got Seychelle Karloff. There's a gun at her head, and one of my people is pressing his resident band to her throat—so no one should trigger that. Tell Blythe she doesn't have the capability to incapacitate us all, and if even one of us goes down, the girl's going to die. Tell her all of that, then feel free to join us. We're taking our home back."

The guard I knew. Gabriela. She worked security and Grandfather's parties and was a fan of old-school hip-hop. She'd turned me onto a group called Souls of Mischief before my family initiated society's collapse. Since, she'd been pleasant. Still waved and asked me how my day was, and I waved back knowing she was terrified of displeasing me, or rather what consequences displeasing me would have for her and her family. She peeked into the car, confirmed I was a trigger's pull away from death, and gave a tight nod. "Be right back," she said.

How would her message be received? Would Grandfather be lucid enough to understand the stakes? If he was, would he care? And Mom, always vocal about getting away. What an opportunity to be rid of the baggage that had *slightly altered* her privileged life.

My family might not bargain for my safety. My grandfather's voice boomed in my head. *Karloff Country does not negotiate with terrorists!*

Most of me, I think, was okay with that possibility. Being afraid was exhausting. No roller coaster should last five months, and Barnabus could issue a command that simply let me off this ride. So to speak.

Gabriela returned with a verdict. It surprised me too.

Soon enough, we were in the study. Me. Mom. Grandfather. Surrounded by our entire estate guard detail, who'd all joined Team Barnabus.

Mom kept her neck stiff and frowned pointedly, the face she put on when we got unacceptable service at a supposedly quality restaurant. "Not a loyal soul among you! We've only ever treated you well here at the estate."

Grandfather stared beyond the walls of our home. Today wasn't one of his good days, then. How bad was that going to make this day for Mom and me?

We occupied three chairs in the center of the room, while Barnabus took Grandfather's big leather beast of a throne, facing us from across the desk. A silver pistol lay next to Mom's laptop.

"Franklin," Barnabus said, sounding tired, "it's been too long."

Grandfather remained quiet.

Barnabus smirked like he was impressed. "You're ice cold, old man. Don't think you can bluff this out like you're swinging those big brass ones around some boardroom. Not this time. Should've kept your promises. Then maybe I wouldn't have come knocking at your door. Maybe—"

Grandpa groaned. A string of drool fell off his bottom lip, bouncing like a bungee jumper before finally breaking and soaking into his lapel.

Barnabus's grin fell away. This wasn't part of any scenario he'd rehearsed. "Franklin. Hey."

"Dad," Grandfather said, mistaking Barnabus for my dead-for-decades great-grandfather, "I want to sit in the big chair one day. I can help."

Barnabus aimed his gun at Mom. I thought I'd gotten over the mortal fear that sank your stomach like you fell off a building. No. It returned with force as I imagined my mother dying before my eyes.

"Blythe, what's wrong with him?"

Mom sneered. "You can't see it for yourself, Mr. I-Got-My-MBA-from-Wharton?"

Barnabus turned the gun on Grandfather. "Franklin, do you see what's in my hand? Do you understand what I can do to you right now?"

Without giving Grandfather a chance to answer, Barnabus aimed the pistol skyward and fired a round into the ceiling. The report echoed, startling me, Mom, and Barnabus's own converts. For Grandfather, it reduced him to tears, followed by the acidic scent of urine wafting through the room.

Barnabus became pure rage. "That's why it's all been going through you. How long has he been like this?" The man's rage shifted to something else. Panic? Fear? "It was *his* plan, Blythe! Start to finish. The world burning is his vision, he's not holding the flamethrower? Do the other Trustees know what you're doing?"

"No," Mom said, watching the barrel of his gun like a field mouse watched a hawk.

"Do *you* know what you're doing?"

Barnabus left the big chair—with the pistol—and went to Grandfather. He crouched so they were eye-to-eye, and he inspected Grandfather's face like something he might have to repair but wasn't sure how. "It's a good thing I'm here now. Blythe?"

"What?"

Barnabus stood to his full height, raised the arm with his resident band. "I'm assuming he never told you that this band wasn't meant for me."

Some of his backup stirred irritably.

Barnabus rephrased. "*Us.* The inner circle. We aren't servants bringing food and drink to his investors. We never should've been treated as such. It was supposed to be for show until the plan was initiated."

The corners of Mom's mouth curled up. Her true happy face. "You assumed he meant that. You claim you're no servant because you didn't bring his drinks. Did you ever refuse him anything else? You didn't bring him drinks because by the time he needed you he wasn't thirsty. That band is the only thing he ever meant for you to have. Now get on with whatever you came to do."

The air sizzled. Barnabus said, "Can the old man provide *any*

304

insight into the plan? Next steps? Codes and access to whatever systems around the property are still functioning?"

"He's not been able to participate for a long time."

"Okay." Barnabus nodded. "Okay."

He fired three rounds into Grandfather's spasming chest, then kicked him, tipping his chair backward, sending his already-dead body sprawling.

Barnabus stood over him, emptying the gun's magazine. He still jerked at the trigger after the slide locked on the empty weapon.

Mom screamed. As did I. Franklin Karloff showed almost total disdain for me, never expressed any pride in my accomplishments, and resented things that brought me joy. Yet, he was a part of me. I wouldn't exist without him. The sorrow of seeing him cast from this world so brutally, while knowing he wholly deserved such a fate, created an unwinnable tug-of-war between my heart and mind.

He was my grandfather and a monster. To grieve him made me . . . *what?*

It might not be a question I'd have to ponder for long.

Barnabus ordered one of his minions to hand over their—presumably loaded—gun. Rearmed, he abandoned the banter with Mom. "Give me your access. I want in on every system, every note, every crumb you use to keep the resort going. If you don't, I'm shooting your daughter in the face. You know I will. Cooperate, and I'll simply place her in the Karloff Wilds with the rest. That's a fair deal, Blythe."

I flinched away from the rifle barrel he leveled at my face.

Mom tracked the blood pool spreading from beneath Grandfather. She sputtered tears and snot. I don't know if she even heard Barnabus's demand. I wondered if his demands were officially the last thing I'd ever hear. Other than the bang.

"Blythe!" Barnabus shouted.

I said, "It's our birthdays. Mine"—I motioned to Mom—"and hers. Probably. She's not very creative with her passwords. That should open up everything."

Mom didn't object to me giving up the big secret. We weren't built for torture, and there was no other play here. Barnabus abandoned her and poked me in the sternum with the rifle barrel. "Unlock the laptop."

Crossing the room to Grandfather's desk, certain I was safe for a few seconds at least, I sat in his big chair for the first time in my life. I keyed Mom's usual password in and got the usual results. "Laptop's unlocked. Should I try the other systems?"

Barnabus leaned in, confirming the desktop was accessible. "Yes, unlock everything and save your mother's life."

Having reversed the polarity of his threat, he aimed at Mom, who still blubbered but was slowly pulling herself together. I typed quickly, unsure how long this man's patience would hold. I'd seen him kill two people today. What was two more?

Minutes later—after I deleted the texts I sent while he wasn't looking and closed the messaging app he could never know I opened—I said, "Done."

Barnabus checked the screen, doing a quick count of all the open apps. "I want you to walk me through how it all works. Power. Security. Any intel from outside the walls."

"I—I can't."

"We're playing games now?"

"I never had anything to do with that part. You think Grandfather would've shared any of this with *me*?"

I pointed at my arm, my *slightly* brown hue. Barnabus huffed, probably understanding the depth of my grandfather's racism better than most.

Mom, her voice so raw, said, "I can do that part. Can we take my dad outside and, maybe, bury him properly?"

"No," Barnabus said. "We can sit down and go over everything I want while my people keep your daughter safe. Only after I'm satisfied will we consider any other options." He motioned to no one in particular. "Somebody take the girl away and keep an eye on her."

Gabriela, the former gate guard, volunteered. "I got her."

I hid the relief I felt that it was a woman, and one who'd been nice to me in the past. I didn't blame her for siding with Barnabus in these extreme circumstances.

Ushered from my mother and the room, I was obedient. No tricks, no mad dashes through the house I knew intimately and that Gabriela had never entered. We were past that. I'd made my one and only move while sitting at that laptop. Either it worked or Barnabus had won.

However things went from here on, I hoped Gabriela knew the worst of this wasn't my doing and I never meant her any harm.

"Is there a room I should take you to?" she asked.

"Down this corridor and to the right is"—almost said *my wing* but sensed it wasn't the right time to claim such ownership—"somewhere to sit."

I sank into my couch. Gabriela remained standing, taking in the vastness of the space. It only ever felt huge to me when I noted someone else's reaction. The way her breathing changed—uneven and rushed—clued me that I maybe should've led us to a guest suite.

"Gabriela," I said, "I want you to know if any of this were up to me—"

I didn't even see the punch. A white starburst exploded across my vision. When I could see again, I was on the floor, Gabriela straddling me while cradling the hand she'd struck me with. She'd likely sprained her wrist, maybe broken something. She was more careful with her other hand when she started in on me, unconcerned with any possible explanations or apologies I might conjure.

Couldn't blame her for that either.

CHAPTER 39

Hearing Connie's voice was the best thing that had happened to me in months, but my body didn't remember how to celebrate. I vomited on the floor.

The sharp twang of my own stomach acid was an improvement over the thick musk here, wherever *here* was. I prayed I'd get used to the smell while dreading I'd be here long enough for that to happen.

"Easy, Jay." Connie steadied me with a hand on my lower back. "You might have a concussion."

"Where?" I managed.

"In your head." Connie flashed that rueful smile I'd never expected to see again, but her mood shifted suddenly, her words dripping with contempt. "Seriously, welcome to Zeke's secret jail for shoplifters. Though I can't imagine he'd thought of something this grand."

We were in a small cell, with a solid wall behind me, and two more on either side. The front was clear glass with an open door. Beyond it a narrow walkway and a safety rail, and beyond *that*, across a ten-foot gap of empty air, was curved mirrored glass set in an ominous column reflecting warped versions of me and Connie.

"The cells rim that column, a full three-sixty. We never know when someone's on the other side of the mirror. So it feels like someone's always there. Watching."

With my head pounding, I trudged onto the walkway for a better look at the setup. Leaning on the safety rail, I peered down, then craned my neck up. We were on the second of four levels. The floor below seemed to act as some sort of common area where other captives shambled about like spirits visible through the thin veil between life and death. The lights were low, creating an unnecessary gloom where the only brightness was the charging resident bands on everyone's wrists.

So many questions. I might've deduced answers on my own if my *head stopped pounding*. Still, I managed to voice a couple.

"What is this, Connie?"

A humorless laugh from her. "A prison. Specifically, a panopticon. Figures."

"Is this where you've been all along?"

"No. At first, I was with my mom. Then they separated us. I don't know how long that's been. Time's funny here."

My eyes adjusted to the gloom, allowing me a better look at her. It took effort not to flinch away.

The skin across her forehead, cheeks, and chin was dry and peeling. Her eye sockets were sunken. Her lips cracked. If ghost stories were true, I might've believed she was visiting me like Scrooge's old business partner in *A Christmas Carol*.

This was real life. People did this to her. Not spirits punishing her for past sins. People.

"Tell me what happened." I nearly added *to you* but backed off, afraid I'd offend her.

"The last night I saw you, my dad burst in panicking," Connie recapped part of the story I already knew. "He'd come from Karloff Manor and asked Zeke to leave."

I'd never forgotten Zeke's recollection of the night. I wished he could hear what happened after he left Connie. I wished Chelle was here too. That wish stabbed my gut with such regret I was forced to return to my cot or wretch again. Closing my eyes, I focused on Connie's voice and nothing else. She told me all I'd missed.

CONNIE

Daddy, still in his white, stained chef's coat, peeked through the curtains, making sure Zeke was gone. "Pack a bag. Only what you need."

"What?" I said, obviously mishearing him. In case I didn't, "Why?"

"Go!"

Daddy never yelled at me. Never yelled at Mama. When he was mad, he got extra quiet and spoke through clenched teeth. He grew up in a house of yellers, where everything began at top volume and strained to go higher. He told me once he didn't know if he *could* raise his voice because of how much he detested his upbringing. "The day you were born," he once said, "when I first saw you, I told myself for me to yell at my beautiful baby girl, the whole world would have to be on fire."

Him screaming, "Now, Constance!" had me peering through the window for infernos.

In my room, I spun in a slow circle, gauging what was valuable enough to fit in one bag. Any trip needed underwear, so I shoved a bunch in a bag. Some T-shirts. My favorite jeans. What else? The things I considered most precious—photos, music—were in my phone. There was a jewelry box on my dresser that I raided. Next to it my Sandrina pyramid chirped on for no reason at all. Its tip glowed purple, listening mode. She was buggy like that sometimes.

The security chimes of the front door opening sounded, and Dad was yelling again, at Mama this time. "Pack one bag" and "only necessities." His voice cracked, shifting to a more recognizable tone seasoned with desperation. "Please do as I say. I'll explain on the road."

Dad talked the entire way toward the Karloff Country gates. "It was dinner for the Karloffs. Same as I'd done a dozen times before. Five courses. Grandeur from the titanium plates to the linen napkins. That's how they do. I didn't even think much about the emphasis on recipes featuring sweetbreads. Maybe some guest requested it. I didn't know. The rich want what they want."

Mama, who wasn't into cooking and swore she didn't marry my dad because he could boil water without having to notify the fire department, interrupted him. "They wanted *desserts* for dinner?"

It was a common mistake. I helped Dad by explaining for him. "Sweetbreads aren't sweets or bread. It's a culinary term for certain parts of the animals you don't usually eat."

Mama looked to Dad, needing more. He clarified. "The throat. The heart. The pancreas. Prepared by an expert, they could be the best thing you've ever had in your life. You'd never know what you were eating. That's what I was asked to do. Make those unusual cuts delicious. I succeeded spectacularly."

We broke from the residential streets onto the wider roads leading to the Karloff Country exit. A few miles to go before we reached the wall.

"I was asked to hang around, as there was future business to discuss. I thought it was about our restaurant. I'd made some expansion requests and hoped my stellar meal might've greased the money wheels with Mr. Karloff. What the rich folks wanted discussed was more recipes. *More sweetbreads.* They asked if I could provide as many as fifty different custom options for every organ.

"They offered a financial bonus and an opportunity to upgrade our home by moving into a new development with mansions on a lake if I could create what they wanted. And soon. They told me we'd be right at home with our new neighbors because they'd be the most talented people in the world."

As usual on a summer night, when the adult venues opened, traffic closest to Downtown Karloff slowed and thickened. Daddy decreased our speed by half, then we were creeping along. It'd be a short delay, only a couple of minutes, but he checked his mirrors like he expected something to leap from them.

"It sounded like a fantastic way to move up. Easy, even. Sweetbreads are considered delicacies across the world, and rich clients wanting unusual food was nothing new. Then someone asked if it mattered what the source of the sweetbreads was. Would it spoil the taste? A good question. I explained environmental factors could certainly alter the taste of any butchered animal. But if we sourced meat from animals in the Vertical Farms livestock tower, for example, taste profiles would remain consistent. That's when someone asked"—Daddy shuddered so violently, he nearly swerved from our lane—"someone asked, 'What if they smoke?'"

Oh God.

OhGodOhGodOhGod.

The car in front of us veered right, clearing the lane ahead, and Daddy stomped the gas. "I didn't get the joke. Because it wasn't a joke. Though people in the room fake laughed and shot dirty looks to the man who said it. I forced an amused smile and said I appreciated the opportunity and that after I cleaned the kitchen I'd be on my way. I immediately sent my sous chef and the rest of the crew home even though cleaning was a team job. I wanted to examine everything.

Particularly the vats my ingredients came in. Because they'd been provided *by Karloff Manor*. Do you understand?"

I don't know if Mama got it, but I did. The sweetbreads Dad cooked were there when he got there. He didn't think to ask where they'd come from.

"I couldn't tell anything from what was left over. I'm a great chef, not a great detective. I had prepared throat, and pancreas, and heart, and never once thought if the animal those pieces had come from might've been a smoker, or a jogger, or great at knitting." Dad cried, "Never once considered it might be a—a—a *person*.

"I don't *know* for sure. Does that make it okay? Will God forgive me if I cooked a man, or a woman, or a ch-ch . . . if I fed monsters what they wanted without knowing?"

We were maybe a mile from the Karloff Country gates. This late, and this far beyond the guest attractions, the road was empty, except for one black SUV on the shoulder. As we passed it, someone stuck their hand from the back window, pointing their phone at us like they were taking our picture.

Dad's resident band flared a cycling red I'd never seen before.

Then he convulsed like he'd touched a live wire.

He twisted the wheel wrong, and before Mama and I could scream, we went off the road directly into a tree.

I hit my head bad, and everything got swimmy. I tracked the SUV coming closer in a series of stuttering snapshots while I blinked in and out of consciousness. Men got out. One went to driver's seat, where Daddy was so, so still. His airbag sagged beneath him, the nylon wet with blood. The man with the phone lifted Dad's head and said, "All you had to do was cook the food."

Barnabus.

Then he pointed his phone at me, while another man pointed a phone at Mom, and he said, "I only wanted to make it nice for whatever time you had left."

Mine and Mama's resident bands flashed red, then pain, then nothing for a while.

But more pain was coming.

CHAPTER 40

Finally learning Connie's truth wasn't the aha moment I'd imagined months ago. The person behind it wasn't even a surprise; Barnabus betrayed me too. The reason her family was torn apart though . . . I nearly vomited again.

She said, "My dad died in front of me. I see it every time I go to sleep."

I knew something about seeing the dead in the dreams.

"I try not to feel sorry for myself," Connie said, in Connie fashion. "Everyone here's got a story like mine. Not the creative-ways-to-cook-humans part, but close enough."

I said, "This is Barnabus's doing, not the Trustees, right? Do you know anything about the endgame here?"

She shook her head. "My biggest fear is there is no plan. Like one day they'll forget about us. Stop feeding us. And a thousand years from now some archaeologist is gonna find the Karloff mummies."

Judging from the haggard condition of Connie and every other kid I saw, we were halfway there.

Connie familiarized me with our new accommodations. There were shower stalls on level one that might as well have been toilets for how clean they were. With little soap, and no such pleasantries like deodorant, mouthwash, or toothpaste, venturing under the lukewarm spray was more symbolic than effective. None of us were clean anymore.

There were children as young as five, all grouped together like ducklings following a freshman girl I recognized from the Academy like she was their nanny. She seemed happy caring for them, and it was the only bit of relief I felt here—that they had each other. The oldest among us was a classmate named Morgan who'd graduated and was supposed to be going to some college out west. Connie said when she first got here she'd tried to organize an escape. "That's why she's limping now."

Guards delivered barely meals on level one twice a day. Usually sautéed vegetables and soup. I'd noted early on the guards were the only adults, and Connie explained that too.

"My mom and I were the first captives, I think. We looked for cracks in the system. Ways to maybe break out. They caught on and separated us, brought me to this facility. Basically, they use our families as leverage. If I'm disobedient, Mom will suffer. And vice versa. The guards told Morgan as bad as her beating was, her parents would get worse. Nobody really tries anything anymore."

I said, "They brought me in from a Trustee's house. My parents would've been at their jobs."

Connie didn't respond.

"You don't think Barnabus would've grabbed them, do you?"

Her pointed stare shut me up. "We're the same here, Jay. The quicker you get used to that, the safer your parents will be."

She didn't have to tell me twice. I adjusted fast, like I always did. Go Along to Get Along Jay.

I never felt more ashamed about it.

ZEKE

"This is very stupid, Zeke."

If Connie were still around, she'd have said it. Jay would've cosigned *after* she said it. Chelle would've offered some safer, smarter alternative. Or roasted me. Probably roasted me. I heard them bickering in my head as clear as the birds singing in the night. They *weren't* around anymore, and the way things were going, I probably wouldn't be either. No way was I sitting by until someone showed up to snatch me.

So, I was going to do the stupid thing and wait here. At night, at the long-abandoned Grand Virginian hotel. In the open. Drone bait. As I'd been told.

It'd been two days since word landed that the Trustee neighborhood got raided. Two days since guys I recognized from that diner meeting with Barnabus dragged Jay's dad from his house in his bathrobe kicking and screaming. Two days since a mysterious text that wasn't Panopticon appeared on my phone.

Unknown Number
barnabus has the missing beneath the karloff wilds

Unknown Number
save them

Unknown Number
but not alone

That *not alone* part was going to be difficult. I was out of friends.

Panopticon/Barnabus ghosted me. He wasn't answering any of my texts. The kids I used to run with, before Splash Zone put the fear of God in most folks, were treating me like a vampire asking for an invite to their house. Dad wasn't acting like my dad anymore. When they took Mr. Butler away, he'd watched through bent blinds, saying, "I knew it. I knew that family was suspect."

"How'd you know?" I asked, trying not to notice how much he sounded like me talking to Jay.

His response: "You could just tell."

I almost reminded him that Mr. Butler was his friend but wasn't a big enough hypocrite to go there.

So . . . my stupidity. After sitting on texts I couldn't ignore for hours, I started looking for the help I'd need. I started asking about the convoy rebels. The ones who broke hands.

Convincing myself I was doing it on the low, I started with a mousy lady in the Enchantria engineering workshop. Like, "Do you know someone who might know someone?"

She skittered away making the sign of the cross.

I tried a couple of others. Someone in food service. A retail worker I'd seen at Jay's mom's book club. The short guy who wore the Becky Bullfrog costume in FuturaScape. I knew the risks and knew I couldn't stop. It didn't take long.

After the next day's shift, I found a note in my locker. My *locked* locker. *Grand Virginian. 9 p.m. Destroy this paper.*

It was cold at 9:17 p.m. in the deep shadows a ways from the drop-off loop, my puffing breaths like little ghosts running away. I was about to give up when I heard a couple of approaching engines. Headlights cruised closer, but the make and model of the vehicles were masked by gloom. More important, I couldn't see who drove them.

The light cut the night close to me but didn't give me away. I thought.

Bushes to my left rustled, and my attacker pounced. The cars were the distractions they'd intended. They were dressed in dark gray that blended better with the night than straight-up black. Rough hands wrenched my arm behind me, then yanked it up, nearly dislocating everything from the shoulder down. I screamed, and that seemed to summon a second, smaller attacker wielding a syringe.

"No, no, don't!" I managed.

A thin silver stream arched from the needle's tip before it stabbed me beneath the jaw. The liquid injected into me burned for a single hot second, then I—

"Wake up," someone said. "Tell us why you're asking for the 'convoy rebels who broke hands.'"

My eyelids were too heavy. The room spun.

"Open your eyes or I'll find a different way to let you know you found them."

"Where—" I said. My mouth tasted like a sock.

"Okay." The voice addressed someone else. "Splay his fingers and give me the hammer."

That someone yanked my arm until my palm was laid flat on a cold surface.

"Finger by finger, until you wake up."

A low, screaming voice in the back of my head warned me to get it together. Fight the drug. My eyelids fluttered, blinking against a blazing light. "Need . . . help."

"Help with what?" A different voice. A woman.

"The missing. I know where they are. We need to save them."

More nothing. At least nothing involving me. My eyelids fluttered open for a few seconds, and I saw my captors speaking in hushed voices. Two of them, a man and woman judging by their heights and shapes. We were in a sea-green room with bright fluorescents overhead and near-empty aluminum shelves surrounding us. Not great clues, but the smell—stinging antiseptics—told me this was the medical center. I tried to stand, but my legs were bound to the chair. My left arm, the one they'd threatened to bust up with a hammer, was my only free limb. Panic had me swiping that through the air like I'd somehow escape one-handed. "I can't be here. Please let me go."

The masked couple turned their attention back to me. The man held my muting fob at eye level. "Where did you get this?"

"Mr. Barnabus. It blocks Sandrina from listening to conversations. Turn it on and it's safe to talk. If you untie me, I'll show you how it works."

He faced his partner. She nodded, and he shook his head in disagreement over something I didn't understand. She overrode his objection and got closer to me. "You said you know where the missing are. Tell us."

"Karloff Wilds," I said, sniveling.

"*How'd* you get this information?"

I told everything. What was the point of secrets now? Told more than I had to. The man, abandoning his tough-guy interrogation voice, stopped me once to say, "We don't need to know what kinds of milkshakes your friends like, kid."

So I skipped that part.

Throughout my recap of Connie going missing, Chelle partying with Trustee kids, Jay being a lesser friend over the last few months, and how that was partially my fault because I'd been shutting him out ever since he became a Concierge and I knew that was wrong now, the woman could barely sit still. She paced, fidgeted, and when I got to the part about Jay's dad being taken, she kicked a depleted shelf. That was the only time she interrupted me. She asked, "Did they get Tisha too?"

I told her I didn't know, and the man squeezed her knee.

The mysterious texts were how I concluded my tale. "If you have my phone, the messages are still there. I think the message came from Seychelle Karloff. I don't know how anyone else could've reached me."

The woman spoke again. "The Wilds was on our short list of possibilities."

The man said, "The kid's saying the intel probably came from a Karloff. Could be a trap."

"Except we were halfway to looking there ourselves. So is it a trap, or confirmation?"

They went back and forth, bickering like my mom and dad used to, and I couldn't help but interrupt because I caught a glint of purple from the corner of my eye. Somehow, I hadn't noticed it before and panicked. "Turn on my muting fob quick! It's not safe to talk freely with that Sandrina pyramid in here."

They did not share my panic. The man grabbed his hammer off the shelf, placed the fob on the table where I'd rested my free hand, then brought the tool down with force. I yelped, snatching my hand to my chest while my fob exploded in shards.

"What did you do that for?" I shouted.

"That fob's a lie," he said. "We've found a few of them in the homes of people who'd gone missing, and it doesn't mute anything. The opposite, in fact. You turn that fob on near a pyramid, and Sandrina flags your audio. The conversation you think you're hiding is suddenly a priority for whoever has access."

The woman chimed in. "Those pyramids are little more than speakers and microphones. The AI spine Sandrina is built on is a decade behind what folks were using out in the world before it all collapsed. Play a song? Sure. Control your lights? Maybe. Conduct automated surveillance? Naw."

"But"—I attempted to put it all together—"I got my fob from Mr. Barnabus. His whole thing was he wanted to get access to Sandrina from the Trustees. Why would he give me a fob that flagged conversations through Sandrina if he didn't have access yet?"

They let me sit with that for a minute.

I said, "Wait. If he already had access to Sandrina, what did he want from the Trustees?"

The man said, "That's an excellent question. I really want the opportunity to ask him myself. First things first, though."

He tugged his mask off, revealing his face. The woman did the same.

"Harry?" I said, then to her, "You're the nurse lady from Mrs. Butler's book club."

"DeeDee," she said.

Harry said, "Because things are moving faster than any of us like now, we're about to let you in on another secret. One that hopefully won't matter for long. Sal! Get in here!"

A door creaked open behind me. Twisting in my seat, I recognized another Enchantria Helper as he leaned over my bound arm, pointing something like a barcode reader gun from a supermarket at my resident band. A red light traced the band, making me nervous. When the band began flashing in an alarming pattern of rainbow colors, I got scared. "Hey! Hey!"

A soft click as my band loosened and the diodes inside deactivated.

Harry unfolded a pocketknife he'd pulled from a holster on his belt and cut the rope that tied me to the chair. I shook away the pins and needles, also my resident band. It slid right off, clattered on the floor.

"How?" I said.

"We've been searching for a way from the beginning," said Harry, "Tried a lot of desperate things that didn't work. Things changed last week with the Splash Zone workers."

It seemed a struggle to finish. DeeDee did it for him. "When they dumped the bodies in Downtown Karloff, they didn't take their resident bands. The security measures deactivate when there are no vitals detected. We were able to . . . acquire some bands to study up close, found a solution. We made their deaths mean something."

All their resident bands were gone; I hadn't noticed before. "When you attacked the Trustee convoy, why did you break their hands?"

"Because one of our people did it to themselves first trying to get their band off. When it didn't work, we thought nothing ever would. So we blew off steam. Tortured our torturers. We didn't think they'd kill people."

Sal, speaking up for the first time, said, "What they did was make martyrs. Power to the cause!"

"Power indeed," Harry said.

Then he told me their plans, and how my "intel" changed things.

I'd found the Helpers I was looking for.

325

CHAPTER 41

Connie had questions. The last she'd seen of the world above, Karloff Country had still been a resort, not a prison where the inmates wore shock shackles. At least we hadn't *known* that's what our home was.

I filled her in on as much as I could recall. Our search for her. The day we were going to fly to Cleveland when everything turned. The aftermath. Somehow I'd focused on my activities. Going from Enchantria Helper to Concierge. She cut me off with a question I didn't want to answer.

"What's up with Zeke and Chelle?"

"I . . . haven't seen much of them over the last few months."

Maybe she knew I was holding back and didn't want to talk about our friends. If so, she didn't call me out on it.

We didn't have much to talk about after that, though.

Two more days passed. I avoided bottomless despair by trying to determine *where* in Karloff Country our jail actually was. Not Enchantria. Unless there were other tunnels under the tunnels I knew. Not Karloff Pictures either. That park didn't have tunnels because the ground was too rocky. Still left a lot of possibilities.

There were absolutely no views of the outside world, so I examined every inch of my cell. Any walls I could touch. Tables, chairs. It took some nerve, but I even examined the central column, where guards may or may not be watching us from. There was only one discovery to be had. The name Greer pressed into a metal plate in the window frame holding the opaque glass in place.

Clint's company had been responsible for this prison.

I wasn't even shocked.

As for the other prisoners, the exact head count was fifty-two kids, who mostly spent days passing time on the first-level common area. Connie spent her time playing cards with the younger ones. I rotated between various board games, trying, unsuccessfully, for fulfillment through variety because a twentieth game of Scrabble in a single day was its own torment.

In the afternoon on that second day, a guard entered and announced, "Everybody to me. Welcome your new neighbors!"

The confusion in the lockup suggested this wasn't normal procedure. These would be the first new arrivals since I'd been here, so I was anxious for the change. We gathered in quiet anticipation. I thought this might be a communal experience, the people who'd been through this preparing to comfort the newbies.

The guards opened the main door with little concern—everyone was conditioned to stand far back, or have their loved ones suffer for their misstep—so the arrivals had a clear path in.

As each entered, the vibes of grim welcome wore off, replaced by angry chatter.

These were Trustee kids.

Each new inmate was the subject of curses, and in the case of Paige Radford, hocked phlegm spat at her feet. The group included every single one I'd seen partying it up on the Karloff Manor months back. The last to enter was their host, Chelle.

Her face was bruised and swollen. A ruby scab crusted her bottom lip. Still, her chin remained high while she stared straight ahead. She hadn't noticed Connie and me.

Another guard followed Chelle into the lockup carrying a cue stick. He cracked it sharply over his knee, splitting the varnished wood in two, then sent the pieces skittering across the concrete floor. "We thought about getting you guys a pool table but figured this would be as fun. Make the newbs feel at home."

The cackling guards sealed us in.

The welcome party began.

There was a moment of stillness among the twenty or so Trustee kids. The phantom sound of those broken sticks clattering across the floor echoed. Then, true to form, Paige Radford, who still looked pristine in teal leggings and a thin pink sweater, said, "Anyone lays a finger on us and my daddy's going to have you hanging from the Ferris Reel."

I don't know what she was thinking. Maybe she'd seen those prison movies that said you had to look tough going into lockup. Given more time, maybe her, or one of the other Trustee kids, would've picked a fight with the biggest among us because that was also prison-movie advice. This wasn't a prison movie.

Morgan limped forward, picked up one of the sticks, then shuffled to Paige while whipping the makeshift club at her head. There was a crack, like an eggshell on the side of a mixing bowl, and Paige collapsed in a pile, the fingers on her right hand spasming.

The other Trustee kids—except for Chelle—seemed horrified, though they didn't help the mean girl. Instead, some resorted to begging, while a few others rushed the gate, screaming for help that wasn't coming.

A big kid who played football at the Academy claimed the other half of the broken stick and chased a couple of Trustee runners. He wasn't alone.

More thuds, cracks, grunts, and screams. Some of it was shouts of joyous revenge. Some was Trustees being beaten within an inch of their lives. Maybe killed.

In the middle was Chelle. Angry inmates flowed around her like a river around a stone.

Connie and I made eye contact, and she whispered, "Get her."

I crossed the opened floor and grabbed Chelle's hand. When she recognized me, she ripped her hand away.

Connie was right behind me. "Chelle, we gotta go."

Seeing Connie, hearing her voice, had Chelle spilling instant tears. She threw her arms around Connie's neck, and Connie dragged her to the showers. It was so nasty there mostly everyone avoided this corner.

Connie directed her into a stall with a crusty floor and sludge on the walls. "We'll stay between you and them. We won't let them get to you."

"*You* won't," Chelle said.

She eyed me like we never knew each other. This wasn't the time for it, but I defended myself anyway. "I didn't set you up. They wanted me to. I was trying to warn you."

Chelle said, "Well, it didn't work."

More pained screams from the far side of the holding area. The pool cues rose and fell, both stained red. Morgan abandoned the Trustee she'd beaten to the ground and pointed her weapon our way. "Is Karloff over there?"

Morgan advanced on us with a small contingent in tow. Maybe eight kids in a bloodlust.

Morgan said, "You two traitors hiding her?"

I put myself between them and Connie while Connie covered Chelle. I couldn't stand by while one more bad thing happened to either of them. Did I owe them? I didn't know. But I loved them, and that was enough.

Dipping into some poor approximation of a fighting stance, I prepared for what came next. Hoped it would be quick.

Morgan raised her stick to strike . . .

The patter of nearby gunfire slowed the small riot. As it got louder, we all stopped moving.

The *rat-a-tat-tat* drew closer still. Necks craned, everyone reaching the same conclusion. There were no real hiding places on this level. The first to act was one of the young kids, sprinting for the stairs. Soon a stampede followed as others opted for the cells on a higher level. Those were all dead ends, but better than sitting still. For them anyway.

Connie held up a halting hand, signaling that we'd be better off hiding in our shower stall.

The gunfire slowed, then stopped. A guard approached the level-one gate in a hurry. A small masked crew trailed, poking him with rifle barrels. He was the same guard who'd provided the cue stick, worse for wear. Blood streamed from a gash at his hairline, and when he keyed open the lockup door, he stumbled across the threshold onto his hands and knees. "Please don't kill me. Please."

A rifle butt to the jaw knocked the guard out, and a mask yelled, "If there are any other guards here, it's best you come out with your hands up. You'll have options that way. We don't want to hurt you."

I recognized that voice.

"Harry?" I lunged into the open with Connie clawing at my shirttail.

He peeled his mask off. He was sweating buckets but managed a half smile when he said, "We're moving up the ranks, Jay. Better late than never."

More people spilled into the space in battle gear. Nurse DeeDee revealed herself. Sal from my Enchantria Helper team. And . . .

Zeke.

He was armed with a golf club, of all things (probably for the best), and couldn't control his shaking hands. Whatever had gone wrong between us, whatever beef we had, I couldn't remember any of it. I nearly tackled him, sobbing into his shoulder. "I love you, bro. I love you."

He squeezed back. "Love you too."

Peeling away, I said, "You need to see someone."

While more rescuers entered and called for those on the upper levels to come out of hiding, I guided Zeke to the shower stall I'd abandoned.

Seeing her froze him. "Connie?"

I don't think he fully recognized her, or even wanted to believe his eyes, because we'd all assumed the worst for so long even though we pretended not to. He broke down crying again but still didn't move. Like one more step and the Connie mirage would vanish. So she took that step for him.

She fell on him, squeezing with strength she didn't look capable of. She did not cry, though. I think she'd run out of tears a long time ago.

Chelle emerged from the shower. "Guess you got my message."

"Yeah." Zeke cast his eyes down instead of looking Chelle in her battered face.

Connie—always the glue—didn't let that ride. She hooked her arm around Zeke's neck, grabbed my wrist with her other hand, then walked us to Chelle. She forced a group hug and said, "Whatever's going on with y'all, it's for later. Not now."

So be it.

How long might we have stood there, together again, if not for Nurse DeeDee calling my name.

"Jermaine." She aimed a weird ray-gun-looking thing. "Where's your mom and the rest of the missing?"

She'd grabbed my hand while she was talking, pointed that gun at my resident band. The band clicked, then expanded. She released my hand and moved on to Connie's band. Mine slid off. It barely made a sound when it hit the floor. My electronic shackle for the last few months was no more than inert trash now, and Nurse DeeDee called my name I don't know how many times to regain my attention.

"Jermaine! Your mom?"

"I don't know." All the relief I'd allowed into my heart, mind, and soul evaporated. Connie told me the rules here early: *They use our families as leverage. If I'm disobedient, Mom will suffer.*

Nurse DeeDee snapped at Zeke. "You said the missing were here."

Chelle spoke up. "He wouldn't have known different because I didn't know. I'm the one who pointed him here."

Nurse DeeDee sneered. "Trying to buy yourself some goodwill, Karloff?"

Chelle backed up a step. Wisely.

Connie said, "They separated the families to use us as leverage against each other."

"Jesus," DeeDee hissed. "Harry! Their parents could be anywhere."

Harry came over while Connie shook her head. "No. Not anywhere. They're in the Vertical Farms. The livestock tower."

This . . . was news. Everyone eyed her skeptically.

"I was there for a time," Connie said. "I knew the smell."

"We have to go there. Now," said DeeDee.

Harry pivoted, observing the emptiness of the holding area. He cursed. "We didn't scout a third location. We can't go there unprepared."

"What about their parents?" DeeDee asked. "Our friends?"

"They could be okay until we're finished." Harry looked sick, but he said the rest anyway. "If not, this is the way they would've wanted it. Their kids safe."

DeeDee seemed set to argue, but I was stuck on one thing. "You said you didn't scout a *third* location, Harry. What are you talking about?"

"The rest of us are moving on the power plant. We take that, and we take Karloff Country."

Connie said, "My mama."

Harry stayed quiet but shot DeeDee a wicked look when she said, "Maybe a small team. I'll lead. There shouldn't be an armed presence in the farm tower."

"After we raided their youth detention? If we're lucky, Barnabus has called all his people there and we won't have any resistance at the power plant."

Connie sucked in breath. My stomach dropped too. I knew Harry didn't mean to suggest that the retaliatory death of our parents might be good for his mission, but . . .

Connie walked away while DeeDee and Harry argued.

She headed toward the exit. Chelle peeled off, chasing her. Zeke and I exchanged looks, then followed.

Several flights of stairs led to a corridor that ended with a mangled door to the outside. The sun dipped, and Harry's people wrapped blankets over the shoulders of shivering children. Some blankets covered bodies of Trustees who hadn't survived their brief time in lockup. I recognized Paige Radford's blond locks, streaked red in sections, spilling from beneath one. The little time I'd known her,

I hated her so much. Seeing her body thrown under a dirty blanket . . . I hated that too. I hated all that had come to pass here.

Hate didn't change a thing. There was only forward.

Beyond the rally area were vehicles. Not the black SUVs the Trustees favored. Sedans, compact, and vans—the vehicles of a homegrown rebellion. Connie went that way, and we chased again. She passed several vehicles, peering inside, until she reached a burgundy Hyundai with the driver's door ajar and the keys in a cup holder.

She started to climb into the driver's seat. Zeke grabbed her. "Whoa. Hold up!"

Connie said, "I'm going to be with my mama."

"She might already be . . . gone."

Connie repeated herself through clenched teeth. "I'm going to be with my mama."

My mom and dad were there too. What about Chelle's people?

What kind of life could I possibly have if I didn't go?

Chelle pushed past Zeke and Connie. "Cool. I'm driving."

Connie climbed in behind her.

So. We were doing this.

I rounded the bumper and got in next to Connie.

Chelle closed the door and spoke through the open window. "You want shotgun or what?"

Zeke looked to the sky for answers and must've got them. "Of course. I have long legs."

He took his seat, and our crew rode.

One last time.

CHAPTER 42

It wouldn't take long to reach the Vertical Farms. The windows were down, and a warm fall breeze scoured our faces. It was impossible not to remember the good times, before. Juneteenth. Zeke's weak game. Milkshakes.

I wasn't the only one thinking it.

Zeke said, "There's an aux cord in this car. I've got my phone."

Connie leaned between the gap in the front seats. "You want me to pick a playlist?"

She grabbed his phone before he responded. Then I took it from her. "We'll be there before you find anything."

She sucked her teeth. I scrolled. "Zeke, I don't see anything on here but your *DeVos* scratch tracks."

Chelle, who'd been grimly quiet, said, "You made scratch tracks for *DeVos*? Are you, like, *singing*? Because I've heard your singing voice."

Zeke clearly wanted off this topic. "Man, get out of Recently Added. Check my library."

Following the instructions led to a revelation. "I Heart the Eighties?"

Zeke twisted in his seat, attempting to snatch his phone back, but I was quick and managed to retain possession.

Connie leaned in, overjoyed. "Oh my. Power ballads."

"I download music for my dad sometimes." Zeke didn't sound convincing at all.

Chelle said, "Oh, that's a playlist. Curated. By you."

She turned us off the main road onto a bumpy, rutted strip. The back entrance to the massive patch of land occupied by the Vertical

Farms. There was a lull in the conversation. All of us recognizing we were close to the end of something now.

Chelle broke the silence. "If we want to hear something, we should choose. It's your playlist, Zeke. Tell us a favorite."

Zeke grumbled. "It's my *dad's* playlist. Y'all know I rock with that gully, grimy rap."

We waited.

"But if I had to choose something from that list, I'd probably pick 'Faithfully' by Journey."

Dead silence.

Then we all cracked up.

"Oh no," said Chelle.

"Save it for karaoke," Connie said.

I said, "How are you this covertly corny?"

Zeke laughed with tears streaming down his face. "You guys are *the worst*. Should've left you in that cage."

The headlights flashed on a horse gate secured with a length of chain and a padlock. Things got less fun as Chelle mashed the gas. "Hang on."

We hit the gate dead center, exploding the chain and throwing it open on stiff hinges. The left half tore loose and flew into high grass. Ahead of us, the tallest structures in all of Karloff Country.

The towers were five-story-tall cylinders, like giant silver oil drums. Few windows broke up the metallic facades, and only tiny directional arrows along the roads identified each tower's purpose. Three crop production towers, a fishing tower that functioned like an aquarium for consumption, and the livestock tower. Each glowed with eerie yellow lights that wavered as the smell overcame us. Earthy around the crop towers, then tinged with sea rot, and manure, and a slight under-smell I wanted to write off as rotting garbage. But everything that ever lived knew that scent of decaying flesh instinctually.

Chelle slowed the car to a creep, listening. I strained too. Detecting nothing but the hum of industrial machinery. Cooling systems and electrical transformers. Not quiet, but not the kind of loud I'd expect after our entrance.

Zeke said, "Is anybody even at work?"

It was a good question. Though we couldn't see inside the farms, it all *felt* empty.

"Doesn't matter," Connie said. "There's the livestock tower."

It was the last structure on this road, where the rot was strongest. Chelle parked by the loading dock, where a Sandrina-powered cargo hauler sat by a half-open garage. "At least we don't have to walk in the front."

Climbing from the car, I spotted company. Four drones hovered.

From the most scared part of me, a thought: *One for each of us.*

Zeke saw too. Stepping in front of me slightly, as if to shield me. Whatever problems we had before, all was forgiven in that one gesture. I clasped his shoulder and sidestepped. "They're only watching."

Chelle shouted at the drones. "Is that you, Barnabus?"

Barnabus's voice squawked through the drone speakers. "Go home, kids. Everything will be fine in the morning."

Connie found a tire iron in the car's trunk. She bypassed the drones for the open garage door. "I'm not going anywhere without my mom."

None of us were losing track of Connie again; as she went, so did we. Chelle ducked under the door, then Zeke. I was last because I watched the drones rotate, tracking us. I crouched, ready to dive into the garage if they attacked. They didn't, though.

They simply powered down and fell to the concrete in a series of dull, metallic crunches.

The scent inside was a physical thing, as heavy as water at the bottom of a pool.

We walked a corridor of white floors, white walls, and white ceilings. Our shadows cowered beneath one flickering bulb but were incinerated a second later. Straight ahead was a set of elevators, one already open. Next to it a sign indicating the departments on each level.

1. LOADING / STAFF RESOURCES / MAINTENANCE

2. GRAZING AND VETERINARY STALLS

3. PRODUCTION / ADMIN

4. PACKING

5. TEST KITCHENS

I asked Connie, "Do you remember what floor you were on?"

"No. They kept our eyes covered most of the time. I remember glimpsing machines once. Maybe the production level?"

"That's the middle," Chelle said. "Nothing wrong with starting there, get a sense of the place, then go up or down until we find them."

"If Barnabus and his people don't find us first," Zeke said.

Chelle stepped into the elevator and thumbed 3 on the touch screen. "Connie's got the tire iron. We're fine."

No music played on the short trip, and when the doors opened, the smell shoved us like a bully. Everything from before—animal, raw, rot—with something else I recognized from the medical center. Sick.

The third floor was an open space, with relaxed amber lighting. Mostly catwalks surrounding and crisscrossing a grazing floor dusted with loose hay below on level 2. Over our heads was nested, ceiling-mounted machinery folded in on itself like giant sleeping spiders. That would be the automated part of whatever happened in this tower.

Below was more massive open space, enough to hold hundreds of animals. Patches of metal flooring were visible. Water troughs were positioned strategically throughout, and less strategic were the sporadic piles of dried manure. There were almost no animals, though. I counted four cows. Two of them had retreated to the corners of separate pens. Of the pair, one's sides heaved with great effort. The other, I thought, was dead already. This looked like the same sickness that hit a lot of cattle throughout the world, something the Vertical Farms were meant to guard against. Another Karloff Country fail.

Across the central catwalk was some sort of foreman's office done in the same white-white-white style as the entrance corridor. Light poured from the windows, and inside was Barnabus. Alone. At a standup computer terminal mounted in a server bank next to a grid of green-tinted security monitors. He typed hurriedly, then left that keyboard for a laptop on the desk, where he continued typing.

"What's he doing?" Zeke asked.

I thought about those drones falling from the sky. "I have no clue."

We trekked across the central, slightly wobbly catwalk toward the office. Barnabus glanced up, spotted us, then left whatever computer work had him so busy to run and lock the door.

We ran too, sending wicked vibrations through the catwalk that felt less sturdy by the second, but it didn't matter. The dead bolt was secure.

"Barnabus!" Chelle pounded on the bay windows with a fist.

Connie brushed her aside and struck the glass with her tire iron. It chipped the pane like a pebble on a windshield. Tough stuff that'd take a half day to break through. Barnabus was safe from us, but were we safe from him? I had serious questions when I saw there were others in the office.

Mostly men, a few women. Some I recognized from our diner meeting but only barely due to their faces being twisted in agony in the moments before they died. Blood leaked from noses, ears, and eyes. Some lips were chewed through from where their teeth clamped involuntarily. One body continued twitching because Barnabus didn't bother to deactivate their zapping resident band.

He'd murdered them all. Push of a button.

The same button he jabbed as he aimed a Trustee phone at us.

My heart seized, remembering the pain of a resident band shock, *feeling* the pain, if only for a second. Then I got a slippery handle on my panic attack. *I'm not dead. I'm not dead.*

Zeke's lip curled realizing Barnabus, a guy he'd once trusted, was actively trying to murder us. Connie swung her tire iron like a hammer, doing less damage to the glass than before. I looped my thumb and forefinger around my wrist, shuddering, relieved Nurse DeeDee saved my life a half hour earlier.

There were vent grates above and below the reinforced glass. The acoustics on this floor were great, so we heard Barnabus fine when he recognized the bands were no longer an issue for us. He said, "Well, shoot."

Disgusted, he shook the phone like the batteries were loose, then tried to kill us again.

It still didn't work, so he tossed it aside and scrambled back to the desk with the energy of someone who decided to ignore the annoying fly buzzing the room.

"Hey!" Connie shouted. "Where's my mama?"

Barnabus answered without looking up from his screen. "Sub-basement. You can go to her now. Everything's fine."

Connie took the first steps of a sprint, but Zeke grabbed her arm. He sensed the wrongness too. "Not by yourself. Not yet."

Chelle said, "Everything's *not* fine. You killed my grandfather."

Barnabus did look up then, indignant, but quickly refocused on the screen while speaking. "He despised you. I'd say you couldn't imagine the things he'd call you when he felt surrounded by like-minded company, but I'm certain *all of you* can imagine it. I did you a favor."

Chelle backed away from the glass. I knew her well enough to tell his honesty hurt her worse than if he'd shown her Franklin Karloff's severed head.

Zeke said, "You're a snake, bro. If you're mad, don't make it seem like it's because you're doing people favors they don't appreciate. Admit you're salty because you couldn't slither your way to the top like your Trustee homeys."

"You're lashing out, Ezekiel," Barnabus said, keeping most of his attention on whatever task he was performing. "I understand if it's because I hurt your feelings not including you in everything."

"Naw. I'm good. I ran a few errands for a liar. So what? You the one out here pulling this fake mastermind stuff with nothing to show. You still got your resident band on. The little minimum-wage Black kids played the game better than you. Can't feel great."

Barnabus ended his keystroke sequence with force, then snapped the laptop shut. He flashed a strained smile. "Okay. I've got some time. Let me show you what's coming, Ezekiel, so you and your friends can see the mistake the Trustees made by not letting this snake in."

He returned to the wall-mounted terminal. Punched up some footage on the monitors. "I used to think doomsday cults were religious crazies holed up in jungle cabins. Or occultists whispering silly spells. When Franklin presented his apocalypse-as-a-business strategy, I won't tell you I wasn't impressed. I *was* promised higher status during his corporatized End Times, but I was always dedicated to my role as a project manager. Franklin and I spent years discussing what rebuilding the world in his image would take, and my leadership role after. The logical steps. Tell me something, kids . . . any of this look logical to you?"

On one monitor, body cam footage from the middle of a riot. Several people being trampled. Some in police and military uniforms. Some in streetwear. It was unclear who were aggressors? Who were defending themselves? Who even recorded this?

Barnabus tapped a key.

In another monitor, on a packed avenue between rows of blackout dark skyscrapers, cars burned and a masked man in a bulky vest dived into the crowd. He exploded in a concussive blast, taking several dozen people with him.

More taps. More carnage.

Phone towers toppled from the weight of bodies shimmying up and over each other like zombies drawn to cellular signals. A passenger plane with stenciled words in a language I didn't know along its side careened down a runway; a rocket zipped into its midsection, tearing it in half with a ball of flame. Hospitals were packed from . . . I didn't know. Could've been some new virus. Could've been some new attack. Zeke had to look away.

These scenes, I couldn't even tell where they were coming from. Maybe everywhere.

Barnabus said, "Startling, isn't it?"

"You all *wanted* chaos," Chelle said.

Barnabus's head was shaking before she finished. "We wanted to *control* the chaos, Seychelle! Then rein it in for a new prosperity. Society was going to collapse anyway. Anyone paying attention knew it. Maybe it would've taken two or three more decades, but then what? Waiting for a building to topple is never better than tearing it down yourself so you can build something newer. *Better.* That's how it was supposed to work. After the more painful parts of the transition, when the world needed saviors with money and big ideas, we were going to provide. Can you tell who or what should be saved in that footage? Because I can't."

He finger-combed his hair like a frustrated teacher lecturing lazy students, started ranting again. "I developed strategies that would've prevented this. Strategies that would've accomplished the goal."

Connie said, "Where did killing my dad because he wouldn't help you make people taste delicious come into your strategy?"

"That plan was supposed to be a worst-case scenario. A lot of things were supposed to be different. But the old man flipped the switch early, then took his eye off the machine. I didn't understand it until I learned of his failing mind. Then it was too late."

Chelle said, "Yes. It's too late for you to rule the world, you sick—"

He keyed up different, daytime footage. Treetops at first, then a swath of mostly clear highway with abandoned vehicles along the shoulder. A group of bikers, maybe twenty or thirty, had set up camp. Their bikes were parked in a line, their various weaponry—guns, huge stabbing instruments—mounted to the frames. We couldn't hear what they were saying, but one spotted the drone. Another had a rifle in his lap, took aim, and the picture went to static.

"That's from the North, probably out of DC," Barnabus said, switching to a different recording. "This is from the South, two days ago."

More road. Rural, but packed by a military convoy. Like twenty jeeps and trucks transporting who knows how many people.

"No one's coming from the East. Yet," Barnabus said. "But the Trustees didn't send any recon drones west, so who knows? Then inside the wall . . ."

Another tap. This drone feed was live. Fighting at the power plant.

"Your people are planning to take the power plant, right? It's a good plan. But what are they going to do about the invaders that will be at our walls within days? What will they do when the real monsters bash in the gate?"

"How do you know they're monsters?" Chelle said.

"Don't be stupid, girl. Don't you see—"

"That they're not you? Yes. You see real monsters because you think you're looking in a mirror. Grandfather thought the same way. I don't have to imagine the horrible things he said about me because he said them to my face at some point or another. I also don't have to imagine that good people might be making their way to Karloff Country." Chelle tipped her chin in Zeke and Connie's direction. Then to me. "I've seen it before."

"That's some serious Pollyanna thinking, Seychelle. I have to say."

"Who's Pollyanna?"

"Children, I—" He stopped talking, his gaze floating past us. We turned to see the second elevator arriving. *Ding!*

Harry exited, sweeping his rifle right to left. Behind him, Nurse DeeDee aiming a pistol she'd acquired, then Sal, wielding a baseball bat. They spotted us immediately and jogged across the rickety catwalk.

"You came!" I said.

Harry said, "When we saw you were gone, well, we couldn't let you do this alone. Could we?" Harry raised his rifle again at the sight of Barnabus.

Barnabus eyed us with hatred I'd seen before. From Farah when she did what she did to Ted. He said, "I wish you'd come alone. I would've left peacefully. You could've at least had until morning."

Harry was beside us. DeeDee wrenched the doorknob. "Locked."

Sal took a home-run swing and spiderwebbed the glass, but no break. Harry touched the center of the crack, testing it. He backed up a few steps and motioned for us to do the same. Aiming his rifle at the damaged area, he said, "Barnabus, we're getting in. Be easier if you opened the door."

Barnabus was already on the move. He snatched a small bag from a desk drawer and retreated through a second door on the other side of the office.

"Cover your ears." Harry squeezed off two rounds that sounded like the universe cracking. The glass exploded, raining shards on both sides of the wall. Sal snaked his arm through the frame and undid the dead bolt.

DeeDee was in first, rushing to the bodies on the floor in case there was aid to be given. There wasn't. Sal ran to the door Barnabus used, now locked. Harry joined him, both ramming their shoulders against the sturdy barrier. A flustered Harry said, "Is this even an exit?"

I nearly called for Zeke so we could help, but something on the floor caught my eye. It was a couple of Karloff candy wrappers. The prismatic red, yellow, purple, and green of the reserve blend that gave people enhanced strength, and perhaps rage, for a time.

"Harry!" I screamed.

The door that wasn't an exit exploded outward, knocking Sal and Harry to the floor. There were showered in splinters, chunks of wood. The least of their—*our*—problems.

Barnabus reentered the room, with veins like wire emerging from his shirt collar and creating a vascular diagram beneath his skin. His eyes bulged like he might never blink again. His hands, face, and teeth stained with gold-flecked chocolate.

He didn't boast. There were no more clever arguments for his actions or supervillain monologuing. The real monster he'd hidden beneath his polished corporate mask was loose.

He crushed Sal's skull beneath his boot.

The sound was like splitting a ripe melon. And the sight . . .

Another person I knew, another life brutally taken. Because Barnabus decided.

There was no time to mourn or be sick or scream, though.

The monster came for us next.

CHAPTER 43

Nurse DeeDee shrieked at Sal's corpse and was too distracted to move when Barnabus charged. He kicked her in the side, a crunching wet punt that sent her sliding into the far wall. She lay there shallow breathing with bloody spittle spattering the floor by her lips.

Harry cleared himself from the door debris and rolled to one knee, aiming his rifle at Barnabus's center mass. But God, was Monster Barnabus quick. He slapped the barrel high, sending Harry's shot into the ceiling, then grabbed Harry by the throat, muscling him to his feet.

No, I couldn't stand by anymore, couldn't continue to not help.

I snatched Connie's tire iron. "Run."

Then I tried to save my friend.

I swung the iron for the roundest part of Barnabus's skull, but he spun Harry at me, forcing me to pull my strike at the last second. Then we were a tangle of bodies and limbs. Harry's back pressed into my chest as Barnabus used him like a plow, forcing us past a horrified Chelle, Connie, and Zeke. The broken window's frame collided with my upper thigh, then Harry and I toppled out of the office and onto the walkway.

The shattered glass beneath us cut and scraped my bare arms. Some worked its way into my shirt, tearing up my back. Harry lay next to me, wincing from his own injuries.

Barnabus leapt through the window frame. He rocked the walkway when he landed heavy, enjoying his new strength. His pale blue button-down shirt and his pleated gray slacks had rips in them, giving the illusion that he'd swollen, grown, gained inhuman mass when really he was the same size, he'd just never been dressed for this kind of exertion. That's what I told myself anyway.

He pawed at Harry again, maybe considering him a threat that needed to be eliminated before us meddling kids. He gripped Harry's throat, cutting off air and turning everything above the neck the color of a bruise. He might've ripped Harry's head clean off if I didn't do the stupidest, bravest thing I'd ever done.

I rushed Barnabus, wrapping my arms around his waist. He was strong but also off balance. Neither of us could correct what I set in motion, so when we flipped over the safety rail and fell twenty feet to the grazing floor, it felt somehow inevitable.

It was a long fall, but I had Barnabus to cushion my impact. Somewhat. He took the brunt of it. I heard and felt things snap within him, but I rolled off him wrong, with too much momentum, and my shoulder twisted in a way it wasn't meant to. The pop sounded as loud as Harry's rifle, and then the pain short-circuited every other sense I had.

Through it, I knew Barnabus would recover. He would come.

Here, there was nowhere to run. By design.

Cattle didn't graze here, they died here.

This was the killing floor.

ZEKE

"I'm going." My boy needed me. I needed to get to level 2.

Chelle grabbed me with both arms, holding me back. "You can't go down there. Look."

She pointed to the exploded door, the closet where Barnabus juiced up. A number of chocolate wrappers littered the floor. Jesus, how many did he eat?

I said, "What does that much Karloff's Reserve do to someone?"

"I don't know."

"We can't leave Jay down there. He's hurt. If I go, I can maybe distract Barnabus, give him time to get out."

Connie, somehow calm in the crazy, said, "There's another way we can distract him. Remember our class project?"

Barely. Whatever she was getting at, I was lost.

Chelle, apparently, wasn't. "The automated systems."

Connie nodded. "Let's turn them on."

CHAPTER 44

Barnabus lurched toward me. I stumbled away past a cow carcass. Another cow that didn't look too far from the grave bleated a weak grunt, like, "See you soon."

Barnabus was between me and the exit. We were both hurt—my shoulder rolling loose beneath my skin was agony, and each wrong twist made me light-headed. But the Karloff's Reserve in his system kept his rage burning. He pointed at me, spitting curses and promises of what I had coming.

"Tear you apart," he said, slobbering. "Lick your bones."

He moved to close the gap between us when the floor shifted.

Hidden compartments opened beneath loose hay. Metal dividers rose, creating a number of geometric pens meant to separate cattle. These new walls put an extra barrier between me and Barnabus. At the same time, the floor began a lazy turntable spin.

Barnabus's head jerked back, forth, up. He sniffed the air like an unsettled dog. This wasn't the elegant manipulator who'd turned on his handlers when he felt his evil genius shunned. I didn't know what he was now.

Way over our heads, the ceiling-mounted machines came to life. Gears and servos and pneumatics shifted in the shadows like grinding teeth. Metal arms with clutching hands and too many fingers unfolded from the AI nest. One-eyed red scanners swept razor-thin laser lines over swaths of the floor. Looking, looking.

Two cows understood this routine better than me and ran as far as their pen allowed, huddling together as a scanner missed them. The scanner closest to me moved toward the dead cow I'd passed. A laser phased over it, evaluating. It shifted to an almost-soothing green, then clutching metal arms seized the carcass and zipped it to some newly opened compartment in the wall with the speed of a hawk snatching a field mouse. The laser returned to red and continued searching. Toward me.

I'd forced myself into motion, despite my shrieking shoulder. The floor continued its slow spin, putting me closer to a glowing exit sign over a door that should lead to elevators. Somehow, I'd forgotten about Barnabus.

Him hopping the nearest barrier and lunging for my neck was an effective, if unwelcome, reminder.

CONNIE

Flipping a bunch of switches in an automated meatpacking facility . . .
maybe not a great idea.

Lights flashed orange and red in the office. Security monitors flitted between multiple cameras and angles, which was generally not
helpful. Messages popped up on the laptop. Chelle ran to the computer, reviewing whatever was there. She said, "I don't know what
any of this means."

"Everything's moving," Zeke said, peering through the window at
the mechanical arms descending from the ceiling.

Harry, battered and bleeding, trudged back into the office, strug-
gling to speak due to his bruised throat. "DeeDee!"

He rushed to the woman on the floor, who had moved from the
spot Barnabus kicked her to. Her ragged breathing hadn't stopped.
That was something.

"What's happening?" Harry rasped while tending to her.

No one answered him, because who could really say?

"Infected carcass!" Chelle shouted.

Everyone stared.

"The message on the screen," she clarified.

Zeke pointed toward the floor. "Look."

A mechanical arm lifted a dead cow up and away from the grazing floor.

Zeke's eyes bulged. He rushed to Chelle, motioning for her chair.
"Let me get right there!"

She didn't argue, leaving the rolling chair so fast, it did a half spin that Zeke had to halt so he could sit. He navigated through the app windows while we gathered around. "It's like the Sandrina resupply protocols for the engineering shop. We give direction on what we need, and the AI looks for it in the stacks." He pointed to some menu he'd found. "This is set for Wellness Intervention. It's looking for sick animals."

"So what?" I said.

He navigated to a different menu, clicked *something*. "This window controls the pen dividers, and those cows know when the arms move it's bad news."

In the security feed, we saw a divider lower. The two not-sick cows made a run for it.

Zeke navigated back to the AI directive menu. "I'm sorry, cows, but it's you or Jay."

He highlighted a new directive and clicked. The system switched from "Wellness Intervention" to "Reaping."

There was a momentary pause in all mechanical movement while the change took effect, then the scanners began a revised search.

I ran from the office to the safety rail overlooking the grazing floor. "Jay!" I yelled. "Run for the cows!"

But Barnabus got to Jay first.

CHAPTER 45

Barnabus squeezed my bad shoulder, and the pain turned the world blank-page white. I thought I'd died. He brought me back with another squeeze. I shrieked.

Leaning into my neck, sniffing me, Barnabus seemed less human than he did even ten seconds ago. Chocolaty drool spilled over his stained lips. The whites of his eyes were gone. There was just blood.

"Jay!" Connie called me. I didn't want her to see me die. "Run for the cows!"

I thought I'd misheard, then a horrified *Moooo!* got suddenly loud and a fleeing cow bumped Barnabus's hip with enough force to loosen his grip. I fell to the ground.

Barnabus seemed confused by the simple occurrence, his rapidly twitching eyes tracking the cows while a scanner and some mechanical arms moved closer with creepy fluidity. Fighting through the pain, I did as Connie said, chased the cows.

Shaking off his confusion, Barnabus followed me. Slowly, though. Stalking. I wasn't moving fast enough to get away, and maybe the sickest part of his humanity was still intact, because he smiled. This was fun.

Until it wasn't.

The scanner swept its thin red laser over him. And flashed green.

The mechanical arms shot forward, grasping him by the base of his neck and his hips. Almost gently. The way you might lift a baby from a crib.

It was a firm grip, though. One his bucking and growling couldn't escape.

I stopped running, watched as another part of Barnabus's humanity presented: fear.

"Wait! Wait!" he screamed, sounding like some mix of animal and man.

A new compartment opened in the wall, somewhere different than where the dead cow had been taken. Somewhere that earned the killing floor its gruesome nickname.

"No!" Barnabus screamed, higher and higher from the floor. "Not me. It's not supposed to be me!"

He was through the wall, his voice distant. Then, no more.

I looked to Connie on the walkway above. She twisted toward the office. "Turn it off. Now!"

The mechanical arms that had taken Barnabus returned empty-handed, and the scanner swept its laser toward me, but the whine of the machine's powering down sounded as all motion on the killing floor halted.

There'd been enough for one night.

CHELLE

"I'm going to get Jay," Connie said. "Then my mama. Y'all coming?"

Zeke continued tapping the keyboard, and I stood over his shoulder seeing, but not seeing, all he was doing. Something nagged.

"Guys!" Connie said.

Zeke shook his head. "Go. Barnabus left over a dozen apps open. I want to know what he was doing."

So did I. But, most likely, my mom was somewhere in this facility too. I said, "I'll go with you."

Harry worked on getting Nurse DeeDee to her feet. She winced with every movement. Her eyes were open; she seemed in less distress. I wanted to feel good for her. Us. We did it. Except that nagging feeling wouldn't shake.

Connie and I took the elevator to level 2 and sprinted to Jay, who struggled with his grotesquely hanging arm. Connie slipped under his good arm, taking a lot of weight, and I tried to be moral support since there was no other way for me to help him along without hurting him more.

I said, "Nurse DeeDee's awake. She might be able to help with your shoulder."

"Not yet," Jay said in pained wheezes. "Sub-basement first. Let's get our parents."

It was the consensus. One of the cows mooed, the sound like a score to the unease that wouldn't go away. Because . . . the thing was . . . when Zeke set the automated system to Reaping, I couldn't understand why it grabbed Barnabus instead of a cow. The AI should've known the difference. Right?

Connie and Jay were halfway to the elevator when a glint of metal on the floor caught my eye. I knelt, brushed aside hay, and pocketed an astonishing gold watch. It was a Patek Philippe, a timepiece preferred by royalty that cost as much as a home. A watch so luxurious it had no business being discarded on what was essentially a slaughterhouse floor. It certainly hadn't come from a cow.

My stomach turned.

In the elevator, I tapped 0 on the touch screen with a shaky finger. We descended.

The doors parted on a concrete corridor. It was a short walk to a heavy door, where I tried an access code that got me into everything else around the resort. We were inside in no time.

There was fencing, and cots, and people. They spotted us from their side and began some concerned murmuring until Connie saw her mother. "Mama!"

They ran to each other and collided with the fencing between them. They touched fingers between links and pressed their cheeks together hard enough to leave faint diamond-shaped impressions in their flesh. The two of them had been in captivity longer than anyone here.

"Jermaine!" It was Mrs. Butler, on the run. His dad trailed. They met at the fence too. Jay's mom's eyes rimmed with tears and horror over his injured shoulder.

"I'm okay, Mom," Jay said through his own tears. "I'm okay."

More adults came forward, necks snaking, curious as if expecting to see their own relatives. When they recognized it was us, then recognized who I was, that curiosity shifted, a range from intense hate to cautious hope.

A woman pushed to the front. "Ms. Karloff, is there any assistance I can offer your family? I'm an excellent cook who worked in the kitchen at Karloff Wilds. I'm happy to do whatever you need; I'd only ask that I see my son."

Others followed her lead, even the ones who looked like they'd wanted to throttle me seconds before. All these people still wore resident bands. Not a Trustee among them. My mom wasn't here.

The gate had a keypad lock. I did my thing and flung it open. "You're all free to go. You don't have to do anything for me. Find your kids; they're probably still at the Karloff Wilds."

The freed captives spilled past me, never sparing me another thought. Connie's mom rejoined her on the preferred side of the fence. So did Jay's parents. They were the last out of the lockup. The squalid, abandoned space mocked me.

I felt concern from Jay and Connie without even looking at them. Their parents, less so. Way less so. I had very few friends left within the walls that bore my name.

The uncomfortable silence was broken by Zeke, broadcasting from unseen speakers like the voice of God. "Hey, guys, get back to the office. Now. We got a problem."

The parents seemed confused, ready to resist, but Connie the Quick Thinker said, "Mrs. Butler's friend Nurse DeeDee is there. Maybe she can look everyone over."

It was enough to sway Mrs. Butler, who convinced her husband. Connie led her mother and the rest to the elevator. They were inside before Jay and Connie realized I hadn't moved.

"Go on," I said, projecting my easy-breezy face, no worries in the world. "I'm going to look around the place some more."

It was a performance worthy of the former child star of cable's twenty-ninth-highest-rated reality show. Which is to say it wasn't much of a performance at all. The elevator doors closed on my cracking facade.

I took the other elevator up. Not to 3, where the rest of them were. To 5, the test kitchen, because my family's access code let me into everything. I persisted despite the mounting dread. Even when something inside screamed for me to stop, *stop now*, I kept on.

I didn't find my mom. Or Clinton Greer. Or the Radfords. Or any other Trustee who might've survived Barnabus's raid on their homes. I *never* found them.

When I opened the test kitchen's massive walk-in freezer, I found meat. Plenty of meat.

Raw, fresh, and red.

Enough to feed an army.

I collapsed in the cold, sobbing, *knowing*. Mourning my mother, even though everyone I knew in the world probably felt she didn't deserve such decency. Even my dripping tears rejected the notion; they were ice as soon as they hit the ground.

CHAPTER 46

Zeke hunched over the laptop looking grim, waving me and Connie over as the adults reunited. The pain in my shoulder had dulled, so I bypassed Nurse DeeDee for the moment.

We gathered behind Zeke, saw what he saw. A countdown.

05:21:25 . . . 05:21:24 . . . 05:21:23 . . .

Connie said, "That doesn't seem good."

"Right," Zeke said. "All I could think about was *Independence Day*, the big alien battleships setting up over the major cities. This ain't that, but . . ."

"Close enough," I said, noticing the name of the app: Greer Development Control Panel.

The only thing more fun than building them up is knocking them down. Wasn't that what Clinton said?

"Is there a map?" I asked.

Zeke clicked through the app menu and showed us Karloff Country, overlaid with hundreds of tiny purple triangles.

"Oh no," Connie said.

Barely any place was untouched except for Karloff Manor, the Trustee homes, and the jetport.

"Mom! Dad!" I called.

They came, as did Harry and DeeDee, skirting the dead bodies littering the floor.

I pointed to the display and explained what I suspected. When I finished, I said, "Barnabus told us we had until morning. Like he was being generous. This is what he meant."

Zeke let loose a humorless laugh. "If he can't have it, no one can, right?"

"Why give that much time?" Mom asked.

Harry said, "A buffer for his own getaway. He wouldn't have expected us coming here to stop it. We wouldn't have if not for the kids. Jesus."

"*Can* we stop it?" DeeDee asked.

Zeke said, "Not us."

He clicked into another app for the intercom systems and triggered a broadcast. "Chelle, we need you, now." His voice echoed around us.

She arrived minutes later, looking lost. Haunted.

Zeke explained the situation quickly and added, "We need to see if your access code works here."

She shuffled over, didn't speak. Zeke returned to the countdown—05:00:46 . . . 05:00:45 . . . 05:00:44—dragged the mouse to a log-in window. He turned the laptop to Chelle. She typed a string of characters.

Access Denied.

She tried again, and again, until a message indicated too many failed attempts and locked the app completely.

DeeDee said, "Figures. Of course a Karloff wasn't going to help us."

Chelle shot the nurse a look that made DeeDee recoil, then said, "Get people to my house and the Trustee homes. However you can."

"In five hours?" Mom said, skeptical.

"Sandrina," Zeke said. "I can probably use the intercom app right here to broadcast to any functioning unit on property. I need maybe a half hour to set it up."

Harry said, "That gives us a little over four hours to move people. Not a lot of time."

I stepped to Nurse DeeDee, offering my shoulder. "We better have something good to say, then. Pop my shoulder in. I got this."

DeeDee looked to my mom for a yea or nay. Dad stepped to me. "Son, I don't know."

Harry said, "All due respect, we wouldn't have this opportunity without these kids. I've worked with Jay for a while now, and there's no job I wouldn't have trusted him with before the Trustees, and my opinion hasn't changed since. If he says he's got it, you can believe him."

Dad looked a little put out, but Mom made the call. "Fix his shoulder."

Harry gave me his belt to bite down on, and DeeDee did her thing. It sucked. But I was only achy by the time Zeke called me over. He gave me the chair and showed me where to click.

I sat, gathered myself, and started the broadcast over every Sandrina device in Karloff Country. "This is Jay Butler of Enchantria, and I'm calling a Code 7. Everyone, wherever you are, please move to either Karloff Manor or the Trustee homes immediately. We believe there are bombs on the premises . . ."

I said more about the umbrella of fear we'd been living under and reassured all listeners that this wasn't a trick, we needed to ride out the next few hours. I was on autopilot, doing it the way I would've if I'd been walking my Dreamscape and thumbing my radio. My attention was divided, though. Because I took a tally of everyone in the room while I talked.

Chelle was nowhere to be found.

CHAPTER 47

03:17:52 . . . 03:17:51 . . . 03:17:50 . . .

We took a detour to Jubilee to drag Zeke's dad from their house. He did not want to go, did not believe what was coming, and he cursed his own son until my dad tore a strip of duct tape off the roll he and Harry used on the man's wrists and ankles to shut him up. After that, we chose Karloff Manor as our temporary shelter. Partially because I never wanted to see the Trustee homes again. Mostly, I hoped I'd find Chelle waiting. I'd hoped for too much.

When we arrived, we found a sparse crowd. I don't know how many people were in the resort these days. Two thousand? Maybe three? But the helpers who met us numbered maybe two hundred. I prayed the rest were on their way or headed to the Trustees' neighborhood. Harry and DeeDee got to work unlocking resident bands, which evaporated only the most resilient skepticism over . . . well, everything. More folks trickled in. Almost instantly it became hard to keep the peace.

01:09:17 . . . 01:09:16 . . . 01:09:15 . . .

A small group formed with a plan to burn down the Karloff house because it was evil. They even found a gas can in the shed Zeke and I once snuck through. Used it to set some shrubs on fire, but the blaze didn't last. Once the flames were done, they dispersed, all out of ideas. Then another group planned to take all the valuables from the home, so they ran in snatching vases and paintings off the wall only to exit the home with nowhere to take their newly acquired wealth. Most of the stuff ended up in a pile next to the scorched bushes.

00:14:31 . . . 00:14:30 . . . 00:14:29 . . .

The time drew near, and the restless mischief tapered. Conversations went from low to nonexistent. There were hills on the estate ground that gave views across all of Karloff Country. Folks chose their spots. No one fought. One loud person yelled, "I bet nothing happens." He didn't sound like he believed his own words.

"One minute!" Zeke shouted. Nervous gasps all around as our little group drew tighter. The sun crested the horizon like a spotlight. Connie started the countdown. "Ten . . . nine . . . eight . . ."

Everyone had joined in by the four count, and part of me wondered if we were wrong. More than anything, I wanted Chelle safe, wherever she was.

"Two . . . one."

The farthest explosions were silent plumes of dust. Splash Zone. Downtown Karloff. Jubilee, our home. That . . . stung. The whole time, Franklin Karloff had a way to wipe us off his personal map, and it wouldn't have disturbed him more than someone swatting a fly.

A little closer, the concussive thuds and crashing debris were like an apocalyptic house party thrown by distant neighbors. The music loud enough to notice, but not so loud you couldn't ignore if you wanted to. That was Karloff Pictures, the Ferris Reel tipping slow at first, with a groan of metal I imagined because it was too far to hear, then falling from view fast. Enchantria, where the pink-and-purple spires of the Sorcerer's Castle collapsed in on themselves like deflated balloons.

Closest: the power plant and Vertical Farms. They went loud, big, and bright. Maybe because of all the chemicals and equipment there. Something from an old Zeke movie came to mind. *The Lost Boys.*

It was about young vampires living forever off the blood and misery of their town. The movie told us that when vampires go, they don't go quietly. Illustrated when a stake through the heart sent a vampire into shrieking convulsions, awaking the rest of its nest.

The power plant, the farms, they were the heart of this place. Barnabus hammered the stake, and Karloff Country shrieked.

What would it awaken?

THANK YOU FOR VISITING!
COME AGAIN SOON!

CHAPTER 48

It didn't take long. Maybe a minute total before the explosions tapered, then stopped, leaving streamers of smoke wicking into the sky. The quiet after felt wrong somehow.

Then a man carrying a toddler ran for the caravan of cars on the estate grounds and took off to wherever. He inspired others, though a bunch of people trying to move crookedly parked cars at once turned Karloff Manor into a snarled, honking traffic jam. Folks argued. A couple of tough guys left their vehicles for a shoving match that devolved into a fistfight. Someone yelled that they'd direct traffic, and someone else replied, "Who made you king?"

I shouldn't have worried so much about the quiet.

Dad tugged Mom and me close to him, so our foreheads touched. The most tender moment we'd had since being reunited. He whispered, "We can't stay here."

"Where are we going to go?"

"First," he said, "Jubilee."

Zeke stayed behind to free his father. We'd taken him into the manor house, a comfortable sitting room where he might cool off. I doubted he did, which had me worried for my friend.

"Dad, we can't leave Zeke," I said.

Harry intervened, though. "DeeDee's inside too. She's not strong enough for another big move yet, so I'll stay."

Dad thanked Harry before I had a chance to object, so I let it be.

"You good?" I asked Zeke.

"I am." He flexed his knuckles for a fist bump. I bypassed it and hugged him hard. The kind of hug you'd give someone you might never see again.

Connie and her mom stuck with us, and we bypassed the vehicular chaos on foot. I knew the trails from here, and we'd rigged a suitable sling for my injured shoulder. We'd make home in no time. What was left of it.

The parents lagged, choosing—wisely—to navigate the rutted trails carefully for fear of a sprained ankle, uncontrolled fall, or worse. Injuries had new stakes since the medical center, and the doctors inside, could very well be rubble now.

Their caution gave Connie and me distance for a quiet conversation. Connie said, "Where do you think she is?"

Chelle could be anywhere. I had no clue. So I said, "Safe. That's where I'm deciding she is."

Connie nodded. "I'm deciding that too."

It was good enough for the moment.

The trails took us to the backside of the Treat. The fields were intact. So was our pavilion, and the restrooms, and the playground. Leaving the park for the neighborhood streets, I braced for the worst. The first bit of home debris we came across was bad, nothing more than a smoldering pile of bricks and splinters. But it was the only demolished house until we turned the corner onto the street to my home. Then we spotted two more demolished houses, directly across the street from each other. Two houses down, there was another casualty. The neighboring house to a demolished one had a patch of roof shingles torn away but was fine otherwise. Connie's vacant home, Zeke's house, and mine were perfectly fine.

Mom spun in a slow circle, confused. "I don't understand. Why did some blow up, but not others?"

Dad looked to Connie's mom like she'd have answers. She shrugged.

Funny thing was, I had a guess.

Having lived with Clinton and Bette off and on for months, hearing him rant about fiscal responsibility, his superior decision-making, and all his other exaggerations about how he became a self-made man, willing himself into privilege, I knew deep down he was a hustler's hustler. The man cheated at Monopoly, cheated in poker. With his company in charge of the explosives around the resort, I suspected he'd cheated there too. Whoever engineered the self-destruct plan, whether it was Franklin Karloff from jump, or one of Barnabus's worst-case scenarios, Clinton hadn't been thorough, though he'd likely charged a thorough price. The scam of scams when you thought about it. If it got bad enough to blow the whole thing up, where, exactly, would you file a complaint?

Dad insisted we stay outside while he checked our home, but he stopped at the door, confused.

"What's wrong?" Mom asked.

He grinned, raised his arm. "No resident band."

Dad thrust a kick near the lock plate, cracking wood, then let himself in. It was the first of many adjustments made during our last days in Karloff Country.

ZEKE

Dad was furious and threatened to disown me. Called me a traitor and Harry ungrateful. We'd ruined everything.

Until Harry removed Dad's resident band, and we finally returned to our intact house the afternoon of the bombings.

Dad calmed down but did not apologize. He retreated to his funky little room, with his funky little CB radio. Good. I couldn't stand to look at the man. I couldn't stand how much of him had been in me. He wasn't *all* of me, though. I'd spend the rest of my life proving that if I had to.

Except, I wouldn't be proving it to the people I wanted to most.

Many of our neighbors who'd found themselves lucky enough to avoid the blasts had the option to stay but decided it wasn't safe. A lot of packing up, a lot of leaving. The front gates were open. No guards, no drones. The caravans Barnabus showed us stayed on my mind. Two groups from the north and south. Maybe more thanks to the smoke signals from the explosions.

The night after the bombings, we met at Jay's house. Me, Harry, DeeDee—moving slowly and wincing from her taped ribs—Connie, and her mom, who were bunking with the Butlers since their house was empty. The consensus was we shouldn't assume those groups coming to our walls were evil and meant us harm. With all that had happened, they should be welcomed, offered shelter.

"That's what the Good Book says," Harry insisted.

Sure, Harry. Cool. The problem . . . we were eight people coming to an easy conclusion over flickering candlelight. Not the boss of anyone. The power vacuum in Karloff Country threatened to snuff those candles.

The explosive damage to the power plant was bad but not terminal. A few engineering veterans felt they could get *some* electricity going again with parts from the not-so-badly-damaged Vertical Farms towers. A group of former Vertical Farms workers didn't want to give up the parts for . . . reasons. Who knows?

"That's not going to end well," Harry said, moving on to the next bit of gossip he'd collected. His report was long and terrifying. For example, the top security officers died helping Barnabus. Their subordinates who didn't get called up to the Super Shady Varsity were currently trying to cut open the secret armory under the mostly intact Enchantria. For everyone's "safety."

That was the worst of the news, but plenty more jockeyed for position.

Mrs. Butler called Harry's list "another set of bombs without timers."

Connie's mom spoke up then, deciding she wasn't waiting for more explosions. "My daughter and I are leaving. Tomorrow."

"To go *where*?" Connie snapped.

It was a question we all had. The mom look Mrs. Chambers gave Connie for yelling at her let me know Connie should've waited for one of us to ask. She backed down, wide-eyed and panicky.

Mrs. Butler said, "I am curious if you have a destination in mind."

"Anywhere but here. This place took my husband. It doesn't get more chances from me and mine." She stood, done. "Excuse me."

She retreated upstairs to the Butlers' guest room. Then Connie stood, I thought to follow her mother, but she stepped outside instead.

That was my cue, then. I was set to chase when Jay grabbed my shirttail.

"Help." He offered his good hand.

I towed him from the sunken couch cushion because his sling arm was aching and slowing him down.

Mrs. Butler said, "Don't go far."

I knew she only meant that for tonight. Jay already told me his parents wanted out of Karloff Country too. That they'd be leaving. Soon.

And I told him I wasn't.

My dad wasn't even considering giving up our home, but that wasn't my reason. I'd been talking to Harry, about all the dangers remaining in Karloff Country. The hidden weapons. Other Barnabus contingencies. Things that would've been better blown up, had the bombs done what they'd been meant to do. All the rumors I'd ever heard about the Karloffs had some element of truth to them. I knew that now. Someone needed to watch this place, someone who'd recognize signs of rising trouble.

We left the adults inside and found Connie on the porch swing, rocking slow, staring at my house. "Pretty sure my mom's walking us through that gate tomorrow to have us get a splinter and die of dysentery. Cool plan, Mom."

I said, "Nothing's final yet. We can— Oh crap, who's that?"

A figure emerged from the side of Jay's house. A no-electricity night was a different kind of dark than a regular night, so dude looked like a living shadow. Whoever he was spoke in a light, lyrical accent. "Connie, Zeke, and Jermaine. I have a message from a friend."

He came closer, his features clarifying with proximity. I didn't remember his name, but he was the Karloffs' pilot. Dude that almost got us to Cleveland.

"Captain Lucio," Jay said.

"Seychelle is waiting at the Retreat. She asks you to come now. If you can."

Jay craned his neck, making sure no parent had overheard. He nodded.

I said, "Say less, bro."

CONNIE

The guy who'd delivered Chelle's message disappeared like a handsome South American Batman, so I had questions, but when I saw Chelle sitting on our table at the Treat, staring at graffiti on the bathroom wall, all I wanted was a hug from my sister.

She saw me coming, hopped off the table, and met me halfway. I grabbed her, spun, and lost my balance so we were rolling in the grass.

The boys were close behind. They helped us up, then embraced Chelle their own way. Zeke patted her back heavily, like he was trying to burp her. Jay lingered, his sling arm pressed between his body and hers in a way that couldn't be comfortable, though he endured.

"Where have you been?" I asked.

"I went to Captain Lucio. He's always been nice to me. He knows I'm not my family."

Zeke said, "What about your mom? You find her?"

Chelle's gaze fell. "Sit. We gotta go over some stuff. Okay?"

We did as she asked. Zeke and me on one side of our table, Chelle and Jay on the other. Whatever anger she'd felt for Jay yesterday, she put aside when she held his hand.

She said, "I love you all. If I could've chosen my family, you all would've been it. The day you stopped me on the bike path was the best day of my life. Thank you."

"You ain't gotta thank us for that, Chelle."

"I want to. Because this is our last time together, but you knew that. Right?"

No one denied it.

"There are a lot of people here who'll kill me if they find me. Captain Lucio is going to take my family's plane up tomorrow. It'll be a transport for a few families looking to go where he's going. He'll hide me in the galley. That's my way out."

Jay's voice cracked, but he eventually managed a word. "Where?"

Chelle looked at me when she said, "Cleveland."

I said, "What?"

"I told Captain Lucio we had to go to Cleveland first. He'd already researched the area for the trip Zeke, Jay, and I never took. Figures there should still be a few places to land even if the main airport's out of commission. If that works out, we'll drop off whoever's on board, then he'll fly me . . . elsewhere."

"Elsewhere?" Jay said.

Chelle kept her eyes on me. "There are two seats on that plane for you and your mother. Don't tell her how that happened. Just tell her that's your way out. If she doesn't believe you, get her to the jetport, Captain Lucio will convince her. You should go talk to her now, though. No time to waste."

I could barely believe what I was hearing. This girl. This. Girl. I circled the table and kissed her salty cheek. "I love you."

"I already know."

I got three steps away from them and froze. This was really it. The end.

Zeke stood. "I'm going to walk her home."

He wouldn't look at Jay. Or Chelle. Or me. But he let out a hitching mumble: "I love you, Chelle."

She smirked. "Facts?"

"Facts."

Then he was beside me, leaning on me, like maybe he needed *me* to walk *him* home. We kept each other upright on the way down the street. Not looking back once. This wasn't the moment to be captured.

The pictures in my head were better.

SEYCHELLE

"Elsewhere?" Jay said again, looking away.

I said, "Yeah."

"Seems that's the destination of choice these days. My parents are taking us elsewhere too."

I pinched his chin and turned it toward me. "When?"

"Day after tomorrow maybe. Mom wants to make sure our car's good. Dad wants to get his hands on more nonperishable food. I'll do whatever they ask."

"You've always been good that way, Jay."

"I'm sorry, Chelle."

"For all the things that aren't your fault. That's a painful way to live, man. I gotta say."

"Think I would've learned by now."

We looked straight at the graffiti-scrawled bathroom wall.

34 Missing Since the Trustees Came
15 Dead Since the Trustees Came
0 REAL Consequences

The last line needed a revision.

I told him, "You and your family have to be careful out there. Find some good people and stick with them. You know."

"Who are the good people?" he asked, and I got his point. You never know for sure. Even if all's good at first, it can change.

I squeezed his hand. "I think we almost had a thing."

He squeezed back. "We did. Almost might be the best thing for us. Because we can always imagine the thrilling possibilities. Like, taking your family's plane to the Bahamas for graduation."

"Where you propose on the beach."

"Right, but I drop the ring, and a crab runs off with it."

"Then we're in one of Zeke's bad eighties comedies doing spit takes and running from gangsters and scamming Wall Street."

He stiffened. "Was that one a comedy?"

"Wall Street from the one with Eddie Murphy and the guy from *Ghostbusters*. Not *Wall Street*."

"*Trading Places*," he said, naming the film while every bit of humor drained from him. "You gotta be way more careful than me, wherever you go, Chelle. We don't know what the world is like. We don't know what they know. Your face, hide it. Change it if you have to."

"I know." I forced a smile and told what was probably a lie. "I have resources. You know how when a billionaire goes broke, that means they've still got, like, ten million dollars somewhere? I'm good."

Honestly, I didn't know what kind of funds were still available to me. Did money even still matter in the world Grandfather lit fire to?

I'd find out soon enough. "Make me a promise. Three years from today, if the world's still spinning, if you can, meet me in Qatar at sunset. At the airport near the city of Doha, at the baggage claim. I'll wear blue."

"The airport? Chelle, there might not be an airport."

"Then that'll save you a trip. Tell Zeke. I'll have Captain Lucio give the info to Connie. They'll have to decide, but you promise me. Okay?"

"Qatar airport. Three years from today. Sunset. I'll wear blue too."
He cried through every word, got me going too.

"Stop that, Jay," I sniffled. "Now our faces are moist, and we don't like that word." I stood, pulled my hand from his with effort. He stood with me, wincing. Maybe because of his shoulder, maybe because separating hurt so, so much.

He wasn't looking at me. He eyed the bike path, where we first met.

"Jay, what are you thinking? Jay?"

CHAPTER 49

She asked me again, what I was thinking. I pulled her into me and said, "I'm thinking about how we find our people. Wherever we go."

My parents allowed us one more night in Jubilee, preferring to get a start at dawn, so we'd have the sun for a long as possible.

The trip to Elsewhere began with a half tank of gas. The Karloff Country gates yawned open. Beyond them, the unknown. We'd find something out there past our little apocalypse, but it wouldn't be like what we had. What we lost. What I lost.

Karloff Country was supposed to be our last, best place. Half of that was always a lie.

Could I say the truth was better? That the lie wasn't worth it?

That would be more dishonest than the Trustees ever were.

Jubilee was a fine place to live in the good days. And my friends, the times we had, they sure were fun.

While they lasted.

ACKNOWLEDGMENTS

A huge thank-you to all those who worked to make *The Getaway* happen:

Editor
Jody Corbett

Publisher
David Levithan

President
Ellie Berger

Art & Design
Maeve Norton
Elizabeth B. Parisi

Production
Erin O'Connor
Melissa Schirmer

Manufacturing
Irene Chan
Katie Wurtzel

Publicity
Seale Ballenger
Elisabeth Ferrari

Library & Educational Marketing
Emily Heddleson
Maisha Johnson
Sabrina Montenigro
Lizette Serrano

Marketing
Erin Berger
Rachel Feld
Shannon Pender
Victoria Velez

Sales

Kelsey Albertson
Holly Alexander
Julie Beckman
Tracy Bozentka
Savanah D'Amico
Barbara Holloway
Sarah Herbik
Roz Hilden
Brigid Martin

Liz Morici
Dan Moser
Nikki Mutch
Sydney Niegos
Caroline Noll
Bob Pape
Jacqueline Perumal
Betsy Politi

Jacquelyn Rubin
Chris Satterlund
Alan Smagler
Terribeth Smith
Jody Stigliano
Sarah Sullivan
Melanie Wann
Jarad Waxman
Elizabeth Whiting

Scholastic Audio
Lori Benton
Paul Gagne
John Pels
Melissa Reilly Ellard

Scholastic Clubs & Fairs
Jazan Higgins
Mariclaire Jastremsky
Lauren McNamara
Stephanie Peitz
Kristin Standley
Anna Swenson
Shelly Veehoff

Subsidiary Rights
Hannah Babcock
Frank Chambers
Adriana Funke
Jennifer Powell
Marco Rodino
Nirmal Sandhu
Rachel Weinert

Andrea Brown Literary Agency
Jamie Weiss Chilton

Film/TV
Jennifer Justman
Mary Pender
Jason Richman

Family & Friends
Adrienne Giles
Melanie Giles
Jaiden Taylor
Britney Williams
Clementine Williams

Writer Crew
Dhonielle Clayton
Tiffany D. Jackson
Karen McManus
Meg Medina
Malinda Lo
Barry Lyga
Ellen Oh
Jason Reynolds
justin a. reynolds
Olugbemisola Rhuday-Perkovich
Nic Stone
Raúl the Third
Jeff Zentner

ABOUT THE AUTHOR

Lamar Giles is the critically acclaimed author of *Spin*, a New York Times Editor's Pick; *Overturned*, a Kirkus Reviews Best Book; *Not So Pure and Simple*; *Fake ID*, an Edgar Award finalist; and *Endangered*, also an Edgar Award finalist, as well as the editor of the anthology *Fresh Ink*. Lamar is a founding member of We Need Diverse Books. He resides in Virginia with his family. Find out more at lamargiles.com.